THE
SHELLY BAY
LADIES
SWIMMING
CIRCLE

THE SHELLY BAY LADIES SWIMMING CIRCLE

SOPHIE GREEN

hachette
AUSTRALIA

For Jen, my Shelly Bay friend

hachette
AUSTRALIA

First published in Australia and New Zealand in 2019
by Hachette Australia
(an imprint of Hachette Australia Pty Limited)
Level 17, 207 Kent Street, Sydney NSW 2000
www.hachette.com.au

10 9 8 7 6 5 4 3 2 1

This edition published in 2020

Copyright © Sophie Green 2019

A catalogue record for this book is available from the National Library of Australia

ISBN: 978 0 7336 4469 6

Cover design by Christabella Designs
Cover images courtesy of Shutterstock
Typeset in Sabon LT Pro by Bookhouse, Sydney
Printed and bound in Australia by McPherson's Printing Group

SPRING 1982

CHAPTER 1

Theresa screws up her nose as she approaches the water. She knows it's going to be cold. It may be spring but the ocean will still be feeling the effect of Antarctic currents. Are they from Antarctica? Someone told her that once. And they're cold enough to be. Or maybe they're from Bass Strait. Or South America or something. She can't remember exactly, but she does remember what it was like all those years ago when she was a Nipper right here at Main Beach, learning how to read rips and run down the sand and swim fast so she could save lives in the water. She never did grow up to be a surf lifesaver but the memories of the water being cold in November have lingered.

She breathes in deeply and clasps her hands behind to stretch out her arms and shoulders. That's what you're meant to do before exercise, isn't it? Stretch? She's seen swimmers do it on the telly, during the Olympics. Lisa Curry, in Moscow. Theresa isn't kidding herself: she's never going to be able to swim like Lisa Curry. But she's here. She's stretching. Small steps.

As she feels the tug around her chest and shoulders she looks towards the horizon, where shades of yellowy-orange are starting to appear. The sun isn't quite up yet but there's enough light for her to see the long stretch of beach to the left of where she stands, all the way to Kings End.

Behind the beach is the concrete that forms the wall and the walkway, and pine trees that are far older than she is but don't belong here anyway, because they're Norfolk Island pines and this beach is a long way from an island that's closer to New Zealand than Australia. Out of sight to her now, but just around the corner, is Little Beach. That's her goal – to swim to Little Beach. Not today. Some day. Soon. She should probably set herself a more realistic goal for today. Maybe swim from this end of the beach to halfway along, then back. That's not too far. Not as far as she used to swim when they went to the pool for school sport. She was all right at swimming back then.

You're stalling.

Ah, yes – there's that little annoying voice she's been fighting all week, ever since it told her she had to start *doing something*. To get fit. To lose weight.

She knows she needs to – it isn't healthy to be overweight and no man would find her attractive if she was. Her mother had told her that each time Theresa had walked into the kitchen in her school uniform and reached for a piece of cake.

Her mother had liked to bake cakes but hadn't eaten them, and had expected Theresa to follow her example. 'You can never be too rich or too thin,' was her constant advice, cadged from the Duchess of Windsor. Theresa's brothers, on the other hand, could eat as much cake as they liked. In fact, the cakes were baked *for* them.

So Theresa knows she needs to lose a bit. She just didn't need her husband to add his voice to the one in her head. But he did anyway.

Andrew – Andy, Ando, Ands to his mates – had sat on the couch a few weeks ago, his newly burgeoning beer gut spilling over the top of his King Gees and out the bottom of the dirty white Bonds singlet he wore around the house, a tinny in one hand and the other idly flipping through the form guide in the paper while he ogled Delvene Delaney wearing a bikini on *The Paul Hogan Show*. He'd looked Theresa up and down as she'd entered the room carrying his dinner on a tray so he could keep perving at Delvene while he ate.

'You're puttin' on a bit,' he pronounced, then looked appraisingly at the food she was offering. 'What are those – cutlets?' Then he'd made a face like he didn't want cutlets, although she knew, because she's been married to him for a while now, that he loves them.

She'd glared at him and slammed the tray down near enough to his testicles to be a threat. '*Yes*, they're cutlets.'

He'd grinned, then winked at her. That grin and the wink had worked better when he used to be handsome. Of course, in his own mind he still was.

She'd spun away from him only to feel his hand grabbing her wrist. 'Hold yer horses,' he said, putting his tinny down on the card table next to him. That's how she knew he wanted to have a serious conversation. 'I didn't mean to upset you.'

Perhaps. But she knew he'd meant what he said. Because he'd said it before, and not just when Delvene was on the screen.

Theresa can't say he's wrong. She's a little plumper than she used to be, but she's had two kids, and they cut the second one out of her, so what does he expect? Still, she's resolved to do something about it. Not because she doesn't like the way she looks, but because she's sick of feeling the way she feels: slow, stodgy – and old. She's only thirty-eight but she feels a hundred most days. She wants to have – *needs* to have – more energy to run around after her children, whom she loves even if they get on her nerves.

She should be more grateful for the kids: her cheeky boy, Oliver, and her sweet girl, Sasha. She almost lost Sasha. When she was born the cord was wrapped around her neck and Theresa saw the end of her dream of having a daughter named Alexandra and nicknamed Sasha. She'd always wanted that, ever since there'd been a Russian girl in her class who was known to all as Sasha – then Theresa had found out her real name. It had seemed so cosmopolitan to have a 'diminutive' name, as she'd also learnt to call it. And she wanted to be cosmopolitan. Still wants to be. She wants to have a racy life. To zip around the world without any cares. Maybe with that dishy Tom Burlinson she's just seen in that new film *The Man from Snowy River*. It wasn't much like the poem she loved so much in school but that doesn't bother her, because sometimes, when she's alone, she thinks about Tom riding that horse straight down that mountainside . . .

So she's decided to take her inspiration from Olivia Newton-John and get physical. Just not the way Livvy did it, with a leotard and sweatband worn like John McEnroe's. Swimming is the only sporting activity Theresa liked as a kid, so it was to swimming she decided to turn two nights ago, when the voice of conscience had a small victory and she made her big decision and hoped she could stick to it. From now until the end of summer she's going to have a sunrise swim. Every day, she's decided. No backing down – not unless the conditions are truly unfavourable.

Andrew and the kids will sleep through the whole thing, up in their little house on the ridge between Kings End and the next beach, Sunrise. And if the kids wake up, Andrew will just have to deal with them. For a change. It's not as if she doesn't have to deal with them most nights of the week when he stays out drinking with his mates after work and comes in smelling of beer and, mysteriously, Brut 33. She's never seen a bottle of it in the house.

This morning she almost decided to make swimming a New Year's resolution instead, but she knows that if she delays until January summer will be almost half gone and she might lose her nerve. This way she has a few weeks of getting in the water and seeing just how fit she can become.

For a second or two, she'd wondered if she should invite a friend to join her – then she'd remembered that all her friends are as wrapped up with their children as she is. None of them has time for each other any more. She's planning to hold on until the kids are in high school and then they can all reconnect. Her mum told her that's about how long it takes for everyone to 'get past the worst of it'.

'G'day, Tess,' she hears from her right, and doesn't need to look to know it's Trevor King, the unelected ruler of the Shelly Bay Surf Club. He's run the Nippers programs for years, and even taught Theresa herself how not to drown in a rip. She doesn't mind him. He's just a bit narrow in his thinking, the way Andrew is. The way she worries she'll become if she keeps hanging around with narrow-minded people.

'G'day, Trev,' she says, making an effort to sound friendly, even though she wants to tell him – the way she always wants to tell him – that she can't stand being called Tess. She is Theresa, like her grandmother. He, on the other hand, has always been Trev, not Trevor; just like Andrew is never Andrew to anyone but her.

'Nice day for it,' Trev says.

It's the same thing he says every time she sees him. Even when she was standing on the sand watching her own kids go through their drills and it was bucketing down, he'd say it was a nice day. But she supposes he's cheerful. Maybe that's not a bad thing.

As he draws close Theresa averts her eyes from his Speedos, which she suspects he's bought a size too small so he can make the most of his crown jewels. Because it isn't the Koh-i-Noor diamond he's got stuffed inside his cossie.

'Too right,' she says with a tight smile and a tighter wave, hoping he'll leave her alone now. She doesn't want to chat. She is standing here in her old one-piece, which has gone threadbare underneath her boobs and won't withstand close inspection. *She* won't withstand close inspection. But all that is going to change. She will do this swim today, and then she's going to get a new cossie at the mall later this afternoon and it will help her feel more positive about this mission she's set herself.

Theresa takes a step into the foam and realises she's holding her breath.

Another step in and the white water brushes against her shins. It isn't as cold as she feared. Not yet.

She watches the waves building. She has to time it right – she doesn't want to get out there and meet the biggest wave of the set. She might never have become a surf lifesaver but she learnt about the water. How to be watchful. How to be cautious. Lessons she sometimes thinks she should have applied to her life.

There's the break in the set she's looking for, so she wades in quickly and dives under. At this depth the water is indeed as cold as she feared and she gasps. Still, this is the price she has to pay to be gorgeous in a bikini. *Cleo* and *Cosmo* tell her that she has to suffer to be beautiful. Which is why she reads the *Women's Weekly* instead and makes biscuits from their recipes.

Nevertheless, she is here now, and she's going to swim a few metres and see how she gets on. She isn't going to transform into an athlete overnight. But if she just keeps thinking about Tom Burlinson on that horse, she's sure she'll have enough motivation to get there soon.

CHAPTER 2

Marie rubs a towel through her hair as she gazes at her unruly back garden. Every day, after she's had her swim and her shower, she dries her hair looking at this garden and she really doesn't know why. Despite the lovely flowers – frangipanis in summer, camellias in autumn, azaleas in winter, plum blossom in spring and hibiscus year round – it's not a pretty picture. The weeds are taking over and she has never learnt to prune the trees properly. Norm used to do that, and after he died there was no one else. Just like there's no one to swim with her any more. Her habit of a lifetime became his too; became theirs. Now it's hers alone once more. As is the garden.

She's thought about getting someone in to tidy it up but she can't afford it. She can't afford much of anything now that she's on the age pension with no savings. Which is her fault. Hers and Norm's. They didn't really plan for the future.

'Charlie Brown, what are you doing?' She bends down to scratch behind the ears of her Sydney silky terrier as he snuffles between her feet.

Marie's best friend, Gwen, brought Charlie Brown into her life. Gwen's daughter had bought a puppy from the breeder who owned him. Charlie Brown was meant to be a show dog but the breeder had decided he wasn't good enough for that. Marie didn't want to know what the breeder had planned for a dog who wasn't show-worthy, so she swooped in and offered to take him. Even offered money, but the breeder refused it, saying that Marie was doing him a favour by removing a problem. Ever since then Marie has counted herself as the lucky one, although she gives Norm the credit – from somewhere beyond he looked after her, she's sure of it. That's why she gave Charlie Brown that name: *Peanuts* was Norm's favourite comic strip.

'I'm going to the shops,' she tells the dog. 'Will you be a good boy while I'm away?'

He looks up at her, his hair – it's too thin to be called fur – flopping near his eyes, and she knows that he will not be good. He'll curl up on her bed even though he's not allowed to, and she will forgive him, as she always does, because he's her only companion now.

Gwen and Marie have lived within walking distance of each other their whole lives, but several months ago Gwen moved into a retirement village a few too many suburbs to the north. Norm's been gone for five years now, and their daughter, Nicole, lives on the other side of town, across the harbour. So Marie's most regular conversations are with the dog. He doesn't seem to mind.

Marie quickly eats her hard-boiled egg on toast and gulps down her tea, wanting to get to the greengrocer when it opens. That's when the fruit and veg will be straight off the truck from the markets. She knows that because Norm used to be the greengrocer in the very same shop. His shop. He sold it seven years ago; two years after that he was gone. So much for a leisurely retirement.

She picks up her string bags from the kitchen counter and tries to stop herself waddling towards the front door. Once she hit sixty her joints started to tighten up, to her dismay. She's been swimming almost every day of her life since she was a child, right here in Shelly Bay, and still her body is ageing. Getting cranky with itself. She's not sure what else she's meant to do to keep it happy. She eats well, she exercises, and she's still getting thick and stiff, just like her mother did, and her mother before her. Maybe she shouldn't bother with the swimming since her genes are lapping her anyway.

Except she loves it. The ocean has always been there for her, on the good days and the bad. There have been a few bad ones in the last five years. And some very bad ones further back in her life. Days she wishes she could forget but which she needs to hold on to, because they are part of her story. Part of who she has become.

Back then, as soon as she was able, she'd returned to the water. Each kick, each stroke, had brought her back to herself; and a couple of years later Nicole arrived in the world and made the sun shine again. She still does that.

'Stay here, Charlie Brown,' Marie says as she gives him a little nudge with her foot and closes the front door on him. He can't come with her because he's not allowed in the shops, and she never likes to tie him up on the footpath. Instead he can have the run of the old sandstone cottage Marie grew up in and inherited from her father because he, too, didn't get the son he dreamt of.

She ignores the out-of-control lavender bushes in her small front garden, closes the gate and sets off down the hill to the village, as the locals call it. She waves to Mrs Morrison on the other side of the road. The older woman's spine makes a C shape but she's still out there, pruning her roses. Putting Marie to shame.

Livingstone Road has been Marie's lifelong artery into the village: it takes her down the hill to the beach and the shops; past the home of the first boy she ever had a crush on; past the playground of her primary school; past the spot on the corner where there used to be a café. She and Norm had their first date in that café. She smiles, thinking of them sitting in the window, him with his big head of dark curls and the scar over his right eye. His brother did it, Norm said, with a cricket bat. He was never sure if it was on purpose or not.

For a while after Norm died Marie couldn't bring herself to go into his old shop, even though it's the closest green-grocer to home. She didn't understand why so she prayed on it, which made her feel better even though she never worked out the reason for her resistance. She went back, and will always remember how happy the new owner was to see her.

As she steps inside today he's organising the peaches.

'Hello, Vince,' she says.

He looks up. 'Marie!' He comes towards her with his arms outstretched, as he always does, as if she's his favourite aunt or something, and gives her a hug, like he's grateful she's in the shop.

What he doesn't know – because it would be too strange to tell him – is that she's grateful he's kept Norm's business going so well.

'What's it going to be today?' he says when he releases her, in that accent he's told her is 'Australian suburbia by way of Calabria'.

She's never told him that she thinks it's taken a detour via dreamy, because what young man wants a crone giving him compliments? She wouldn't want to make him uncomfortable, plus she's never been the flirty kind. She just misses the company of men. Of one man.

'Half a dozen oranges, please,' she says, and he starts to pick them up and put them in a basket.

'You been for a swim this morning, *signora*?'

'Every morning, Vince.' Which he knows, because he always asks her. She appreciates the banter, though.

He smiles and shakes his head. 'I don't know how you do it. Even in winter?'

'Even in winter.'

He shakes his head again. 'It's too cold for me *now*, *signora* – and it's almost summer!'

'The water will warm up soon. You should give it a try.' She nods towards the end of the street, where pine trees guard the beachfront at almost exactly the spot where she starts her swim each day at sunrise. 'It's so close. You could run down there after work. Daylight saving.'

He raises his eyebrows at her.

'Four bananas,' she says, and he nods as he selects them carefully.

'Two tomatoes.'

'Only two?' He frowns. 'What kind of pasta sauce can you make with only two?'

She laughs. It feels good. And rusty. She doesn't laugh much these days. No one to laugh with. It's another reason to be grateful to Vince. Although that doesn't mean she can afford more than two tomatoes.

'You know I'll never be able to make a proper sauce,' she chides gently. 'I'm not your nonna.'

He winks. 'She makes the best sauce.'

'I know. You always tell me.'

She's almost at the end of her list, after which she'll turn around and go back up the hill, wearing out that short track her life runs on. Her world has become smaller these last few years. If only she'd learnt to drive a car, but she never needed to; Norm took her everywhere she wanted to go. Now it's too late to learn, even if it meant she could drive to see Gwen. And Nicole. Her daughter doesn't live far away as the crow flies, but it takes an unreasonably long time to get there when Marie has to take the ferry then the bus then walk a few hundred metres. It uses up the whole day, going to see Nicole and her kids. Marie knows she has whole days to spend – she has all the time in the world – but she's still not visiting. She should make herself, before she gets stuck further in the sludge she sometimes feels is building up around her feet, holding her in her old ways, not letting her move on.

'Thanks, Vince,' she says as he loads her purchases into her string bags.

'It's lovely to see you, Marie.' He pecks her on the cheek. 'I'll look forward to the next time.'

He's such a charmer, and he knows it, but he's made her day. Little points of light are what she lives for now. She gives him a last wave as she steps onto the street.

She can just make out the glint of the sunlight on the ocean, past those pine trees, and for a second she contemplates having another swim today. She might just do that. Or she could go for a walk up to the headland. Give her hips something to really complain about.

She has time. So much time. She should start doing something with it.

CHAPTER 3

'**K**eep your head down. That's it. That's it! Now kick. Kick!'

Leanne can hardly hear the swimming instructor yelling to her. She has cotton wool doused in lanolin stuffed in her ears and a cap over her head, and the water is rushing past her face as she tries, clumsily, to pull her arms through the water and move her feet at the same time. Freestyle doesn't feel so free when you're still learning how to do it.

She thinks Matt says something like 'Breathe' but she still can't hear him. Then she feels his hand on her shoulder and she stops.

'You're not breathing,' he says when she lifts her face from the water. 'You'll pass out if you keep that up.'

'Sorry,' she says, feeling abashed. She forgets to breathe every single time she's in this lesson, but never when she's practising on her own. Perhaps she's concentrating so hard on what he's saying that she forgets. Or perhaps in his presence she's just more self-conscious about doing things right or wrong.

'No worries,' he says, his grin wide, his sun-darkened skin looking as though it might crack. His shaggy brown hair hangs almost in his eyes, and he has what appears to be encrusted salt on his eyebrows and eyelashes. He's like so many of the young men she sees in the area, although they're usually nearer the beach than this council pool.

It took Leanne many months to get used to how different life in Shelly Bay is to where she grew up, in a landlocked suburb far from the sea where she wasn't the only child who never learnt to swim. Her mother didn't swim either. Her father and brothers did, but they were expected to; her father told her brothers that they'd never grow up to be lifesavers if they didn't. Which was a strange statement, because he wasn't a lifesaver, they never went to the beach and her brothers showed no interest in learning how to save anything. But that's what Aussie blokes did, apparently: they became lifesavers. It was important to her father that her brothers became Aussie blokes. Sometimes Leanne wonders if that's how they turned out, but it's been several years since she has seen any of her family.

'Let's try again,' Matt is saying, although through the cotton wool it's hard to make it out. 'You're doing really well, all right? We just don't want you to drown.'

He laughs and it sounds almost like a honk. She's grown used to his laugh over the past few weeks. He's been her only instructor for the lessons she decided she needed.

As she pushes off the wall and tries to time her strokes properly, she thinks he's probably being kind about her progress. But she's not going to stop just because she's not Shane Gould. She lives in a beachside suburb now and if she can't swim she's not making the most of it. Half of the residents of Shelly Bay are in the water each morning, it seems; each time she goes for a run she can see them ploughing up and down offshore. She wants to try that too. All her life she's been active, and never baulked at a challenge; swimming the length of the beach seems like something she should try. And it will make her a proper local.

Shelly Bay is as different as Leanne could imagine from the place where she grew up. Home was full of streets tightly packed with dark-brick houses and gardens of English plants that usually weren't tended to. There were parks that were mostly patches of dirt with the occasional swing; playing fields that were teeming with rowdy boys on weekends; and streets that were quiet enough for her and her brothers to play cricket on without worrying about cars.

In Leanne's suburb, people mostly stayed inside their houses. It was hot in summer and cold in winter, and those dark bricks were meant to keep everyone's temperature even. In Shelly Bay, the residents seem to be outside all the time. The streets are wide and the houses are set further apart than she's used to, creating a sense of airiness that makes the whole place feel relaxed. And there is so much light: the houses are built of sandstone if they're old, or weatherboard if they're not. Where there's brick, it's blond. The gardens are full of trees and flowers that look like summer: frangipanis with their yellow and white faces; strelitzias, lavender, and freesias on the nature strips. There is scrubby bush nearby, covering the headland and encroaching into people's lives; eucalypts are on every street and there's the occasional stray native plant in front gardens. Leanne grew up with kookaburras and magpies and miners, but here there are more colourful birds too – cockatoos and rainbow lorikeets and king parrots. They obviously prefer the seaside.

Leanne's move to Shelly Bay happened when she took a job at Northern Hospital up on the hill – her first after she finished her nursing degree. She liked paediatrics the best when she was training, so getting a position in the paediatric ward was a dream. And she was glad to move out of the dense city-bound suburbs near the university to the roomier Shelly Bay. She took a flat on her own and still enjoys the freedom it brings her, to make decisions for herself and how she wants to live.

This place has changed her perspective on life. Before, she felt hemmed in by the past and the decisions she'd made that shaped it. The further away from it she has moved, the more she has begun to believe that she can be a different person – the sort of person who lives in a bright, happy place filled with friendly, open people. With Matt as a prime example.

'Right!' he says, tapping her on the shoulder as she reaches the wall. 'That was pretty good. How are you feeling?'

'Fine,' she says, sniffing water up her nose and tasting the chlorine as it trickles down the back of her throat.

He honk-laughs. 'You don't say much, do you?'

'Not really.' She half smiles but is sure it looks like a grimace.

'I think that's enough for today,' he says. 'But it would be good if you could get some practice in before the next lesson. Okay?'

She nods once, definitely. 'Okay.'

He grins. 'See you next week.'

As Matt heads in the direction of the office Leanne wades to the steps, avoiding a more vigorous swimmer whose freestyle is smooth and swift. She wants to swim like that one day. Soon. Or even just a bit like that, so by the time summer starts she can swim in the ocean and be one of those locals churning their way through the surf.

Maybe then she'll feel like she's really home.

CHAPTER 4

Thwack. The ball hits the net and Elaine winces. Another double fault. She risks a glance at her doubles partner and can see how unimpressed she is. As she should be: they've lost two games already because of Elaine's serving.

If Elaine could only work out what she's doing wrong she'd fix it, except she was never this lousy when she used to play at home. Since she and her husband moved to Australia a few months ago, she's lost . . . something. Not her abilities: she refuses to believe that. She's been playing tennis since she was a child and her game is automatic now. Perhaps that's the problem: it was automatic *in England*. A change of country has changed all the parameters she's used to. She's not so much a fish out of water as a mermaid marooned on dry land. Or so she'd like to think. It's a more glamorous idea than the truth, which is that she's wretchedly miserable living in the southern hemisphere and the deficit in her tennis game is the least of it. Yet it's the most tangible part of it, so it's what she's working on. Even if there's been no improvement since last week's ladies doubles round robin.

'How about I serve from now on?' Marguerite says with a pinched look on her face, and although Elaine wants to protest, and make it clear that she's not usually this hopeless *really*, it wouldn't be fair. Because she's hopeless right now.

'Sure,' she replies breezily and forces a smile that she is sure looks as fake as it feels. 'I'm clearly having a bad day.'

Marguerite sniffs and Elaine thinks she can translate: in short, Marguerite doesn't believe that she ever has good days.

It gives Elaine no satisfaction that while Marguerite can serve the ball over the net, she isn't much good at hitting it thereafter, so they lose the match anyway.

'Thank you,' Elaine says as she shakes hands with their opponents over the net, then with Marguerite. 'Next week?' she adds.

She really doesn't want to play with them again, but she hasn't managed to find another group activity that suits her, and if she doesn't play tennis she will have absolutely no one to talk to apart from James, who works all day and half the night. Not that she isn't used to it. He did that in England, too, and she didn't expect that returning to his homeland would change him. A surgeon's work is never done, or something like that. His wife's wait is never over.

'Um, well . . .' Marguerite exchanges looks with the others. The sorts of looks normally seen on cruel schoolgirls in a playground. 'The thing is, Elaine . . .'

Marguerite pats her on the arm, a gesture that Elaine finds both patronising and intrusive. Playing tennis together does not confer a level of familiarity that allows for patting. She wonders if shifting away from Marguerite will look rude.

'We have a friend who wants to play with us,' says one of the others – Cheryl, Elaine thinks it is.

Cheryl and Beryl. Elaine thought it was a joke when they told her, but apparently not, and ever since she has rarely been able to remember which one is which – a predicament not helped by the fact that they are both bottle blondes, both play tennis wearing, improbably, boob tubes in combination with tiny ellesse skirts and socks with pink pom-poms on the backs, and both have husbands called Barry. They go to 'the Services' on the weekend – a club, Elaine believes, on the bluff at Sunrise Beach – where the Barrys play 'the pokies' and bet on 'the dogs' and 'the trots'.

Marguerite's husband is known as Bluey. This, Elaine has learnt, is because he has red hair. James tried to explain it to her but she felt too overwhelmed to understand; the steep cultural learning curve she has found herself on ever since moving to Australia has generally had the effect of making her feel simultaneously stupid, tired and resentful. But she's persevered these last few weeks, despite not having anything in common with these women apart from the fact that they have all played tennis since childhood, and now here they are turfing her out of their foursome. She wishes she felt more relieved because she doesn't want to play with them again, either, but being rejected is never pleasant.

'Is that so?' she says, trying to sound nonchalant but instead sounding like she's swallowing a plum.

'Yeah.' Cheryl – or Beryl – inspects her chipped fingernail polish. 'Kel. You met Kel. She plays mixed doubles sometimes.'

Elaine recalls a tiny woman with a perm growing out and a faded navy-blue Lacoste T-shirt. 'Right. Kel.' She smiles quickly. 'So I imagine that leaves no room for me?'

'We'll call you if we have a spot,' Marguerite says, and Elaine steps away as she sees another pat coming.

'Fine.' She tries to smile brightly but feels she probably looks startled instead. 'Thank you for letting me play with you.'

'No worries!' says the other Cheryl/Beryl. 'See you round.'

You will never see me round, Elaine wants to snap. She has never been round in her life apart from her two pregnancies. Well-brought-up young ladies aren't supposed to eat. That's why they drink instead – the calories have to come from somewhere.

It's a drink she's thinking of as she almost trots away from the courts. Her daily gin-and-tonic ritual that she never used to let herself start before six o'clock. It's been creeping in earlier – only because she's lonely, and bored despite the plethora of novels she's been ploughing through; and so many nights she's already asleep by the time James gets home, which means he's not likely to find out that she's drinking more than she used to. Unless he's checking the bottle she keeps on the sideboard. She'll have to start using a decoy bottle.

She walks back up the hill to Francis Street, wishing that she'd brought the car. But that would make her lazy: the courts are only ten minutes' walk from home. Not that their proximity matters any more. She's hardly going to look for another group to play with.

Perhaps there are other courts nearby . . . But then she might face the same problem: women who don't really want her there, and her game not up to scratch. There's more entertainment to be found at home with her books. Maybe she should get a dog. They haven't had a dog since the boys were little.

As she reaches the top of the hill she sighs and turns around so she can look past the rooftops of the village shops and flats, past the spire of the church, St Mary's Immaculate, to the ocean. Today it is a rich blue and, given the warmth of this November day, looks incredibly inviting.

She can take up swimming. It was her favourite sport at school, and she was good at it. Not a group sport, true, so she's not going to make friends by swimming on her own. However, she hasn't made friends trying to be part of a team. She was always a better singles than doubles player – she should have remembered that.

Tomorrow morning she's going to get in the water. Or maybe the day after, because she'll need a cap and goggles if she's going to take this seriously and that requires a trip to the shops.

This afternoon, the only thing she's going to take seriously is that gin and tonic. She sets off in strides towards home, with quinine and slices of lemon on her mind.

CHAPTER 5

The water looks murky this morning with the sky closing in. Those aren't rain clouds up there, Theresa tells herself, just those humid puff balls that promise a lot and deliver not much. The sea isn't its usual appealing blue. She just has to talk herself into going in. She's made it down here, after all. Now she just has to get in the water. It's not so hard! Really, it's not!

The cool air on her shoulders tells her otherwise and her resolve wavers yet again. She was cosy in bed, even if Andrew managed to turn triple somersaults in his sleep and kept her awake half the night.

'G'day, Tess.'

'Hi, Trev,' she says, keeping her eyes on the water as he draws up next to her. It looks cold and she's still wondering if she can talk herself out of going in.

Not that she can say that to Trev, because he's proud of the fact he swims year round, 'even when it's so cold me apricots turn into peanuts!' he said the other day, chortling while she blushed. Theresa's no prude but she doesn't know him well enough to talk about his gonads. She's still trying to work out how to talk to Oliver about his, and that's *after* he came home from school one day asking her what 'balls' were.

'Watcha lookin' for, Tess – Jaws?'

Trev laughs as if he's said the funniest thing ever. But Theresa doesn't think it's funny. It took her more than a year to get back into the ocean after she saw that bloody movie.

'Have you ever seen a shark out there?' she says.

'Nah.' Trev shakes his head. 'Not often.'

'Not often?' she squeaks.

'You'll be right.' He sucks in his belly and hikes up his Speedos before turning to look over her shoulder. 'G'day, Marie.'

'Trev,' comes the response.

Theresa turns to see an older woman with a strong jaw and thick grey hair cut in a bob. She looks like a swimmer: broad shoulders atop a muscular frame, even if some things are sagging. Not that Theresa should judge.

Marie steps away from them before she slowly takes off her T-shirt and shorts.

'Swims every day of her life,' Trev says quietly with a note of admiration. 'Been doing it since she was a little tacker.' He nods slowly. 'Her husband was taken by a shark.' He jerks his chin. 'Out there.'

'What!'

Trev starts with a small laugh that develops into a roar. 'Geez, you're gullible, Tess.'

Theresa feels an urge to punch him, because she knows she isn't gullible, just trusting. It isn't always the same thing.

'Nah, he died of a heart attack or somethin'.' Trev looks almost misty-eyed. 'Five years ago, I think. She's been alone ever since. Swimming alone too. They used to come down here together. She was always better than him, but. Anyway,' another sucking in of the belly, 'I'm off. Gotta train for the surf comp. Cheerio.'

Theresa is glad she isn't required to speak because she really wants to scream at him for letting her think, for even a second, that a lethal shark attack happened right here, where she swims.

She glances over to Marie and sees she's being observed.

'Morning,' Marie says, raising a hand.

'Hi!' Theresa says, quickly putting on her cap. She's been stalling long enough, and if this Marie can swim every day of her life *for years*, through all the seasons, Theresa should be able to manage to get in today.

'I'm Marie,' says the other woman as she comes a little closer. She pronounces it 'Mah-*ree*', the French way, not '*Maah*-ree' like Trev.

'And I'm Theresa.' She smiles broadly.

'Not Tess?'

Theresa laughs. 'No. Trev likes to call me that, and I guess I can't blame him when I've never corrected him.'

Marie nods. 'People can be too familiar. Anyway, I'm going in.'

Theresa smiles again, hesitantly, wanting something but not wishing to seem too forward about it.

'May I follow you?' she says. 'I mean – if you don't mind. It's just a bit lonely out there.'

So what if she's also thinking Marie can be shark bait instead of her? She has a survival instinct just as much as anyone. Besides, she might learn something from Marie, who is likely to be a much better swimmer.

'Sure,' Marie says, and offers Theresa a cautious smile.

'Thank you!' Theresa hurriedly tucks in her hair. 'I'm really bad so I'll be slow. I won't even try to keep up. It's just nice to, um . . . nice to have someone else there with you, isn't it?'

'Rightio,' Marie says with a nod.

Maybe Theresa has pushed her luck – she's foisted herself on this stranger who's probably too polite to tell her to get lost. 'Do you really not mind?' she asks as she folds her sarong and puts it under her towel.

Marie gives her a quizzical look. 'Why would I mind?'

'Okay!' Theresa beams and follows Marie to the water. Marie strides in almost with a swagger while Theresa wobbles on the uneven sand. How embarrassing – Marie has about twenty-five years on her and she's so much stronger.

You just have to keep it up, Theresa. Keep coming down here every day and swim as hard as you can, and you'll get good.

The motivational speech to herself doesn't last very long, because once she's flailing along in Marie's wake, trying out freestyle because her breaststroke is too slow, all she can think is: *No sharks. No sharks. No sharks.*

Of course, she could ask herself why she's in the water at all if she's so worried about sharks – and the answer might be that she's trying to use the sharks as a reason not to swim when she knows she needs to. Even though she's been swimming for only a little while, she's feeling better already. When she arrives home afterwards she's in a good mood and less likely to get upset that Ollie has managed to crease his school uniform again. She's sleeping more soundly too. Andrew is still getting on her nerves, but that's married life, isn't it?

As she nears Little Beach – which she reached on her fourth day of swimming by breaststroking slower than a turtle – the water becomes shallower and she can see the fish she's noticed before. There are quite a few little silvery-white ones with yellow fins on the bottom and a black ridge on the top fin. They like to dart around. And longer silvery-white ones with yellow tails. She wonders if they're related. Even though she had goldfish as a child Theresa has never been as interested in fish as she is now she's sharing their world.

She jerks as she sees a small brown stingray. It's harmless – and nowhere near her – but it still looks a bit creepy. It's territorial, always in the same spot each day. Maybe that's a characteristic of stingrays. She should go to the library and find out.

As her feet find the bottom she decides to take a breather on the beach. She's surprised to see Marie standing on the sand.

'Thought I'd wait for you,' Marie says, looking at her curiously.

'That's nice! Thank you.'

Theresa is conscious she's a little breathless. Over time that will improve. She'll swim this far with ease and be so fit she'd be able to carry on conversations if only she could talk underwater. Which is what her mother used to say about her: *Theresa could talk underwater.* Then her father and brothers would snigger.

'I'm not holding you up?' she says as she positions herself next to Marie and admires the view back to Main Beach, the blond sand sweeping up to the wall, little dots of people already visible on it, walking and running. She wonders, sometimes, about the people she sees at the beach. About their lives. Did they grow up here? Are they new? Do they travel to the city for work? Most of her own adult life has been spent in and around this beach. If it were a forest perhaps she'd have worn a path in it; instead, the waves make sure there's nothing to suggest she was ever here at all.

She can't see her house from here, but she knows the kids will be waking up soon and Andrew will be grumbling about making their breakfast. But he'll do it because he knows the kids' hungry whingeing will be more punishment than getting their food. Then, if he's in a good mood, he'll make coffee for Theresa's nonna and take it to the granny flat.

'From what?' Marie says. 'My dog's the only one waiting for me.'

Theresa feels stuck in the kind of moment that happens sometimes: when you know something about someone but you're not sure whether to reveal that you do. Because what if they want to tell you themselves? Or they don't want you to know at all? Just because Trev likes to gossip on the beach doesn't mean that Theresa should know that Marie's husband is dead.

'Oh?' is the response she decides on.

Marie puts her hands on her hips, and for a second Theresa thinks of Yul Brynner in *The King and I*: his proud stance, feet astride, bare chest . . . She has to stop herself giggling.

'I used to swim with my husband,' Marie says with a quick, sad smile. 'But he's gone. Dead, I mean.' She pauses. '"Gone" is a bit too soft, isn't it?'

Theresa starts a reflexive reply.

Marie frowns. 'Don't say you're sorry. You didn't know him. I don't expect you to be sorry.'

Theresa opens and closes her mouth, feeling like a guppy. She doesn't know what she can say if 'sorry' isn't available to her.

Marie exhales. 'Sorry. That was tough.' Her laugh sounds dry and unpractised. 'Now *I'm* the one saying sorry. I'm just not used to meeting people who don't know that Norm's dead. A consequence of doing the same thing every day and never leaving the suburb.'

'My husband's not dead,' Theresa says, thinking that at least they have husbands in common. 'But he's hardly around.'

Marie raises her eyebrows.

'He's out a lot. With his mates.' Theresa shrugs. 'All the blokes seem to do it.'

She doesn't know if all the blokes sit around the house doing nothing useful while their wives cook and clean and do the washing and watch the kids, but she suspects so. The going-out-drinking and the doing-nothing-at-home seem to be a matching pair.

'Do you have children?' Marie asks.

'Two.' Theresa can't help smiling when she thinks of them. 'Oliver, he's eight. Sasha's five. My nonna lives with us too.'

'Nonna, eh? You Italian?'

'Yep. She's a bit of work, but it's great for the kids to have her around. She speaks to them in Italian sometimes.'

'That's the best age to learn a language.' Marie glances towards Main Beach. 'We should get back. You probably have to take those children to school.'

'I do.' Theresa's skin has dried while they've been standing there and she's not relishing the idea of the sting of the cold again.

'I swim from Main Beach every day at sunrise,' Marie says as they walk into the water.

'So do I. You can probably tell I haven't been doing it very long, though.' Theresa feels the nervousness that comes with trying to make a new friend. It's hard when you're an adult. So hard she rarely tries it, and it usually doesn't stick anyway.

'Well . . .' Marie stops and turns to look at her. 'If you don't want to keep swimming alone, how about we swim together every day?'

Theresa feels the way she used to in primary school when she was given a certificate for being the neatest or the kindest or the most helpful with other children. 'I'd love that!' she says and it comes out almost like a squeal.

Marie winks. 'Great. See you back on the beach.' She pulls her goggles down and dives out.

Theresa knows she won't catch her on the way back – and she also knows she doesn't need to. Because Marie is going to be there tomorrow, and the next day. That's all the motivation Theresa needs to keep turning up.

CHAPTER 6

When Leanne wakes up she can't work out if it's Tuesday or Wednesday. The alarm pulled her out of a dream that she wanted to stay in, and it takes her a while to orientate herself. Finally she makes out the familiar lines of her small bedroom in this small flat. She's never needed much space. She doesn't have knick-knacks; she doesn't hang on to books after she's read them. The kitchenette and cramped bathroom aren't ideal but she's not much of a cook and she takes quick showers, so they're not too great an inconvenience.

She thinks about going for a swim – maybe in the ocean. Then she feels the hesitation. No, it's stronger than that: it's fear. What if she's not good enough? What if she struggles or fails without Matt there to keep an eye on her? Practising in the pool is one thing; swimming in the actual ocean is another. She's not ready.

When she was a child – even as a teenager – she didn't know this kind of fear. She would climb trees and swing off branches; climb rocks and jump off them. She used to win running races too. She was fast back then, accustomed to racing her older brothers through the streets, used to them egging her on half out of love and half out of spite, the way most brothers would. 'C'mon, Lee!' they'd call as they sprinted ahead of her, their spindly legs disappearing around corners as she tried to keep up. They didn't make any allowances for her because she was younger or a girl, and she never cared. In fact, she loved it. She loved the challenge. Not that she had ever managed to catch them, but she grew strong and fast in the trying.

As she moved deeper into her teens, she lost that comfort in her body. Then one day it was gone for good. Taken from her.

Now she's twenty-five and she thinks of her body as a foreign land for which she doesn't have a passport. She should get one, though. It's been a long time since she's moved her body just to feel it move instead of trying to control it – or forget it. For years running has been her way of keeping it in check, and she's used that time and the kilometres to travel away from the past.

Swimming is bringing back some of that childhood exhilaration of using her body to go further and climb higher. She's pushing herself, even though sometimes she thinks her swimming prowess is coming along too slowly. But learning something new requires courage – she knows that. It's the same courage she needed to start her life over, to go to university, to move to this suburb where she knows no one.

She still doesn't think she's ready for the ocean, though, so this morning she goes for a run instead, then eats her one piece of toast and Vegemite, and drinks her black tea with half a sugar, before she puts on her nurse's uniform and walks the ten minutes up the hill to Northern Hospital.

Leanne goes into the bathroom for one last check that her hair is neat and tidy, and her uniform as it should be. Matron likes her nurses to be just so and tells them if anything isn't right. In front of the mirror, Leanne pulls her uniform down a little and tucks some stray hairs into her bun. The problem with fine, dead-straight hair is that it slips out of bounds easily.

As she pats it down at the sides she sees flashes of her mother in her face and feels a tug in her heart.

The door opens and bangs against the hand-towel dispenser, and a breathless, bustling figure comes into the bathroom.

'Hi, Leanne!'

'Hi, Theresa.' Leanne smiles tightly, not wanting to encourage chit-chat. They're likely to be here a while if Theresa gets started.

Not that Leanne dislikes Theresa – no doubt she's perfectly pleasant – but she likes to ask questions that Leanne has no intention of answering. *Where did you grow up? Did you always want to be a nurse? Have you lived in Shelly Bay long?* Theresa likes to get to know people and Leanne isn't ready to be known. She's spent the last few years actively trying to not be known. Luckily Theresa only volunteers a couple of days a week so Leanne doesn't have to avoid her too often.

Theresa smiles as she drops her handbag on the counter and starts rummaging through it. 'I rushed here. Had to get the kids to school. Didn't do my make-up.' She rolls her eyes. 'I'm always playing catch-up.'

Leanne glances quickly at Theresa's face and doesn't know what she is worried about. Theresa has thick, long, wavy brown hair, big brown eyes and long lashes; her lips are naturally a deep pink and she has olive skin. She doesn't need make-up. Whereas Leanne thinks her own black hair, black eyebrows, small eyes, small nose and small mouth make her look severe and mean if she doesn't at least use a bit of blusher.

'I have to start my shift,' she says with a small smile. She may not be willing to chat but she wants to be polite.

'Oh!' There's a flash of something that looks like disappointment on Theresa's face, then her big smile is back. 'Before you go – did I see you running on the beach this morning?'

Leanne isn't always conscious of the routes she runs – her legs take her where they want to go – but she remembers thinking that she needed to push herself and run in the soft sand. She didn't think she'd had a witness, however; the idea isn't welcome.

'I was on the beach,' she says.

'I knew it! I told Marie it was you.' Theresa pulls a lipstick from her handbag. 'A-ha! There it is. It's my favourite. They discontinued it. Don't you hate it when that happens? You should join us,' she adds through stretched lips as she applies the hot-pink colour.

Leanne, about to turn to go, feels the peril of having to consider an invitation she doesn't want.

'Me and Marie,' Theresa continues, blotting her lipstick with a tissue. 'We swim every morning at sunrise, to Little Beach and back. It's great!'

Leanne thinks of the swimmers she's seen off the beach; how naïve of her to never consider that she might know one of them, given how many local people she encounters at the hospital.

Then she thinks of the lessons she's been taking just so she can be one of those swimmers. Now Theresa is giving her a chance to put her plan into practice. If Leanne were an ordinary person, the kind who talks easily to people who aren't her patients and who, therefore, aren't children, she'd probably leap at it.

'No pressure,' Theresa says with a note of uncertainty, her smile slipping.

Leanne's silence seems like a rejection, no doubt, but she just can't say yes straightaway. That once-spontaneous person doesn't exist any more.

'I'll – I'll think about it,' she says. 'I'd better go. Matron gets upset when we're late.'

Theresa nods quickly. 'I know! She can be a bit of a dragon, can't she?'

Leanne smiles, and emerges into the corridor. She can hear the high-pitched hum of children talking. It's nice when the patients get to know each other. She was talkative as a child, once she started. Her father said she didn't talk for so long they thought she might have a problem, then she talked so much they just wanted her to shut up. That was a long time ago.

She walks towards her station, priming herself for the day ahead. She loves her work, but she can find it overwhelming too. There are some children who take so much of her time that she feels like she's neglecting others. There are some who, after spending weeks here, go back to places where she knows they won't receive the care they need. But she didn't get into this job to be comfortable. If she'd wanted to be comfortable she could have chosen a nice, quiet job in a bank or an office, a job she could leave behind when the working day was over. One that didn't involve witnessing hurt and pain and sadness. But comfortable isn't what Leanne wants. Comfortable isn't who she is.

'Good morning, Sister,' Matron says.

'Good morning, Matron.' Leanne hurriedly puts her handbag on a shelf, and tucks up another stray hair she can feel tickling her neck.

'I can't seem to find the night nurse so I'll take you through handover. If you're ready.' Matron gestures with her hand for Leanne to follow her.

'Yes, Matron.'

The young voices grow louder as they approach the first room. Leanne has no idea what to expect from these children – she never does, and that is part of what keeps her job interesting. But she knows there will be the chance to help them, to make their lives better, just as she has wished someone would do for her. Except she would never ask for help, and she has become so good at hiding her need for it that she can't blame others for not noticing.

As Leanne walks through the door behind Matron she sees five faces – some with teeth missing, some with hair like a bird's nest, all with eyes bright – and she remembers something else she loves about this job: the chance to start over, for these children, and for her. Each day anew. Each hour an opportunity for things to be different. Better.

One day it will come true.

CHAPTER 7

'Are these your famous Anzac biscuits, Marie?'

Father Paul gives her a wink as he picks up another biscuit from the plate. That's his third, and Marie can't help feeling chuffed that he's enjoying them.

'I don't know if they're famous,' she says, wishing that false modesty wasn't a quality she'd been taught to cultivate from childhood. 'And I haven't made them for a while, so they probably aren't.'

'I've heard talk at the church.' Father Paul smiles as he bites into the biscuit. 'Dulcie even sounded somewhat annoyed that she hasn't been able to guess your recipe.'

Marie picks up a biscuit for herself. 'It's all in the sugar, Father. I don't use the same sugar as everyone else.'

She closes her eyes as she takes a bite and remembers her mother churning out Anzac biscuits by the dozens. Her mother once confessed that after Marie's father returned from the Great War the only way she could cope with his long silences was to bake. It was also the only way she could show him that she loved him; saying it back then wasn't really acceptable behaviour.

Marie's parents never told her they loved her either, although she knew they did. Just like she never told Norm too often, although she loved him. Still does. Nor did he say it to her, yet she knew how he felt by the way he looked at her and took care of her.

Marie regrets not saying it more, but it simply wasn't done. The fashion these days for verbal declarations of affection stems, she is sure, from those ridiculous television shows everyone is watching. Those soaps. Nothing wrong with a good book, and it lasts a lot longer and gives more comfort than an episode of *Days of Our Lives*. She has to be careful about expressing that opinion, though, because she knows some of the ladies at the church are fond of the shows.

Not that she sees those ladies as often as she used to. Morning service at St Mary's Immaculate, twelve minutes' walk from her house after she showered off the salt water, used to set her up for the day. But she's fallen out of the habit. She's been trying to work out if it's laziness, old age or something more sinister that has her stuck in this position of wanting to keep doing what she's always done but feeling less willing to expend the energy required.

Going to church means talking to a lot of people who aren't friends – people who say all the polite things but aren't genuinely interested in her wellbeing. She used to care about them – when she said, 'How are you?' she meant it. Although it doesn't come back in the same measure; and she no longer has the inclination to give it out when it's not returned. She's not cut out to have a bottomless well of compassion and regard for her fellow man – and she knows that means she's letting down her faith. Her God. That requires a reckoning between her and Him, but she doesn't want to do it with an audience. So she doesn't go to church every day any more.

There is also the fact that, most days, going for her swim is as much as she can manage. Gwen once told her that grief would track her down, just when she thought she'd outrun it. Gwen's first husband died suddenly, so even though her second is still very much alive Marie takes Gwen as an authority on the subject of being a widow. She wants to ask her friend if grief feels like a weight you drag around, a weight that holds you back – holds you under sometimes. But she hasn't been to see Gwen in too long and it doesn't feel like the sort of conversation you can have over the phone. One day, maybe, she'll get herself to Gwen's retirement village and ask her in person.

It's the dragging around that Father Paul has noticed. As well as her absence in the mornings. He took her aside last Sunday and told her that he was always available for her if she wished to talk. 'I may not be a doctor but I can make house calls,' he said – and here he is, doing just that and taking another bite of the biscuit.

'I suppose you're not going to tell me which sugar you use?' he says, and smiles at her in a complicit way.

Marie smiles back. 'Only if you can get me into Heaven.' She's grateful he's made the time to visit her: she feels better already.

'I'll put in a word.'

Father Paul sits deeper in the armchair that Marie keeps telling herself she'll throw out. It was Norm's favourite, and even though it's seen better days she likes the memories attached to it.

She hears the scratch of doggie claws on the floorboards in the hallway.

'Charlie Brown,' she says sternly, 'you know you're not allowed in here while I have visitors.'

The scratching stops.

'I don't mind if he comes in,' says Father Paul, leaning out of his chair towards the doorway, where one of Charlie Brown's paws is visible. 'I like dogs.'

'It's good for him to have a bit of discipline,' Marie explains. 'He has the run of the place usually. I can't let him think he can get his way all the time.'

Father Paul looks amused. 'You don't think it might be too late for that?'

Marie thinks of Charlie Brown sleeping on her bed, sitting on her lap when she's on the couch and standing next to her while she cooks.

'Probably,' she concedes, smiling sheepishly.

'It's good to see you smile, Marie.' Father Paul puts his cup and saucer on the coffee table and sits back, crossing one leg over the other and brushing his hair out of his eyes. He has a good, thick head of hair – like John F Kennedy's. Irish hair. Presidential hair, you might even call it.

'It's good of you to visit, Father.'

They sit looking at each other, and she's aware that she doesn't know how to have a conversation with him like this. He's never visited her at home; they've only ever talked at the church. She's not sure if she's meant to treat this like a casual confessional or chat about the weather.

'I haven't heard you mention Gwen lately,' he says.

'That's because she . . .' Marie stops, surprised to find herself feeling emotional. And embarrassed about it in front of the priest. He may be here because he's concerned about her but it feels impolite to fall to pieces.

'She and her husband moved away,' she goes on, collecting herself. 'To a retirement village in the northern suburbs.'

Father Paul nods slowly. 'Life continues to change, doesn't it?'

This doesn't appear to be an existential statement so much as a personal acknowledgement – or maybe that's how Marie wants to take it.

'It does,' she says, her voice catching.

As he picks up the teapot Father Paul looks at her enquiringly and she nods. He fills her cup just enough to allow her room to splash milk into it. What a thoughtful man.

Marie hasn't known that many men – there was Norm, of course, but she didn't have a brother. There was one boy cousin, but she lost touch with him years ago. She went to a Catholic girls school on the other side of St Mary's. Fraternising with boys was discouraged there, and at home. She barely spoke to young men her age, so when she met Norm she didn't know how to talk to him. Her mother had sent her down the road to buy fruit, and there he was in his shop. He was tall, and she didn't mind that he had a little stoop. Tall men do sometimes. He asked her name, and she told him. He said he recognised her from church, and she couldn't believe, first, that he was Catholic – that seemed too easy – and, second, that she had never noticed him. He told her, well after it was too late to matter, that he'd never been confirmed; he went to mass because he liked the ritual. She'd never seen him because he sat up the back and never came forward to take the sacrament.

'You must be lonely in this house sometimes,' Father Paul says, sipping his tea, 'even with Charlie Brown.'

She nods quickly. It's the first time since Norm died that anyone has acknowledged what has become her natural state.

'I know all this loss has been hard,' he continues, 'but I fear that Gwen's departure might have been one loss too many.'

'She hasn't died,' she says, almost too sharply.

'No, but you have known her longer than you've known your daughter, or your husband. She's – what did you call her? Your bosom friend.' He smiles. 'Like Anne of Green Gables and her friend Diana.'

'Yes,' Marie says. She and Gwen had both loved the book and seen themselves in it: young women fancying themselves headstrong and bright. She isn't sure, now, if that assessment was accurate but she enjoyed it at the time.

'I know how *I* would feel if my bosom friend left and I wasn't able to see her easily. Especially if my other loved ones are far away.' His eyes hold hers and are full of understanding.

Marie has let herself grieve for Norm, even on days when the grief felt like it might consume her. She's let herself miss Nicole, and she knows her daughter isn't too far away. What she hasn't done is allow herself to feel what Gwen's absence really means for her day-to-day life. They saw each other almost every day from childhood, and spoke on the phone in between. She was more honest with Gwen than she was with anyone else – including Father Paul. They'd shared all the ups and downs of a normal human life.

'Have you been to visit her since she moved?' Father Paul asks.

'No.' She sighs. 'That's bizarre, isn't it? That I haven't visited my best friend. I mean, she hasn't moved to Mars!'

Her levity is false, and she can tell that he knows.

'Perhaps you're angry at her for leaving you, in a way you don't feel you can be angry at Norm and Nicole.' Father Paul's eyes search hers. 'But I think it's more likely that you simply need to find a new way to stay in contact with her,' he continues. 'Communicating with Gwen was a matter of course for you when she lived nearby. It was part of your routine for decades. It makes sense that you're having trouble adjusting to life without it.'

This is a kindness he's offering her: letting her off the hook for moping around because her friend has done a perfectly reasonable thing in moving to a different place.

'Don't you think she may feel the same?' Father Paul says. 'She may be having trouble adjusting to life without you.'

'I doubt it!' Marie says, but she doesn't really know. She presumed that because Gwen made the decision to go, she would be fine with whatever resulted from it.

'What makes you think you're so easy to forget, Marie?' Father Paul's face relaxes into a smile. 'I'm sure she misses you just as much as you miss her. Why don't you visit her?'

Marie feels something stuck in her throat. An admission, perhaps, that she's scared to see Gwen in case Gwen's new life is just wonderful without her.

'I should,' she finally gets out.

'Yes, you should.'

As he looks at her she wonders how he became so wise at such a young age. He can't be older than forty, yet he is more understanding and compassionate than she believes she will ever be.

'You're still swimming, I take it?' he says.

'Yes.'

She thinks of this morning's swim, with Theresa attempting a faster freestyle and instead looking like the Tasmanian Devil in a Looney Tunes cartoon, arms and legs thrashing around and hardly any progress being made. Marie had laughed so much she swallowed water, and her body hummed with the joy of it as she walked home up the hill.

'You're smiling,' Father Paul says. 'I take it that means you're enjoying it.'

Marie nods. 'I am. I have someone to swim with. For now.'

'For now?'

'Who knows how long she'll last? I see a lot of people who are very keen for a couple of weeks each spring or summer, then you don't see them again until next year.'

She can't understand why that happens – why anyone would drop a new habit so quickly, especially when it's so beneficial – but she hopes Theresa won't be amongst their number. She is finding her to be good company.

'I have faith,' Father Paul says, gazing at her. 'I'm sure she will enjoy swimming with you so much that she'll have no trouble continuing.' He takes another biscuit. 'Now, are you sure you won't tell me what sugar you use in these?'

They smile at each other. Yes, he is a thoughtful man. Thoughtful and kind.

And Marie has learnt at least one thing today. While Gwen may not be down the road any more, she still has a friend nearby.

CHAPTER 8

The children are still asleep when Theresa checks on them: Ollie lying on his back with his arms and legs flung out, Sasha curled around her favourite teddy bear. It took ages to get them to this point – they each wanted two stories read and to have their backs rubbed. Theresa understood: she'd like to have someone rub her back too.

They're always like this on the nights when Andrew doesn't arrive home in time for dinner. They never say anything about him not being there, yet they cling harder to her. They want all of her time, and they'll fight sleep to get it. It eats into the time she has to potter around before bed but she finds herself thinking that she *should* mind that more than she actually does. She is lucky to have her children, and doesn't take them for granted. One of her sisters-in-law has been trying for years to get pregnant and it hasn't worked; and someone Theresa knew at school had a baby who only lived for a few weeks. There are reminders everywhere that motherhood is not always easily come by or kept.

She pushes open the kitchen's screen door and steps down to the path that takes her to the granny flat. Everyone they know in Shelly Bay has a house like this: one storey, three bedrooms, half brick, half fibro, with a reasonable back garden and some room out the front for rose bushes or whatever else people like to plant to make their place look nice from the street.

When she and Andrew bought the house, not long after they married, the granny flat was a shed. Andrew had liked the idea of a place to store the lawnmower and his surfboard, and it was somewhere to keep the gardening equipment. On weekends he'd disappear into the shed and do god-knows-what. Once Theresa found some girlie magazines, some empty tinnies and three packets of Benson & Hedges. She threw out the tinnies, and the next time she came looking for a trowel the girlie magazines were gone.

Three years ago the shed became a flat when Nonna came to live with them.

Andrew had protested when Theresa said that her grandmother would have to move in.

'Why do I have to support your family?' he'd said, in a way that made her wonder if he even resented having to support their children. 'Why can't she live with your parents?'

Theresa had pointed out that Nonna was an elderly woman who had lived on the northern beaches for decades; her friends were here, and she knew no one on the Central Coast, where Theresa's parents lived. Nonna could no longer be at home alone but that was no reason to uproot her entirely.

'Besides,' she'd said, 'she can watch the kids after school while I'm—'

'Getting your nails done?' he'd said, and she'd wanted to burst into tears.

'No, Andrew. While I'm shopping and cooking and cleaning.'

'That's your job.'

'I realise that, but you don't have to do your job and also look after the children.'

He had looked momentarily stumped. 'You could give up volunteering. Then you'd have more time to do everything else and watch the kids.'

Volunteering at Northern Hospital was the only thing in Theresa's life that was just for her – until she started swimming. She feels competent at the hospital, and gets to talk to people who have ages in double digits. Yet she knew Andrew wouldn't understand; and she also knew not to say anything that might sound defensive because she wanted something from him.

'It's important to give back to the community,' she'd said as calmly as she could, 'so I'm not giving that up. Nonna won't get in the way. If anything, she'll be a help to us.'

He'd snorted. 'And you'll have even less time for me.'

She didn't know what he meant – he never asked to spend time with her. He went to work, came home and went to the shed. But there was no point trying to bargain further. 'Please,' was all she'd said.

He'd agreed – after a few days.

Now he seems to like having Nonna there, because she's happy to talk about the cricket and she's an excellent cook. Andrew prefers Nonna's lasagna to anything Theresa makes. But at the time he'd whinged his way through each day of painting the walls and putting in a shower and toilet for her. He'd done it all himself, which surprised Theresa – she hadn't known he had those kinds of skills – but he'd brushed aside her thanks. She knows she's never able to say things in the way he wants her to, but she doesn't know how else to say them.

The air feels humid as she makes her way to Nonna's door. She thought there might be a storm tonight but it seems to have passed them by and left only its heavy promise behind.

She knocks softly. 'Nonna?' Her grandmother is usually still awake at this time of night but she never likes to presume.

'*Si*, Theresa,' comes the rich voice that has deepened with the years and Nonna's fondness for menthol cigarettes and afternoon aperitifs.

Theresa opens the door and finds Nonna with a ciggie in one hand and *La Fiamma* in the other.

'Can I get you anything?' she asks.

'No, thank you, darling.' Nonna wafts the ciggie in the air. 'I have everything I need.' She smiles and her face turns into a concertina, folds enveloping her eyes.

Theresa doesn't remember what her nonna looked like before she wrinkled, and can't help wondering if that's what she's going to look like herself one day. The only difference between them is that Theresa only smoked for a few years and quit before she got pregnant the first time. Nonna smoked through all her pregnancies and the breastfeeding too.

'Are you playing cards tomorrow?' Theresa asks, leaning in the doorway.

There's a regular game of poker at the house of one of her grandmother's friends; it has proved to be a source of funding of presents for Ollie and Sasha.

Nonna exhales smoke and nods. 'Yes. I need to have a victory.'

'Don't you have one every week?' Theresa raises an eyebrow. 'You're bleeding those old coots dry.'

Nonna smiles mysteriously. 'They deserve it.'

Theresa laughs. 'I bet they don't. I think you just like to win.'

'Don't you?'

Theresa hears the front door slam and winces. Andrew should know the kids are asleep by now. The noise could wake them.

She looks at her grandmother and wiggles her eyebrows.

Nonna shrugs in response. 'He's your husband,' she says and takes another drag on her cigarette.

Theresa makes a face and steps out of the doorway. '*Ciao*,' she says as Nonna waves her off.

Inside, she can smell Andrew before she sees him: hops mixed with the smoke cloud that hangs in every pub. As she walks into the living room he's already slumped on the couch and turning up the volume on the television.

'You'll wake the kids,' she says, and can hear the irritation in her voice. She shouldn't have to talk to him like he's a kid himself, yet that's all she seems to do, especially when he isn't sober.

'Hello to you too,' he says and she feels the rebuke in it. She knows she forgets to say hello and goodbye to him most days, but he doesn't say anything to her either.

'Andrew – the volume.'

'They'll live,' he says.

Theresa's shoulders hunch and she feels her jaw tense. She doesn't want to be like this around her own husband – she wants to welcome him with open arms and a big kiss, but he makes that impossible.

Not once has he arrived home and said he's happy to see her. In the early days she used to say she'd missed him and he'd wink and slap her bum, although he'd never say he missed her too. It took her a while – perhaps too long – to realise that he never says anything much that could be construed as affectionate or appreciative. He doesn't even tell the children he loves them.

She'd asked him about it once and he said she was spoiling them by telling them all the time. 'You'll make them sooks,' he'd said.

She shouldn't have been surprised, because 'sook' is his father's favourite word. Andrew was a sook of a kid, apparently, until he learnt to harden up. Andrew's father believes that Oliver is heading the same way: too sooky because he always wants his mum, but 'he'll grow out of it, mark my words'.

Theresa has never marked any of her father-in-law's words but she knows Andrew does.

Looking at Andrew sitting on the couch, his face half in shadow because the bulb in the lamp is near the end of its life, Theresa thinks he looks like his father. He's getting the same jowls. She can't say she's ever found jowls sexy. Combined with the fact that she's exhausted all the time and seems to have three children instead of two, it's no wonder they haven't been naked together for so long she can barely remember what he looks like. Maybe it was New Year's Eve. Which makes it . . . almost a year. Cripes. According to *Cleo* it should be a lot more regular than that if she wants to 'keep her man'. Not that he's making the prospect appealing.

'Where have you been?' she says, because she still cares about what he does even if he doesn't care about her.

'Out.'

She counts to five so she doesn't come back with a retort that would only earn her an argument.

'The kids missed you.'

'Yeah?' He sinks a little further down but doesn't turn to look at her.

'I'd really like you to be here to have dinner with them.' She tries to sound assertive. She's read about that in *Cleo* too.

'They eat pretty early,' he says. 'I'm not hungry then.'

Another count to five.

'Fair enough. But they'd still like to see you before they go to bed.'

'And I'd like you to be here when they wake up,' he says.

Now his bleary eyes are turned her way, and she can't tell if he's angry with her or simply saying something true. They stare at each other as a movie plays on the TV. She thinks she can hear John Wayne talking.

'You get to do your swimming,' Andrew says, 'and I get to go out with the boys. Fair's fair.'

There's a certain logic to it, she has to admit. But if she starts to do the maths on what she does versus what he does and who comes out in front, they'll get stuck in the same muck they've been in for a long time – too long. Their marriage is a push-and-pull of who wants what and who doesn't get what they want. Each of them feels hard done by. She feels like if she's awake she's working to look after this house and their children; and he says he has all the financial burden and that should count for a lot.

She can't escape the conclusion that the only way out of it is for her to give up the fight. To stop asking for things. To stay quiet. To be the obedient little wife and maybe then Andrew will start coming home early enough to see the kids. He's never going to change, so she has to be the one to do it. It would be less stressful, that's for sure.

Except she's not giving up the swimming. She has come to need it. When she does that swim she achieves something, and Theresa doesn't feel like she achieves anything else in her life apart from just getting by. Maybe when her children reach adulthood in one piece she'll feel like she's accomplished something, but that's a long way off.

'I'm going to bed,' she says, as she does every time.

'Right,' he says, his head already swivelled back to the TV.

Slowly, Theresa makes her way to their bedroom and undresses. Andrew will probably sleep on the couch tonight, like he's been doing lately. She doesn't miss him thrashing around in the night but she's not rapt about the development. It doesn't feel like a temporary situation.

Once upon a time she thought the sun shone out of Andrew, and believed he thought the same of her. Each night now, as she's waiting to fall asleep, she tries to figure out how they can get back to that, because it would be a more peaceful way to live.

There's an obstacle, though, that she just can't shift: for her, the sun now shines out of Oliver and Sasha. If she'd once thought her love for Andrew was endless, she found its limits – but she knows, with each cell of her body, that her love for her children is as big as the universe. She can only hope, for Andrew's sake, that he feels the same.

CHAPTER 9

While swimming each morning might have seemed like a good idea in theory, Elaine isn't convinced that it's one in practice. Not when she's spent the night before drinking gin and tonics while waiting for James to get home from work – which he did, late, kissing her once and falling asleep sprawled across her torso. Luckily he was too tired to notice that she was drunk, or there would have been words. Each time he sees her with a drink he counsels her to 'slow down', but it's all right for him with his twelve hours a day at work while she's at home, missing her children and the business she used to run and the friends she used to see, and the parents she used to pop round to visit and do the crossword with and take to the doctor.

Elaine's sister has to look after their parents now. All Elaine has to do is try to adjust to this new country that is not new to her husband, who has picked up again with all his school and university friends, and whose mother is delighted to have her only son back home. Precisely no one is delighted to see Elaine. Except James, when he's conscious. She supposes she should feel grateful for that – she knows more than a few women whose husbands are boors, and bores, and neither party is delighted to see the other, ever.

Not that it's stopped her drinking too much. She knows it's too much, but what started as a way to pass the time, and distract herself from the fact that the housework does not at all fill her day, has become a habit she can't seem to break. Which is *ridiculous* because it's not as if she doesn't have willpower. She has exercised it almost every day of her life since she was a teenager, including throughout her pregnancies. Her food intake is monitored in what one might call an ascetic fashion. Booze, on the other hand, is proving harder to control.

This morning, that lack of control has left her with a pounding headache to match the pounding waves that she's trying to avoid thumping into her as she swims back to shore. She must be foolhardy to attempt to swim at all in this surf. She grew up swimming in nice local lidos and on beaches in Norfolk. James tried to warn her about Australian surf, but she breezily informed him that she had several blue ribbons in all sorts of swimming strokes and she would be *fine, thank you, darling, just fine.*

Today's definition of *fine* includes wanting to vomit – because of her hangover and the panic resulting from the tug at her feet that is a rip or sweep or whatever Australians call it that carries people out to sea. She's fighting it to get back to the beach. She's stronger than this. *Fitter* than this. She shouldn't be having so much trouble.

'Oi! Marie!' she hears a man call as her feet find purchase on the sand and she uses her hands to pull herself through the water. 'Bloody tourists!'

Elaine looks to her left, where an older gent stands with arms folded over a hairy suntanned chest and tight swimming costume.

'They all think they can swim,' he goes on. 'Getting into trouble all the bloody time.'

'Shut up, Trev,' says a woman with grey hair who, Elaine can see now, is hauling a teenage girl out of the water. 'You could give me a hand, you know.'

'You're doin' all right,' he says. 'Besides, I've done me back in.' He winces in an exaggerated fashion and puts a hand to his hip.

Elaine can see that the girl's eyes are closed and her body is limp, so that Marie – she presumes it is Marie carrying the girl – is struggling with her. Finding some speed, Elaine steps onto the sand and hurries over.

'Can I help?' she says, picking up the girl's legs and seeing the relief in Marie's eyes.

'I'm coming, Marie!' Elaine hears from behind, and glances over her shoulder to see a younger woman having the same trouble she did getting out of the surf.

'Watch behind you,' Elaine says as Marie starts to stumble up the sharp incline of sand carved out by hard-crashing waves.

'Thanks,' Marie grunts, adjusting her grip under the girl's armpits as Elaine tightens her own on the ankles. Above the water's reach, she adds, 'Let's put her down. Easy.'

Once the girl is on the sand, the other woman appears. 'Sorry – so hard to get in,' she says breathlessly. She kneels down and puts her cheek next to the girl's mouth. 'She's breathing, but let's get her on her side.'

Elaine can only watch as Marie puts her hands under the base of the girl's head while the other woman looks as if she's about to wrestle with her, her arms wrapping around, then she rolls the girl onto her side. Much to Elaine's shock, the next thing she does is put her finger in the girl's mouth.

'Clearing the airway,' Marie says, catching Elaine's eye. 'In case there's sea water or anything in her mouth. We don't want her to *stop* breathing.'

Elaine nods, struck mute by the choreography of this unlikely scenario: two rescuing women, an unconscious girl, a man standing by and doing nothing. And her, also doing nothing because there's nothing she knows to do. These women seem to have some intrinsic knowledge about how to save a life. Perhaps that's something else that comes with living in Australia.

The girl coughs and moans, her eyelids fluttering.

'Hello?' says the woman. 'Can you hear me? What's your name?'

The girl coughs again. 'Kathy,' she says croakily.

'Kathy, you got into some trouble in the water,' Marie says, stroking the girl's forehead. 'How are you feeling?'

'Um . . . a bit strange.' Kathy attempts to move.

'Stay there,' says the woman. 'Don't rush anything. You've had a bit of a shock.'

She and Marie look at each other.

'Theresa, you go,' says Marie. 'I know you have to get the kids to school.'

Theresa's forehead crinkles. 'I don't want to leave her.'

'I'll stay with her,' Marie says.

'I can stay too,' Elaine says. It's the least she can offer.

The woman – Theresa – smiles at Elaine. 'Thanks for your help before.'

Elaine makes a noise of disbelief. 'I hardly did anything.'

'It helps just to know someone else cares.' She stands up. 'I'm Theresa. This is my friend, Marie.'

'I'm Elaine,' she mutters in the shy way of a new girl in the school playground.

'Thanks again. But I have to get going. Maybe I'll see you tomorrow?' Theresa doesn't wait for an answer as she bustles over to a nearby towel folded on the sand, picking it up as she wrests her swimming cap off her head. 'Bye, Marie!' she calls as she almost skips over the sand towards the stairs.

Marie waves and turns her attention back to the girl, who is now pushing herself up onto one hand. Trev, Elaine realises, has disappeared.

'Here,' she says, offering her hands to Kathy, who is slowly getting to her feet.

Marie takes the girl's elbows. 'How are you feeling?' she says.

Kathy blushes. 'A bit embarrassed. I thought I was okay.'

'We all think that, love,' Marie says kindly, 'until we're not. Just take your time. See how you feel standing up. There's no hurry.' Her eyes catch Elaine's and she nods her head to the side. 'Let's give her a second,' she says softly.

Elaine steps away and Marie follows, both of them keeping watch on the girl.

'You swim often?' Marie asks.

'Hm?'

'I saw you here the other day.'

'Oh – yes. I've started coming down in the mornings.'

'You may prefer to swim on your own, but if you don't Theresa and I are here at sunrise each day. You're welcome to join us. We swim to Little Beach and back.' Marie smiles. 'I don't know how Theresa fits it in. She has a lot to juggle. Kids at primary school. She volunteers at the hospital. I know she skedaddled this morning, but she's usually very friendly.'

Elaine feels something like shame. Theresa has a life full of obligation and she still managed to take care of a stranger in distress. Elaine has a life full of emptiness and can't manage her way out of her own distress.

'And I think I know her well enough to say she'd welcome another swimmer,' Marie adds, looking at Elaine as she smiles.

'Thank you,' Elaine says quickly, not sure whether to believe Marie. What if Theresa wouldn't want her to join them? Elaine doesn't want to be tossed out of yet another group.

Kathy stands up a bit straighter and turns to look at them.

'Are you all right to walk?' Elaine calls and moves towards her.

Kathy nods. 'Yes. Thanks.'

'Can I walk you somewhere?' Elaine asks, happy to have a potential task.

Kathy nods again. 'Yes, please. My bag is at the surf club.'

Marie smiles approvingly. 'Thanks, Elaine.'

'It's nothing. Honestly.' She puts her arm through the girl's.

'See you,' Marie says, and Elaine isn't sure if it's meant for her or Kathy.

Elaine only glances back once as she carefully escorts Kathy to the club. She sees Marie walking slowly, deliberately, her head bowed as if she's examining each footstep. Perhaps she's someone Elaine could get to know; someone who might like to get to know Elaine. But if Elaine doesn't turn up to swim with Marie, neither of them will ever find out.

SUMMER 1982-1983

CHAPTER 10

'Morning, Theresa.' Marie's smile is just visible in the dawn light but Theresa would recognise those broad shoulders anywhere.

'Good morning, Marie!'

Theresa feels almost as happy to see Marie as she does to see her children every day after school: it's the warmth of knowing you like someone enough to miss them and then enjoy their company again.

At least, Marie gives the impression that she likes Theresa. Each morning whoever is there first waits for the other, then they swim together, striking out for Little Beach. Sometimes they stop offshore and tread water for a while. Marie says it's good for the legs. Theresa's legs already feel like they're getting enough exercise with the swimming, but Marie looks athletic for an old duck so who is Theresa to doubt her word?

And she really shouldn't think that Marie is old. She's just *older*. Theresa knows that Marie is in her sixties, because once she said something about being in her twenties during World War II. Theresa's idea of people in their sixties used to be that they were glued to their favourite armchairs, doing the crosswords and reading the death notices in the *Herald*. That's because her father's parents used to do that, and Andrew's parents still do.

Nonna doesn't, though, so Theresa should remember not to make assumptions about people before she knows them. It's a bad habit and she's always done it. She could blame her mother for telling her over and over that girls whose skirts were a certain height above the knee were 'cheap' and if their hair was dyed a certain way they were 'common'. It's not that her mother is mean, either; it's what she and all her friends think. Theresa has no idea where they get it from but it infected her for a while. She's making herself stop. You have to take people as you find them. That's what Marie did to her, and she's doing it to Marie. No judgements. The way friends should always be with each other.

Theresa snaps back to attention when she realises that Marie is sighing as she looks at the water.

'What was that for?' she asks as she tucks her hair into her cap.

'Hm?' Marie turns to look at her.

'That sigh.'

'What sigh?'

'You *sighed*. It was loud. You didn't notice?'

Marie frowns briefly and Theresa worries that she's put her foot in something she didn't even know was there.

'It's . . .' Marie sighs again and shakes her head. 'It's a day.'

'What do you mean?'

Marie's lips part and close, and her shoulders slump a little. 'I had a boy.' She keeps looking at the ocean but Theresa wishes she'd look at her, because she sounds so sad. 'He was stillborn. Today. Thirty-three years ago.'

Now she gives Theresa a smile, except Theresa feels like crying for her instead.

'He'd be thirty-three. Obviously.' Another sigh. 'I don't think of him all the time, but on this day I do.'

Theresa puts her hand on Marie's arm. They may be friends now, but she doesn't think she knows her well enough to hug her. 'I'm so sorry,' she says, and it sounds hollow. Meaningless. Especially when Marie told her once before not to say sorry about her husband. 'It's not the right thing to say but I never know what the right thing is.'

'There is no right thing.' Marie looks at her kindly. 'And there's no wrong thing, either. It's nice for me to be able to talk about him to someone. Norm and I . . .' She pauses. 'Well, we didn't talk about it. And Nicole can't remember it – she was only two. So I don't like to talk about it with her. My friend Gwen was a godsend at the time, but we haven't spoken about it in years.'

Theresa nods because she's not sure what to do apart from acknowledge what she has heard.

'Time's a funny thing, isn't it?' Marie goes on. 'It seems like yesterday that he was here. And it seems like another lifetime. In my head I'm still that young.' She shrugs. 'Yet most days I feel old.'

Theresa takes her hand; *that* feels like the right thing to do. 'What was his name?' she says softly.

'Duncan.' Marie squeezes her palm. 'Thank you for asking.'

They stand there for a minute, maybe two, maybe three, as the sky turns their faces orange. Normally Theresa is keen to get in the water because she knows how much is waiting for her at home. Get in, get out, choof off, plough into the day. Today, though, she's happy to be still for a while.

'Er . . . hello?'

Theresa turns to see the lady from last week – the one who helped with the half-drowned girl. She looks nervous.

'Elaine, isn't it?' says Marie, and Elaine's face relaxes.

'Yes. Hello . . . Marie. And Theresa.'

'You can come closer – we're not that scary,' Marie says.

Theresa wants to laugh at that. Marie can seem imposing sometimes – she looks like a warrior walking out of the water, and she doesn't smile that readily.

Theresa knows she gives her own smiles away perhaps too much, although that's what she was told to do when she was a little girl. *Smile, Theresa, no one likes to see a pretty girl with a scowl* – her mother's broken record. It didn't matter who they were with, Theresa had to smile while her brothers could just be themselves. She can feel the unfairness of it still – but she's used to stuffing those kinds of feelings down.

'Do you mind if I join you?' Elaine asks, and Theresa can't help the instant pang of – what? Jealousy? No. It's . . . disappointment. She won't have Marie to herself, and she's become used to that.

Ah well, life is nothing if not change. Nonna likes to say that, and she's lived through two world wars so Theresa thinks she should believe her.

'I told Elaine we wouldn't mind a third,' Marie says, and her eyes look like they're pleading a little bit.

'It's fine!' Theresa says. 'You look like you're fitter than me – you can probably keep up with Marie.' She rolls her eyes. 'I can't. She's *so* much better.'

'No, I'm not,' Marie says with what sounds like a *tsk-tsk*. 'I'm just more experienced. I'm guessing from your accent that you probably didn't grow up swimming in the ocean, Elaine?'

'No, I didn't. And I haven't been in Australia long enough to get much practice.'

'What brought you here?' Theresa asks.

'My husband is Australian. We met in England – we've

always lived in England.' Elaine's face clouds momentarily. 'But he wanted to come home.'

Marie's eyes narrow a little. 'That can't be easy for you. Do you have kids?'.

'Two sons. They're grown-up so . . .' There's the cloud again. 'They stayed in the UK.'

'Oh no! You must be so sad,' Theresa says, unable to imagine not having her children nearby – in fact, she's not even going to try to imagine it. But maybe she's making it worse for Elaine by reacting so strongly? She should have thought before she opened her mouth.

Elaine looks almost relieved, however. 'I am,' she says, with a small smile. 'I miss them all the time. But they have their own lives now. We couldn't expect them to rearrange everything just because their father quite rightly wanted to be near his family and friends for a change.'

'I think a daily swim is just the thing for you then,' says Marie. 'It's a good discipline. A good . . . distraction. I'm speaking from experience.'

The look on Elaine's face shows that she understands. 'I've been enjoying the swimming so far,' she says. 'Although I had a shock the other morning – it was harder to manage than I'd expected.'

Her eyes flit from Marie to Theresa, almost as if she's seeking approval.

'A word of caution, then,' says Marie. 'Always respect the ocean, and never turn your back on a wave.'

Elaine frowns. 'But how do you—'

'Get out?' Marie smiles. 'Keep checking over your shoulder. Even when the surf is small, there can be one that surprises you. Like today – they're mostly small but each seventh wave has a kick to it.'

'Seventh wave?'

'Seven waves in a set. The last one is usually the biggest.' Marie winks. 'Stick with me, you'll be right.'

Elaine nods. 'I will.'

'And I'll be watching from far, far behind,' Theresa says as she removes her sarong and folds it up, putting it under her towel. Elaine hurriedly puts her own cap on.

'Ready?' Marie says.

'Ready,' Elaine says emphatically.

'Lead on, Macduff!' Theresa says, giggling.

She walks slowly so that Elaine can accompany Marie into the surf, her earlier disappointment put aside. It's been lovely – a privilege – having Marie to herself but she's really too special to hoard. Besides, Theresa likes Elaine already, in the way that you just know you like some people even if you can't say exactly why. *Kismet*, you might call it. She read that word in a book once. It was kismet that she met Marie, and now it might have happened again, and she's not going to argue with that.

CHAPTER 11

Today is the day. After her lessons, and Matt's reassurances that her freestyle is 'coming along nicely', Leanne is ready to swim in the ocean. With Theresa and her friends.

She hasn't arrived at this decision lightly; she could even say she's capitulated to it. To Theresa's bouncy campaign to persuade her to swim in the ocean instead of the pool. 'Beautiful morning,' she might say as she passes Leanne in the corridor. 'The water is so warm now – almost like a bath!' Then she'll keep walking, as if she's doing nothing more than giving Leanne a weather report. But the next day there'll be something else: 'I can't believe how good I feel swimming every day.' Or: 'It's so much fun swimming with other people. I don't have time to think about whether or not I'm getting tired.'

Leanne has been nodding along to these statements as if she's a bystander, not their intended audience. She's impressed by Theresa's willingness to persevere. It makes her think that she really wants her to come swimming.

The only clue Leanne has as to why Theresa might be doing all of this came a couple of weeks ago, when Theresa asked if Leanne was seeing her friends on the weekend. Leanne was looking through a file at the time and only half listening, which is why she didn't have time to obfuscate as she normally would.

Because there aren't any friends. Instead she has a small garden to tend; on Saturday mornings she goes to the local library to stock up on books for the week, and on Sunday afternoons she attends the local cinema.

'No,' she replied.

'Why not?' said Theresa, and that's when Leanne realised her mistake.

'Because, um . . .' She'd turned away and hoped that Theresa wouldn't press the issue – which was completely irrational, because Theresa is the last person who would let that kind of thing go.

'Leanne?'

'Hm?' She kept her back turned, which was rude, of course, but she didn't want to engage.

'You never talk about your friends,' Theresa says, and it's not an accusation. She sounds curious, and maybe a little sorrowful, as if Leanne should be pitied.

'Because that's nothing to do with work,' she'd said as strongly as she could, thankful that Theresa couldn't see the lie written across her face.

'Okay,' Theresa said meekly, and left, and Leanne felt bad.

After that Theresa started asking her the occasional question: What would she be doing on the weekend? Had she seen such-and-such movie? It didn't sound like concern so much as nosiness, yet Leanne knows that Theresa isn't so pointed.

Or maybe Leanne just doesn't want to believe that the campaign to persuade her to come swimming is born out of pity – but she can hardly ask, and she won't let it stop her. In order to get herself here today, she's had to trust that Theresa means well, and no more than that. Whether or not Leanne joins her little group, it's clear she has friends to swim with and doesn't need Leanne. So it's altruism that's motivating her. Or maybe she likes to have a lot of friends. Leanne can't imagine why Theresa would want to be her friend, given how difficult she can be, yet she's persisted.

She didn't tell Theresa that she would be joining her today. Or any day. She didn't want to feel locked in – and if she'd made a promise, that's how she'd feel. But a couple of days ago Theresa mentioned that she and Marie now had another person with them, Elaine, and that Elaine had only just started swimming in the ocean. Leanne felt reassured: she wouldn't be the only novice. That's when she realised she was truly ready – or as ready as she could be. Leanne has learnt to love the liberation – the disembodiment – of being in the water, and she wonders how much greater it might be out there with only the horizon to limit her.

Except now she's holding her breath as she stands on the sand and waits for Theresa. She's bought a new swimming costume for the occasion: a plain black one-piece. And a cap – also black. She bought it at the pool, along with the goggles that don't fit perfectly, but they'll do.

It's a Sunday, which Leanne chose because if she's slow – if she takes twice as long as the others, which she suspects she will – she doesn't have to rush off to work. She's going to say something like: 'You go on without me.' It sounds almost noble. Not that she is noble. Or generous. She's had to preserve all of her energy for herself these last few years so she's hardly been offering it to others. But it won't cost her anything to tell them to go ahead – indeed, it will free her to paddle around behind them.

When she got out of bed before sunrise she felt almost excited to be testing her new abilities. Except now, looking at the water that is still dark in the pre-dawn light, she can't help thinking about what it can hold: mysteries, obviously, and also terror. Once she was walking on the beach and saw the lifesavers rush to pull someone from the water. A girl whose family were shrieking on the sand. What's the line between having a lovely morning swim and being carried from the surf?

'Leanne!'

She turns and sees Theresa waving from a few metres away, a sarong tied around her waist and a towel over her shoulder. Theresa often talks about how she's 'let herself go', but Leanne doesn't see that. She thinks Theresa looks strong as well as voluptuous.

'You didn't tell me you were coming!' It might have been an admonishment, but Theresa is beaming and Leanne feels pleased – satisfied, even. 'Marie will be happy.'

'Will she?'

'Oh look, there she is – yoohoo, Marie!'

In the growing light Leanne can see the older woman walking slowly but confidently over the soft sand, her bare feet sinking into it.

'Hello, Leanne,' Marie says, her voice throaty. 'Theresa's told me about you. I'm glad you decided to join us.'

'I'm – ah, so am I.' Leanne feels nervous even though she knows it's ridiculous. Just because there's no black line to follow doesn't mean she won't be able to swim just the way she does in the pool. Matt told her it would probably be easier because salt water is more buoyant. 'I'll be going slowly,' she adds quickly. 'I haven't been swimming for as long as you have.'

'That's quite all right,' Marie says. 'We won't make you go fast. And I'm sure you're better than you think.'

'I'm sooo slow,' Theresa says, making a face. 'Poor Marie! She must get sick of it.'

'Not at all,' Marie says and her voice sounds firm and calm. 'I can go as slow as anyone wants.'

Leanne senses someone near her shoulder and turns to see a tall, lean, middle-aged woman dropping her towel next to them.

'Ladies,' she says.

'Hi, Elaine.' Theresa grins. 'I'd like you to meet Leanne. She's going to join us today. Maybe every day!'

Theresa looks at her hopefully and Leanne feels her resolve weaken. She hasn't made plans beyond today, and she's not at all sure she wants to turn up *every* day. That would involve a commitment to people she hardly knows.

'We'll see,' she says.

'How do you know Theresa?' Elaine asks, and now Leanne can hear an accent. English.

'I work at the hospital. Theresa volunteers on my ward.'

'Leanne's a nurse,' says Theresa with a note of pride. 'The children *love* her.'

'I don't think that's true,' Leanne says, feeling self-conscious.

'It is! You're their favourite. But I don't tell the others or they might get jealous.'

'Sun's coming up,' says Marie.

Leanne looks towards the horizon and half closes her eyes against the intense golden light that looks as if it's opening up the whole world. The bay seems enormous: the pool is a contained space and she realises she's built her confidence within those constraints. But now, with an ocean that reaches the horizon and beyond, she's not feeling so sure. Then there are the waves, which aren't as big as she's seen them, but as she's used to the flat pool, they seem like an obstacle.

'How, um, how far do we swim?' she says, swallowing.

Marie points towards Little Beach, where Leanne has run many times along the path. 'Over there and back. It's not as far as it looks once you're used to it.'

'If I can do it, *anyone* can do it,' Theresa says, giving Leanne's arm a reassuring nudge. 'Honestly. I'm so unfit.'

'Not any more,' says Elaine, smiling. 'You keep a very good pace.'

'Don't worry – I'll swim alongside you,' says Theresa. 'These two tear away pretty quickly.'

'We always come back though,' Marie says with half a smile.

'As you're passing me in the other direction!' Theresa sounds indignant but she's grinning.

Leanne glances from her to Marie to Elaine and sees them all smiling at each other, their body language indicating their ease. Meanwhile she feels like a spinning top wound tightly and about to be released. She's not sure if that's a good or a bad thing.

'Anyway, not much of a rush today – I don't have to get the kids to school.' Theresa sighs and gazes at the sea. 'It's a luxury.'

'Do you have children, Leanne?' Elaine asks.

Leanne almost rears at the question, although it's a reasonable one: she's the right age to have children. She just hasn't put herself in the position to be asked about it for a long time. She avoids social gatherings when she can, and doesn't say much if she does have to go along. If someone persists, she knows that the easiest deflection is to ask questions about them: most people will cheerfully talk about themselves for hours. Theresa, she knows, isn't like that – she likes to ask questions – but at the hospital her questions are easier to contain. Now Leanne has three people staring at her, waiting for an answer to a question that is, no doubt, kindly meant, but that doesn't mean she wants to respond to it.

'No,' she says, looking down, hoping that will end the conversation.

Elaine tries again. 'A husband?'

'No.'

'Nor do I,' says Marie. 'He died. Very thoughtless of him.'

Leanne meets her eyes and sees understanding in them. She's been let off the hook, and she appreciates it.

'Come on, into the water!' Theresa says, sounding as though it's the most inviting place in the world.

Leanne presses her hair into her cap, picks up her goggles and follows the others as they wade in. The water is surprisingly cold against her skin. She's used to the pool, which catches the sun's rays during the day and holds the warmth for her post-work swims.

A small wave crashes against her belly and she gasps with the impact, which is harder than she'd expected.

There are larger waves rolling towards them, and she sees Marie dive under one, then Elaine, so naturally that they look like porpoises. Leanne can't do that. She can't dive under a wave. She has no experience in the ocean and was stupid to think she could manage this.

She doesn't want to panic, but her mouth opens and she starts to breathe so quickly it's like panting. She stops and wonders how badly Theresa will think of her if she turns around and goes back. The pool is safer. Contained. While she likes gazing at the ocean, the reality of being in it is too overwhelming. This is wilderness. This is not something she can control.

'Leanne?' Theresa has stopped and turned around.

'I . . .' She swallows.

'It's normal to be afraid,' Theresa says, wading towards her. A wave unfurls against her back but she doesn't move even a millimetre and Leanne wonders how long it takes to become so used to the surf. 'I was.'

'I'm not afraid,' Leanne snaps, but doesn't know why she said it. Why is she worried about what Theresa thinks?

Theresa pushes her goggles up onto her head so Leanne is looking into those deep, sympathetic pools she sees at the hospital.

'It's not like anything I've done before,' Theresa says. 'But I did go to the beach as a child. You didn't do that, did you?'

'No,' she says, scrunching her toes into the sand to try to stay calm.

'You don't have to do anything, of course,' says Theresa. 'You can wait for us on the beach. Or go home.' She looks out to sea. 'Like I said, I was scared too. But it's the best thing I've ever done, Leanne. When you're out there, all your troubles disappear.' As she turns back to Leanne there's kindness in her smile. 'We all have troubles, don't we?'

Leanne can't imagine what troubles Theresa has; she always seems carefree. Yet she's aware that nothing about her own behaviour tells the story of her past. She is diffident with adults, and more so with men than women. She knows – because Matron has told her – that her more lively behaviour with the children is noticed, but no one has ever asked her why. She doesn't know what she'd tell them if they did.

'I guess,' she says.

'The ocean may not be the right thing for you, Leanne. And that's okay. But if you do want to go in, I promise I won't leave you.'

The water is still running past her thighs and Leanne feels how her body has adjusted to the temperature. It didn't take long. Other adjustments may not take long either.

'All right,' she says, trying for a smile.

'Really?' Theresa looks like she's been told that Santa Claus is real.

Leanne nods and hears a strange sound rising from her chest: a laugh. 'Let's go!'

Theresa pushes her goggles back down, takes Leanne's hand and leads her towards deeper water. As the next wave rolls in, Theresa grins at her then dives underneath it.

Leanne follows her and feels how this world is familiar yet strange: not the warm cocoon of the pool but not unlike it either. She opens her eyes and sees the wave rolling over her, the curve of its action making a shape so perfect she can't believe it's real. She sees gradations of light and sand being churned. She feels suspended inside a story that has no beginning or end.

Then she sees Theresa, pushing up towards the surface. Putting her feet down, Leanne erupts into the air, gulps a breath and dives under again straightaway.

CHAPTER 12

The room is almost oppressively hot. Elaine clutches a glass of tepid riesling with one hand and tugs at her dress with the other. Why on earth she chose to wear something *lined* she cannot imagine. It's summer, it's humid, and she's in a small room with no air conditioning in a cocktail dress with lining – she has clearly lost her senses. If she perspires any more, her make-up will slide off. She's given up on her hair, which is clinging to her neck and feels like it's plastered to her scalp. So much for hairspray. Before she left England she had it cut short, in the style of the Princess of Wales, because she thought that would be more manageable in a subtropical climate. As it turns out, thick hair at any length isn't comfortable in the subtropics.

'Hello, darling,' says James as he reappears beside her. 'Are you enjoying yourself?'

She feels her eyes form a shape that is en route to a glare and stops herself. She's at this wretched function to support her husband and that's what she's going to do. He doesn't need to know that she's been standing on her own since he left her to chat to some urologist and another fellow with a job title she can't remember. Precisely no one attempted to talk to her in that time, and it only took her about a minute to feel mortified enough to render her incapable of approaching strangers to say hello.

Elaine was brought up to be more socially adept than this – she knows how to talk to people. She can even be charming when she wants to be. However, it seems that all those skills work only in an environment in which she's comfortable. Here, thousands of miles away from it, she's starting to suspect she's a failure.

She isn't even making much headway with her swimming group. Granted, there isn't a lot of conversing to be done when they're all in the water, but she hasn't had much of a chance before or after the swim either. Clearly, she put her foot in it *colossally* when she asked Leanne if she had children. The poor girl looked as if she'd been shot. There must be a reason why, but Elaine may never have the chance to find out if she can't work out how to be less gauche.

'Somewhat,' she says, her voice thin. 'You?'

He looks bemused. 'Only with certain people. Those orthopods are like rugby players with hacksaws – I wouldn't want them coming anywhere near my bones.'

Elaine smiles as if she understands what he's talking about but she's never really known all the different medical disciplines. James does hearts – that's the only thing she's sure of.

'Mr Schaeffer, good to see you,' says a tall, bullocky man as he grasps James's hand and almost wrenches his arm out of its socket.

'Neville, good to see *you*.' James smiles broadly and Elaine marvels at his ability to tolerate certain people. She knows who this Neville is – a colleague of James's who hasn't been very kind to him – yet here is her husband acting as if he's delighted to see him.

'And this is the little woman, eh?' Neville turns his half-lidded gaze and ruby nose her way.

Elaine glances at James and sees him widen his eyes, and knows why: he doesn't want her to make a fuss. So she won't; she'll find a compromise.

'I'm quite tall actually,' she says, smiling as sweetly as she can and throwing in a flutter of her eyelashes for good measure. Over the years she's learnt what that combination, added to her good posture and shapely bosom, can do to a man.

'So you are.' Neville looks her up and down quickly. 'Now, what's this James tells me about you being an *interior decorator*?'

He says it slowly, as if he's talking to a toddler. Accordingly, Elaine wants to kick him in the shins. She stretches her face into a smile so forced she feels her eyes almost disappearing inside it.

'I was. At home. I had a business. I sold it when we were planning to move here but I'm still interested in interiors.'

'A *business*!' Neville's laugh rumbles up from his substantial belly. 'How on earth do you have time for that with James doing what he's doing? My wife certainly doesn't have time for a *business*. I need her to be at home.'

James squeezes her elbow and while she knows it's partly to encourage her to be civil to this uncivilised man, she also knows it's a reassurance. He's reminding her that he's on her side. So she does the only thing she can to keep herself quiet while buying some time to formulate a response: she drinks her glass of wine in one gulp, grimacing at the taste. At room temperature and no doubt out of a cask, it's not her preferred drop.

'Elaine is a woman of many talents,' James says, smiling and wrapping his arm around her waist. 'I could never have managed my working life without her, but it's important that her life isn't all about me.' He peers at Neville over the top of his glasses, one of his grey curls falling onto his forehead. 'I'm sure you'll agree that as much as we like to think we're the centre of the universe, it's not actually true.'

Neville's laugh is louder than before and he claps James on the shoulder so hard that James staggers. 'I like to think it is,' he says, and his face shifts into another, nastier gear. 'And you'd do well to remind your wife who pays the bills.'

Elaine weighs up whether or not to mention that *she* was the one paying the bills while James studied in his specialty, then did all his years of training without much of an income while they had two small children. This is a battle she knows she can never win, however. James's world is full of Nevilles, all convinced of their own importance and blind to the assistance they've had along the way.

For all Elaine knows, James is a Neville himself when she isn't around. But she's never seen it; and before he told her that he wanted to move home to Australia he had never directly asked her to sacrifice anything for him. The sacrifices, such as they were – she knows she was lucky to have the business and to have her parents helping her with the children – were made by her willingly.

'I need another drink,' she says to the air. 'James, would you like one?'

He frowns at her and she remembers the conversation they had in the car: he asked if she'd already had a G&T today, and she lied and said she hadn't. Of course she had – she'd no intention of facing a room full of strangers without some kind of assistance.

'No, I'm fine,' he says with a meaningful look.

She knows he won't tell her not to drink any more – not in front of Neville. So she's in the clear, for now.

'I'll leave you to it. Neville – *enchantée*.' She smiles her sickliest smile, then strides towards the drinks table.

There is the offending cask, but she doesn't care. She wants to anaesthetise herself against this room, so she pours one glass, drinks it quickly and pours another. There's no one to see her – everyone is caught up in their conversations.

She takes her glass and pushes her way through the throng until she finds a doorway. Outside there's the cool breeze she's come to expect of this city in the evenings. She sees a step, and sits on it, and this time drinks her wine slowly, closing her eyes and thinking of her sons.

Henry is tall like her but he looks like James; Marcus isn't quite as tall and resembles no one so much as her grandfather. She did a good job, she thinks, with them. They are kind men. Rational. Patient. Actually, now she thinks about it, those are James's qualities.

She's never had so much time to contemplate her children as she does now, in her absence from them. It wasn't until she and James had been in Australia for a few days that she felt the pain – the intense, jagged pain – of leaving them behind. It feels more acute than any grief she's known. No wonder she wants to dull her senses each afternoon.

Her eyes shoot open as she feels a warm hand on her wrist.

'I've been looking for you, darling,' James says as he slides his hand up her arm and down her side, sitting next to her as he does so.

'Sorry.' She grimaces. 'I'm just not the party girl I used to be.'

'I've noticed,' he says, putting his hand on her thigh and kissing her neck, his way of making sure she knows he's not being critical. 'But I blame Neville. He's a dickhead.'

She gasps out a laugh – James is usually so polite. 'It's not just Neville,' she says.

James's nostrils flare as he inhales. 'I know. Australia is full of dickheads.'

She laughs again, despite a minor flash of irritation that he's deliberately moving her away from the truth.

'I'm sorry,' he says. 'I'm making light of something that's not light.'

Ah, so her irritation has shown on her face. She's never been quite as practised at hiding her feelings as her mother would like her to be.

'It's not your fault,' she says. 'I'm still adjusting to . . . being Australian.'

'Oh darling,' he says, squeezing her thigh, 'I hope you never are. I love you being you, English and all. And I am grateful – in case I haven't said it before – that you're here with me. It was a lot to ask.'

'You stayed in England for me,' she says, smiling as warmly as she can. 'So I'd say we're even.'

She takes a sip from her glass, but the wine is beyond tepid and she makes a face.

'Let's go,' James says. 'I'd rather be home with my beautiful wife than here with Neville.'

He stands and offers her a hand. She takes it, and wishes that her next thought isn't one of regret that she's leaving the wine behind and won't be able to have a drink when she gets home, because James will be watching. And she wants him to watch; she wants him to notice what she does. Mostly, though, she wants distraction. A temporary oblivion. The absence of longing for her sons, for her home, for the person she was when she was there.

But it's not coming tonight, so she holds her husband's hand, and smiles and waves as they exit the party, then rests her head against the car window as he drives them home, past jacarandas in bloom and bushes full of white stars of jasmine, along streets that look like nothing she knows and nowhere she's been, and tries not to wish that everything was different.

CHAPTER 13

When this sandstone cottage was built it was probably the only house within cooee, surrounded by trees and rocks and wildness. Certainly, there aren't a lot of sandstone places in Shelly Bay and their distinctive blond colour marks them as residences from a much earlier time. The sandstone was hewed out in the local area and used to make houses and larger buildings. A century or more later it has proved its durability, the only sign of possible weakness the metal brackets on each side of the cottage that prevent the stone from bulging. Marie has long thought that the potential to bulge suggests that the house is alive, or still part of the earth it came from.

She loves this house, even if it has witnessed her sadnesses over the years: the loss of her baby boy; Nicole's struggles at school when she couldn't make friends and couldn't get good enough marks to satisfy her teachers, and Marie was helpless in the face of her distress. Norm's death. The years since. Not so many sadnesses in the context of a long life – not compared with those of other people she has known – but enough to make the house sometimes feel like it is full of shadows.

She doesn't give in to them, though. One whistle to Charlie Brown so he will hop up on her lap and she knows she can distract herself long enough to prevent her mind going down a dark path.

There's another reason too: Theresa. She has a habit of enlivening every day – not that Marie knows how she can fit in a swim given how much running around she does. The addition of Elaine and Leanne to their little group hasn't diminished her appreciation for Theresa and the light she brings. It's made everything seem more manageable.

Not that Marie would tell Theresa that because it sounds like it's an expectation, that Theresa is responsible for her happiness. Marie knows she's responsible for her own happiness; it's just that Theresa makes it easier to think that each day brings possibilities instead of drudgery.

One morning not long after they started swimming together, as they were drying off afterwards, Theresa talked about going home to the children and Marie said she was only going home to Charlie Brown. It was an offhand remark – or so she thought.

'You've said that before,' Theresa murmured.

'What?'

Theresa's eyes were shiny, as if she was upset. 'You say it almost every day. That there's only Charlie Brown at home.'

Marie shrugged. 'Because it's the truth.'

'I hope . . .' Theresa hesitated, then smiled wistfully. 'I hope you know you're not alone. That you don't have to be alone.'

'But I am,' Marie said quickly.

'You're not!' Theresa's tone was one of defiance. 'You have me!'

In Theresa's eyes Marie saw not a neediness so much as a fervent wish: that Marie would be her friend perhaps. At the time, she wasn't sure what to do with it.

'That's kind,' she said, and Theresa's face crumpled a little. 'I mean,' Marie added quickly, 'you don't have to say that.'

'I know I don't,' Theresa said, then she smiled, and there was such kindness in it that Marie felt as if she was being blessed. 'I just wanted you to know that I like you. That's all.'

It was so simply expressed – the way one child might say it to another – that Marie couldn't believe it was that easy to make a new friend. But it was, because Theresa had made it so.

And Theresa is the reason that Marie has been delaying having the conversation she needs to have with Nicole, about what's to happen with this house. Because of Theresa and their swimming together, Marie has been lulled into thinking that her life might hum along again and she won't have to deal with the problems she knows are there. Rather, the one big problem: money.

She can't wait any longer, however, because it's not going away. Her cupboard is bare, sometimes literally. That's why she's invited Nicole over today, to have a chat about the plan she's formulated. She even said that: 'Let's have a chat.' It's not a phrase she's used before, so Nicole is probably thinking Marie wants to talk about Christmas presents or whether they have hard sauce with the pudding this year. 'Having a chat' sounds benign. What Marie wants to say won't sound benign, though, and it's something Nicole has to manage on her own. If her brother had lived, she wouldn't have to. That was a big reason why Marie had wanted another child: so Nicole would have a friend in childhood; and, in adulthood, someone to work with to manage all the decisions that come with having ageing parents.

After Duncan, Marie and Norm talked about having a third child, although Marie never told him that she wasn't sure if she could bear it. She feared that she'd spend the whole pregnancy worrying about what would happen; she fretted that she'd always think of the new child only as a replacement.

Then the doctors found a growth in Marie's uterus and out it all came. No more babies. Just comments from supposedly well-meaning people who'd ask her when she was going to have another child, or say, 'You only ever wanted the one?' And the guilt – oh, the guilt that still visits her sometimes. She thought the hysterectomy was punishment for losing her son, although his death wasn't anyone's fault. She just couldn't shake the idea that she should have been able to save him.

Now, Marie's one child is watching her own child playing in the garden. Marie's often thought that Nicole is a blessing, and she's never taken her for granted. Which is why she wishes she didn't have to create a burden of decision for her.

'Jessie, darling, don't do that,' Nicole says as she waves a finger at her six-year-old daughter, who is attempting to pin down a little skink.

'But he wriggles!' Jessie looks delighted as she keeps trying to grab the lizard.

'That's because he doesn't want to be caught.' Nicole gives Jessie a warning look.

Marie smiles, a little sadly, to hear her own firm parenting tone coming out of Nicole's mouth. Was she really so strict? She knows she was a cautious parent. She'd thought that caution came with parenting, or you weren't really doing a proper job.

'Tea ready, Mum?' Nicole asks, smiling at Marie.

'Should be.' Marie lifts the lid on the pot and glances in. 'It's had a few minutes to steep.'

'Jessie, do *not* pull up that plant.' Nicole is waving a finger again.

'It's all right, love,' Marie says. She knows how hard it is for little people to keep their hands to themselves.

'I'm trying to teach her to be careful, Mum. Since it seems to be too late for Toby.'

Nicole smiles at Marie, and a lifetime of their own exchanges is in her eyes: all the times Marie told her to be careful because she wanted to protect her. Because she didn't want to lose her.

'What are Toby and his father up to?' Marie asks.

'Playing cricket at the local park. If we're lucky Toby won't break anything this time.'

Nicole makes a *what am I going to do with him?* face. Toby has always been an active child, and there's nothing malicious about his propensity to damage property and himself – it just seems to happen.

'He's a good kid,' Marie says.

'Most of the time.' Nicole reaches over to pour the tea. 'So you wanted to have a chat?'

'Mm-hm.' Marie takes her cup, which has just the right amount of milk in it. Nicole has always been precise. She thinks about how to start the conversation, as if she hasn't been thinking about it for weeks now.

Nicole suddenly looks stricken. 'Are you sick?' she says, her voice tight.

'No,' Marie says quickly, feeling foolish for not thinking her daughter might leap to that conclusion. 'It's not that.'

'Oh.' Nicole's face relaxes.

'It's the house.'

'Has that bloke from up the road been pressuring you to sell again?' Nicole looks amused.

Dimitri, the man's name is, and for the last couple of years he's stopped by every now and again to see if Marie is interested in selling. His wife loves the house, he says, and he'd like to buy it for her. Marie's always said it's not for sale, which has been the truth. Although in her current predicament it's starting to look like an easy, if distressing, solution.

'Not lately,' she says, attempting a smile. 'But I . . .' She swallows. Last night she tried to convince herself that something that scares you is less scary when you actually do it. In practice, this is not proving to be the case. 'I think I need to sell anyway,' she says in a rush.

Nicole stares at her, only stopping when Jessie lets out a cry. 'I got him!' she says, holding up the skink.

'Jessie, put him down,' Nicole instructs, met by a pout from her daughter. Then she turns back to Marie. 'Why, Mum?'

'It's too expensive to run. The work . . .' Marie throws her hands in the air and is surprised to feel tears in her eyes.

This discussion was meant to be calm and considered. She doesn't want to get emotional in front of Nicole, because that will set off a loop of concern: she'll be upset that Nicole is upset, and Nicole will be upset because Marie's upset, and so on. It's a loop she's been caught in before, and she has to be the one to break it because she's the parent, even if the roles are reversed sometimes. That seems to happen with mothers and daughters. Gwen's daughter took to mothering her as soon as the first grandchild arrived. It's as if once their daughters have children they find it easier to mother everyone instead of differentiating between age groups.

'Mum,' Nicole says, her voice warm with concern, 'it's okay. Don't get upset. I'm sure you don't need to do something as drastic as sell.'

'The front path is cracked. That needs fixing,' Marie says, embarking on the list she's been keeping in her head. 'The roof leaks over the bedroom whenever it rains. That shed,' she points to the contraption Norm built when Nicole was a child, 'is about to fall over so I either need to tear it down or fix it. But I can't . . .' Her voice catches. 'I can't afford to do that. So I've got a ramshackle old thing in my garden and it's ugly.'

'It was always ugly,' Nicole says wryly.

'I know! But . . .' Marie swallows her emotion. 'My point is that this house will continue to fall apart if I can't afford to stop it. And the pension doesn't cover home repairs. I can barely afford to buy new underwear.'

'That can't be true!' Nicole says, looking incredulous.

'There are council rates,' Marie goes on, 'quite apart from the other bills. It adds up. I don't have any savings.'

She stops, believing she's made her point, and from the look on Nicole's face, she's right.

'I had no idea,' Nicole says, looking to the garden. 'Jessie! Do *not* pull up Granny's plants!'

Marie sees her granddaughter with a primula clutched in one hand and wants to tell Nicole, again, to go easy. But she won't be able to buy plants to replace anything Jessie pulls up, so perhaps she should be a little more firm.

'Just put it there, Jessie,' she calls. 'I'll plant it again later.'

'Sorry,' Nicole mutters. 'She's never like this at home.'

'The garden will survive,' Marie says reassuringly.

'Don't sell.' Nicole sounds fervent now. 'Please. I know you love this house. *I* love this house. And it's your home.' She pauses and looks thoughtful. 'Let me talk to Pete and see if we can't help you out with the rates and the jobs that need doing. I also think you could use a hand taking care of the garden.' She raises her eyebrows.

'It's a bit messy, isn't it?' Marie says. Nicole's own garden looks like a mini Chelsea Flower Show, with topiary and all sorts of plants that are improbable in a subtropical Australian suburb.

Nicole looks sheepish. 'A bit.'

'I don't want you to pay for so much, though,' Marie says, and she means it. That's a lot of money for her son-in-law to come up with.

'Mum, just let us help. You took care of me – isn't it time I took care of you?'

Marie sighs. 'I didn't realise I'm so old I need taking care of.'

'Oh *gawd*.' Nicole looks momentarily exasperated. 'Stop being pathetic. We're not putting you out to pasture. Just paying some bills.'

Marie feels gratitude, and also embarrassment that it's come to this, yet she's in no position to refuse – unless she wants to leave the place that has been her home since she was born.

'Thank you,' she says, and relief melts the tension in her neck and shoulders, down her torso and all the way to her toes.

'I just wish you'd told me sooner,' Nicole chastises, 'instead of getting your knickers in a knot about it. If anything like this comes up again, *please*,' she grabs Marie's hand, 'say something.'

Marie nods and leans over to kiss her daughter on the cheek. Then they sit back, hands still connected, and watch Jessie rub dirt on her face.

CHAPTER 14

Elaine has grown to love Shelly Bay's tough little trees, kept small and made hardy by the buffeting coastal winds. She's even grown used to their leaves, which have a strange hue of emeralds that have been left too long.in the sun. The native bushes and their almost aggressive-looking flowers are charming in their way, although she misses the abundance to be found in English gardens. All that rain – she had no idea how much of a difference it made until she moved to Australia and learnt that torrential downpours every now and again don't have the same effect on plant life as the steady drizzle of home. Despite that, there are gardeners in Shelly Bay who make the most of the conditions and produce lovely, ordered plots that offer some relief from the tangled mysteries of the bush at the water's edge.

However, Elaine hasn't ventured much past Shelly Bay; she hasn't really had reason to. James's parents live in a country town to the south-west, but they always come to the city to see him because James isn't able to take enough time off work to make a visit worthwhile. Three hours in the car means you want to stay overnight before driving home, and he's had so many commitments that it hasn't been feasible.

Yet as Christmas is approaching and his parents are planning to spend the day with James's sister and her family on a property even further west, James decided that this weekend they should make the effort.

Elaine relished her swim this morning, knowing there wouldn't be another until Monday. She'll miss it; she's started to look forward to seeing the other women almost as much as she anticipates the thrill of diving under the first wave of the day. As someone who has never experienced the surf before, she's surprised by how much she likes it.

'Penny for your thoughts?' James's voice brings her mind back to the car.

'They're worth considerably more than that!'

'I'm sure they are,' he says. 'But I'd still like to know what you're thinking about.'

'If I said I was wondering if turkey takes less time to cook in a warm climate, would you believe me?'

It's not too far from the realm of probability: this year will be the first time Elaine has been responsible for a Christmas feast, ever. Her mother has always been the cook, with more time to spend planning and shopping and creating. Elaine would work up until Christmas Eve and arrive at her parents' house on Christmas morning limp and exhausted, with two excited children and a similarly exhausted, overworked husband. She thought that would never change, so never learnt how to do all the things her mother makes look effortless.

'No, darling, I would not,' James says. 'But I would like to note, for the record, that I don't expect you to cook a turkey. We don't need to replicate your parents' lunch. The boys won't be with us, so . . .'

As he stops, Elaine bites her lip and looks out the window. They are passing land that is yellow and brown and khaki.

In the distance there's a brighter green rectangle, but it looks like a misplaced patch on a sad quilt. It doesn't belong. And neither does she. Her children are in another hemisphere and James is right: without them, there's no need to have an elaborate Christmas. Except that's the main reason she wants to do it – she will feel closer to them if she has the same kind of experience they'll be having with her parents. Or maybe it's because she feels guilty she won't be there with them.

'We should have gone back,' James says gently.

'We decided it was impossible.'

'*You* decided it was impossible,' he replies, his voice still mild. 'I would have found the time.'

But she'd known when they spoke of it, when she thought about it, that going home would mean she would never want to leave again. To travel all that way for a week – and that's all it would have been – then return to this alien place with its humidity and flies and hailstorms, with its vast distances that mean that in the time it takes them to reach James's parents, she could drive from her own parents' home to Scotland . . . She couldn't do it. They had to stay put.

'It's done now,' she murmurs.

She loses track of the kilometres as they pass caravans and horse floats, and signs that display names of places she's never heard of, and some she has because they're replicas of place names she grew up with: the transplantation of Britishness to this decidedly un-British place.

It's only when the car comes to a halt that she realises she either dozed off or was in a trance, for she's jolted back to the present as James hops out of the car and opens a gate.

'Not much further now,' he says with a grin as he gets back into the car, puts a hand to her cheek and kisses her strongly, lingeringly. 'I know this isn't your ideal way to spend a weekend. Thank you for coming with me. Mum and Dad are really pleased you'll be here.'

He looks into her eyes and she realises something that hasn't occurred to her before: she made a choice to be with her husband, to leave her children to the lives they had already established, because she made a commitment to him many years ago, as he did to her. These past few months she's been thinking about what she's lost – wallowing in it, actually – without stopping to consider what she still has. She is still married. She is still loved. And she loves in return.

'My ideal way to spend a weekend,' she says softly, 'is to be with you.'

He looks surprised for a second, then he kisses the tip of her nose and puts the car into first gear.

As his parents' house appears at the end of a driveway so long that it's almost a road, Elaine is taken aback as she sees that it's not as big as the surrounding land suggests. All those hectares yet their home is about the size of her own cottage in Shelly Bay. Rather, James's cottage. Having grown up on the land, when he moved to the city as an adult to study and work he fell in love with Shelly Bay and the water all around. He bought the white weatherboard-and-brick cottage not long before he moved to England, thinking he'd be gone for only a year or two. As his life took root overseas he put tenants in, and luckily they took care of the place, keeping its gardens neat and its neighbours onside. There is space enough for two of them now, Elaine thinks, but it's just as well they didn't try to raise children in it: the boys would have outgrown it before they reached their teens. Still, it's large enough to feel empty when she's home alone for hours.

'Hello, love,' James's mother calls as she opens the front door onto the verandah.

'Hi, Mum,' he says, enfolding her in a hug and raising one hand to greet his father as he appears around the side of the house.

'Elaine, love.' His mother offers a twinkly smile and a kiss on the cheek. 'Come in. Good to see you. How was the drive?'

'It was fine, thank you, Amy – interesting. There's so much land between here and the city.'

'Too right,' James's father, Tom, says, kissing her hello. 'How else do you think we keep you city slickers at a distance?' He winks. 'Here – let me.' He opens his hand towards James, who gives him one of their bags.

'I know it's probably early for a drink,' says Amy, 'but I know you like a G&T, Elaine, so we're all set up. It's after midday, so we're in the clear, I reckon!'

Elaine meets James's eyes and sees the suggestion of concern. She hasn't thought about having a drink once today, and that's an achievement – even though it's entirely due to the fact that she's been distracted thinking about all the people and places she's missing. That's not a long-term solution, though: she can't make herself miserable in order to stop drinking.

'Thank you, Amy,' she says. 'I can wait a while.'

James is still looking at her and now she can't read his expression. She doesn't want to worry him; she doesn't want to worry herself. Yet if his mother has noticed how much she drinks, they're probably past the point of worry and tipping over into a problem.

'Suit yourself,' says Amy. 'Anyway, let's get you inside and unpacked, then we can have a nice chat.'

Elaine follows them towards the house, through dirt that clings to the white sandals she's foolishly worn. It infiltrates the spaces between her toes and under the soles of her feet, and she knows that her carefully chosen outfit is going to wilt in the heat of this place. For a second or two she lets herself feel wretched. This country is not hers, and she doesn't understand it. She's not sure she ever will.

'Darling?' James calls, and that's how she knows she's been dragging her feet, probably literally.

'Yes,' she says wearily, and lets him take her hand to lead her up the stairs and into the house.

CHAPTER 15

'Andrew, can you get the phone, please?'

Theresa has her hands in a rissole mixture as she hears the *tring-tring* continue.

'*Andrew!*'

With no response, she uses her least-sticky hand to pick up the receiver in the living room and hears her father on the end of the line.

'Hi, Dad,' she says and tries to keep her voice light even though her parents know this is the worst time of day to call: Theresa is making dinner, the children are always running amok because she can't watch them at the same time and Andrew can never seem to manage it either, while Nonna observes the whole thing. Theresa just knows her grandmother thinks it should all be better managed. That in her day the children wouldn't be unsupervised while Mamma worked in the kitchen. Well, in Nonna's day there were grandparents around to help – all those generations living in the one house – but Theresa's parents decided to move away when Oliver was born, so she has no help. Not from them, not from Andrew, and not from Nonna either for that matter, although she doesn't expect that. An elderly woman should be allowed to be elderly, even if she wants to use her time to drink Italian aperitifs and smoke the strongest cigarettes she can find.

'Are you busy?' her father says, sounding tense, and again Theresa has to restrain herself, because when is she not busy?

'No, it's fine,' is what she says instead.

'I need you to come here for a few days,' he says, and that's when Theresa realises the trap she's walked into. The question about her being busy didn't refer to *right now*. It was a bigger question about life. So her answer should have been 'yes'.

'What for, Dad?'

'Your mother's hurt her back.'

Theresa pauses. Her mother's back has been a problem off and on for years. Normally she goes to the doctor for some painkillers, then takes to her bed for a day or so and that tends to set her right for a while. Theresa isn't sure why that means she has to go to their place.

'I'm sorry to hear that,' she says. 'But I can't fix it for her.'

'Not that,' her father says with irritation. 'You need to come and do the housework and cooking. I can't manage it.'

'Dad, you've been fine in the past. And you know it will only be for a day or two.' She's trying to keep her voice even as she thinks of the mince going brown in the kitchen and the time elapsing before her ravenous children start complaining they want dinner.

'My knee's playing up,' he says. 'I can't do everything.'

Theresa takes a deep breath, her training to be a good daughter warring with her instinct to tell him to grow up and take care of himself. He's almost seventy years old and he's acting as if he's Oliver's age. But she has to take that back, because Ollie knows how to switch on a vacuum cleaner and use the washing machine. She's shown him because he's interested.

'Dad, your knee won't stop you cooking,' she says slowly.

'What about the rest of it?' he sputters.

'Mario lives five kilometres away from you – ask him!'

Her oldest brother followed her parents up the coast, and she knows he has the time to help them because he doesn't lift a finger to help his own wife with the kids and the house, and he's always boasting about how little time he has to spend at his business because he has staff to run the place for him.

Her father makes a sound that could be disgust, but it's hard to tell over the phone. 'He has enough to do. I can't bother him.'

'Dad!' Theresa says, exasperated. '*I* have enough to do!'

'It's your duty to help your parents,' he counters.

'And it's not Mario's?'

'He has his own family to worry about.'

'What about *my* family, Dad? Who's going to look after my house and kids?'

'Theresa, it is your duty. You must come.'

The buzz in her ear tells her that he's hung up on her. The other sound she can hear is rage bubbling inside her. She knows her mother will have listened to the whole conversation and likely condoned it, because she would rather have her daughter turn up to run everything than her husband attempting to do it. Theresa was always the one to take over when her mother needed help, and not just when she had a bad back. When Nonno was still alive, and Nonna asked for a hand with something, her mother would go and it was simply assumed that Theresa would do whatever was needed at home. Well, now she has Nonna and her own children, *and* she lives two hours' drive away, so she doesn't see how it's reasonable that she's the one who has to drop everything.

That won't get her out of it, though, so she's at least going to have to go through the motions of telling Andrew.

She puts the receiver back in the cradle and closes her eyes, remembering how happy she was, oh, only twelve hours ago. She was catching up to Elaine as they rounded the point on the way back to Main Beach. Finally, Theresa is getting faster. Even though she didn't quite catch Elaine, she wasn't far behind by the time they reached the beach, and the others were happy for her. There was laughter, and Marie pinched her cheek and told her she was a 'little champion'. Theresa achieved something, and she has a goal to work towards. Not like here, at home, where everything runs on an eternal loop and she never gets ahead but it certainly feels like she could fall behind.

'What's goin' on?'

She opens her eyes to see Andrew standing in front of her wearing a clean shirt and his newest jeans. Half an hour ago he arrived home in his dirty work clothes and headed out to the garden to see the kids.

'Why are you wearing that?' she asks.

'I'm goin' out.'

Theresa holds back the heavy sigh that wants to escape from her chest. 'Where to?'

'Just out.'

She looks at his shirt again. 'Who are you going out with?'

'Why don't you stop askin' me so many questions?' he snarls.

'Because I'm making dinner for us all and you're going out. Again.' This time the sigh can't be held in, and brings with it tears that hover inside her lower lids. 'Don't you want to spend time with your children?'

'I've already spent time with them,' he says dismissively. 'Besides, they've got you.' His lips press together and his eyes go dark. 'And that's who they really want, isn't it?'

'Don't be silly,' she says, trying to keep her voice light although she knows what he says is true. But it's only true because he's never here any more, so the children are getting used to him not being around.

'They love you,' she adds.

He looks sceptical and turns away.

'I need to talk to you about something,' she says quickly.

'What?' He sounds irritated.

'Dad needs me to stay with him and Mum for a few days.'

'Why?'

'Mum's hurt her back. He wants some help around the house.'

'Why does he need you? He can bloody do it himself!'

Theresa almost smiles at this. Andrew, who has never done a skerrick of housework in his life, is judging her father for being the same.

'Well, he can't,' she says. 'He's insisting.'

'And who's meant to look after *this* house? What about the kids?'

'School's almost over for the year – I could take them out early and we could stay up there for a few days.'

'And what am I meant to do?' He sounds pathetic but Theresa's sure he doesn't realise it.

'You're never here anyway,' she says slowly. Deliberately. She wants him to appreciate the impact of what he's been doing lately.

His eyes flicker and she can tell he's trying to come up with a different argument.

'So you're goin' to leave me here with your nonna?' he says.

'She can manage. Although I'll need you to take her to her poker games.'

'Fucked if I'm goin' to do that.' Andrew squares his shoulders, as if he's ready for a fight.

Theresa pauses. She doesn't really want to go to her parents' house but feels the obligation to do so. There's also a part of her that wants to make Andrew take care of himself for a few days. And another part that knows she'll have several days without a swim, without seeing the others. The one part of her day that gives her space, the part she needs to cope with all the rest, will be taken away.

A noise at the back door makes them both turn their heads.

'I can *hear you*,' Nonna says as she steps inside the kitchen, her eyes narrowing.

'Sorry, Nonna,' Theresa says, embarrassed.

Nonna turns a steely gaze on Andrew. 'And the children can hear you.'

Theresa wants to melt into the floor. She thought the children were down the bottom of the garden, where they usually play.

'You're not goin',' Andrew says. 'I'm not goin' to live in a dump just because your mother can't be bothered lookin' after her own house. Sort it out with your father.'

Without giving either of them a chance to respond he picks up his car keys and slams the front door behind him.

Theresa and Nonna stand looking at each other. Outside, Sasha and Oliver have gone back to their noisy playing.

'The men always want control, *mia* Theresa,' Nonna says, putting one hand on the kitchen bench. 'You cannot let them have it. You have to be smarter. You have to control first.'

'That's just not me, Nonna,' Theresa says sadly. Besides, she thinks, the time for controlling Andrew is long past.

'That's because my daughter did not show you how.' Nonna throws her other hand in the air. 'That father of yours, she lets him be in charge. *Stupido!* I did not bring her up like this.'

'I'm sorry,' Theresa says. 'I didn't mean for you to hear that. I don't know what to do with him any more.'

Nonna grabs both of Theresa's arms with the same strong

hands that used to play piano for hours when they were all younger. Much, much younger.

'You *take control*, Theresa,' she says hoarsely, then lets her go. 'That is all I am going to say.'

As she turns to leave she gives what looks like a dismissive wave – the same wave she'd use when Theresa was a child and had done something naughty.

Back then, the punishment was scales on the piano for half an hour. It took Theresa a few years to realise that the punishment was actually an education and it made her a better pianist. She hasn't played for years though. Andrew wouldn't let her have a piano. It took up too much space, he said, and he wanted a big couch.

'Dinner's in half an hour,' she calls limply.

Theresa hears the strike of a match.

The smell of cigarette smoke wafts in the back door as she wets her hands and goes back to making rissoles.

CHAPTER 16

Marie tries to keep her face in a neutral expression as she removes her T-shirt, but Theresa spots the truth straightaway.

'What's wrong?' she asks, her eyes wide.

'Nothing,' Marie says, hiding her wince behind the garment as she struggles to get it over her head.

'*Marie.*'

'I've hurt my shoulder,' she confesses, huffing as she drops the T-shirt on the sand. 'I was pulling out weeds. I was . . . a little too enthusiastic.'

She remembers the exact moment the muscle in her shoulder told her that she'd done the wrong thing. Charlie Brown was the only one there to hear her cry out, but she still felt like a fool as she fell out of her crouch and onto the garden bed.

'I thought Nicole was organising someone to help with that?' Theresa says as she waves to Elaine further up the beach.

'He can't start until the new year,' Marie says, frowning. 'Who knew that gardeners are so in demand?'

'I can help,' Leanne pipes up, and Marie swivels to face her. The girl is so quiet a person can almost forget she's around.

'If you need some weeding done,' Leanne adds quickly, then turns away to pick up her cap and goggles. 'I live near you.'

'Do you?' Marie can't recall them ever discussing where they live – and she would, because she hasn't had many conversations with Leanne at all.

'You're in the sandstone cottage near Livingstone Road?'

'Yes.' Marie can't remember mentioning it, but she must have. Or perhaps Theresa told Leanne.

'I'm at the other end – the harbour side. Just around the corner on Elliott.' Leanne gives a quick smile then looks away again.

Honestly, it's harder to hold that girl's attention than it is to get a cat to like you. Which is why Marie's never had cats: they're too standoffish. She glances at Theresa, who looks fascinated by the exchange. As she would be, because it's the most Leanne has ever said in a morning.

'Well, it's kind of you to offer,' Marie says, 'but I think I'll wait for the gardener now.'

Leanne looks briefly crestfallen and Marie wonders if there was another motive for her willingness to weed.

'Good morning, ladies,' says Elaine, striding towards them.

Marie envies those long legs: Elaine makes walking on soft sand look no more difficult than a ship sailing on a calm sea.

'Marie's hurt her shoulder,' Theresa announces.

'I see.' Elaine's eyebrows lift. 'So this is my chance to lead the pack. At last.' She smiles mischievously.

To date Marie hasn't had an ego about the swimming, but now she feels a ping of umbrage that tells her that's only because she's always been in the lead. She's not keen on the idea of being slow. It reminds her too much of getting old. If she's out in front she's still not old – or that's her rationale, at least. And, just maybe, she likes to win. Small victories are the only ones she's ever had.

'Indeed,' she says. 'But don't get too used to it.'

'Actually . . .' Elaine says, drawing it out in that cut-glass accent: *Acc-tuu-a-llyyy*. 'I think we should all swim breaststroke. That's fair.' She smiles at Marie. 'It's easier on shoulders than freestyle.'

'Oh no,' Marie says, wishing she'd been better at hiding her impediment from Theresa. 'I'll just go slowly.'

'I like breaststroke!' Theresa says brightly.

Leanne looks almost relieved. 'I like it too.'

'So we'll swim together, then?' Elaine says. 'How convivial.'

'Morning, ladies. Long time no see.'

Marie sighs as she sees Trevor King on the approach. 'We've been here, Trev. You must have been slacking off.'

'Did me back, didn't I?' he says, putting a hand to his side.

'Oh, that's right,' Marie says drily. 'I remember you being in pain the day we pulled that girl out of the water.'

Trev shakes his head. 'Geez, it's been bad. Couldn't get out of bed. Couldn't even get a beer!' He laughs as if this is the funniest sentence imaginable, then turns his gaze Leanne's way. 'Hel-lo. You've got a new one.'

'This is Leanne,' Theresa says. 'She's a nurse at the hospital.'

'Where you from?' Trev asks.

'I live on the other side of the hill,' Leanne replies, her voice even.

The look on his face suggests that he thinks she's an idiot. 'No,' he says, shaking his head. 'Are you one of those boat people or something?'

Leanne's face doesn't move, and Marie wonders how many times she's heard this over the years. None of them has asked Leanne about her background – Australia has people from all over, and Leanne's accent is as Australian as they come, so as far as Marie's concerned she's Australian.

Heat erupts on the younger woman's cheeks and Marie

can't stand the fact that stupid old Trev King has made Leanne feel embarrassed.

'What on earth do you think you're talking about, Trevor?' she snaps.

'You know,' he says, gesturing towards Leanne.

'No, I don't know. Do you know, Theresa?'

'No.' There's a fierce look on Theresa's face that Marie has never seen before.

'How about you, Elaine?'

Elaine's chin goes up and her shoulders back. 'Not a clue,' she says.

Marie turns a dazzling smile on Trevor. 'Sorry, we have no idea what you mean, and we're sure Leanne doesn't either.'

Trevor's frowning as he looks from one to the other, but not at Leanne. 'Oh,' he says and seems to shrink a little.

Marie keeps smiling. 'Off you go. We're late for our swim.'

He again looks at each of them, but this time he glances at Leanne too, with confusion. 'Right,' he says, then turns and shuffles away.

'Dickhead,' mutters Marie.

'Sorry about that,' says Theresa.

Leanne shakes her head. 'It's not your fault. And it's not as if I haven't heard it before.'

'I'm still sorry,' Theresa says.

Marie nods ahead of them. 'Come on, let's leave him behind and get in the water.'

'This will be fun!' Theresa says in Leanne's direction, a little too eagerly.

Marie has to admit to herself that breaststroke will be a lot easier. Her shoulder isn't ruined, just sore. By tomorrow she should be back to normal and back to freestyle, but it will do her good to make an adjustment today.

The water has lost some of its bite, she notices as she submerges up to her shoulders. Not only is it warmer than it was yesterday but the swell is almost non-existent, meaning they can breaststroke their way out.

'Thank you, Elaine,' she says as she draws alongside. 'This was a good idea.'

'I have them occasionally,' Elaine says, but she doesn't sound convincing.

'I didn't ask you how your trip to the bush went,' Marie adds, keeping pace with Elaine's graceful strokes.

Elaine sniffs. 'It was all right.'

'Oh?' In Marie's book, 'all right' doesn't mean 'good'. But because she can't see Elaine's eyes behind the goggles she has no idea what she's really thinking.

'James's parents are lovely,' Elaine goes on, her voice firmer. 'But I . . . the countryside – it's so . . . drab.'

Marie wants to disagree – to say that Australia is beautiful all over – yet to an Englishwoman she knows it wouldn't be. No point being patriotic if it's only going to make someone else feel bad.

'Sorry,' Elaine adds. 'That sounds mean.'

'It's brown,' Marie says. 'There's no getting away from that.'

'And there's a lot of it!' says Theresa. She's drawn level with Elaine's other side, while Leanne is next to Marie. 'The first time my parents took us to that part of the state there was so much brown I thought there'd been a fire.'

'There probably had been,' Marie says. 'Or a drought.' Her shoulder pinches a little and she reduces the amount she extends her arm when she strokes. She glances at Elaine. 'It must make you homesick. Not at all what you're used to, eh?'

Elaine shakes her head and appears to swallow some water, coughing before she answers. 'I kept thinking about my parents' place in Kent. Of course, that led me to think about them. And my sons, spending time with them while I'm here, not spending time with any of them.' She exhales loudly through her mouth, as if in distress.

'It's hard when you miss people,' Marie says. 'How about we stop here and tread water for a bit? It's a beautiful morning. Let's take it in.'

Elaine frowns, as if Marie is suggesting a punishment, but Marie's motives are pure: she thinks Elaine may become even more upset and swallow more water, which won't improve her morning. They form a little circle off the point, in the spot where the water is shallowest near the rocks. Without waves this morning, they're not likely to be swept against those rocks. Usually they have to be careful not to get so near.

'There's a few people I miss,' Marie says. 'My husband, obviously, and I can't do anything about that. But my friend Gwen – she moved a few suburbs away and I miss her, but I just haven't gone to visit her. I can't work out why.'

'Maybe you're having so much fun with us you don't miss her like you used to,' Theresa says.

It's a good point. Marie thinks of Gwen but she doesn't miss her as much as she did a few weeks ago. There's now a new emotion: guilt.

'Perhaps,' she says. 'You *are* very entertaining.'

Theresa looks pleased.

'But that's no excuse for me to let the relationship go,' Marie continues. 'I've been slack. So I'm going to visit her soon.'

'You're good,' Theresa says. 'I was meant to go and visit my parents – well, Dad asked me to go there for a few days and help. I said no.'

'As you should have,' says Marie. 'You have a lot of responsibilities here. Too many, I'm prone to think.'

Now Theresa is the one to show guilt. 'I'm a bad daughter,' she says.

'You!' Elaine bursts out. '*I'm* the daughter who lives half a world away from her parents.'

'But you'd visit if you could,' Theresa says, sounding miserable. Or perhaps self-pitying, although Marie doesn't think that's her style.

'If they lived nearby, probably not,' Elaine says. 'I'd be wrapped up in my own life, as I used to be.'

'What about you, Leanne?' Marie asks. 'Are your parents close by?'

Out of the corner of her eye she sees Theresa shaking her head vigorously.

'Um . . .' Leanne says, and her mouth disappears under the water. She bobs up. 'Yes.'

Marie glances at Theresa, whose eyes are now wide with what looks like alarm. She presumes that Theresa – being Theresa – has already tried to get information out of Leanne about her family and perhaps been unfruitful. That's no reason, however, for Marie not to try.

'Do you see them often?' she asks.

'No,' Leanne says, swimming a little more towards Elaine and away from Marie. Perhaps, Marie thinks, so she doesn't have to look at her.

There's clearly a story there. Leanne strikes her as a fairly solitary person and she wants to know why, because she's too young to be alone for the reasons Marie is.

'May I ask why not?' she says.

Leanne treads water, looking up at the sky. 'They don't want to see me,' she says, still gazing up.

'That can't be right,' Marie says quickly. 'You're a lovely girl.'

Leanne drops her head, but with the goggles hiding her eyes Marie doesn't know what's going on. 'Maybe I'm not as lovely as you think,' she says, her voice tight.

'Of course you are!' Theresa says. 'You're wonderful with the children.'

Leanne says nothing.

Elaine's head swivels from Leanne to Marie and back again. 'I think I need to keep swimming,' she says. 'Shall we move on?'

And Marie notes that her lovely manners have probably salvaged an awkward situation.

Leanne moves away and kicks herself into a freestyle action, leaving them behind.

'Oh,' Theresa says, 'she's going on ahead. Marie, you can't . . .' Her forehead wrinkles.

'Let her go,' Marie says. 'I pushed too much. I've upset her.'

'Don't worry, I've done it too,' Theresa says. 'It can be hard to know when you're past the point of just being friendly.'

'I'd say she has burdens we can only guess at,' Elaine says, moving slightly ahead of them. 'But I'll keep her company, if you don't mind?'

Marie nods. Her legs make their frog kick, and she and Theresa carry on in silence.

CHAPTER 17

'Good morning, Leanne.'

'Good morning, Dr Jacobs.' Leanne nods at the paediatrician as he strides past her station. She watches as he disappears inside Matron's office, then lets her shoulders drop. Whenever there's a doctor around she feels like she's on guard – like she'll be told she's doing the wrong thing.

She's had a lifelong fear of doing the wrong thing, which can't be traced back to her upbringing because her brothers did plenty of wrong things before she came along, and afterwards, so she knew it was possible to do the wrong thing and survive. There was no incident that made her this way; her parents never imposed the belief on her directly. Yet she has screeds of memories of desperately wanting to be the best-behaved student, of wishing her brothers wouldn't misbehave, of trying to teach her younger sister to be good.

It hasn't escaped her attention that what brought her life undone was a monumental exercise in someone else not doing the right thing, to her, and she took the only course of action she thought could set it right. She knew she might pay for it forever. But it was what she had to do. Years of hearing her mother issue judgements about 'bad girls' – girls who had found themselves in similar situations to her – told her what was necessary.

Now it's easier to be alert to other possible missteps and never put herself in a position for them to happen.

'Sister?' Matron calls from the hallway.

Leanne scurries towards her.

'We have a new patient arriving today,' Matron says. 'Dr Jacobs has just told me she's to be transferred from the Children's Hospital.'

Leanne frowns: it's unusual for a child to come *from* that hospital, the only dedicated hospital for children in the city.

'She's from this area,' Matron explains, 'and her parents want her to be closer to home. She has kidney disease. They're keeping her in while they work out the best course of treatment.'

'Okay,' is all Leanne can say. She isn't sure why she's being given a briefing now when everything she needs to know will arrive with the patient.

'She needs to be specialled,' Matron says impatiently, as if Leanne is being deliberately dense. 'We'll be looking after her as normal during the day, but the parents want someone with her at night. I'd rather it be someone already on staff.'

The request is unusual – most parents don't even know they can hire a nurse to look after their child alone within a public institution. Leanne has never done it before; she's never been asked. She's not even sure she's being asked now.

'So do you . . . want me to organise someone?' she says.

'No, Leanne, I want you to do it. If you have time. The parents have asked for you.'

Leanne is taken aback – how would anyone know to request her specifically? Children come in and out of here with regularity but no pattern; some of them leave alive and some of them don't. She is professional at all times, but would be hard-pressed to remember the names of the children's parents. Although she always remembers the children.

'How could they – I mean, why?'

'You nursed the eldest child two years ago. Brain tumour.' Matron looks at the file in her hands. 'Daphne Sullivan.'

Leanne recalls a pale child with green eyes and mousey-brown hair and a smile that transformed her face, although they saw it rarely. She never made it home. Leanne also remembers a younger sister, Imogen, and the pang that came when the little girl told her – with the pride children have when they announce their age – that she was born in July 1976. She was the same age as Leanne's baby. The baby who is the reason Leanne is isolated from the people she loves, the family she grew up in, the brothers and sister who were her best friends and who she's left behind. She has spent the last seven years constructing battlements, and for good reason: to keep out the memories that could destroy her.

Except that on the nights when she has trouble sleeping it is always because of the one memory that resists all her attempts to keep it out.

'How could you let him do this to you?' her mother says to her in this memory, over and over. 'How could you let him touch you? Put his filthy hands on you? Who else have you allowed to do this?'

It's a question Leanne won't answer because she knows that any number she gives – even one – is wrong, and 'no one' will not be believed.

In this memory she feels her father's palm hitting her cheek. The sensation is a different pain to twisting an ankle or grazing your shin. Those pains tell you that something is going wrong and it needs to stop. But the pain in her cheek is the pain of letting down the people she loves, even though she hasn't done anything wrong – not in her own eyes. She didn't want that man – her oldest brother's friend, someone she trusted – to put those filthy hands on her. She didn't want anyone to find out.

'I didn't allow anything,' she says softly, hoping her parents believe her.

Her mother's eyes show flint and outrage. 'And how are we meant to believe that?'

'Because I'm telling you.'

But Leanne knows that the truth – her truth – isn't going to be enough of a defence and she can feel her life not so much shattering as disintegrating. The structure that has held it together since her birth has become dust, and she will never be able to rebuild what she has always known.

'That's not what we heard,' her father says, so angry that his face has become ugly, and he has never been ugly.

'But I'm the one involved, and I'm the one telling you,' Leanne says as firmly as she can muster. She may be alone in this confrontation with her parents, but years of having older brothers have taught her how to stand up for herself. 'No one else knows.'

'Apart from *him*,' says her mother, and Leanne can see her lip trembling.

Each time, in that memory, she sees her mother's lip trembling – except Leanne doesn't know if it's because her mother is worried for her or disgusted by her.

She and her mother have never been close the way some mothers and daughters are, but their relationship has been harmonious. Leanne would like to think that her mother has only concern for her, but she knows she's also concerned about what other people think, and will be worrying about that now. Because they found out from someone else that Leanne is pregnant. Because Leanne trusted one of her brothers with the information and he betrayed her. And Leanne knows that as much as her mother is horrified about the pregnancy, she's also aware that her son didn't keep this most private of secrets. So he'll probably have told other people. Told them a portion of the story but not the full story, because only Leanne knows that. Only Leanne and the man who did it to her.

When she replays the memory, Leanne tries not to go further. She tries not to remember the calculations she ran through that day. The decision she made, in the middle of all that upset, to leave and never go back. No – it's easier to cut off the memory at the point at which she opens the door and walks out.

She realised long ago that she replays it mostly because it's the last time she saw her parents' faces. The last time she heard their voices. The decision to leave them behind was hers; she didn't ask them what they wanted. Perhaps they have been relieved, all these years, to not have to deal with her. They probably think she has a child, on her own: a living symbol of her bad behaviour.

Except that baby never became hers. Leanne felt so trapped that she freed herself the only way she could, like an animal gnawing off its own foot. So she could survive. But she knew there would be a price to pay. What she did tipped the scales somehow, and there had to be something to balance them. So she decided on the price: to never let anyone get close to her. If there is a God, or some being who decides the way things work, she hopes it's paying attention to what she's done. Because she's alone now. She doesn't have friends; she has acquaintances.

Theresa has tried to be her friend, over and over. Now Marie and Elaine are trying too. Leanne has never let anyone get that far, though, because friendship requires reciprocity and while she is interested in other people and their lives, she doesn't want to share hers. There are stories that she wants to keep to herself. Histories that she doesn't want to repeat.

Except it's hopelessly naïve to think you can evade the past. Even her attempts at remaining alone have failed, because something in her wants that connection with other people – why else would she have joined Theresa and her friends? There are days when Leanne is a mystery to herself; many days, in fact. Perhaps she should stop trying to work herself out and just give in to being human.

And here is a child the age her own child would be now.

'Yes, I remember Daphne,' she says to Matron. 'And Imogen is her sister.'

Matron looks pleased. 'She is. Coming here this afternoon. I don't expect you to special her every night – you'll wear yourself out if you do that, and I need you in tip-top shape. Why don't you work it out with the parents, then let me know what you've decided?'

'All right. Thank you.' Leanne nods deferentially and walks back to her station.

She hears Matron talking to Dr Jacobs again, and takes the opportunity to slip away to the kitchen so she has a minute to herself. She could refuse the extra work, come up with an excuse – although she knows there isn't one. Her life isn't so full of commitments or hobbies that she can't spare the time. The extra income would be useful – her rent won't stay where it is forever and she doesn't have many savings. Perhaps she could even have a holiday somewhere.

Yet she wonders what it will be like to sit with a sick child – *that* sick child – each night and not be able to do anything other than make sure she is comfortable and not afraid.

She doesn't know what Imogen will be like, but it's clear her parents are already concerned. Leanne has seen it before:

a run of bad luck that can seem like a family curse. She can't remember if there were any other siblings; as she saw only Imogen, she suspects not. Imogen's parents will be blaming themselves, as so many of the parents here do. But there's no blame, and no responsibility either; only that trite but true phrase – the luck of the draw. Leanne has four brothers and a sister and none of them had a serious childhood illness. But here is Imogen, already without her one sister and now sick herself. If Leanne were religious she might believe it was God's will, or God's work. As she isn't, she can see only random chance in any of this.

It's a comfort, and also not, to think that the same principle applies to her own life.

So Leanne will special this child, and try to improve her odds of getting better, of going home well, of simply sleeping through the night. Just as she has tried to improve her own odds, each day of her life, by getting up and working hard, by doing all the right things and staying away from the wrong, so maybe, one day, she will believe that her slate is clean.

CHAPTER 18

This Australian tradition of having a hot Christmas lunch in summertime is something Elaine will never understand. Hot food is for cold climates, and as she feels sweat trickling down the back of her neck and running towards her bra strap she wants to kick the oven door.

'Let's have a few friends over,' James had suggested. 'People who can't be with their own families on Christmas Day.'

As Elaine doesn't have any friends in Australia – at least, not people she knows well enough to consider asking to her house for Christmas – he obviously meant his friends. She had presumed that anyone who couldn't get to their families for Christmas must be from overseas – maybe there would be a European or two with whom she could chat about northern-hemisphere things. But, no, they were Western Australians and Queenslanders with not enough leave over Christmas to make it home.

She can hear them now, laughing in that loud way a lot of Australians do, especially the men. When they first arrived here she found herself flinching whenever she was around a group of them. Then she heard cockatoos for the first time and understood: Australians are loud because they're competing with those parrots. Cockatoos, kookaburras, random other native birds – they're so noisy that sometimes she can't hear herself think. Between the birds and the sharks, and the possums in their back garden, she has become convinced that Australia is a giant free-range zoo.

Their Christmas guests started arriving at eleven o'clock and immediately opened cans of beer and bottles of wine. James never drinks beer – not that she's seen before – yet there he was, pulling the ring on a 'tinny', as he called it, and knocking it back as if he was the Sahara and it was a downpour. He was even slapping men on the back and calling them 'mate'. Over the past few months Elaine has seen her husband in the company of colleagues and a couple of friends at a time, but has never seen this version of him. It's at odds with the man she's known for twenty-five years in England. It's possible he's putting on an act, trying to be a proper Aussie bloke for his *mates*, yet it happened so naturally, and quickly, that she's secretly convinced that he's been pretending to be someone else for the entire time she's known him. It's not a comfortable idea.

'You're dreaming!' she hears one man yell, then there's laughter, something that sounds like a chair falling over, and high-pitched giggling. That would be Joanne, the new second wife of one of the mates.

Elaine didn't ask for a background briefing on today's guests, and so feels foolish as she tries to navigate the possibility of children who are absent because they're with first wives, and attendant sensitivities. She shouldn't have presumed that she knew who James's friends would be – and he shouldn't have presumed she knew either. They're here now, though, expecting turkey, ham, roast vegetables, plum pudding and who knows what else.

'I hope there's a pav!' one of them had declared as soon as he'd stepped in the door.

James had looked at Elaine apologetically and said nothing. She has since deduced – after numerous hints from Wayne, as she thinks his name is – that *pav* means pavlova: a meringue-based concoction that is best not made in the sort of humid weather they're having today. She's going to have to let Wayne down by revealing that there'll be no pav because her husband told her that plum pudding would be fine.

More laughter, another thud.

Elaine reaches for the glass of Champagne that has grown warm in the kitchen and gulps it down. If she has to be in here doing all the work, she may as well entertain herself, and she's certainly not sharing the Bollinger with the guests.

Another glass, and this one she drinks faster so it doesn't have time to get tepid. Right, what should she be doing? Stuffing. Gravy.

She hiccups and tastes some of the Champagne again. Whoops – too quickly consumed. She turns on the tap and fills a water glass, drinking slowly this time.

'Are you all right in here, darling?' James is standing in the doorway, looking bleary eyed.

'What if I said no?' she responds, feeling bolshie.

'Oh.' Uncharacteristically he pouts, then walks over and plants a sloppy kiss on her cheek. 'Does that make it better?'

'Not really.' She sniffs. 'But if you give me a hand, that might.'

James looks around the kitchen and she appreciates, as she often does, his lovely face. She knows it was shallow to marry a man partly because of his face but she rationalised it to herself – still does – by saying that it's not a classically handsome face. It's a nicely arranged face: he has a good nose, and eyes that are closely set but not so much that he looks odd instead of intense, which is the usual impression they give. He has surprisingly delicate cheekbones and strong brows. Skin that tans easily, and he does like to be in the sun – an ongoing issue when they lived in a country that rarely saw it. Mainly, it's a *kind* face. That's what first attracted her to him when they met.

A friend of her parents' had asked if they could 'take care' of a young Australian doctor who was doing some training in London. He didn't know anyone. Might they show him around? Her parents had deputised Elaine, satisfied that James was a friend of a friend so no chaperone would be needed. They'd been comfortable with each other straightaway, talking easily, sharing their memories of wartime and how their countries had changed since. He said he'd resented having to leave Australia to further his career – and that should have been her first clue that he would want to return eventually. But he'd slipped into London life so easily that she didn't think he belonged anywhere else.

Today, seeing him with his friends, she considers the possibility that he may be able to slip into many circumstances with ease – not in a disingenuous way, because that's not his style, but with a fluidity that she lacks. That is, no doubt, why it was so easy to get on with him when they met, and a central component of their success as a couple since. He's the charm, she's the follow-up. After he made new contacts, she was the one to organise lunches, dinners, picnics, outings. It looked like she was the friendly one but it was all him. Besides, she had her own friends and parents, and her children to worry about. And now that they're here, in a place where he's laden with friends, she's deficient.

'So what can I do?' James says, hands on slender hips, looking from one side of the kitchen to the other. He points to what remains of the Champagne. 'Have you drunk that *whole* bottle?'

'Not the whole bottle,' she says, because it's the truth. She's drunk most of it. That's all.

He frowns. 'Darling, it's barely afternoon. Shouldn't you slow down?'

'Shouldn't you?' she snaps. 'I think you've been indulging too.'

'I haven't drunk as much as you,' he says, in that infuriatingly rational way he has.

'Well, I'm in here *alone* while you're out there with your *friends*.' She sounds drunk even to herself. Perhaps she has gone too far, but he shouldn't have abandoned her.

'They're your friends too.'

'No, they are *not*.' She's being snotty but she can't seem to help it. '*My* friends would talk to me.'

She's aware she's waving a carving knife in the air, and puts it down.

He walks over and puts a hand on hers. 'It's fine to indulge on Christmas Day. We all do. But I'm worried about how much you're indulging at other times.'

Her shoulders hunch around her ears – her only form of defence against the ugly truth. Because he's right – of course he's right. James would never say anything like this just to make a point or to hurt her. He's better than she is, clearly, because she's just said things to hurt him.

'Don't get upset, darling,' he says softly. 'I care about you. That's all.'

'I'm not indulging too much at other times,' she says brusquely. 'I'm having just the right amount.'

She hears him inhale and he takes his hand off hers. 'All right,' he says. 'I don't want to push.'

'Good.' She yanks open the oven door and, without thinking, puts her bare hand on the roasting dish. '*Shit!*' she cries as her skin registers the heat.

As she pulls her hand back her mind goes blank. What is she meant to do now?

'Here,' James says, coming to her swiftly and taking her wrist as he turns on the cold tap in the sink. He holds her hand under the water and tears spring to her eyes.

'God,' she says, feeling foolish. She's never burnt her hand cooking in her life. Once on an iron, and she felt just as foolish then.

'It's all right,' James says, although he's not looking at her and she can tell it's because he thinks she burnt her hand because she's drunk. He's wrong: she's not drunk, just stupid. 'Keep your hand under the water.'

She yelps as the pain resurges.

'I need to get the turkey out,' she says, wincing. 'It will be dry if I don't.'

He lets go of her and picks up two tea towels, using them to grab the roasting dish. 'There.' His smile looks forced as he puts the dish on the stovetop.

'Thank you,' she says.

'Let's have a look.' He takes her wrist again. 'I'll get you something to cover it. Put it back under the water.'

She nods and tries to look contrite, although now the Champagne is really going to her head so she thinks she looks loopy instead.

From the sitting room she hears him telling their guests there will be a slight delay with lunch. She sighs, wondering what they're all thinking of her, and wishing she didn't. She'll get the lunch on the table, and then she'll clean up later. She wants to keep being a good wife to James, even if she is drinking too much. Or so he says. Right now, she thinks the Champagne is helping to dull the pain so it's actually proved to be very useful.

When she inspects her hand and sees the big, angry red welt, she decides she deserves another glass for her trouble, and there's just enough left in the bottle. Before James returns it is poured and consumed, and she feels better about how the rest of the day will run.

CHAPTER 19

Theresa is sure she broke the speed limit driving down the hill to the beach. She just couldn't wait to get here and have some time to herself. Her parents and brother and his family have taken over the house and she's been desperate to get away from them. Christmas Day – no chance, even though Marie said she'd be swimming that morning. Boxing Day – forget it, they all had to go to church, and the only bright spot was seeing Marie in the congregation. Although Theresa decided just to wave and not inflict her family on her friend, because then her mother would get nosy and ask questions, such as why was Marie there on her own? Did she not have a husband? Where were her children? Her mother *is* nosy sometimes, and, yes, Theresa is aware that she's nosy herself but she doesn't do it to be rude. Her mother does it to judge. If she had met Marie, and Marie had said she was a widow and her daughter was with her husband's family, as soon as she walked away Mum would have said something like, 'What kind of daughter leaves her mother alone at Christmas time? Clearly she wasn't a good mother.' Then her father would have an opinion, and so would Mario, all of them conveniently forgetting that Theresa's other brother, Angelo, moved to Canberra a decade ago and has never once come north for

Christmas. He keeps saying Canberra is beautiful in summer. *As if.* Still, he gets away with it.

The beach, by comparison with life with her family, is paradise. Mostly empty. And she's early, so she has time to sit in the half light and watch the waves. There are surfers out there already. What did Andrew say once? Surfers on dawn patrol are shark bait.

Andrew used to surf once upon a time. He'd been surfing the day they met around a bonfire on Killarney Beach, not far from Shelly Bay, where he and his mates had gathered, and her friend Sheryl had basically ordered Theresa to accompany her because she was going out with Andrew's friend Bonza. Andrew told Theresa that the 'hot chicks' never went for him but here he was talking to her, so maybe his luck had changed. She was twenty-two then but still unsophisticated enough not to question whether he was lying about there being no other 'hot chicks'. She was a good girl – she'd never gone anywhere near a boy, because her father and brothers would have killed her. So when Andrew said she was hot that's all she needed to hear. Later she thought he was a spunk and a good catch because he had his own business – car repairs, in his own garage – and he pulled out the chair for her in restaurants and said he wanted two kids, just like she did. She's wondered, many days since then, how she could have thought that was enough to build a marriage on. Because it wasn't.

'Oh – I thought I'd be the first one here.'

Theresa's view of the ocean is blocked by the tall figure of Elaine who, even in the kind light of dawn, looks a wreck. Her face is blotchy, her shoulders slumped and her hair is standing half up on her head. Usually she glides onto the beach looking like she's the teacher of a deportment class.

'Good morning!' Theresa says. 'We're both early birds.'

'Yes. So it seems.'

Elaine looks almost as if she's scowling, but that's a really un-Elaine thing to do. Looking stern is as far as she goes. So Theresa decides there's something wrong.

'Aren't you feeling well?'

'Why would you say that?' Elaine asks, a little too quickly. Now Theresa is *sure* something is going on.

'You just look a bit . . . off. Sorry. I shouldn't have said anything. I just worry too much.' She busies herself playing with the edge of her sarong.

Elaine says something that sounds like 'hmph', but she drops onto the sand next to Theresa and wraps her arms around her legs.

'How was your Christmas?' Theresa asks, trying a different tack.

'Interesting.' Elaine is looking at the surf. 'How was yours?'

'Full of noisy people I didn't particularly want to see.'

'Ah.' Elaine smiles her way, but it looks like it hurts. 'It sounds like we had the same Christmas.'

'Oh, right.' Theresa tries laughing as a way to move on from her awkward inquisition. She really doesn't want to upset Elaine, who intimidates her just a little bit. Elaine is elegant and graceful and sophisticated in that way only non-Australians can be.

'You're right,' Elaine says, 'I am a bit off. I, uh . . .' She squints, then relaxes her face. 'I drank slightly too much over Christmas and now I'm paying the price.'

'I don't blame you! I wish *I* could have drunk too much. It would have helped!'

'I was feeling sorry for myself,' Elaine says. She shrugs. 'Moping, I guess. I'm homesick. I miss my children. I miss having work to do each day.'

Theresa's surprised at how readily the confession tumbles out: Elaine doesn't seem like the confessional type. Not like Marie, or Theresa herself. That's what a lifetime of being marched into an actual confessional once a week will do; they spill their guts without much prodding.

'You don't like having a rest?' Theresa asks. 'I know I can't *wait* for my kids to grow up and not need everything done for them any more. Of course, Andrew will still want to be taken care of.'

She sighs, thinking of the chores waiting at home. Truthfully, being with her children isn't amongst them. That's a pleasure, most of the time, even if she does sometimes get annoyed by the fact that motherhood is a seven-day-a-week job. Why doesn't anyone warn you before you give birth? She hasn't had a day off in eight years.

'I was lucky – I had help with the children. Because I had my business. Now . . .' Elaine's eyes close briefly. 'It all seems somewhat empty.'

'Can I send my husband to you for a while, then?' Theresa says, nudging her gently. 'Because he's one child too many.'

Elaine laughs, and Theresa is glad she's been able to shift her mood.

'Oh, look,' she says, 'Marie and Leanne are here.'

Elaine turns to look in the same direction. 'Leanne's quiet, isn't she?'

'Only around adults. She's great with kids, but she doesn't like adults.'

Elaine looks surprised. 'She's here, isn't she?'

'Yes, but I think that's because she wants people to swim with. So we're . . . what's the word? Convenient.' Theresa frowns. 'No, that sounds mean. She just doesn't want to be friends. And that's okay.'

'Is it?' Elaine is looking at her with amusement. 'I suspect you like to be friends with people.'

Theresa laughs, although she wishes she wasn't so easily found out. It's always been that way though: her mother told her she should learn to control her emotions better because everyone could see them on her face. Theresa tried for a while but it was too exhausting trying to not be herself.

'You've been very friendly to me,' Elaine goes on. 'And I appreciate it.'

Theresa feels warmly pleased, like she did when a teacher at school gave her a good mark. 'I like you,' she says, and is surprised when Elaine looks as if she's going to cry.

'Do you?' she says.

Theresa puts a hand on her arm because there's no time to say anything more: Leanne and Marie are upon them.

'Well – look what the cat dragged in,' Marie says to Elaine, who appears confused. 'Did you have a big night?' Marie goes on, her eyes narrowing.

Elaine swallows. 'What do you mean?'

Marie looks at her askance. 'I think you know.'

'Not big. Just . . . long,' Elaine says, her voice light.

'Right,' Marie says slowly.

'Hi, Leanne,' Theresa says. 'How was your Christmas?'

Leanne's smile is brief. 'Quiet.'

Theresa knows that's as much as she'll get out of her for the moment. She wants to find out more, though; she worries that Leanne is lonely. Even if she doesn't really like talking to adults that much, she's so different with the patients that Theresa can tell she has a warm heart. Which means she likes connecting with people. Which means she might be lonely if she doesn't have anyone in her life.

'Shall we go in?' Elaine says, getting to her feet. 'I'm keen to start.'

'Good idea,' Marie says. 'Let's wash off the residue of Christmas.'

Elaine's eyes go round but she says nothing.

'Last one in is a rotten egg!' Theresa cries, then remembers that because she has the longest hair it's going to take her the most time to put her cap on properly. Which makes her the rotten egg.

She doesn't mind, though, and she's not long behind the others as they make their way through the waves, striking out for Little Beach and the day ahead.

CHAPTER 20

When Gwen had first said she and Fred were moving to a retirement village she'd sounded so pleased, as if she was going on a lovely vacation. But Marie shudders each time she thinks of a retirement village. She can't bear the idea of being surrounded by old people, even if to the untrained eye she looks like an old person herself. She doesn't want to look old, think old or feel old, even if the walk up the hill from the beach each morning causes her knees to complain and she puffs a bit more than she used to. She's fit from the swimming – as she's always been and intends to stay – and likes to think it's helping her not need to move to a place where she'd have to meet a bunch of new people and learn new routines. The routines she has still serve her well.

But she misses Gwen after so many years of knowing each other, even though she's not sure that Gwen misses her. They speak on the phone, but the easy rhythms of the past are no longer there. What did they have to say to each other all the time? The more they saw each other, the more they seemed to have to talk about, yet now they're stuck in conversations about their grandchildren and the government. Marie doesn't talk about what's happening in Shelly Bay because it won't interest Gwen any more, and she doesn't know what to ask about the retirement village because she hasn't been there yet.

So she's decided to remedy that today with a visit. It's a long bus ride and a train trip, then a kilometre's walk downhill from the station, causing her once again to rue the fact she never learnt to drive. It was so easy to have Norm drive her everywhere, and for some reason it never occurred to her that he might drop off the perch first and leave her without a ready means of transportation.

The streets on the way to Gwen's new home are quiet, populated mostly by trees that crowd into the front gardens of the heavy-bricked homes. This is the same city but a world away from Shelly Bay. Here, there's a sense of being hemmed in; there, a sense of unending sky and ocean. It amazes Marie that her friend could grow up in Shelly Bay, live there as an adult, raise a family there, then want to leave. Marie is so attached to the place that she's convinced her blood is really sea water, and feels personally acquainted with every grain of sand on the beach.

The retirement village is all new buildings in a tortoiseshell brick and immature bushes in neat garden beds. Gwen told her that she has a little duplex. Marie finds the number she's been given and presses the doorbell.

She hears slow steps inside, then the door opens and there is Gwen, smiling toothily the way she always has.

'Oh, Marie,' she says, opening the door and hugging her. 'I've missed you.'

Marie holds the hug for longer than she ever would have before. It feels like she's clutching on to the past, as if letting go of Gwen will mean they really have to move on into this new phase where Gwen lives here and she lives there. When Gwen moved, Marie never imagined they wouldn't see each other for this long, but she's been forced to realise that her life is narrow. She wears out the same track around the bay, and it is Gwen who has been the adventurer.

'I'm so sorry I haven't visited earlier,' Marie says, embarrassed now that she knows the trip, while long, wasn't difficult. 'It's not as if I don't have time to come here, I've just . . . been slack.'

Gwen smiles kindly. 'We've known each other a long time, Marie, and I'm not going to stop being your friend just because we don't see each other every day.' She scrutinises her. 'You're looking well. Still swimming?'

'Of course,' Marie says, not without pride. She doesn't know many people who exercise regularly – though she's met a few who talk about how they'd like to. 'And I have some people to swim with now,' she continues.

'Really?' Gwen looks uncertain.

'New friends!' Marie says brightly and sees Gwen's uncertainty grow. 'I'm sure you've made some friends here too?' she adds.

How silly, she realises, not to think that Gwen might be as worried as she is about their friendship not surviving the move.

'Some.' Gwen's smile is brief. 'No one like you.'

Marie puts a hand on her arm. 'And I haven't met anyone like you.'

That's almost a lie, she thinks: her affection for Theresa is deep, and she's fond of Elaine and Leanne. But Gwen doesn't need to know that; and none of them will ever be her friend for as long as Gwen has been.

'Is one of them a man?' Gwen says hopefully.

'No!' Marie splutters. 'Thank goodness. I can't be bothered with that any more.'

'Oh?'

Marie waves a hand. 'Imagine having to train someone new. No, thank you – I'm too old. Speaking of men: am I seeing Fred today too?'

'No,' Gwen says, looking guilty. 'He's playing canasta with some people at the club. He said to say hello.'

Marie isn't surprised: Fred has never really taken to her. She thinks it's because she has known Gwen far longer than he has, and he's jealous. Or perhaps he simply doesn't like her.

'That's all right,' Marie says. 'I'm here to see you anyway. Now, why don't you show me around?'

Gwen gives her the tour: bedroom, sitting room, kitchen, bathroom, small courtyard out the back.

'Quiet neighbours,' she says, gesturing over the back fence. 'I'm starting to think they're all dead!'

Marie smiles then stops herself, because for all she knows it could be true soon enough.

They sit, and Gwen bustles around filling the kettle and bringing the tray.

'How's the house?' she says as she makes Marie's tea just the way she likes it, with a splash of milk and a dollop of sugar.

'Still there, and still costing me money. I need to get some new braces for the sandstone or the walls are going to bulge to a point beyond decency.'

Marie smiles to make light of it, even though the subject is serious. The house was built in 1878 and, like any centenarian, needs regular, expensive upkeep.

'You should sell it,' Gwen says, pushing the cup and saucer towards Marie.

This is a subject Gwen has been fond of for a while, dating almost to the time of Norm's death. She told Marie then that it would be hard to afford the upkeep. Marie hadn't wanted to listen. She could be obstinate when it suited her – as Gwen knew – but in this case her resistance was because the subject upset her.

'I'm not quite there yet,' she says now.

'Marie, you know you should.' Gwen sighs, picking up her own teacup and sitting back in her chair. 'It's causing you stress. It's mucking up your aura.'

Ah yes, her aura. About five years ago Gwen's eldest child, Bronwyn, had decided she was psychic and started telling Gwen – and anyone else who would stand still for five minutes – about her aura. Gwen was wholeheartedly persuaded that her daughter's new beliefs were right, did her own exploration of mysticism and other things, and now declared her religion to be 'New Age'. Which Marie found curious when Gwen decided to move to a Uniting Church–run retirement village. That isn't to say that Marie dismisses Gwen's beliefs. Her friend is good at diagnosing when Marie's out of sorts just by looking at her, although Marie doesn't know whether that's because of her aura or the fact that she looks haggard and worried.

'Well, I don't want to muck up my aura,' she says, sipping her tea and only half trying to be sarcastic.

'*Marie.*' Gwen frowns at her.

'I'm not making fun of you,' Marie says. 'But I don't know how to fix my aura.'

'I'll ask Bron to give you a call. Or we can talk about selling that house. That'll do the trick.'

'Nicole would never let me.'

'She doesn't get a say.'

'It's her inheritance!' Marie protests. 'Besides, I don't want to move if I can avoid it. And Nicole and Pete are very kindly helping me out with some bills for a while.'

'You can't live there for the rest of your life,' Gwen says. 'On your own,' she adds pointedly.

Marie looks away, at Gwen's collection of family photos. At her life, crammed into one sitting room, one bedroom, half a kitchen and a small bathroom. She thinks of her own cottage, which isn't huge but it's her home.

'I'm doing all right,' she says quietly.

'Really?' Gwen emits something like a snort.

'I have Charlie Brown.'

'Marie! You're going to trip over that dog one day and you'll break something and lie there for who knows how long until someone finds you.' Gwen huffs. 'It's not *safe* being there on your own.'

She knows Gwen has a point, because this same point has occurred to her. Each time she gets on a stepladder to change a light bulb she considers the possibility that she'll fall and not be able to reach the phone to call for help. If she lived each day worrying about it, though, she'd never do anything.

'It's safe enough,' she says, although she could have made herself sound a little more convincing.

They sit in silence for a minute or so, drinking tea and eating biscuits.

'It's only because I worry about you,' Gwen says, and when Marie looks at her she can see it's true.

She laughs. 'I worry about me, too, but not about tripping over the dog.'

'What's your biggest concern?'

Marie has a list of concerns, but she doesn't want to burden Gwen with them. Gwen has simplified her life by moving here; she doesn't need it cluttered with Marie's petty problems.

'Nothing I can't handle,' she says.

'Don't be like that.' Gwen reaches over to pat her knee. 'A problem shared is a problem halved.'

If only that were true. Marie doesn't think she'll miss Norm less if she talks about him; she doesn't think the cost of living will decrease if she tells people that staying alive is expensive. But she knows the sentiment behind it – and Gwen is just trying to help. If she stops telling her friend what's really going on in her life, they won't be friends for much longer. Since Gwen's move Marie has learnt that the intimacy of friendship requires careful tending, and it's always vulnerable. You can't take anyone for granted – especially the very people you think are rusted on to your life. As the last few years have shown, even they can be removed suddenly and soon the whole structure of your existence is starting to wobble.

'The money is a problem,' she admits. 'There's too much going out and not enough coming in.'

'You have paintings you could sell,' Gwen says, looking pleased at coming up with the suggestion. 'Those ones your mother left you.'

Marie's mother had friends who were artists working nearby around the turn of the century, some of whom became quite famous. Her mother would never say much about them, although Marie suspected she painted herself. When she was younger she used to think that some of the paintings were really her mother's, signed with another name, but she had no proof. The paintings bear mostly the names of those famous men and Marie's aware she could get a few dollars for them, but they're all she has left of her mother. Besides, if she sells them she'll have nothing on the walls.

'I'll think about it,' she says to Gwen, because she appreciates that her friend is trying to help.

'If you moved in here you wouldn't have to worry about anything!'

'I don't know if my place would be worth enough to get me in here.'

Gwen shrugs and sips from her cup. Marie has no doubt she'll try that line again before the visit is over.

'Tell me about the kids,' she says, feeling that the topic of her house has been exhausted for now.

Gwen's face transforms with a beaming smile. 'They're wonderful. They were just here yesterday.'

Marie sits back into the couch and relaxes a little. As Gwen talks she remembers what it's like to spend time talking of subjects that seem small but say so much: grandchildren, family, shared experiences and laughter. It's a reminder that she shouldn't leave it too long before she visits again.

CHAPTER 21

The balcony doors on the surf club's expansive first floor are open but the air inside is still hot, and heavy with cigarette smoke. Theresa tries breathing through her mouth, which achieves precisely nothing because she can still smell the smoke. Once upon a time she wouldn't have noticed – she might even have enjoyed it – because she would have been amongst the smokers. Everyone she knew smoked. She only gave it up when she became pregnant for the first time, because she decided her baby should have a choice about whether he or she would be a smoker. The withdrawal was worse than the morning sickness, and now the sensations of both are intertwined so the smoke inside the club is making her feel like she's going to be sick.

'Here,' Andrew says, pushing a plastic cup filled with pale liquid into her hands before walking away.

Theresa was surprised when he was so keen to come to the party – they never usually do anything on New Year's Eve apart from pass out with tiredness; that same tiredness every parent she knows seems to have.

She wishes she was already asleep tonight – she's been more tired than usual lately – but Trev trapped her into coming to this party, the other day when she was waiting for the others to arrive for their swim.

When she mentioned it to Andrew she hoped he'd kick up his usual stink – as happens any time they have to go to an event at school, for instance – but he said, 'Oh yeah, I heard about that. Should be good.'

'How did you hear?' she asked, risking his irritation with her questioning.

'Chook, down at the garage. He's a member.'

It's Chook who Andrew rejoins after presenting her with this unidentifiable beverage, and now Trev is approaching and she's going to be stuck. She's also busting to do a wee and she just knows that Trev is going to keep her from getting to the ladies.

She looks towards Andrew and his friend, but they're play-shoving each other and cackling about something. The only other person she knew at the party – Brian, from across the road – has disappeared. What she really wants to do is go home, but she doubts she'll prise Andrew away.

'G'day, Tess,' Trev says, standing a little too close.

'Hi, Trev,' she says weakly.

'Nice evening for it.' He looks her up and down and gives her what can only be described as a leer. 'You look nice too.'

'Thanks,' she says.

She doesn't want to sound too grateful for the praise, because that might encourage Trev to step even closer. But Andrew hasn't said a word about how she looks, even though she's pleased that her dress is hanging a little looser than the last time she wore it. The swimming is paying off, in lots of ways. In the water she feels carefree, graceful, strong and brave. Out of the water she's sometimes tired and sore, but that's part of the deal, and in exchange she's in better shape than she has been in years.

'Is your wife here?' she asks Trev, drinking quickly from the cup and making a face, because whatever's in it doesn't taste like something she wants to drink.

'Yep.' Trev nods towards a woman standing near a potted palm. She has a close-set perm and a polyester dress that doesn't belong inside a stinking-hot surf club. Then he hikes up his pants just the way he does with his swimming costume. 'That's the little lady. Nance.'

Theresa's mind whirrs with conversational options: the cricket, the surf club, the brawl that broke out inside the pub last night. But before she can land on one she notices Andrew and Chook walking away, out of sight. Typical of Andrew to leave her stranded. He does it every time they go somewhere.

'So where's your husband, Tess?' Trev asks, with a return of that leer.

'Um, he . . . he just went somewhere. I should go and find him.'

She starts to walk away but Trev grabs her arm. 'Hang on – come and meet Nance.'

Theresa tries to look happy about it, but she doesn't want to be friends with Trev, nor does she want to meet Nance. Yet here Nance is, smiling and taking her hand with that lady's half-handshake that Theresa has always found weird – why can't they just shake hands like men? – and asking her about her children, not noticing that her husband is still leering.

Maybe five minutes go by but they feel like fifteen, and now her bladder really is protesting. 'Sorry,' she bursts out with what she hopes is an apologetic expression on her face. 'I really have to go to the loo.'

'Oh.' Nance looks offended – but Theresa is telling the truth.

'Sorry,' she says again. 'Two kids – you know how it is! I can't keep it in.'

Trev goes red and mumbles something inaudible. Theresa knew that suggesting she has a weak pelvic floor would be a get-out-of-jail-free card. She puts her drink down on a trestle table and sets off in search of the loo, which she's pretty sure is downstairs.

As Chook passes her, going in the other direction and on his own, Theresa stops. 'Where's Andrew?' she asks.

Chook shrugs and avoids her eyes. 'Dunno.'

Theresa resists the temptation to get cross at him, because it's not Chook's fault that her husband has, in all probability, left her there and either gone to the pub or gone home.

She trots down the stairs and goes to turn right to the toilets when she sees him. Him and someone else. A female someone else. A girl. Or young, at least. Younger than Theresa. She's blonde. Her hair is straight. She's slender. She's nothing like Theresa. Of course.

It's the perkiness of her boobs that makes Theresa think she's younger – and it's hard to avoid noticing them because Andrew has his hands on them.

There are people going past her, up the stairs, and all she can think is thank god her neighbour Brian has gone home, and that Trev and Nance are still upstairs, so there's no one to witness this.

No one apart from her.

Now one of Andrew's hands has slipped between the girl's legs.

He must be drunk. She hasn't seen him drink much tonight, but it makes sense, right? At a New Year's Eve party people get drunk and do stupid things. Which doesn't mean she isn't mad but it's an explanation. She might have flirted with a bloke at a Christmas party one year after one glass of spumante too many, so she's in no position to throw stones in this particular glass house.

Except she's stuck here, gripping the banister and realising she can't go to the loo because her husband is kissing another woman in front of her, and she can't confront him because that would draw attention to the scene, and she sees how they're looking at each other. Staring into each other's eyes as he gropes her and she slides her hands down his back.

They know each other already.

It's there in the way the woman is stroking his cheek. More than that, it's in the way Andrew looks at her: the way he used to look at Theresa several years and two children ago. His face is soft. His smile is sweet. He looks like a teenager in love.

Theresa thinks about the past few months – all the nights he's been out with his mates. The Brut 33 that he doesn't have in the bathroom cabinet, but which is on his skin when he comes home. She wants to laugh – out loud, and at herself. She's been ticked off that he's prepared to doll himself up for nights out with his mates but not for her. How stupid – *how stupid* – could she be to not realise that it isn't his mates he's interested in impressing? To *believe him* when he told her he was drinking with the boys at the pub? He knew she'd never check. She can't leave the kids at home alone to trot down to the pub and find out where he is.

The front door is right in front of her. The night air is so much cooler than the shame that is heating her cheeks and making her want to throw up. She flees outside – to the bushes next to the club – and up come the sausage roll and party pie and whatever the cheese on the Jatz cracker was. She hasn't thrown up like this since . . . since she was pregnant with Sasha.

As she thinks of her babies, at home with Nonna watching over them, she wants to scream. How could Andrew choose that girl over them? How could he prefer to spend time with her when his children love him unquestioningly?

As Theresa straightens up she's vaguely aware of people walking nearby, talking – perhaps about her – but they leave her alone. She's grateful. She needs some time to think about what to do next. She doesn't want to confront Andrew. Not here.

Then something else clicks: he was making no effort to hide himself. So maybe other people know. Maybe everyone knows.

If she had anything left to throw up, she would. Shame is an emotion that her religious upbringing encouraged, but Theresa can't remember feeling this way before. Shame about sinful thoughts is one thing; shame because your husband is making no secret of his affair, in front of people you know, is another.

What is she meant to do, though? Leave and go home on her own? Then what – have it out with him later, while her children are asleep, and risk them waking up and hearing her accuse their father of cheating on her?

No. She's not going to do that. She needs to work this out. Because it's not as straightforward as telling him what she saw. If she accuses him of cheating on her, he'll fire back with his usual complaint about how he's had to work so hard for years to 'support my family'.

Theresa wishes she could give him an invoice for everything she does around the house. If he had to pay for someone to cook, clean and wash his clothes, let alone raise his children, he wouldn't be able to afford it.

And to think she almost had a teaching degree to qualify herself for all of this. She wanted to finish the degree, but Andrew asked her to marry him and that was that. Andrew hadn't wanted her to work – like what she does every day of her life in their house isn't work! And her mum told her it was her 'duty' to make a home for her husband. Theresa had wanted to ask about her duty to herself, but life didn't go like that, did it?

She didn't completely listen to her mother: she worked in the bakery down the street until she fell pregnant with Ollie. Then she had to leave – Andrew had insisted.

Now she can see how she's trapped herself inside a world of his creation. All this time she's been telling herself that despite the fact she earns no money of her own, the house, at least, is her domain. But it's not, because he's brought whatever he's been doing into their house, their marriage and their family. It can't be her domain when someone else can infiltrate it so easily.

She sits on the low brick wall outside the club and closes her eyes. The night air is like a balm, and the sound of the waves just a few metres away reassures her. They're her constant, those waves. Tomorrow morning she'll be in them again. Tomorrow morning she will have time to think. Maybe time to talk. Because she needs advice from someone wiser. Like Marie. She's seen more of life than Theresa and she's a sensible woman.

Theresa doesn't feel she can tell Marie about it yet, though; it seems too soon. Or maybe it's that telling Marie would make it absolutely real.

After a while she walks back upstairs and sees Andrew standing with Chook by the drinks table. Chook must know what's going on; that's why he couldn't look her in the eye. She feels sick again, but she's not going to run. That's not the solution – not tonight.

'We've had a record number signing up for bronze medallion training,' she hears Trev say as she walks up to him and Nance.

'Sorry for running off,' she tells them.

'No worries,' Trev says, looking at his feet.

Andrew appears at her side. 'Ready to go?' he says.

From deep within her, Theresa summons the best acting performance of her life – better than when she played one of the seven dwarves in a school play. 'Yes,' she says, smiling at him. 'I am.'

The whole way home she lets him talk about Chook and the garage and how he should maybe join the surf club because there are 'good blokes' there. It's proof that he didn't see her standing at the bottom of the staircase, watching him. If he had, she doubts he'd be so talkative.

When they arrive home she checks on the children, then goes to the bathroom to have a shower and scrub off the cigarette smoke and the shame and the stink of vomit that Andrew didn't notice.

Afterwards she finds him sprawled on their bed, taking up all the space, so she turns on the TV in the lounge room and doesn't notice the time passing until the dawn light appears through the windows.

CHAPTER 22

As the morning light spreads over the water like a cheerful blanket, Elaine keeps her head up and breaststrokes for a while. It's too beautiful not to look – and this way she can keep an eye out for bluebottles. They had blighted the first few days of January, in what Marie called an 'unseasonal infestation', and Elaine's first experience of them came one morning when Marie bent over to examine the wet sand where it met the dry and made a 'hmph' sound.

'What is it?' asked Theresa.

'Bluebottles,' Marie said, straightening. She sighed and looked at the water. 'The tide's going out so they may all be on the beach.'

Elaine glanced at Theresa, who looked startled. 'Um,' she said, her eyes moving from Marie to Elaine to Leanne before landing back on Marie.

'Is there a problem with bluebottles?' Elaine asked, noticing brilliant blue flecks on the sand near Marie's feet. 'What do they do?'

'They sting. I usually go in when they're about, but this one,' Marie jerked a thumb towards Theresa, 'may not feel the same.'

'I got stung when I was ten,' Theresa said, grimacing with what looks like a memory of pain. 'It was not good.'

'What are the chances of getting stung?' Leanne said quietly as she bent to examine the specimen.

Marie shrugged. 'Who knows. It's not pleasant when it happens, but in all my years I've only been stung twice. So . . .' She looked meaningfully at Theresa. 'Our odds are pretty good.'

'Then I'll go in,' said Elaine.

'That's the spirit,' said Marie, pulling her T-shirt over her head.

Elaine had noticed she wears the same one every day; it bears the legend *Life. Be in it*. Given that Marie's husband is dead, she wondered at the meaning behind it.

'I will too,' Leanne said. 'I'm so slow that I'll see them.'

'What about you, Theresa?' Marie said as she kicked off her shorts.

'Well, I don't want to stay here on my own,' Theresa said uncertainly.

'I'm sure Trev would keep you company.'

'I'm coming.' Theresa whipped off her sarong and tied her hair back.

'Just a little tip,' Marie told them all, 'keep an eye out for them. Most of them are on the beach, I'd say, but it can't hurt to be wary, especially as we're heading out through the waves.'

Elaine took heed and swam through the waves instead of going under them.

This morning they saw only two bluebottles on the sand but Elaine is still swimming with caution, even now that they're past the breakers, and with the sunlight on the water it's easier to see what's about. She thinks they're in the clear but it's no hardship to keep her head above water for a while. She rolls over a bit and sidestrokes, something she hasn't done for many years. It takes her a few metres before she swaps sides.

She hears splashing water and Theresa pulls up beside her. 'You're sidestroking!' Theresa says, breathless. 'I didn't think anyone remembered how any more.'

'Sometimes I like to try different things,' Elaine says with a smile as she rolls back into a breaststroke.

She feels her hips expand with the frog kick, and her chest open as she pushes her hands out and around. It's a lovely stroke – she's always enjoyed it – just not as efficient for the purposes of exercise. Freestyle – the Australian crawl, as she first learnt it – is more vigorous and challenging, and you can swim further faster. If she were to breaststroke every day all the way she'd be out here for hours.

Up ahead, Little Beach beckons. It's their regular destination, but Elaine usually has her head in the water so she's never had a chance to see what's around it. The small beach is guarded by a ridge of rock on one side, covered by houses, and another curve of rock on the ocean side, giving it protection from the wind. There are no waves here either.

Behind the beach there's a grassy area with picnic tables that are unoccupied at this time of day, but when Elaine has walked around here on the occasional weekend she's found the place packed. To her right she can see the kiosk with its advertisements for Paddle Pops and Schweppes soft drinks. It's closed now; she's not sure it opens on weekdays anyway.

On the ocean side, the rock leads to scrubby bush: the light green, low, hardy plants that are typical of the coastline here, able to withstand salt and wind. Somewhere back there are spots for cars, she knows – all those visitors have to park somewhere.

With the rest of Shelly Bay at her back, it's possible to pretend that Little Beach is part of a village far from the city. Although some of the appeal of this whole place for Elaine is that it *can* feel like this yet still be part of Australia's largest city.

Marie has already turned at the beach to head back. Usually Elaine isn't far behind her but today she doesn't mind being the one to lag. Rather, she doesn't mind too much: there's a little competitive streak in her that she has never encouraged but which likes to remind her it's there. Consciously, rationally, she doesn't care if Marie beats her back to Main Beach; subconsciously, that competitiveness tells her she will always care. She likes to think it keeps her sharp, and stops her from doing nothing but lying around at home dreaming of gin. If she didn't feel that niggle to be better and do more, she couldn't imagine who she'd become.

'I'm going to freestyle back,' she announces to Theresa as they near Little Beach.

'Okay! I will too.' Theresa sounds cheerful but looks more strained than usual.

Elaine has heard of the demands on Theresa's time, and as much as she misses her sons she's pleased that she's past the stage of having to get children fed, bathed, clothed and out the door each day, let alone checking on a grandmother who sounds as though she thinks smoking is the secret to eternal youth.

By the time they're back at Main Beach and emerging, bluebottle free, onto the sand, Elaine feels invigorated – but Theresa looks even more weary.

'Are you all right?' Elaine asks as they walk slowly to their towels – just as a dripping Trev passes them at a clip.

'Feeling better, love?' he calls.

It's not clear who he's addressing but Theresa turns her head away.

'Who are you talking to?' says Marie.

'Tess.' He winks at Marie. 'Think she had a few too many sherbets at the New Year's Eve party.'

'Oh yes?' Marie looks barely interested.

Theresa, on the other hand, looks like she hopes quicksand will suddenly form and swallow her whole.

'She was vomiting in the bushes, wasn't she? That's the rumour,' Trev says a little too gleefully, and Elaine is horrified that he's been so indiscreet.

'Who hasn't done that?' she says, wanting to deflect attention from Theresa. 'I've been known to not even make it to the bushes.'

She glances at Marie, who is frowning at her, then at Theresa, who looks like she wants to cry.

'Like to get on the turps, do ya?' says Trev, hoisting the back of his Speedos so they hug his groin a little more tightly.

Elaine smiles and makes sure it doesn't reach her eyes.

'Off you go, Trev,' Marie says.

He chuckles as he toddles up the beach, swimming costume wedged up his backside.

Marie turns to Elaine. '*Do* you like the turps?' she says, and Elaine colours.

'Sometimes. Anyway, I should get home to see James before he leaves for work.'

'Thank you,' says Theresa limply.

'No need to thank me,' says Elaine, wrapping her towel around her waist.

'And what happened to you, Theresa?' Marie asks. 'That sounds completely out of character.'

Of course – Elaine should have asked that. Instead she was self-centredly trying to escape scrutiny of her own behaviour. She glances towards Theresa and sees Leanne looking at her with a slight frown, as if she's disappointed.

'Oh – ah – just ate a bad prawn!' Theresa says with a high-pitched laugh, and it's clear she's lying.

'But we saw you the next day,' Marie says slowly, 'and you didn't look like someone who was recovering from food poisoning. Or someone who'd had too much to drink the night before.'

'Food poisoning sounds so dramatic!' Theresa says as she ties up her sarong in record time and picks up her flip-flops. 'Anyway, must run! School holidays, you know. The kids are probably already tearing the house apart.'

'The-*reeee*-sa,' Marie says.

'Cheerio!' Theresa moves faster over the sand than they've ever seen her.

Marie glances at Leanne, then towards Elaine. 'Something's wrong,' she says. 'Leanne, any chance you can get it out of her at the hospital?'

Leanne shakes her head quickly. 'She's not rostered on this week. Or next. Because of the holidays. And I, uh . . .'

'Wouldn't ask?' Marie makes a face. 'We're all too bloody polite, aren't we? Not a criticism. Just a comment,' she adds as Leanne's face falls.

'I imagine she'll tell us in her own good time,' Elaine says, 'if she wants to.'

Marie turns completely towards her. 'Yes,' she says. 'I imagine she will.' Her gaze is piercing and Elaine feels completely exposed. 'I imagine we could all do that if we want to. Since we're friends here now, aren't we?'

Elaine knows exactly what point Marie is trying to make, but if she thinks Elaine is going to declare anything right here, on the sand, she's wrong. Declarations are not part of her genetic make-up. But she doesn't want to ignore the hand of understanding that Marie has extended.

'We are,' she says after a few moments have passed.

Marie nods as if satisfied. 'Right.'

'I have to go,' Leanne says. 'Early shift.' She nods to each of them and slips away in her quiet Leanne fashion.

'I'm going too.' Marie wraps her towel around her neck. 'And you should get home to that husband. I'll see you tomorrow.'

'Goodbye.'

Elaine watches as Marie walks in a plodding, determined way over the soft sand and up onto the promenade. It takes her a few seconds more to realise what was acknowledged between them this morning: that they are friends. That they are all friends.

While Elaine revealed more of herself than she intended, she can't chastise herself for it. She has made friends in this place where she was, not so long ago, friendless. It's a moment for being gloriously, ineffably pleased with life.

CHAPTER 23

The staff roster has been all over the place since the new year arrived, and some of her colleagues appear to have forgotten what time their shifts start, so Leanne feels like she almost has the hospital to herself today.

After placing her handbag in her locker she rolls her shoulders back and forth, feeling the effects of the swimming. After the first couple of days in a row she was sore in muscles she didn't know she had; but it's been weeks now and she's still discovering new parts of her body that ache. It's good to put her lessons into practice, though, even if she hasn't actually been for a lesson for a while.

She's going to head to the pool after work today, because there was no ocean swim this morning, or yesterday. Heavy rain two days ago means a risk of pollution, and Marie has always been clear that they need to wait two days, at least, until they swim again – 'unless you want to inhale a poo', she said. The warning was effective enough for Leanne to stay away. Although she suspects that Marie doesn't take her own advice, because she's been in the habit of daily swimming for so many years it's hard to imagine her not doing it.

Marie is the sort of swimmer Leanne dreams of being, instead of the uncoordinated mess she feels like. She was never this uncoordinated as a child. Some days during a swim she'll wish she'd stuck to dry land, but then she'll have a day when it all clicks and she'll feel capable and accomplished. The others are so much faster, though, and more at ease – even Theresa, who says she's hopeless but clearly isn't. Leanne wonders if she'll ever swim like that.

Walking towards the station desk all she can hear on the paediatrics floor is quiet. Several patients were sent home for Christmas and New Year – either returned for good, or taking an authorised break from their treatment – and the influx that is surely coming hasn't yet started. That means she can give more attention than usual to the children who are here. And there's at least one person she wants to see: the same person she has spent nights sitting beside, watching her sleep, listening to her breathe. When Matron asked her to special Imogen she knew the job wouldn't be hard so much as long, because mainly she's providing reassurance for Imogen's parents – and she knows the form that reassurance takes: they want to know that their child is still alive. So Leanne sits and listens to that breathing throughout the night; she sacrifices her own sleep because she, too, wants to know that Imogen is alive. She cares for all her patients, of course, but she can't help feeling just a little more attached to this one.

'Hello, Imogen,' she says as she approaches the wan child. She's in a room on her own, with three empty beds.

'Hello, Sister!' Imogen smiles, and Leanne marvels, as she has before, at the girl's ability to stay cheerful throughout harrowing treatment.

She smiles back. 'You can call me Leanne. We know each other well enough now, don't we?'

Imogen nods and hugs her doll closer. The doll belonged to

her sister – Leanne remembers it because it has one eye missing and its hair chopped diagonally.

'What's your doll's name?' she says as she picks up Imogen's wrist to measure her pulse and covertly observe her breathing.

'Bunny.'

'Bunny!' Leanne counts the beats in her head. 'She doesn't look like a bunny.'

'No!' Imogen's nose wrinkles and she scrunches her mouth into a smile as her eyes roam over Leanne's face. 'Your hair is very black.'

Leanne places Imogen's hand on the covers. 'It is.'

'And very straight.'

'True.' She fills Imogen's water glass.

'My hair is curly.'

Leanne smiles. 'Yes, it is.'

'At my school my friend has hair like yours. She's from Japan.' Imogen looks as if she's delivering serious news. 'Are you from Japan?'

Leanne shakes her head quickly. 'No. I'm from Australia. Don't I sound Australian?'

'She sounds Australian too! But she says her parents are from Japan.' Imogen puts her head to one side like she's thinking about something.

'Did you eat all your breakfast?' Leanne asks, trying to appear as if she's in charge even as her young patient steers the conversation in a direction she's not sure she wants it to go. She doesn't talk about herself to the children or their parents, even though a lot of them ask. It's better to maintain a barrier.

Imogen makes a face. 'I don't like porridge.'

'So you didn't eat it?'

Imogen drops her head as Leanne shakes out a thermometer and puts it in her armpit. 'Hold still for me.'

Imogen's eyes go to the top of Leanne's head. 'Are you sure you're not from Ja-paa-aan?' she singsongs, and Leanne knows she'll need to say something or Imogen will keep asking. She's as curious as most children her age, and sometimes a little more so.

Yesterday she asked Leanne why her sister died because her parents wouldn't tell her. In the end Leanne had to make up a line about how we don't always know why things happen the way they do. It was too vague to satisfy anyone, let alone a bright six-year-old, but she could hardly tell Imogen the truth when her parents clearly don't want her to know.

'I'm not from Japan,' Leanne says, keeping her voice light. 'My mum is from Korea. That's why I have this hair.'

'And your eyes are funny. Not like mine!'

Leanne thinks of the teasing she endured at school about her eyes. Back then the taunts were all variations on her being from China, not Japan, not Korea. She figured then, and still does, that for all the sarcasm Australians like to indulge in, they're lazy with their insults.

'That's true. They're not like yours,' she says, removing the thermometer. Thirty-eight degrees. So she wasn't imagining that Imogen looks paler than usual. She reaches into her pocket for some paracetamol. 'They're like my mum's.'

'Do you have any brothers and sisters?'

Imogen has already asked this question, several times, and Leanne has told her yes, but demurred when it came to giving a number. Not only because she wants to keep it private, but because she thinks it's unkind when dealing with a child whose only sibling has died.

'You know I do,' she says. 'Now, I have some medicine for you. I'm just going to find some orange juice for you to take it with. Will you keep Bunny company while I'm gone?'

Imogen wrinkles her nose again and nods quickly. 'Mm-hm.'

Leanne reaches out and pats the side of her head. 'Good girl.'

She walks quickly towards the kitchen, her heart beating a little faster. If Imogen's temperature is up, something is going wrong. They've just stabilised her and now she's going backwards. It's what Leanne has worried about some nights as she's sat beside Imogen's bed, then she's chastised herself for being too attached. Imogen is one patient out of many. If Leanne worries about her more than she does the others, she's not doing her job.

After she's administered the paracetamol she calls the registrar and asks him to come and check on Imogen, then continues her rounds. At the end of them she finds Imogen asleep, and a note on her chart indicating that paracetamol was given. Now all she can do is wait and hope that Imogen improves.

The day passes quickly – they all do when she's here, in constant motion – and once her shift is over she walks briskly home to pick up her swimming gear and head for the pool.

It's one of the advantages of living in Shelly Bay that everything is in walking distance, yet it doesn't seem like a small place. There are so many different people coming and going from the hospital, and tourists ebbing and flowing on the weekends, that there are always new faces. Shelly Bay expands and contracts to fit the people who need it. Like her. Without her realising, this place took her into its care and has kept her there.

As Leanne reaches the turnstiles at the pool she feels a fat drop of rain on the back of her neck. If it becomes heavy she can add another day onto her forced exile from the ocean. The pool is an acceptable alternative, although she prefers to come after work when there are fewer agitated men in the fast lanes trying to get in their twenty laps before the day starts. She made the mistake of turning up in the morning yesterday, and even the 'moderate' lane was full of hazards. It wasn't pride so much as practicality that kept her out of the slow lane: that's the domain of breaststrokers, who are lucky to do fifty metres in under ten minutes. She knows she's faster than that. She's come a long way in just a few weeks and she deserves to be in that moderate lane – at a time when there are fewer rivals for it. So she sighs with relief as she sees that there are two moderate lanes this afternoon and only one person in each.

She has no idea how many metres she swims between Main Beach and Little Beach each day, so she's trying to match the time: forty-five minutes or thereabouts. Swimming in chlorine is harder because there's no salt to buoy her, so it's a more tiring forty-five minutes, but it still proves to her that she's achieved something – even if she sometimes does the last few laps as breaststroke. A fast breaststroke.

She ducks into the change room and peels off her uniform. She always tries to be quick even if there's no one else around. Her parents didn't encourage their children to walk around the house nude so she learnt to scurry from bath to bedroom. She's never seen any of her family naked, not even her siblings.

When she swims at the beach she never feels as exposed as she does at the pool. Perhaps it's because the other women are so relaxed about their bodies. Theresa makes cracks about hers, but she's still out there in a swimming costume. Marie may be in her sixties but she's proud, Leanne can tell, of the achievement of making it that far in life and of her years of swimming. Elaine is so lissom that Leanne doesn't believe she could have had a self-conscious moment in her life.

As she emerges from the change room, spitting rain gets in her eyes and she looks around for a place to put her bag and towel. There's one table with an umbrella up and she almost sprints towards it before anyone else can have the same idea. With her eyes half closed against the rain, she doesn't see the person she collides with.

'Whoops!' says a man's voice, and Leanne is mortified to find that it's Matt. The same Matt she hasn't seen for lessons for a while.

'Leanne,' he says, his face transforming into a smile. 'I didn't realise you missed me so much.'

Leanne has no idea how to respond. She hasn't missed Matt – although she sometimes wishes he was in the water with her, giving her tips on improving her stroke – but she doesn't want to say that. If she was Theresa she could come up with something light-hearted. Instead she emits half words, then tries smiling, although she's sure she looks weird.

'Sorry,' she says. 'I was hoping to get these things under shelter before it starts to really rain.'

'Oh.' He looks at the belongings in her hands. 'I'll put them in the office for you.'

He beckons her to follow him before she has a chance to protest.

'You're looking well,' he says over his shoulder, then a shy expression crosses his face. 'I mean, you look in good shape. Have you been swimming a lot?'

'Yes. Every day.'

He nods in a way that suggests it's an answer he expected.

When they reach the office he takes her things and puts them behind the door. 'We don't lock it, so just come and get them when you're ready.' He grins.

'Thanks,' she says, starting to shove her cap over her hair and wondering if it's rude to turn around and walk away from him.

'So how have you been?' he asks, and the matter is decided for her.

'Fine. The swimming I'm doing – it's in the ocean. So it's toughened me up a bit, I think.'

Matt nods vigorously. 'I thought I hadn't seen you here lately.'

'Oh, I was here yesterday.' Leanne tucks in the last of her hair.

'Right.' He nods again, looking crestfallen. 'So . . . no more lessons?'

'I'm good for now. Thanks.' She half smiles.

'Right.' He has a funny look on his face but she has no idea what it means.

She has to think of something to say to end this conversation or she may never get in the pool. 'You were such a great teacher that I'm swimming really well. And I can keep up with the ladies I swim with. They're really good. Experienced.'

Something crosses his face then and she thinks it's genuine pleasure. If only she'd thought to tell him this earlier – she feels almost cruel not letting him know that he's helped her so much. She has been grateful, but mainly only aware of it when she's in the sea, far from being able to tell him.

'That's really terrific,' he says softly. 'Good on you.'

She smiles as fully as she can. 'Thank you.'

'There's, um . . . something else I'd like to ask you.' He fidgets with the handle on the office door as she looks at him expectantly. 'It may sound a bit strange, because of how we met, but, um . . .' He looks flustered. 'Would you like to go out for dinner one night?' he says, then seems relieved, as if he's finished a three-hour exam.

Leanne is too surprised to know how to respond. She had no inkling that he thought of her as anything other than a student – although she supposes that means he did his job professionally. Should she be upset that all the while he had other designs on her? No, probably not, because she doesn't know if he did, and it's not as if he called her home number – which he could have, because it's in the office records. So he's not a creep. And she doesn't want to think he's a creep. She's just not sure if she wants to think he's anything else either. He hasn't been someone she might consider going on a date with.

Not that she's thought of anyone else that way. That hasn't been part of her life. Until right now, she thought it never would be again. Men don't ask her out – that's what she's always told busybodies at work when they've asked why she 'doesn't have a fella', and it's easy to say it because it's mostly the truth.

'Leanne?' Matt says gently. 'Sorry – did I say the wrong thing?' He looks worried.

'No, you didn't,' she says. She takes a breath, because she feels, all of a sudden, the past seven years running up to meet her.

Seven years of not sitting across the table from a man, making conversation. Seven years of thinking that she would be a spinster forever and it would be all right. Seven years of sometimes longing to feel the touch of someone else's skin, then remembering what the cost of that has been in the past. She has, for those years, believed that men can't be trusted because they want to hurt women. They want to hurt *her*. Even her father and brothers, in the end, hurt her.

It's not feminism that's made her like this. She isn't inclined to read *The Female Eunuch*, even though Marie has encouraged her to, and she put aside Simone de Beauvoir's *The Second Sex* on her sole attempt at reading it. Leanne doesn't think she needs books to tell her that women deserve the same rights as men. She knows they do. And she also knows that in life it seems impossible to achieve.

Yet here is Matt, with warmth in his voice and kindness on his face. He is happy for her that she's swimming regularly and he helped her achieve that.

There has to be a point, Leanne knows, at which she decides how much she wants to keep hold of the ideas she has; how much they are worth to her stacked up next to the life that's still ahead of her. And she needs to be brave if she is going to mark the end of those seven years. She needs to believe that her future can be better than her past. And she does believe it, because she has already made it so.

Matt may not be the man of her dreams; then again, she's never had one of those. She hasn't let herself wonder or daydream about a man she might form a life with. Matt may not turn out to be the man of her immediate future either, but she won't know if she doesn't start.

'That would be lovely,' she says, and gives him her best smile, the one she's been trying to use more often. Inspired by Theresa, who smiles so readily.

'Really?' Now he looks as excited as a child who's won a prize at the fair.

She nods. 'Really.'

'Great. Great. That's really great. Can I – um, you need to swim. Can I call you later?'

'Sure.' She smiles again.

'Well, uh . . . have a good swim then.' His smile is broad and she feels pleased.

'I intend to,' she says, and turns to walk towards the pool, out into the warm rain that is now falling steadily. She barely notices the change as she slips into the pool, under the surface and pushes off the end.

CHAPTER 24

'Jesus, Andrew, don't let him do that!' Theresa feels like stomping the way her children sometimes do, and not just because she's annoyed that Andrew's not stopping their son from decorating the kitchen with the mayonnaise she's trying to put into the potato salad.

She still hasn't said anything about what she saw at the party and the compulsion to do so is reaching a high-tide mark inside her. She worries that it will flow out of her mouth in front of the children if she doesn't say something soon. Yet they're at her parents' home for a few days, and before that they were in the car driving here, and before that the only times she was alone with him were the seconds when they passed each other in the hall. She's been asleep each evening when he's arrived home.

Theresa's been falling asleep earlier and earlier each night, and she's not sure if it's because she feels exhausted – which is the case, but she's been exhausted for years – or because she's been subconsciously avoiding the very conversation she needs to have.

She glares at her husband but he doesn't even register her request.

'Andrew – *please* help me,' she says. She pushes her hair back from her sweaty forehead and realises she's smeared herself with mayo.

'That's a good look,' Andrew says, picking up his tinny and taking a long swig.

'I swear to God—'

'God, Jesus – you're havin' a good run of it.' He takes another swig of his beer, which makes her want to scream.

But Sasha is standing by her legs, looking up at her with those gorgeous brown eyes, and her lips are quivering the way they always do when her parents fight.

Oliver is high on the rapture that comes with being in his grandparents' home, from the bowls of jelly and ice cream her mother always gives him. And Theresa knows Andrew won't do anything to stop him misbehaving, because he never does.

Andrew never used to be like this. When it was just the two of them he'd tell her to forget about the ironing and the washing up and come to bed. As soon as Oliver was born he changed, and she slipped into chains she's never managed to break.

'Mamma,' Sasha whimpers.

Theresa wipes her hands on her apron and bends down to pick up her daughter, wincing as Sasha presses against her breast. That breast has been so sensitive lately, and Theresa's tried to work out if she's using one arm differently when she swims. But she's no expert, and the effort of trying to analyse her freestyle stroke while actually swimming freestyle has been taking a lot of fun out of the whole experience.

'It's all right, darling,' she whispers, kissing Sasha's temple twice before putting her down again. 'Why don't you go and see what Nana is up to?' The atmosphere in the kitchen isn't likely to become less tense and Sasha will be better off in another room.

'What's going on?' Her father is in the kitchen now, carrying his own tinny.

Theresa sighs and forces a smile. 'I'm trying to get Ollie to calm down. He's throwing food everywhere.'

She offered to make lunch so her mother could have a break from Nonna, who has been demanding games of backgammon because she's missing out on poker by visiting her daughter – but didn't count on having to wrangle her children while she did it.

'Oliver,' her father says, putting his shoulders back the way he's always done when he wants to command authority, 'how about some cricket, eh? Your nana put the bat and ball somewhere in the garden. Once we find it, we can have a hit.'

Oliver grins.

'Ollie, put the jar on the bench, please,' Theresa says, only to see her son drop it on the floor as he runs towards the back garden. Mayonnaise spatters across the kitchen cupboards.

She lets out a shriek. 'OLIVER!'

'Leave him alone,' Andrew says, drinking more beer, burping. Charming. 'It's his school holidays. Only a few days left.'

'That doesn't mean he's allowed to do whatever he wants,' Theresa says, picking up the Chux from the kitchen sink and wiping down the cupboards. 'And it's not you cleaning up the mess.'

'Because that's your job,' he says, not even looking at her. 'I do enough as it is.'

Of course: he does so much; he does it all. He pays for everything. She does nothing. The housework is easy. Looking after the kids is easy – until he has to do it and then it's all too hard. She's sick of it.

She's not going to get upset, though. It doesn't get her anywhere. So she stuffs the anger back down, throws the Chux into the sink and turns on the tap, dousing and wringing the cloth.

'Dad,' she says, hanging the cloth over the tap, 'aren't you going to play cricket with Ollie?'

'Oh. Yeah.' Her father nods to Andrew and leaves the kitchen.

Theresa turns to face her husband, who is gazing at her with what might be called indifference if Theresa was being kind to herself, but is more likely to be something stronger.

'Are you having an affair?' she blurts.

Andrew stares at her. 'Don't be bloody ridiculous,' he says, but she hears a quavering in his voice.

'I saw you,' she says, feeling bolder.

He glances away then back to her. 'I don't know what you're talkin' about.'

Because she knows he's lying, somehow it allows her to feel calmer. She's the one speaking the truth. Why didn't she do it earlier?

'At the surf club party,' she says. 'By the toilets. You were . . .' How can she describe the spectacle she saw? 'You were groping a woman.'

'Was not.'

He sounds like Oliver when he's denying something that he's definitely done. Trying to get her son to admit the truth never works, so Theresa doesn't like her chances with his father.

She didn't think about what she'd do if Andrew denied her accusation – she just wanted to get it out of the way. But if he insists there's no affair when she knows there likely is, or something close to it . . . what will she do next? How is she meant to keep living with her husband knowing he prefers another woman, and he knows that she knows?

'Fine,' she says, because it's all she can come up with.

Andrew looks stunned. 'Fine?'

'Why don't you join Dad and Ollie outside?'

She picks up the Chux and drapes it again. Picks it up. Drapes it. If he doesn't leave, she worries that she'll say something else – scream it, maybe – and she doesn't want to fight any more than they have. She wants her children to enjoy their time here – the garden is twice the size of the one at home, there's a swing on one of the trees, and her father has limitless patience with his grandchildren. It is, as Andrew reminded her, their holidays. She has happy memories of summer holidays, and Ollie and Sasha should have the same.

She stays facing the sink but feels him close behind her.

'It didn't mean anything,' he says.

She can smell the hops on his breath and her stomach turns, but not because of the smell. 'So you're not denying it now?'

She doesn't want to look at him so she's going to stay here, where she can see her father and son through the kitchen window.

He sniffs. 'What's the point?' he says wearily. 'But that was the only time.'

'You knew her,' Theresa says. 'I could tell.'

'She's Chook's sister.'

Of course. Which means Chook is a party to her humiliation as well, just as she suspected.

'I didn't know she'd be at the party.' He sniffs again. 'I just . . .' His exhalation is ragged. 'She's had a thing for me for a while.'

As if that explains it. Except it's the excuse he's allowed himself, so clearly it does.

'And that meant you should do what you did?' she half whispers.

'I just . . .' He sighs. 'Gave in.'

In all the scripts Theresa's run in her head about this situation, she never once had Andrew saying he'd given in. He was meant to tell her that he's in love with this woman, at least. In one of the scripts he's going to leave her because the other woman is pregnant. Or there's already another child and that's why he's been gone so often. Theresa wanted a drama to match her reaction that night. Something big. Now she feels something very much like disappointment mixed in with the churn of embarrassment and betrayal.

She turns to face him. Wants to see how he reacts as she says, 'You were right there in front of everyone. Didn't you care who saw? Didn't you care if *I* saw?'

There are clouds in Andrew's eyes, and she notices that he's unkempt. He hasn't shaved in a while. His hair is in need of a cut. The skin on his forehead is peeling because he never wears a hat when he's working outside and she stopped, long ago, trying to make him. He looks uncared for, and she hasn't seen it because she hasn't looked at him closely for a long time. Maybe she looks the same; she doesn't really take the time to check each day.

'Of course I care,' he mutters. 'Why do you think I did it?'

Theresa feels like a hot wind has blown into her eyes, so she half shuts them against the world. 'You wanted me to see?' she says hoarsely.

'I wanted you to *react*,' he says, an edge to his voice. 'But you didn't. Not until now. And now is . . .' He looks like he's sneering, then he shakes his head and it's gone. 'You used to think I was hot shit. You could never get enough.'

She has a memory – an image that flashes in and out of her mind – of Andrew telling her she was the most beautiful girl on the beaches. 'I could say the same about you,' she says quietly, although she knows she's not that girl any more. Besides, she doesn't believe that he still wants her. If he did he wouldn't have looked elsewhere for company. He'd have stayed loyal to her. But she doubts he'd buy that argument.

'You stopped wanting me first,' he says, swallowing. 'I never stopped.'

His eyes are red-rimmed but she doesn't think he's about to cry. She's never seen him cry. Truth be told, she's never wanted to. She's never liked to see men cry because she wants to believe they can be stronger than she is; strong for her when she needs them to be. Crying is weak, isn't it? That's what the magazines say.

'Andrew,' she says, 'most of the time I'm so tired I don't know what I want.'

'Yeah, well . . .' He picks at the ring-pull on his tinny. 'A man's got needs.'

And a woman doesn't? She can't say that, though, because she knows the answer, and it's *no*. Her needs are secondary to everyone else's.

'I'm sorry you're feeling that way,' she says, because keeping the peace is another of her jobs. 'I'll try to make more time for you.'

'You could stop swimming,' he says quickly, as if he's practised saying it. As if he's been waiting for the chance to say it again.

'What?'

'Instead of rushing out every morning, you could spend a bit longer in bed.' He looks at her suggestively.

Once upon a time she'd have taken up his invitation, but now her immediate reaction is to want to tell him to get lost. Swimming is the one thing she has for herself, to herself. In the water she's free. Accomplished. Capable. All the things she doesn't feel on dry land.

Yet if she refuses his request, he can say he's tried to fix things and it's her not making the effort.

'Mu-um!' Sasha's voice rescues her from Andrew's checkmate.

'I'd better go,' she says.

'What a surprise.'

'I'll – I'll think about it,' she says, although she's lying. She just needs time to come up with a compromise.

'Sure.'

'Mu-uuuum!'

She and Andrew stare at each other for a few seconds, then Theresa rushes from the room.

CHAPTER 25

When Marie arrives home from her swim there's a message on her answering machine. She knows it will be Nicole, because Nicole is the only one who leaves messages.

Hi Mum – I forgot to tell you that your new gardener is starting today. His name's Gus. I don't know what time he'll be there. I said you'd be home. You will be, won't you? Love you. Bye.

Marie looks outside and sighs. The arrival of the gardener is sorely needed: her garden is on the verge of being ramshackle and she knows Norm would hate it. This Gus will probably think she's lazy or useless, but she can't be worried about that because he's probably young and will barely notice she's there. That's what happens when you start to go grey and your posture's not as straight as it used to be: you become invisible. As far as most people are concerned Marie's an old lady; and she may as well be a ghost as she passes them on the street, so intangible does she feel. Luckily she wasn't invisible to Theresa when they met.

Marie smiles as she thinks about this morning's escapades, with Theresa swimming underwater for as long as she was able before popping up next to Elaine, who yelped.

'You could have been a shark!' Elaine cried, as Leanne looked on with amusement.

'But I'm not,' Theresa said, gasping as she trod water. 'I'm not as good at that underwater thing as I'd like to be, though.' She started to float on her back.

'You'll go out to sea if you try that,' Marie said as she swam back towards them, for once not so interested in getting to her destination.

'I need a rest,' Theresa said weakly.

'You should have come up for air earlier, you fool,' Marie chastised. 'People can blow valves or something if they hold their breath too long.'

Around them the water was rolling slowly with the motion of the waves that would break on Main Beach but never manifest right where they were. They were about fifty metres from the walking path; there were people jogging and strolling along it, some with dogs. It was one of those perfect mornings when the sky is cloudless and the light is golden, turning the leaves on the nearby trees a more lustrous green and the sand a richer hue. Marie has been looking at this place her entire life yet she doesn't always see it. Too much time has passed since she's stopped to appreciate it.

She's still thinking about it as she showers and makes her breakfast. The whole day seems suffused with the glow of the morning and she feels like it's seeped into her marrow.

The click-clack of claws on her kitchen floor snaps her back to the present. 'What is it, Charlie Brown? Have you finished your breakfast already?' She bends down to scratch behind his ears.

'Knock knock,' she hears, and straightens up to see standing on her verandah, by the back door, a man with a full head of salt-and-pepper hair and a slight stoop to his tall frame. He has grey-green eyes set in a complexion that's either olive-skinned or browned by the sun, and he's looking at her with curiosity.

'Hello?' she says, her heart beating fast at the sight of a stranger in her home, even if she's sure this is the new gardener.

'Are you Marie?' he says, smiling – and, she notices, still standing outside. At least he has the manners to wait for an invitation.

'I am,' she says.

'I'm Gus. Nicole sent me. Sorry for surprising you – she said to take the side gate.' His crow's feet crinkle in a way that suggests he smiles a lot.

He's older than she was expecting and looks nothing like a man who's spent his life doing manual labour. For one thing, he's wearing a linen shirt with the sleeves rolled up, tucked into moleskins that are secured with a new-looking belt. He's wearing boots, though, so that's workmanlike. Around these parts a lot of the tradesmen wear thongs. She once had a man cleaning gutters while wearing thongs and spent the whole day expecting him to fall off the ladder.

'Please – come in,' she says.

As he steps inside, Charlie Brown starts to dance around his feet. 'Who's this?' says Gus, bending down to bring his face closer to the dog's.

'Charlie Brown. He runs the place.'

She watches as Gus holds the back of his hand towards Charlie Brown, the way someone used to dogs would.

'Do you have a dog?' she asks.

'I did, a long time ago.' He stands up. 'An Alsatian. Lovely fellow.'

He extends his hand towards her and she shakes it, feeling the dry warmth of his skin, conscious that hers will feel cold to him. *Cold hands, warm heart*, Norm used to say.

'Lovely to meet you, Marie.'

There are those crinkles again and he's looking at her more intensely than any man has since Norm died. She doesn't quite know what to do with it, especially as he must be at least a decade younger than her, so she's sure he doesn't mean it in the way Norm did.

'I suppose you saw the garden on your way in,' she says, nodding towards the back, reminding herself why he's here.

'I had a glance. But I'd love you to show me properly.' He has the modulated tones of someone with training in received pronunciation.

Marie smiles quickly and steps around Charlie Brown, who then hangs off her heels as she walks onto the verandah.

'How did Nicole find you?' she asks over her shoulder.

'My son knows her husband,' Gus says as he follows her down the stairs to the garden path. 'And he mentioned I've been doing some gardening work around the place. Nothing too fancy.' He flashes her a smile as he stops beside her. 'I should warn you that I'm self-taught, but I haven't managed to butcher a garden yet.'

She looks up at him. 'Well, I've almost managed to butcher this one, so you can't make it worse.'

He puts his hands on his hips and looks around. 'I think you're being hard on yourself. Everything's in the right place – it just needs a bit of attention.'

Their eyes meet.

'Don't we all?' he adds smoothly, and she doesn't know whether to be shocked or pleased that he seems to be if not flirting with her then allowing her to believe he is.

Marie breaks his gaze and gestures towards the shed. 'I'll show you where the tools are. My husband kept them in there.'

She doesn't know why she's mentioned Norm – there's no need to tell Gus that the tools were his.

'Nicole told me that he died several years ago. I'm sorry,' Gus says, and he sounds genuinely concerned.

'It's not your fault.'

He laughs. 'That's what I say when people say that about my wife.'

Marie feels a pinprick of jealousy – something else she hasn't experienced in a very long time.

'You're widowed too?' she asks.

Gus nods. 'Around the same time you were. That's when I started this.' He opens his arms to the garden. 'I spent years in the law and I lost my taste for it. It's satisfying when you have a victory, but the rest of the time you don't feel like you're doing much good. However, it did give me enough of an income that I could step back and do what I pleased.'

He looks abashed. 'I ran on a bit there – I apologise.' He looks at her with that intensity again – the same look as when he arrived. 'I suppose I feel like I know you because I've heard about you from Peter. Forgive me.'

Marie raises her eyebrows. 'There you go again, saying sorry.'

She hears a noise and follows it to where Charlie Brown is digging up a flower bed.

'Charlie Brown!' she says crossly. 'Stop that.'

Gus strides over and picks up the dog in one easy movement. Charlie Brown looks too surprised to protest and Marie is much the same.

'Let's see these tools,' Gus says, walking towards the shed with the terrier tucked under his arm. 'Then we can talk about the amount of work involved.'

Marie fights the impulse to want to be tucked under his other arm and follows him into the shed.

AUTUMN 1983

AUTUMN 1983

CHAPTER 26

This morning's swim was sublime. Almost effortless, right up until the point Elaine decided she'd attempt to catch up to Marie – who still has the advantage most days – only to feel her shoulders protest, reminding her that while she may think of herself as being athletic, she hasn't been swimming for as long as Marie.

Nor can she really call herself athletic with the amount she's drinking. It's become more than a bad habit now. For so long she has kidded herself that gin has been keeping her company in the late afternoons while she waits for James to come home from work, and after he falls into bed exhausted.

Occasionally he wants to make love and she never minds that – she welcomes it, in fact, because it gives her a chance to forget herself. On those nights she doesn't drink nearly as much and she doesn't miss it. On those nights she tells herself that she doesn't need to drink as often as she does; she can do without it.

Then the next afternoon arrives and she thinks, *Just one*. Then, *Just another one*. Her body is so used to it now that it takes more and more to achieve the same small oblivion she's always looking for.

And now that James has noticed she's drinking a lot, she's become sneaky. Starting to drink earlier in the day so she can sober up a bit before he arrives home, then creeping out of bed to have a tipple or two late at night.

She's hiding a huge part of her life from her husband and part of her relishes it, because it makes her feel like she has some control again. Not of him, but of her circumstances. It also makes her homesickness disappear. Most of her, though, detests what she does yet feels completely out of control. She wants to stop, but can't. She doesn't want to stop, and doesn't.

She tops up her tonic to dilute the gin, and turns down the radio in the kitchen. The hour of music has turned into talkback and she flinches at the sound of some of the flatter Australian accents of the callers. They say inscrutable things such as 'I dint come down in the last shower' and 'He was all over the place like a dog's breakfast'. They talk about the 'gummint', which, after some study, she believes to be the *government*.

The male callers – and they're mostly men – use the term 'mate' a lot, especially when they're being hostile. She has realised that Australians use this term as a friendly greeting and as a warning. Deciphering its intention is all in the tone. When it's friendly, the speaker tends to use a rising inflection, as if there's an exclamation point: 'Mate!' If it's a warning, the tone is usually lower and the word spoken more sharply, almost like it's 'met': 'Listen, *met*.'

Clearly Elaine has too much time on her hands if she's trying to decode local speech, but she knows it's useful. For example, when she met James's colleagues she noticed that they didn't use the term 'mate'. They addressed each other by name. That's led her to a theory: that for Australians who aren't any good at remembering people's names, 'mate' serves as a useful substitute. If everyone uses it, who's to notice that you're forgetful? Although, more likely, it's deployed as a weapon of faux egalitarianism: everyone's a 'mate'. Except they're clearly not.

She's heard Australians railing against the English class system yet she only has to look at the social pages in the Sunday newspapers to see there's at least the pretence of such a system here. There are Ladies who are wives of Sirs rather than being born with any blue blood. For example, Lady Sonia McMahon, who's a regular in those newspapers and given prime position in the layout. Elaine is quite sure she's not the daughter of an earl, like the former Lady Diana Spencer, yet she's fawned over like minor royalty.

Elaine's tennis ladies had their own idea of a class system. Someone's daughter was being given a better start in life because she was going to a private school rather than a public school. Yet another's son was in a selective public high school, which was better than the other public high schools yet not as prestigious as the private school. Humans strive to sort themselves into strata wherever they find themselves – even, or perhaps especially, in a former penal colony.

The only group where she hasn't found that is in her little swimming circle. Marie, Leanne and Theresa don't seem to mind where she's from or what she did before they met. They're all equals in the water: each of them wanting to be out there, feeling the embrace of the ocean, the power of achievement, the sun on their faces as they dry off afterwards.

Elaine takes another long sip of her drink as she thinks about her new friends. Theresa: so vivacious yet Elaine can see a vulnerability behind her bright smile and determination to be happy every day. Leanne: giving the appearance of being closed off to the world yet she keeps turning up to swim with them each day, so perhaps she doesn't really know what she wants, or she's telling herself a story about it. As for Marie – Elaine knows she's a widow and there's a layer of sadness there, yet she's a sturdy type, and not just because she's so fit.

Elaine looks at the clock on the kitchen wall. It's almost five and James said he'd definitely be home for dinner tonight, so she needs to start thinking about what she's going to cook. She puts her drink down and yanks open the fridge door. She has some spinach and tomatoes. No meat. And James does like his lamb chops. *Why* didn't she check this before?

There's a butcher at the bottom of the hill who sometimes stays open past five. If she hurries, she can make it. Her keys and handbag are by the front door. She almost runs to the car, turns on the engine and pulls out of her parking spot.

Her head feels a bit light and she probably shouldn't be driving given how much she's had to drink, but if she walks to the butcher she's never going to make it in time. And she can't give her husband spinach and tomatoes for dinner, because then he'll know she's slipping up and wonder why she's not as attentive to home duties as she should be, given she has no other duties. If he doesn't already suspect why.

Not that Elaine has ever pretended to be in love with home-making. In their former life she had a housekeeper to keep things running while she took care of her business and of being a mother. She always felt that mothering needed to take up all the time her work didn't, and cooking and cleaning shouldn't distract from it. That excuse doesn't exist any more with her two grown sons still in the northern hemisphere. So she really should be better at homemaking. She should have noticed she didn't already have chops.

Suddenly she feels an impact and hears a scraping sound, but she's not sure if it's real. It seems like it's happening somewhere else, to someone else. Except her head is ricocheting on her neck, and when it stops she can see she's driven into the old Mercedes-Benz that's always parked at the end of their street, just before the T-intersection. It's the car that's stopped her, not her foot on the brake, because she didn't get around to that.

There's a *thud* now. Fainter than the first sound. Faster. Her heart. She can't get her breath. She's gulping in air but it's not going anywhere.

Her car is poking out into the street and she can see in the rear-vision mirror that another car is coming. She's sure it won't be able to get past her. This is a mess. She's caused a huge mess. And her head feels funny.

The other car manages to squeak past, and she recognises Colin from up the street, frowning at her. Wonderful – now she has an audience.

Colin stops his car and gets out. Now his car is also blocking the road and it's all her fault. She would be mortified if she weren't feeling so appalled.

As Colin approaches her side of the car she rolls down the window and summons the smile she's been trained to give since childhood: the everything-is-lovely smile common to her people; a cousin of the stiff upper lip.

'You all right?' Colin says, bending down and looking around her car's interior.

'I'm so *silly*,' Elaine says slowly, controlling her words, conscious that she may slur them otherwise. 'I wore heels to drive the car and I slipped on the brake.'

She hopes he doesn't look too deeply into the footwell to see that, in fact, her heels are sensibly low.

'You hit your head?' he asks.

'Oh no – no!' she trills. 'Nothing like that! Sorry to disturb.'

He narrows his eyes and nods slowly. 'Need a hand moving it?'

'It will be *fine*. Honestly. Please, you go. I'm holding you up.'

Mea culpa always works as a social strategy, especially when it's the truth. Besides, she has to fix this. Right now. Before James gets home. He can't see what's happened, otherwise he'll want to know why.

As Colin gets back in his car and drives off, thoughts are moving around inside her head like a murmuration of starlings. So much for alcohol dulling her senses: she is vibrating with alertness.

What can she do? Who can help her? Who is nearby?

Theresa. The name pierces the fluttering in her brain.

She pushes open the door, dragging her handbag and the keys with her. Her neck is telling her she shouldn't move so quickly but she needs to get help. Shoving the door closed, she walks as fast as she can back to the house, drops the keys twice trying to get them in the door, and flings her handbag onto the floor as she moves towards the sitting room to make the call.

'Hello?' says Theresa's voice on the other end of the phone.

'Theresa – it's – it's me,' Elaine says, simultaneously thinking that's a ridiculous thing to announce: *me* could be anyone.

'Elaine?' There's concern there.

'I – I need help.'

'Give me your address,' Theresa says and after she has it she hangs up.

She didn't ask why, or what sort of help. Elaine feels tears stinging her eyes at the idea that someone could be so generous.

Theresa arrives with an apron over a cotton dress and a smile that is lower in wattage than her usual.

'I'm drunk,' Elaine says, figuring that Theresa will smell it on her breath.

Theresa's face doesn't change. 'Okay.'

'I crashed the car.'

Now there's a small wrinkle on her forehead. 'Are you hurt?'

'I . . .' Elaine exhales through her mouth. 'I don't think so. Maybe a bit of whiplash.' She swallows. 'The car – it's up the street. And James will be home soon and I don't have his chops.' Her face crumples.

'Don't worry about the chops,' Theresa says as she puts her arm around Elaine's shoulders.

'I have to!' Elaine says, sniffing back the sob that's in her throat. 'If I don't have his dinner right he'll know I've been doing nothing except drinking!'

Theresa squeezes her closer. 'I'll call Marie. She'll have chops.'

'No! Please. I don't want her to know.'

Elaine can't bear the idea of Marie judging her for being drunk in daylight. She saw the look on her face the other day at the beach when Elaine only hinted at drinking too much from time to time.

'Elaine,' Theresa says in a tone of voice that Elaine presumes she uses on her children, 'there are a few things that need to happen and we're going to need more help. I'm going to call Leanne to come over and check that you're not hurt. And Marie can help with the car. And the chops.' She smiles that sweet, reassuring smile that always makes Elaine think everything will be fine.

'Okay,' she says.

'Good. Now – where's the phone?'

Elaine lifts her chin in the direction of the sideboard. While Theresa makes calls she slumps onto the couch.

'What am I going to tell James?' she moans when Theresa hangs up.

Theresa comes over and sits next to her, taking her hand. 'How about the truth?'

Elaine starts to shake her head but the pain in her neck stops her. 'I can't. He already thinks I drink too much and now . . . well, there's proof, isn't there?'

She closes her eyes, trying to picture what it would be like to have that conversation with James, and the thought is more alarming than the memory of the crash.

'Then . . . maybe you need to think about what you can do?' Theresa says. 'You're my friend and I don't like to see you in this much distress.'

'You're so kind,' Elaine whispers. 'If I were you I'd judge me fairly harshly.'

'It's not my place to judge,' Theresa says. 'But it is my place to help. What can I do?'

'You've helped already.' Elaine rests her head against Theresa's briefly.

'What about AA? It's meant to be really good.'

'I'm not an alcoholic,' Elaine says sharply, and regrets it instantly because Theresa looks hurt. 'I mean – I drink too much but I haven't been doing it for long enough to be an *alcoholic*.'

It's the label she's been resisting all this time because she can't bear the idea of it being applied to her. Alcoholics are old men in falling-down trousers with straggly beards as thick as forests. They're sad women who sit alone after a lifetime of no husband and no children. They're people who *can't cope*. That isn't her. It simply cannot be her.

'It could still be good,' Theresa says. 'You might get some tips that could help you. Or you might realise you're not as bad as you think.'

Elaine looks sceptical. 'Maybe. But I don't know that I'm good in groups.'

'You're good in our group,' Theresa says gently, 'and I guess it can't hurt to try.'

Elaine emits a sharp laugh. 'I wouldn't know where to begin.'

'I'll find out! I think I saw a sign when I walked past that church on the plaza.' Theresa puts her arm around Elaine again. 'You're not alone,' she says.

As Elaine looks into Theresa's eyes, she knows it's the truth. What she doesn't know is how to stop feeling so alone that she wants to drink the day away. Or maybe the wanting is the key. And if it is, perhaps she is an alcoholic after all.

'Thank you,' she says. 'If you could find out some information I would appreciate it.'

Theresa nods once then stands up. 'Come on. Let's go and look at this car.'

As much as Elaine wants to crawl into a hole and let the others deal with the problem she's created, she knows she has to face it. And keep facing it. Each and every day until she feels as though she has a handle on this problem that's overtaking her life.

If only it were that simple.

CHAPTER 27

The pleasant morning temperatures can't last much longer now they're halfway through March and almost at the equinox. Australia marks its seasons by months but autumn doesn't really start until the equinox. So there's no chill in the air yet, but there will be in another fortnight or so, most likely, and then they'll start to sniff Easter, and then it will be winter. Leanne imagines they won't keep swimming as a group once the weather turns, although Marie has made it clear that she swims all year round. What Leanne can't work out is if Marie disapproves of people who don't – and she finds herself caring if Marie disapproves of her or not.

Leanne's the first one here this morning, so she closes her eyes and feels the breeze on her skin. After she moved to Shelly Bay she learnt that living by the water means living with the elements – earth, water, air, ether. No fire, not yet. She hopes never. There are bushfires on the outskirts of the city each summer but none has erupted in this little peninsula. Instead there is wind, each afternoon, so regular she could set her watch by it. In fact, she's been by the water and felt the wind come up and assessed that it's likely one o'clock. The mornings are rarely still, either, but they have a breeze instead of wind.

She opens her eyes to take in the earth element: the plentiful trees that line the beachfront and the path around to Little Beach. They're not all native to this place, or to this country, but they're thriving.

And the water is there, beckoning her. Since that first day in the ocean she has craved it. If only she'd known there was so much joy to be had by diving under a wave, by swimming out so far from the shore that you feel like the world has unlimited bounty, she would have done it sooner. She's tempted to blame her parents for not introducing her to the ocean, but she doesn't think they knew either: they didn't grow up near the beach.

Perhaps she's fibbing to herself, though, because it was at the pool that she first came to trust herself in the water – to believe that she could move in it, keep herself safe in it. That was thanks to Matt and his encouragement, as well as the way he taught her. He never let her feel that she wasn't learning at just the right pace. He would smile at her with such reassurance.

She flushes as she thinks of that smile, and the one he gave her the other day at the pool when she saw him again. He smiled at her like she made his day, but she doesn't know if she deserved it, because she hasn't arranged to see him since, although he's been calling. Despite her determination that day to be open to what he was offering her, once she was out of his sight she lost her nerve. And it's only because of him, really, that she's standing here, taking in this view she loves so much, craving that salt water on her skin.

She knows she is made of mostly water; all humans are. But that was just an idea – a fact – until she found out what it really means to her. The ocean calls her, and she wants to respond.

It's a point of commonality with Marie that binds them, even if they don't know each other well enough yet to talk about it.

She can see it in Marie's eyes each morning – the recognition of home – and she hopes that Marie sees it in hers too.

'Magic, isn't it?'

That's Marie's voice, and for a second Leanne wonders if she's daydreaming. But Marie herself steps next to her, real as the day.

'Yes,' Leanne murmurs. 'It's . . .'

She tries, every day, to think of the best words to describe what these mornings are like. She can't. Perhaps those words haven't been invented. Perhaps no one in charge of words has stood on a beach at dawn in early autumn and tried to conjure just the right combination of vowels and consonants to describe what it feels like. There are words for the sights: sunlight, water, waves, foam, sand, ocean. And for the sounds: seagulls calling, waves crashing, the hissing of water on sand, the susurration of other humans nearby. But she has searched her mind and her memory for a word to describe this feeling and found nothing appropriate.

Maybe she's being unfair. The word she's searching for could be particular to her experience of being here on this exact beach each day, with women she is learning to appreciate more and more for their friendship offered so unquestioningly and the gifts they've given her of company and comradeship. Also for their personalities, their histories, and how all of them understand that this time in the water together is a capsule of belonging that is just for them. They part each day knowing that they can take the morning with them, and tomorrow they'll be here again to repeat the actions but have a different experience. Each day is precious, new. Each morning is alive with vigour and a certain rapture.

For the first time since she was eighteen Leanne feels like she belongs in her body again. It is not a territory invaded by an enemy; it is not a hollowed-out ground for something she could not bear to nurture. She loves her job yet she knows she's been play-acting: there's a version of herself that's great with the kids, and another that deals with the adults, and neither has been really her. The real her – the essence of her – has been trapped in a reservoir. She doesn't know if she did this to herself, or circumstance forced it, yet now she feels it bubbling up towards the surface. Her hard-baked surface that she's taken so much care to guard against cracking. She should feel scared of it splitting and exposing her after all this time hidden away. But she doesn't. She feels brave. What was trapped in that reservoir were all the things she was as a child: the fearless girl who climbed trees and hit cricket balls and rode bikes and ran with her brothers for hours, tired and exhilarated. She was in her body then, and she didn't even question it. Now, as she returns to herself, she's not questioning it either. This is where she belongs: in this shell called Leanne. That's what these days have taught her; this is what the ocean has given her.

'Hello! What a beautiful morning.' Theresa is pushing herself through the soft sand, her sarong flapping open.

'I'm here too,' says Elaine as she arrives from the other direction. 'I know I'm a bit late.'

'We're not sticking strictly to the clock,' Marie says, smiling.

'I know. But still . . .' Elaine sighs as she drops her towel on the sand.

'Are you all right?' Marie asks.

'I'm fine.'

Marie looks dubious and Leanne knows why: they didn't see Elaine yesterday, or the day before. They haven't seen her since Theresa asked them to help her out of that mess with the car. Leanne's job has inured her to surprises – she's shocked sometimes, but rarely surprised, simply because she sees so many different things in that hospital. But she was surprised that day.

She'd always thought of Elaine as being somewhat untouchable: tall and glamorous, with lovely elocution. The woman she saw that day seemed small and lost and rumpled. Vulnerable.

'Honestly,' Elaine says, although she looks tired.

'What did James say?' Marie asks, and Leanne is glad someone did, because she imagines they're all wondering.

'He was cross,' Elaine says. 'But he sorted it out with the owner of the other car, and he's taken mine in for repair.'

'What did you tell him?' Theresa joins in.

Elaine's eyelids flutter. 'Not the whole truth.'

Theresa looks disappointed but Marie seems unsurprised.

'He'll have guessed,' she says. 'He's just not saying anything.'

Elaine's smile is tight-lipped. 'Perhaps. Shall we swim?'

Marie half rolls her eyes. 'Sure.'

She and Elaine look as though they're having a race to be first in the water, but Leanne hangs back and is glad that Theresa does too. She wants to talk to her.

'Theresa?' she says tentatively, and is rewarded with an expression on Theresa's face that looks like shock. Which Leanne supposes is reasonable: she's never initiated a conversation with any of the three women.

'Yes?'

Leanne gestures to the water. 'Let's, uh . . . I'll talk while we walk.'

Now Theresa looks as if Leanne has given her a present.

'I – I need some advice,' Leanne says as they walk slowly.

Marie and Elaine are already a few metres offshore with arms and legs working hard.

'Oh? Yes?'

'I got asked out to dinner.' Leanne has wondered how to start talking about this subject and this seemed the least inflammatory way.

'You mean, on a date?' Theresa says, her voice going up an octave.

'Maybe.' Leanne stops. Perhaps she doesn't want to talk about this after all. Theresa is an understanding person, but private things should stay private. Shouldn't they?

'Who is it?'

Leanne starts walking again. 'His name's, uh, Matt. He works at the pool.'

'I know him!' Theresa says, and Leanne feels instantly the cold sweat of embarrassment. She didn't think she'd be asking advice about someone Theresa knows – and there's no way to back out of this conversation now that Theresa has a stake in it.

'He taught the kids to swim,' Theresa goes on. 'He's *lovely*. Handsome! How do you know him?'

'I . . . took some lessons from him.'

'He did a good job with you too, then – you're swimming so well.' Her smile is encouraging.

'Thank you,' Leanne says.

Now they're in the water and she has no idea if it's cold or not because she's focused on controlling this conversation.

'So when's the dinner?' Theresa asks as they breaststroke through the small waves.

'That's just it – I've been putting it off.' Matt has called her three times to ask when she is free for dinner and she kept saying she'd check her diary; by the third call he sounded confused. No doubt he would be, as she hasn't returned to the pool either.

'Why?'

'I don't think I should go on a date with anyone.'

'Why not?'

'I don't . . . I don't have a lot of luck in that department.' Leanne dives under a wave so she has no idea if Theresa says anything right away.

As soon as she pops up she hears, 'How would you know if you never go on a date?'

'Well, I did,' Leanne says quickly, because this is the point she wanted to reach yet she's also scared about saying anything out loud. 'Once. When I was eighteen. He, uh . . . wasn't nice.' She can hear her voice faltering.

'Stop!'

Leanne obeys.

'Take those goggles off and look at me,' Theresa orders, and lifts her own.

Leanne hesitates to remove hers because she's mortified to realise that she's crying. She never cries. Crying is for people who are emotional and that's something she's trained herself not to be. If she got emotional about her patients, for example, she'd never make it through the day.

'Lee-*anne*.'

She dunks her head under the water, hoping it will stop her crying, but it doesn't and she can't stay under here forever.

'Whatever you're avoiding telling me is obviously bad,' Theresa says, but she doesn't sound bossy any more, just concerned.

'Sorry,' Leanne says. 'I didn't mean to get upset.'

'No one ever *means* to get upset,' Theresa says. 'But I'm not fit enough to tread water for a long time, so you need to talk.'

Leanne gulps a breath. Of course this was going to be hard to talk about when she's been avoiding it for such a long time. She should have realised that.

'I went on a date once,' she says. 'He was – he was a friend of my oldest brother's.'

'Mm-hm,' Theresa says, her face uncharacteristically devoid of expression.

'I never had a boyfriend in high school,' she continues. 'I was . . . too busy. Playing sport. You know. I wasn't really interested.'

Theresa says nothing, but what is there to say, really?

'So this was my first date. And he . . .'

She stops, her mouth open, feeling her breath catching in her chest. She's trying to gulp in air but it's getting stuck. Now she's sinking, and her arms start to flail.

Then she feels Theresa pulling her over onto her back and placing her hand underneath her, making her spine arch. Leanne remembers this: it's what Matt did when he taught her how to float.

'Breathe,' Theresa whispers in her ear.

She feels more hands beneath her and hears Marie and Elaine muttering to Theresa. Or maybe they're not muttering – maybe her hearing is distorted, because it sounds as if she's inside a speaker and looking out through a fishbowl. She's panting and still Theresa is whispering, 'Breathe. Slowly. That's it.'

'She's panicking,' she hears Marie say. 'What happened?'

'She was telling me a story. She just . . .'

'Let's take her back to shore.'

That's Elaine, Leanne thinks, and feels the thud of a decision within her.

'No,' she says, moving herself so she's upright once more. She sees three faces that look as worried as those of most parents she deals with. 'I need to keep swimming,' she sputters.

The others are silent, and she knows their legs are moving like egg beaters underwater. She's delaying them. She's delaying herself.

'Please,' she says.

'All right.' Marie turns and kicks herself into a breaststroke for a few metres, then a freestyle. Elaine follows. Only Theresa is left.

'I think I know what you were going to say,' she says, floating on her belly now, her goggles still on the top of her head. 'And that's awful. Terrible. *Terrible.*' She shakes her head. 'No one should have to go through that.'

Leanne hiccups with the surprise of acknowledgement after all this time. And no judgement – but what did she expect? Theresa was the one she wanted to tell because Theresa is the one she knew wouldn't judge. All this time watching her at work has taught Leanne that.

'So I think you're brave if you go out to dinner with Matt,' Theresa goes on. 'But I also *know* you're brave, Leanne. You could barely swim when you started with us! And now . . .' She gestures to the horizon in front of them. 'Look where you are. No one else did this for you. You did it for yourself.' She laughs. 'I did it for myself too. We're all brave! Except Marie. Swimming is her habit.' She wrinkles her nose. 'But I think she's brave too, sometimes.'

Theresa rolls onto her back and makes a shape like she's sitting on a lumpy banana lounge, her knees out of the water while her arms drape just under it.

'You don't have to go,' she says. 'But I will tell you this: Matt is a good person. He's not going to hurt you, I'm sure of it. And if you're really worried, I can be your chaperone.' She winks.

She and Leanne look at each other for a few seconds. Out of the corner of her eye Leanne can see Marie and Elaine receding and she wants to start after them. She wants the water to carry her along and wash the past away.

'Thank you,' she says.

'No worries.'

Theresa yanks her goggles down and rolls over once more before she puts her head down and starts to kick. A second later her arms pull through the water and she's off.

Two seconds later Leanne joins her.

CHAPTER 28

It's weird, sitting here in the dark. Theresa has only just realised that in her thirty-eight years on earth – thirty-nine in a few days, on May the fifth – she's never sat in the dark. Although it's not completely dark: the television is on. She thinks it's showing a re-run of *Quincy, ME*, but she's not really paying attention. The sound is off. That's another weird thing. She's never sat in front of the telly with the sound off. Because there's no point in that. Is there?

She licks her lips. Can't remember when she last drank some water. Or had a cup of tea. Or coffee. Maybe this morning? It must have been this morning, after she dropped the kids at school and Brian from across the road came over, looking nervous as he found her in the back garden hanging out the washing.

'Theresa,' he said, and smiled in that way people have when they don't really want to smile.

'Brian!' She put the washing basket down. He'd never come past her front fence before. Usually they chat about his roses and his porcelain collection, and he asks about the children. Once he gave her a recipe for his favourite lemon syrup cake and asked her not to share it with Muriel down the road. He said Muriel had been after it for years but he only gave it to special people. Theresa felt like she'd been inducted into a club she hadn't known existed. Even then, though, he hadn't left the footpath.

'How are you?' he said nervously as she tucked the pegs into her apron.

'I'm well,' she said, because that's what she always says when someone asks her that. It's the polite thing to do.

'Good.' There was that strangled smile again. 'Look, I, ah . . .'

'Are you okay, Brian? You've gone pale.'

'Oh – well – ha! Ha! I am okay, thank you. But, I, uh—'

'Theresa, who is it?' Nonna said, appearing from her granny flat.

'It's Brian,' she called over her shoulder. 'From across the road.'

'Ah.' Nonna waved. 'Thank you for the tip, Brian. You were right about that horse.'

She waved again then retreated into her flat, leaving a mystery behind. Since when had Nonna and Brian ever spoken? Truly, her grandmother could be running a small country from that flat and she'd never know.

'So, Brian, can I . . . help with something? Is my grand-mother being a pest?'

'Oh – no.' He shook his head. 'Nothing like that. I just . . .' He sighed. 'I was in the hotel last night.'

'The Ox?' That was the pub all the locals went to.

'Yes.' He looked at her as if she was meant to guess something, but her mind was still trying to grasp why he was telling her about his evening.

'Okay,' she said, hoping he'd take it as a prompt.

'I saw your husband.' His eyebrows formed an upside-down V.

'Yes, he likes it there. I can never go . . .' She gestured towards the house. 'The kids.'

'Yes. Well . . .' The eyebrows were now in a pincer movement. 'He was with a woman.'

And now the eyebrows were almost at his hairline. That's what Theresa noticed, or made herself notice, so she could ignore the fact that her heart felt like it was wedged between her collarbones and beating at a mile a minute.

'Was she . . .' She swallowed. 'Blonde?'

His face fell. 'Yes.'

That was all she needed to know. She can't remember what she said after that, or what Brian said to her, but she remembers feeling alternately grateful that he told her and humiliated that he saw her husband being so obviously not with her.

She ignored Nonna's questions as she went back inside; it was only later that she remembered the washing and saw that it was all pegged up. Nonna must have done it.

Nonna would be the perfect person to consult about all of this: she's lived through two world wars and narrowly missed Mussolini's rule, so she knows things. She's seen things. Probably all of the things. But Theresa also knows what Nonna will say: *Get rid of him.* Nonna can be ruthless, and she's never been that fond of Andrew. She thinks he's lazy and selfish, and Theresa can't say she's wrong. She's not ready to be so ruthless, though. Not yet. She has to consider her children. She has to consider herself and how she – they – can afford to live if he's not around.

Except perhaps he's a step ahead of her. He might be planning to come home and tell her that he's leaving. Or that she has to.

Andrew is out. As usual. Drinking with the boys, he said, but he must realise that Theresa knows that's a lie. Or maybe he thinks she's gullible. Or stupid. Actually, yes, he must think that, to carry on with his girlfriend in front of other people in a place where her neighbour could see them. Did see them. Who knows how many other places they carry on in.

Maybe he'll try to force her out of the house to move his blonde in. Theresa's pretty sure he won't want the kids – they're too much work for him, and she knows his mother won't help him look after them – so she's going to put her foot down to stay if it comes to that.

Thinking all that through has been easier with the lights off and Jack Klugman on.

Theresa jumps as she hears Andrew's key in the door. There was no sound of a car. Not that he'd be driving, because he's probably drunk, but she would have thought he'd take a taxi home.

'Hello?' she says as the door opens, so he knows she's there. She may be plotting the next phase of her life without him but that doesn't mean she wants to scare him when he walks inside.

'Oh – hi.' He steps inside and flicks on the light. 'Why are the lights off?'

Theresa shrugs. 'I felt like it.'

He drops his keys on the coffee table.

'How's the blonde?' she says, as breezily as possible.

'Wh-what?' He staggers a little as he steps towards her.

'Chook's sister,' she says, flatly this time. 'Your girlfriend.'

'What the fuck are you talking about?'

Despite his language, he sounds more wounded than angry. As if she's accused him of something unfairly. Theresa sighs. He's clearly going to make this hard.

'The woman you were with in the pub last night.'

Now he looks indignant. 'I don't know who you're talking about.'

Theresa sighs again. He's definitely going to make this hard. Draw it out. Why would a man cheat on his wife and then try to deny it when she raises the subject, thereby making the whole thing more difficult than it already is? Does he want to cheat and keep cheating and just never get caught? She supposes so. That means the denial is selfish, in the service of wanting to continue cheating. In other words, just what she'd expect of him. And she's sick of it.

'Andrew,' she says, walking over to the television to switch it off because she's getting distracted, 'a friend saw you with a blonde woman at the pub last night. And I saw you with a blonde woman at the New Year's Eve party. Remember? I asked you about her.'

His right eyelid twitches and he looks away. When he looks back she sees defiance in his eyes. Ollie gets that look too, except he's usually defending his right to have Froot Loops for breakfast.

'Yeah,' Andrew says slowly. 'Okay.'

'Okay?' Theresa's laugh is hollow. 'You told me it was a one-off at that party. Now it's clear that you've had a girlfriend for however long and it's meant to be *okay*?'

'So what? You still haven't gone anywhere near me. What am I supposed to do?' His words are nonchalant but the sound of his voice suggests that he's scared. It makes her feel like she has some power here, but that's a trick, because she has none. She probably never had it. That other woman has the power in her marriage now. Part of her wants to give in to it. Or give up. But there's still the part of her that sees their marriage as a long-term project – that's what they promised each other on their wedding day, that they'd be together through good times and bad. These years of the children being young, of her being too tired to be a full-service wife, won't last forever, then they could have more time together. Maybe she should have told him that. Yet, once more, she feels the utter exhaustion of the responsibility of making their marriage work being entirely on her. And she realises that it will always be. She can't make him do his share.

'I'm sorry I can't take care of everything you need,' she says at last, 'but you could have given me more time.'

'I did,' he says, his chin jerking a little. 'You didn't bloody change. And Susie was still keen, so . . .' He shrugs one shoulder. 'She takes care of me.'

So she has a name, Chook's sister.

Theresa thinks of all the things she'd really like to say to Andrew now – about how obviously Susie can take care of him because she's barely out of puberty and therefore doesn't have children; about how that would change if she and Andrew did have children and then he'd find himself in the same cycle – but she knows it would be fruitless. He doesn't care about her any more. She doesn't know when he stopped, and she doesn't want to try to figure it out. Her earlier indecision has fallen away and her world has come into focus. The children are what's most important to her, just as she told him, and she needs to concentrate on them right now.

'Then you should be with Susie,' she says softly.

She can see from the look on Andrew's face that he wasn't expecting this response.

'I imagine you won't mind if the kids and I stay here,' she goes on. 'At least while we work out what to do next.'

Andrew's mouth opens. Then he shakes his head. 'I didn't say good night to them.'

'I'll tell them you've had to go and see a friend.' She smiles sadly. 'That's kind of the truth, isn't it?'

'I didn't, um . . .' Andrew squints and scratches his head. 'I just wanted a bit of attention, you know?'

So do I, Theresa feels like saying to him. Screaming at him. But he'd no doubt say she has attention, from the kids.

'I understand,' she says instead. She nods towards their bedroom. 'Why don't you pack enough to last a few days and we'll work out when you can pick up the rest?'

He nods, and now he can't meet her eyes. She doubts he's ashamed. Maybe he's just feeling stupid for getting caught before he was ready.

He used to be handsome, her husband. Now he looks like a washed-up fool trying to relive his glory days by clinging on to someone who's too young to remember them.

She turns the TV on again, and the volume up. A different show is on. It could be a movie. Maybe with Jane Fonda in it.

Theresa leaves the lights on, and doesn't hear Andrew when he leaves.

CHAPTER 29

'Can I give you a lift home?' Theresa says.

Her face looks pinched as she stands before Marie in her tracksuit, her arms folded tightly across her chest. Marie is still getting used to seeing the others in clothing rather than swimming costumes.

The colder weather has led to a group decision to walk up and down the beach for the same amount of time they'd swim, although Marie was happy to keep going once it turned cool. As soon as the water temperature hit seventeen degrees, though, she had trouble convincing the others. So this is the first May for many decades that she hasn't spent in the water. She can't say she's missing it. In fact, the walking has reintroduced her to her calf muscles and she is surprised they complain so much.

It's possible Theresa's body is complaining too. She's been looking tired the past few days – or perhaps not tired so much as worn out. Marie is trying not to worry about her because it feels almost like an intrusion, but Theresa has become a good friend in a short period of time and it's hard not to wonder what's causing such a marked change.

Marie thinks about the offer of a lift. She always walks home from the beach. Theresa knows this and has never before offered to drive her. Usually she's sprinting off to get the kids ready for school, although today is Saturday so Marie supposes she can afford to take more time. Still, the only conclusion she can reach is that Theresa wants to talk to her about something – and she's not going to deny her.

'Sure,' she says.

'Oh.' Theresa looks relieved. 'Good.'

They say their goodbyes to Elaine and Leanne, then get into Theresa's car. The drive up the hill won't take long, so if Theresa has something to say she's unlikely to get it out in those two minutes.

'Maybe you could even come in for a cuppa,' Marie says as they head away from the beach.

She glances at Theresa, whose face looks like it's about to dissolve.

'That would be . . .' Theresa swallows. 'That would be lovely.'

Marie nods. She doesn't want to press Theresa to say anything now. Time and care and attention are no doubt required, and if she doesn't afford her that, Theresa may keep her mouth shut, to her own detriment.

Once out of the car, they walk through Marie's front gate and the small garden with its camellias in bloom and azaleas starting to show buds.

'Oh! This is your house?' Theresa stops before they step onto the verandah. 'I've always loved it. Not that I . . . I mean, I haven't been staring at it. I've just noticed it whenever I've been up this way.'

'Theresa, it's fine,' says Marie, turning the key in the lock. 'This house stands out. Sandstone, on a corner, across the road from the milk bar – people notice it. Every time I go over there for the paper someone asks me about the history.' She arches an eyebrow. 'I usually tell them it was the first gaol in Shelly Bay – and they believe me.'

The hallway is cool and dark; Marie gestures for Theresa to walk down it and through to the living room.

'I think we'll sit in here,' she says. 'Not as hot as the back garden. Even in autumn it can be like a cauldron back there.'

Theresa nods and sits on the couch. That pinched look is back on her face.

Marie sits next to her and pats her hand. 'I don't think we really need that cuppa, do we? You want to talk.'

Theresa's breath catches and her eyes blink rapidly, the irises shining. She looks like a naughty child at the headmistress's office.

'Yes,' she says, nodding quickly.

Marie takes her hand properly. 'Whatever's the matter?'

Theresa squeezes her fingers. 'Andrew's having an affair.' She blinks again. 'I think . . . I think our marriage is over.'

'All right,' Marie says carefully.

She's been in situations before where women have said things about their husbands – things that make the husbands sound like very unsympathetic characters indeed – and Marie has learnt not to express an opinion, let alone a judgement, because those women rarely leave those husbands, and Marie will end up seeing the men at a social function, knowing what they've done and having to watch her friends acting as if the husband is the best thing since Cary Grant.

'I've been wanting to tell you. Since I saw him with – with her.' Theresa's breath catches again and Marie pats her hand. 'I've been trying to work out what to do. What to say . . .' She shakes her head. 'I feel like such an idiot.'

'Why on earth would you feel like that?'

Theresa looks up, surprise on her face. 'Because I should have known. Because I should have been brave enough to say something to him the first time. Because it took my neighbour – *my neighbour* – seeing them together *at the pub*. Because I . . .' She stops, something that looks like embarrassment taking her over.

'Caused it? Is that what you think?' Marie hopes that her expression strikes the balance of showing Theresa that she thinks she's being ridiculous and wanting to be supportive.

Theresa looks to the ceiling and blinks several times, but the tears roll down her cheeks anyway. 'I haven't had time for him,' she says, shaking her head again.

'Bullshit.'

Theresa makes the small noise of someone unused to hearing a woman swear.

'You've been raising those kids and running that house,' Marie goes on. 'All he has to do is fix cars and drink beer with his mates. *You* don't have time for *him*?' She huffs. '*He* doesn't make time for *you*. And if he chooses to run off with someone else because he's feeling neglected at home, that's not on you. Has he ever tried to make you feel wanted?'

Theresa shakes her head.

'Does he tell you you're beautiful? That he loves you?'

More shakes, now accompanied by sniffles.

'But I . . .' Theresa stops, and sighs. 'I don't tell him that he's handsome. So maybe someone else did.'

'Or maybe he's an idiot.'

Theresa opens and closes her mouth, and it reminds Marie so much of the goldfish Nicole used to have that she starts to laugh.

'What?' Theresa says, looking hurt.

'Oh, love.' Marie pats her cheek. 'I'm not being mean, I promise.'

They sit side by side while Theresa sniffles and Marie tries to think of what to say next. How much of her own experience to share – because everyone's life is their own, and things she knows may not apply to what Theresa is going through. Or they may, in which case she has a duty to say something. To make sure Theresa knows she's not alone.

'Marriage is hard, isn't it?' Marie says eventually. 'Living with anyone is hard, but at least with your kids you love them unconditionally.' She makes a face. 'We're *meant* to love our husbands unconditionally but I don't know who came up with that rule. It's ridiculous. You have to choose to love them, every single day of your life, and you know they have to do the same thing. For two people to keep choosing to love each other, three hundred and sixty-five days a year, for decades – well, that's a bloody miracle. And miracles aren't that regular.' She smiles ruefully. 'I should know,' she says, picking up Theresa's hand again and holding it in hers. 'Norm had an affair.'

'*What?*' Theresa clutches on to her.

Marie nods slowly. 'We were at about the same stage you and Andrew are. Nicole was young, and I was tired all the time – and that was with one child, so I don't know how you do it with two, especially with your own mother not close by.'

Theresa's eyes are round and she pushes her hair out of them. 'It's been tough at times,' she says softly.

'Too right.' Marie sighs. 'Anyway, it was messy because she was married to one of his mates. Their marriage broke up. Ours didn't.'

'Why not?'

Theresa leans towards her, and Marie can see that she genuinely wants to know the answer. She wants to find a way out of the situation, but Marie isn't sure she can give her one, because not everyone is prepared to do what she did.

'I forgave him,' she says. 'And I also told him that if he did it again he'd be out of the house, out of the marriage, and I'd tell Nicole all about it.'

Theresa looks impressed, and slightly scandalised. '*Really?*' she says, almost whispering, as if Norm is still around to hear her.

'It wasn't easy,' Marie admits. 'And it wouldn't work for everyone. But he never strayed again – as far as I know.' She laughs. 'Maybe he did and he just got better at keeping it a secret. At any rate, he seemed to respect me more after that. Like he'd been waiting for me to lay down the law. Like he wanted it.' She considers something for the first time. 'Maybe he had the affair to test me. Push me.'

She and Theresa look at each other; she can tell that Theresa doesn't approve of her late husband and Marie understands: at the time, neither did she.

'If that's the case, it worked,' Marie continues. 'But I don't know what your Andrew's reasons are. And you may not want to know.' Theresa's tears have returned and Marie wipes them from one cheek. 'As I said, marriage is hard. And you need to do what's right for *you*.'

Marie is only slightly surprised when Theresa grabs her in a hug.

'I wish I knew what that is,' Theresa says into her ear. 'I wish I knew what to do next.'

Marie hugs her tighter, then lets her go. 'Keep swimming. That's how I worked things out.'

She remembers the days she spent churning up and down the beach, telling herself that she had to come up with a solution for what to do about Norm, eventually emerging with her decision.

'Of course, we're not going in the sea at the moment but sometimes I find that just looking at it does the trick. The ocean is more vast than our problems, my girl,' Marie adds. 'Trust it to help you.'

Theresa is regarding her with something that resembles hope.

'He hasn't been home for a few days,' she whispers. 'I kind of told him to get out.'

Marie wants to offer more advice, but she never reached this point with Norm. She's not sure what to tell Theresa now without it sounding like she's giving her instructions.

'Time's a funny thing,' she says at last. 'A few days – a few minutes: when you're hurting they can feel about the same. Don't think anything is over until it's over.'

Theresa blinks and nods.

'Now,' Marie says, 'it's the right time for that cuppa.'

WINTER 1983

CHAPTER 30

The piece of paper says that Alcoholics Anonymous meetings are held every Tuesday at 7 p.m. at St Vestey's Church on the plaza. It is Tuesday today, and it's six-thirty. Elaine feels a clutch at her throat. The first time at anything new is hard, she tells herself, but it's only the first time once. It sounds trite, but she has no licence to be snobbish about motivational phrases.

It seems incongruous that a bunch of drunks would meet in the house of the Lord. Or perhaps it's poetic. They're meant to offer themselves up to a higher power, after all. That's what she's heard.

Not that she's heard much. She hasn't paid attention to any details about AA before now, and if Theresa hadn't suggested it she's not entirely sure she would have found her way to a meeting – even if it has taken her several false starts to get here. Nor does she know what she would have done otherwise. Because she's a coward – that's what she's realised about herself. She's been drinking to run away from reality, and she was too ashamed to tell James the truth about why the car was dented. It wasn't even brave going to Theresa, because she knew Theresa was the one person who would be kind to her. Theresa wasn't the only person who could help her, though: James could have done that. Except she didn't tell him.

And now she has to, because he's home unexpectedly early and she isn't going to use that as an excuse to miss the meeting. On top of the excuses she has already made, that is. Just as she became an expert at lying to herself about how much of a drunk she was, she grew adept at telling Theresa she was 'definitely planning' to attend a meeting. Until yesterday, when Theresa was uncharacteristically firm and told Elaine that she had to go and she wouldn't accept another excuse. She also asked for a report tomorrow morning.

'Short day, darling?' she says after he kisses her hello – always on the lips. 'Relatively speaking, that is.' She hopes she sounds light, carefree, blasé, but is sure she doesn't.

'There was a meeting but it's been moved. What's that?' He points to the piece of paper in her hand.

'It's, ah . . .' She gives him the fake smile she's used on his colleagues in the past, to suggest, in what she hopes is a playful manner, that she's about to say something awkward. 'It's the details of an Alcoholics Anonymous meeting that's on tonight. Shortly, actually.'

She drops the fake smile and swallows her nerves. James may make the occasional comment about how much she drinks but he's never called her a drunk. And in front of him she's never claimed the label either.

He puts his keys on the sideboard. 'Oh?' He looks like he's about to laugh. 'Who's that for?'

She blinks. 'For me,' she says, trying for a real smile this time. 'I . . . thought I should go.'

He perches on the sideboard and folds his arms. 'I see,' he says softly.

Moments pass as he inhales and exhales, his gaze on the ground.

'I'm not an alcoholic,' she says in what she hopes is a convincing tone. 'But I don't want to *become* one. That would be . . . inconvenient.'

James sighs. 'I knew it was going too far,' he says, his voice still low. 'I should have said something earlier. But I . . .' He glances at her, then out the window that reveals their back garden. 'I felt bad. I made you move here. It hasn't been easy, I know. If you needed a drink here and there, well . . .' His eyes are dark as they meet hers. 'Who hasn't, from time to time? But if you're doing this . . .' He sighs again and shakes his head. 'I've let you down.'

While she loves this man, Elaine can't help feeling a tingle of anger towards him. *It's not about you*, she wants to yell. *It's about me!* Except she's lived with him long enough to know that he sees her problems through the prism of his experience. Most people are the same. It's another reason to feel grateful for the friendships she's forming with Theresa and Marie: not once has either of them tried to interpret anyone else's life by looking at their own. In Theresa, it seems to be the result of a surfeit of compassion; in Marie, of a long life and what Elaine suspects to be some hard times. Even Leanne, in her self-contained way, is supportive.

So she can't blame James for looking at her problem and taking it on as his own. Perhaps she should be grateful that he wants to bear that much responsibility, even if what she needs – what will help, she thinks – is to claim that responsibility for herself.

She remembers that old joke: *How many psychiatrists does it take to change a light bulb? One, but the light bulb has to want to change.* She wants to change. Thus far she's lacked the tools to do so, but she thinks that going to this meeting may give her what she needs.

'You haven't let me down,' she says firmly. 'And I haven't let myself down either. I've just gone off the rails.' She walks over to him and puts her hand on his shoulder. 'It's time to get myself back on.'

He puts his hand over hers and pulls her towards him with the other, narrowing his eyes. 'What's changed?' he asks.

'What do you mean?'

'You've been moping around.'

She opens her mouth to say that 'moping' is too strong a descriptor, then he kisses her nose.

'Don't disagree with me,' he says. 'I've seen it. You know it's true. I should have said something about that too.'

'I'll accept "moping",' she says. 'I think it's normal for a mother who's away from her children to mope.'

'Especially a mother who is half a world away from them.' He hugs her to his side. 'I'm sorry I've done that to you.'

She goes to say, *It's all right*, but that would be a lie that serves neither of them. Instead, she chooses to answer his question.

'You asked what's changed. I have friends now. I think.'

He pulls back and looks at her, almost with confusion. 'Who?'

'You know I've been swimming each morning. Now walking because it's cold.'

'Mmm.' He pats her bottom. 'It suits you.'

'Thank you,' she says. 'I think it suits me too. And it's so nice being with the others.'

'Theresa and . . .' He stops. Frowns.

Elaine's mentioned their names several times but she doesn't expect him to remember them. He has so much on his mind. He couldn't remember her parents' names for several months after he first met them. But he always remembers his patients' names. Once she told him it's because he relies on her to remember the details of their domestic life so he can focus on his work. He hadn't disagreed.

'Leanne and Marie,' she supplies for him now.

He smiles. 'That's right. So you all get along?'

'Yes,' she says emphatically. 'It's not like the tennis debacle—'

'It wasn't a debacle,' he cuts in. 'Those women just weren't right for you.'

She smiles, appreciating his kindness in the face of the facts. 'Perhaps. Anyway, they're lovely. We don't spend a lot of time talking each day but all those little bits add up. I've become . . .'

She was about to say that she's become close with them. To admit that she went to Theresa for support about her drinking before telling James. But no matter how much he loves her she's not sure what he'll think about that.

'Yes?' he prompts.

'They're very kind. And open. So I think we're friends now.'

The memory of a late-summer swim pops into her mind. In the midst of a rough surf, there was Marie pulling a jelly-fish out of her swimming costume and brandishing it before flinging it into the ocean, and Theresa fishing seaweed out from the back of her costume and asking if she should use it to make a bikini, while Leanne hid her smile by putting her mouth underwater. If Elaine existed just in those moments – if all of them did – life would be easy. Together they have created a bubble of light, and that is what illuminates her path now.

'I'm so glad.' James kisses her again. 'People deserve to know you. Even if I do want to keep you to myself sometimes.'

He hugs her and she feels the relief of not carrying a secret, and of knowing that for all her missteps she is loved. That can be hard to remember when she's feeling out of control of behaviour that's damaging her; she will have to keep reminding herself, she is sure, over the weeks ahead. Because even now, as James holds her and she sees on her watch that she needs to leave for the meeting right away, she is thinking about having a drink. Rationally, she doesn't need one, but her habit is pounding beneath her skin and that is what she needs to conquer.

'May I drive you to the meeting?' James says.

'That would be lovely.'

Still holding the piece of paper, she takes his hand as they walk to the front door.

CHAPTER 31

Marie is sure that Gus hasn't needed to be here two days in a row. Very sure, because she told him so. In the time he's been doing work at her place he's made every single garden bed tidy. He's pruned the bushes that need pruning. Yesterday he said he wanted to clear the gutters now, before spring arrives, so he would come again this week, but she told him they've been full of dead leaves for five years so they could wait until next week.

Not that she wanted to wait until next week to see him again. She's been enjoying having him around. They converse easily – banter even. Norm wasn't much for talking, and while that didn't stop them being close she sometimes thought it stopped them really knowing each other. He loved her, she was sure of that. Just not that intrigued by her. She never stopped wanting to know about him but eventually she stopped asking, and as much as she loved him she did sometimes wonder if she had imagined him to be a more complex man than he really was. Perhaps there were no depths there to explore. Not that Norm ever said there were.

Once she'd mentioned to Gwen that she thought Norm's lack of curiosity about her meant he didn't really care.

'That's just how some men are,' Gwen had said. '*Most* men, don't you think? Do you know any who like to chat? I don't.'

Marie could think of one: Bradley, a sweet young man she knew at church – he was the sort who never had a girlfriend and her mother would have described as 'precious'. Even Father Paul, for whom talking was part of his job, never seemed quite as at ease with it as Bradley. The last she'd heard of Bradley he'd moved to a country town to take up a teaching position. She missed his conversation.

It's conversation Marie needs to feel the connection of close friendship, and because Gus loves to talk she's aware that she may have a false idea of how friendly they've become. Except he does seem to be genuinely interested in her life. He's made it clear that he wants to know about her because he asks her questions. Sometimes she finds herself rambling on and stops, self-conscious that she's doing all the talking, as she's been doing today.

Despite Marie's protests, Gus turned up this morning saying that her gutters absolutely need to be cleared: she lives in a bushfire zone and her house will be a 'tinderbox' if she has leaf litter.

She told him that she can't recall there being a bushfire in Shelly Bay in her entire lifetime, but he insisted.

So now he's up and down a ladder, clad in long work shorts and an open-necked shirt with its sleeves rolled up, and she's doing everything she can to not watch him as he stretches and reaches. Because it feels rude to stare, for one thing, and because she shouldn't be observing him so closely. He's her gardener. She hardly knows him.

Yet she's caught him looking at her too. Right from the first day.

The second time he came, she made an effort to wear clothes that weren't shapeless from too many turns round a washing machine, and was rewarded with an admiring glance.

'You're pretty fit, aren't you?' he said, and she could have sworn he looked her over like he was a judge at the Royal Easter Show assessing a cow. She could also have sworn that she enjoyed it.

'What do you mean?' she said, because she was a little flustered and really wasn't sure what he meant.

'You're . . . fit.' He smiled, and the skin at the corners of his grey-green eyes crinkled, and she felt a little flutter in her belly. 'You look like you play sport or something. Do you?'

'Oh, well, I . . . I've spent most of my life swimming every day.' She felt ridiculous – she never stumbled over words like this. 'Most of the year, that is. In the ocean.'

'Really?' he said with an admiring tone. 'Down at Main Beach?'

'Yes.'

'I've probably seen you. I kayak there sometimes. What time of day do you go?'

'Sunrise,' she said, so breathlessly it sounded like she was issuing him an invitation.

'Yeah,' he drew out as he bent over to pick up sticks, 'I would have seen you.'

He gave her a look that suggested he already knew her and liked what he knew, although she can't recall being aware of a kayaker, and she's sure if she saw him on the beach she'd have noticed.

Or maybe not. Marie stopped looking at men *like that* a long time ago. Not when she married – it's one thing to pledge your life to someone but that doesn't mean you turn off the tap. Eyes can see and hearts can race; that's all part of being human and alive. For her, being married meant choosing not to let it go further than that; you've made a commitment to someone. So she'd noticed attractive men over the years, but noticing was as far as it ever went.

Norm didn't make the same choice on at least one occasion, but she understood it. He was human too, and as wounded as she felt at the time she didn't condemn him for not doing what she did. Her faith, her upbringing, taught her that adultery was a sin, but in her heart she couldn't write off a man she loved simply for making a different choice to her. And according to her religion, she should never have looked at another man either, even if it was impossible to switch off those human impulses. So she'd made a deal with herself: she would keep her faith but adjust it for the realities of life. Norm wasn't a priest and she wasn't a nun.

Once she reached her fifties, though, her hormones slowed their merry dance, and if she saw a handsome man she noted he was handsome and nothing more. She and Norm were still physical – she enjoyed that – but it lost its urgency. After Norm died she thought about whether or not she should seek out a new companion, but it was an intellectual exercise, not a yearning, so she left it alone. Besides, she still felt married to Norm because she didn't choose to end the marriage. Death was another state of being, not a divorce.

It's been five years, though, and she has felt him slipping further from her. She doesn't think about him multiple times a day any more. But that doesn't mean she was looking for anyone else, so it's a shock to find herself paying attention to Gus in a way that conjures memories in her body.

Marie's conscious that her desire may look obvious to him, which is part of the reason why she keeps talking and talking – to deflect from it. Just now, for example, she's telling him about how Charlie Brown came to be her dog, and Gus is smiling and nodding as she recounts how he wouldn't leave her alone for the first few weeks and she thought she'd never get out of the house.

'He seems settled now,' Gus says as he stuffs dead leaves into a garbage bag. 'He's quite a happy little fellow.'

Charlie Brown stands up from the spot in the garden bed where he's been sitting.

'Yes, mate, I'm talking about you,' Gus says with a laugh.

He's even easy with the dog. Marie wonders if there's anyone Gus *can't* talk to.

'Just let me know if he gets in your way,' she says.

Gus gives her that wondrous smile. 'I doubt he will.'

'I hope you don't have much more to do. So you can get on with your day,' she says in a rush.

'This is my day.' He puts his hands on his hips and gives her a funny look. 'It's not a hardship to be here.'

'This garden can't be . . .' She looks around. 'The prettiest you've been in.'

'That's why I'm here – to make it pretty. That's what I do.'

He takes off the gloves he was wearing to gather the leaves and places them on the edge of the verandah. As he bends over she admires the length of his back, and isn't quick enough to hide it as he straightens and catches her looking.

'Th-thank you for coming back so soon,' she says, flustered, glancing towards the roof. 'The gutters are grateful.'

He laughs. She likes the way he laughs: his head tilts back and his laughter seems to come from deep in his chest, almost like a wave rising.

'I am too,' he says. 'It gives me another opportunity to see you.'

He smiles and Marie wonders if she's heard him right.

'To see *me*?' she says, determined to make sure.

Gus laughs again. 'Well, I'm fond of your azaleas, Marie, but not half as fond of them as I am of you.'

Her mouth hangs open, and she shuts it before he thinks there's something wrong with her.

'I enjoy your company,' he says. 'It's become . . .' He pauses. 'Addictive. I think that's the word. It's been a long time since I've found someone so easy to talk to. And so easy on the eye, if you don't mind me saying so.'

They stand looking at each other, and Marie is aware that he's offered her something and she needs to decide if she's going to accept it or reject it. If she reacts in a way that isn't true to what she feels and thinks, she may never have another opportunity.

'I think the same of you,' she says, feeling bold. 'About being easy on the eye, I mean. You're a shocking conversationalist.'

His eyes widen, then there's that laugh again.

'I'll try harder,' he says. 'Maybe if we have dinner this Saturday I can get in some practice?'

He looks at her with confidence and expectation, and Marie appreciates how much this is smoothing the way for her. He is making it clear that he's interested in her and this frees her to express interest in him. They are, as others might term them, senior citizens. There's no place for false coquettishness on her part, trying to hide what she really wants because that's what nice girls do. How marvellous to have left that stage of life behind. How extraordinary to meet someone else who has arrived at this new stage.

'I'd love that,' she says.

'Wonderful. May I pick you up at seven?'

'You may,' she says, wanting to turn away so she can smile as widely as she wants to. 'For now, though, how about a cup of tea?'

'Yes, please.' Gus's smile makes her feel warm all the way to her toes. 'I'll just take these leaves to the bin.'

She nods, breathing faster to match her heart beating, and turns to walk inside. As she approaches the back door, she permits herself a little jig.

CHAPTER 32

The nerves are to be expected, Leanne supposes, because of her past, but she tries not to go too far down that memory rabbit hole as she dresses for her date with Matt. Her dinner. It doesn't have to be a date, although she's sure he doesn't want to be just her friend.

She spends half an hour trying to work out if she even has the right clothes to go out to dinner. Her life is so circumscribed that she has clothes to take her to the beach and the shops, and for the occasional walk, but nothing that could be described as remotely fancy. In the end she chooses one of her two A-line skirts, a shirt that she rolls up at the sleeves and pairs with the only necklace she owns, and flat shoes she once wore to a work function. They do have functions occasionally – usually when a ward is being opened by a local politician. Leanne always thinks it would be more appropriate for the nurses to wear their uniforms to those things, but apparently it isn't. She obviously doesn't know what is appropriate, hence her lack of suitable clothes for dinner.

Matt seems to appreciate them, though. 'You look lovely,' he says when he picks her up at exactly the time he said he would.

She doesn't think she's meant to say he looks lovely too, except he does. He's wearing a crisp shirt open at the neck, underneath a blazer, with slacks and lace-up shoes that don't quite go together but are the sort of thing a man used to living in shorts and thongs might wear to dinner. He's made an effort, that is clear; he's made the effort for her. And, she realises, she's made an effort for him.

He drives her to a small French restaurant in the next suburb, hesitantly chatting about the weather and the dramatic change of leadership of the Labor Party from Bill Hayden to Bob Hawke just before the March election, and Hawke's subsequent elevation to the prime ministership. Matt likes 'Hawkey', thinks he's a good bloke, but still says he voted for the Liberals, because the local seat has been Liberal since Moses was a boy, and why change it if you don't need to?

Leanne listens but doesn't comment, because she's never paid much attention to politics. She reads the newspapers and listens to the radio, sometimes even watches the news on television, but most nights she's reading Georgette Heyer and the occasional crime novel. These past few years she's preferred escapism to reality.

Now, with their first course in front of them, Leanne knows she has to initiate some conversation. Matt has been doing all the work, just as Theresa, Marie and Elaine do all the work at the beach.

'I'm glad you're doing lots of swimming,' he says, picking up his knife and fork. 'Most people who come for lessons just have a couple then don't do anything.'

'Really?' Leanne thinks that's a waste of everyone's time – and she should say that, because that's how you have a conversation, but she's so used to keeping her opinions to herself that it feels like this one is stuck in her vocal cords, waiting for something to propel it out.

'Yeah.' He puts a small piece of chicken in his mouth and chews with his mouth closed. For some reason that makes her feel relieved. 'They think they're going to keep swimming,' he says after he's swallowed. 'Or maybe I should say they *want* to think that. But they don't stick to it. You stuck to it, though.'

He grins and his face changes – his eyes seem full of light, and he has too many crinkles around his eyes for a man so young but it's a sign that he smiles a lot, and she likes that.

'I love it,' she says, and his grin grows bigger still. 'It's, um . . .' She searches for the right word. 'Liberating. But I think those people who have lessons with you and don't keep going are wasting your time.'

There, she's said it.

He shrugs. 'I guess so. But I'm used to it now. And I can usually pick 'em. You looked like you were taking it seriously and paying attention. Some of 'em – even some of the little kids – think they know more than me.'

'Even kids?'

'I think they get it from the parents – they're usually around. I tell them that the kids can goof off if they want, but it won't be funny if they think they know more than they do and drown because of it.' He winks. 'That usually gets them good and unhappy.'

Leanne gasps and it turns into a laugh. She didn't realise he's audacious. He has only ever been respectful to her.

'So how come you never learnt to swim as a kid?' he asks.

'My parents didn't push us to and I didn't really think about it.'

'Us? You have brothers and sisters?'

He's leaning towards her so she can tell he's genuinely interested, but she genuinely doesn't want to discuss this and shouldn't have slipped up like that, even if it's normal to talk about your family. Or so she supposes.

'I do,' she says. 'Do you?'

'One brother,' he says, his expression changing. 'But we don't get on.'

'Oh?'

She hopes he'll let her keep prompting him to keep talking, because then she won't have to. Despite her resolve to make conversation, it's hard work.

Matt sits back in his chair and glances to the side before picking up his cutlery again. 'He's a bit older than me. Bigger, you know what I mean?' His eyes are bright as they meet hers. 'When he hit his late teens he, ah . . . he got a bit *angry*. With our parents. With the world. But he took it out on me.' He bends over his plate so Leanne can't see his face properly. 'I was so careful not to do anything to set him off, y'know? Never worked. Anyway,' he says, his head still down, 'he's not like that now, but I haven't forgotten. Or forgiven.'

Now he's looking at her again and he's no longer happy-go-lucky Matt, but she thinks she likes this Matt more. This Matt is someone whose life isn't as one-dimensional as she assumed. And she shouldn't have assumed, because she's met enough people through her work to know that there's never just one dimension.

'Do you talk to him at all?' she ventures.

'Only at Christmas.' He spears a green bean and pops it in his mouth. 'I keep the peace, for my parents' sake. They want us to be happy families. But that puts all the pressure on me and none on him. So I can only do it for one day.' He sighs. 'But you don't want to hear about that. It's boring.'

'No, it's not.'

She wants to tell him that she understands about family relationships going wrong, but to do that she'd have to tell him why hers did and she doesn't want him to know the story. Not yet.

'I'm surprised you don't have a boyfriend,' he says, smiling at her again. 'You sure you don't?'

'I'm sure,' she says, and feels her cheeks colouring.

'You're so pretty,' he says.

She knows that's her currency – it's all women's currency – but she can't help feeling a little disappointed that it's the reason he's asked her out.

'That came out wrong,' he continues. 'I mean, of course you're pretty. It's hard not to notice. But I liked the fact you always paid attention in the lesson. You're serious.' He nods slowly. 'I like serious. It means you won't laugh at me if I tell you I play chess.'

He looks a little nervous and she finds it charming.

'Do you?' she says, slightly incredulous because he keeps dismantling her preconceptions.

'Yeah. My brother taught me before he turned aggro. I'm always looking for people to play with. You play?'

She shakes her head. 'Never.'

'Want to learn?' He's looking at her with eagerness mixed with a trace of those nerves.

This is a point, she thinks. A significant point. If she says yes, she'll see him again and that may lead to seeing him after that too. If she says no, that's probably the end of it. She doesn't think he's doing it to trap her, though – he seems to actually want to play chess with her – so she'll respond accordingly.

'I haven't thought about it before,' she says slowly. 'But . . . okay.'

'Really?' His grin returns.

She nods.

'I reckon you're going to love it,' he says.

As they continue with their meal they talk about hobbies and games. She tells him about being athletic as a teenager, and they compare notes on childhood broken bones earned from adventures up trees and in dry creek beds. Two hours pass and she realises he hasn't tried to get her to talk about anything she doesn't want to talk about. He's let her guide the conversation without doing it obviously. And when he drives her home and walks her to her door, after they've arranged a date to play chess, she is disarmed when he kisses her hand.

He may be the first man she's had anything to do with in years, but she's prepared to believe that Theresa was right. He is a good person.

CHAPTER 33

'So then me wife left me. Said it was her or the dogs.' The man scratches his beard. 'I've been bettin' on the dogs all me life.' He shrugs, and Elaine realises with a small shock that this man in her AA meeting chose betting on greyhounds over his marriage.

It was a surprise to her when she arrived at her first meeting and discovered she was expected to stand up in front of strangers and say her name and also say that she's an alcoholic. Because that's not a word she wants to apply to herself in front of strangers. It's the word for a long-term problem, whereas she has a short-term problem, and the better noun for that is 'drunk'.

When she hesitated to say it, that first time, the man running the meeting – Gerard, who runs every meeting, as she's realised – smiled at her condescendingly and said, 'All in good time, Elaine.' She wanted to hurl her cup of weak tea at his head, followed by her milk arrowroot biscuit. He doesn't know her, so how can he know what will happen in her good time?

She doesn't even know herself, as it's turned out. The Elaine she thought she knew would never have crashed into someone else's car because she had too much to drink. That Elaine wouldn't have foisted herself onto a friend she doesn't know well to ask for help. She's grateful that Theresa lent her a sympathetic ear but Elaine had no right to do that to her. The only explanation is that she was desperate to talk to someone, which doesn't excuse it. Talking about herself that much – it's not something that comes easily to her.

It comes even less easily in a room full of strangers, so Elaine hasn't yet stood up in front of these people. But there's no shortage of others willing to share their stories, like this fellow before them now.

'That's when I started drinkin',' he says, scratching the other side of his beard. He laughs, a deep rasp. 'I gave up the dogs not long after.' He makes a face that seems to say: *What can you do?* 'Should've kept the missus instead but . . .' Another shrug. 'She didn't want a bar of me. 'Specially once she found out about me twelve beers a day. I tried to tell her it was cheaper than the dogs.'

He laughs again and Elaine almost joins him, because somewhere inside that man's paradox she can see the humour.

'Anyway, she took the kids and moved to South-A-bloody-'stralia. Got a job workin' for Holden.' He rolls his eyes. '*South Australia.* They only just got rid of that Don Dunstan. I told her if she likes a man who wears pink shorts, I can see why we didn't get on.' Another rasping laugh, and this time he grips the sides of the lectern. 'Point is, if I don't stop drinkin' I don't get to see me kids. She'll let them come and visit if I'm off the beers. So I'm givin' it a try. That's all.'

He glances at Gerard, who nods slowly. 'Thank you, Walter. Very insightful. We're all here to support you.'

There's a smattering of applause; Elaine perfunctorily joins in. She's yet to fully embrace these meetings – partly because she feels like a fraud. Afterwards she goes home and all she thinks about is having a drink. Still. She hoped that going to the meetings would be enough to stop the impulse, but it's as powerful as ever.

Derek – the one person she's chatted to in the group – told her that's normal and she should prepare to feel that way for the rest of her life. Elaine's opinion is that she should be strong enough to *not* think about drinking every day. Derek told her she will, at some stage, come to accept that she's an alcoholic and then she'll understand.

But Elaine doesn't want AA to be a lengthy commitment. It's not as if she's been drinking for years. She was just drinking a lot for a short while. And, yes, drinking a regular moderate amount before that, but that wasn't a *problem*.

The length of time doesn't matter, Derek said, it's more to do with her behaviour around alcohol. So she can never drink again.

Elaine's been able to honestly tell him that she's stayed away from gin since she started coming to meetings, but she hasn't told him that her abstinence has been made easier because she's started some projects. She suspects that keeping busy may be a better solution to her drinking problem than coming to AA, but she hasn't seen that anywhere in the twelve steps.

'Who else would like to speak?' Gerard says, looking around the room.

Elaine ducks her head because she doesn't want him to call on her.

'Claire?' he says to a mousey-haired woman at the end of Elaine's row who shakes her head vigorously. Claire is newer than Elaine is, so she can get away with 'no', for now.

'Elaine?'

'What?'

Elaine realises her mistake: because she was thinking about Claire she didn't say 'no' straightaway like she usually does, and now she's opened a conversational opportunity for Gerard.

'Would you like to share anything with us?' He's looking at her with a combination of superciliousness and insistence.

Elaine has, on occasion, wondered if Gerard's not really an alcoholic but rather an actor paid to run these meetings. He seems to know just which expressions to use to get the outcome he wants – and today his expression suggests that he's not going to accept her 'no' any longer.

'Not particularly,' she says, almost swallowing it. She likes to kid herself that she can stand up to people, but she does have a tendency to wilt in front of authoritative individuals.

'That's an advance on your usual position.' Gerard smiles, showing his teeth – a rare sighting.

'Is it?' Elaine looks around the room, catches Derek's eye.

He's grinning at her, the bastard, because he's been waiting for this day. He spoke at his first ever meeting and thinks her reluctance is partly snobbery – she thinks she's too good for this crowd. That may be correct, but it's also because she wasn't brought up to share sob stories with strangers.

Derek nods his head towards the lectern.

'Elaine?' says Gerard.

For all her resolve to not speak, she's battling with another part of her nature: the library monitor, the school prefect, the vice-captain of the hockey team. That girl did what was expected of her. That girl didn't let people down. Perhaps Elaine's problem started as a way of rebelling against that girl, because *she* would never dream of drinking gin at two o'clock in the afternoon. *She* wouldn't have sulked about moving to Australia; she would have just got on with things.

But at this point in her life, Elaine realises, it's irrelevant whether she was trained to be that girl – as her mother and grandmother were before her – or whether that girl is who she really is. She can't tell the difference any more. What she knows is that if she accepts her nature, life may be easier. She's had her little rebellion against what's nice and normal for a girl – a woman – like her, and it hasn't worked.

The thought is enough to lift her to her feet, along with the knowledge that if she doesn't get this over with, Derek and Gerard will keep hectoring her.

She clears her throat and stands as straight as she can. Shoulders back, stomach in, sternum lifted, just as she was taught in ballet classes. She almost turns her feet into first position just to feel more at home.

'My name is Elaine,' she says.

'Hello, Elaine,' comes the chorus back.

'And I'm . . .'

She falters. For all her resolve of mere seconds ago, she doesn't want to say these words. She is not this person. She is not weak. She is not out of control. She is not a *failure*, and that's what these words would announce.

Except she is. Or she feels like it. She's let her life turn into a mess because she's failed to control it. She couldn't get on top of her misery when they moved here. Up until a year ago she'd led a charmed life, really – by anyone else's account, and often her own. And there was one hiccup. *One*. She couldn't even handle that.

Elaine knows that people have suffered far worse than she has. She was a child during World War II, and read the newspaper stories about the Blitz while she was tucked up in her grandparents' home in Devon, far from danger. Yet she's allowed herself to wallow. To *indulge*. She has been miserable because she wanted to be, not because misery was imposed on her. She drank because she wanted to. So she can stop if she wants to.

'I'm an alcoholic,' she says.

SPRING 1983

CHAPTER 34

'Come on, put your back into it!' Marie yells from behind, and Theresa is tempted to turn around and poke out her tongue.

It was Marie's idea that they try a bushwalk today instead of walking on Main Beach or around the path to Little Beach, as they've been doing over winter. It'll be easy, she said. Up and around the headland. So pretty. So wild. You'll love it.

She failed to mention that it involves several steep parts and some clambering over rocks, as well as some dodging of scrubby trees and spiky native bushes. Theresa has never been agile – she tried ballet for a year but the teacher told her mother that Theresa would be better off playing Dumbo in a school production – so she is lumbering from rock to rock and feeling cross.

Leanne and Elaine are athletic – you can tell that by looking at them. Theresa, on the other hand, is fit and trying to keep the kilos off. It's a different proposition altogether. The others don't even look bothered by what Theresa would define as climbing, not walking. Look at them! They're laughing, joking. *Talking.* Either the swimming didn't make her as fit as she hoped or she's lost a bit of stamina over winter.

Two hands attach themselves to her bum and she yelps. 'Marie! What are you *doing*?'

'Giving you a shove. You look like you're reluctant to get up those rocks.'

'That's because I *am*.' She makes a noise of exasperation but lets Marie push her along.

'Are you keeping up?' Marie asks, more seriously, and Theresa knows she's not just talking about the walk.

'I don't know,' she says honestly, looking ahead to where Leanne and Elaine have stopped at a level spot, their hands on their hips, looking across the sea.

'Isn't it glorious?' Elaine says, grinning at Theresa once she arrives.

'Yep,' Theresa says, trying to get her breath back. 'Lovely. Wonderful.'

Elaine gives her a funny look.

'The perspective sure is different up here,' Marie says. 'When you're in the water the horizon doesn't seem so far away.'

'I've never been here before,' Leanne says. 'And I live just over there.' She turns to indicate behind her, and looks sheepish. 'I should come here more often.'

'It's a great spot,' Marie says. 'I'd walk up here with Nicole after school. Thought I was giving her an appreciation of the natural world.' She shrugs. 'Now she lives in a terrace house in a cramped suburb and has one geranium to her name.'

'I'm sure she does appreciate it,' Theresa says. 'She'll come back one day, I'll bet.'

Marie sighs. 'I'd like that. I'd get to see her more often.'

Theresa's face clouds. 'I guess that means once Ollie and Sasha grow up I'll hardly see them, either.'

'You're not getting enough of them now?' Marie says pointedly.

Theresa knows what that point is: they've discussed her telling the others about what's going on in her life. Marie says they deserve to know, and she's right, they do, because they hear all the boring details about the books Sasha is reading with her teacher and the footy team Ollie likes, and how Nonna has made enemies out of every aged pensioner with a gambling streak within a two-kilometre radius because she keeps beating them at cards – yet she's been keeping the most fundamental detail of her life from them. Because telling them is going to make it real. She hasn't even told her parents. Only Nonna, Marie and the kids know, and she's kept it that way for months now.

She glances behind her and sees a natural seat formed of rocks. 'Can we sit for a couple of minutes?' she says, looking at Marie.

'Sure,' Marie replies, and the others smile mildly as they stretch out their legs and keep their eyes on the horizon.

'Not too long! We don't want to get cold!' Elaine says cheerily.

She's been gradually more cheery since she started going to AA and sometimes Theresa misses her occasional moroseness, because the cheeriness has the gleam of a cult about it. She's proud of her, though, for making the commitment and sticking with it.

The only other person Theresa has known to have a drinking problem – apart from Andrew and his mates, although they always say it's 'just blokes being blokes' – was her Uncle Mario, and the way the family handled it was to never mention it. They'd just hide the alcohol at family gatherings and hope he wouldn't realise it was to stop him drinking it all. Except once her grandfather had called him an *ubriacone*. Only the once. Theresa had pretended not to know what it meant because she was sure Nonno hadn't meant to say it out loud. Uncle Mario is the reason Theresa is glad she was able to help Elaine, as modest as the help was. If only someone had helped Uncle Mario instead of judging him, if only they'd talked about the problem, maybe he wouldn't have fallen out with his children and ended up dying slowly as his liver packed up on him. They were all afraid to say anything, but not saying anything meant he thought no one noticed. Or that no one cared.

Elaine can be in no doubt that they all care about her. And Theresa should be in no doubt that it's reciprocated.

'What I have to say won't take too long,' she says.

Leanne bites her bottom lip. 'That sounds . . . ominous.'

Theresa releases a nervous little sound that's halfway to a laugh, although a laugh would be inappropriate. Unless it's gallows humour. A requiem for the end of her marriage.

'It kind of is,' she says, her voice small.

She exhales loudly and looks at the ocean. A year ago, she never would have imagined she would voluntarily swim in that. It is terrifyingly large – yet to her it seems like home. She has made friends because of that ocean. She's had the chance to make friends with herself too. The Theresa who first yanked a cap over her springy hair would never, she thinks, have stood up for herself the way she has over the past months. That's what Marie said too.

That Theresa owes a lot of her new self to the three people who've been showing up for her and with her day after day. In the past she's never had a reason to contemplate the idea that families aren't necessarily made from blood. The relatives she has are enough of a handful. Now she knows that the family you create, voluntarily, can bring joy instead of pain, and support and love and strength. They're who she chooses to be with.

'Andrew left a few weeks ago,' she says, looking from Elaine to Leanne. 'Months, actually. He's not coming back.'

'No!' Elaine gasps, and Leanne draws back, her eyes hooded.

'I haven't told you because . . .' Here Theresa falters. How to describe shame? Or the concern that you've failed at one of the two roles society has assigned to you: wife and mother? Even when you believe your friends love you, that doesn't stop you worrying about their reactions.

'Because the dickhead got himself a girlfriend and you shouldn't have to explain that to anyone,' Marie says decisively. 'It's not your fault. And I *know*, Theresa, that even though you're in a better place now there's a little part of you that's taking the blame. It's called Catholic guilt, and listen: I'm a good Catholic but I don't think the guilt is reasonable.'

Theresa presses her lips together, trying to control the emotions she's been keeping a lid on while she's helped the children adjust to their new life.

She remembers how Nonna reacted when she told her that Andrew had gone to be with someone else.

'Stupid boy,' she muttered, taking a drag on her cigarette. 'He thinks he should be the centre of the universe.'

When Theresa had protested, still trying to defend him for no reason other than habit, Nonna had added, 'They all think that. Some are just better at hiding it than others.'

She needs to keep remembering that, because it's the answer to sloughing off the guilt: Andrew's behaviour is all about Andrew; Theresa's is mainly about others. So he's responsible for everything he's done, and she owns none of it.

'I'm sorry,' Leanne says.

'It's not your fault,' Theresa says, then looks at Marie and laughs. 'I'm stealing your lines.'

'You're welcome to them.' Marie smiles at her the way Theresa wishes her mother did. Then says to Elaine and Leanne, 'She's been a brave girl.'

'You know I'll support you,' Elaine says, reaching over to place a hand on Theresa's wrist. 'Whatever help you need with the children. I have time, after all. I'd welcome the job.'

Theresa's nose twitches – her usual sign that she wants to cry and is trying not to. 'You're very kind. But I've been doing it all on my own for years anyway.'

'It doesn't mean you have to continue,' Elaine says, smiling reassuringly. 'Honestly, let's make a time to talk about it.'

Theresa nods. 'Shall we keep walking?' she says, sniffing and wiping a finger under each eye.

'Sure,' Marie murmurs and they all stand.

Elaine leads them off, and Marie follows, so they don't see Leanne wrap her arms around Theresa and squeeze her before letting go. Theresa doesn't think she's been more surprised in her life.

'I really am sorry,' Leanne whispers. 'You're so kind to other people. This shouldn't happen.'

'No, it shouldn't,' Theresa says, and Leanne looks so young and vulnerable that she feels a big-sisterly urge to take her hand as they start to walk along the path. Although she doesn't do it, because Leanne is a grown-up and she may not appreciate being treated like a child. 'And don't let it put you off men,' she continues. 'Not that I presume it would.' She shakes her head. 'That was a strange thing to say.'

Leanne flashes a smile. 'No, it's not.'

'Anyway!' Theresa straightens, feeling her shoulders begin to release some of the burden they've been holding. 'They're not all like Andrew. And I have no idea if you're seeing Matt, because I don't want to pry and you haven't said anything, but I can't imagine him ever behaving the way my husband has. Ex-husband. Or can I not say that yet? We're not divorced.

Oh!' She throws her hands in the air. 'Who cares. Ex. Now, let's catch up to the others.'

Theresa and Leanne increase their walk to a trot. The wind from the ocean hits them and Theresa giggles at the surprise of it. Up here, out there, the world keeps doing what it's doing, and her life is just one of billions moving in and out of the planet. She knows she's going to be fine. Eventually.

And if she never has another relationship with a man again, she won't care. She has three friends who are very good company.

CHAPTER 35

Leanne has to admit it to herself: the paediatric ward has been a lot quieter without Theresa, and also not as pleasant a workplace. It's not that work has to be fun – Leanne has never expected that – but having been the beneficiary of Theresa's sunniness, the place is gloomy without it. But Leanne understands that her friend needs to reduce her responsibilities for a while: Theresa doesn't know if she can stay in the house, for one thing, and she is trying to work out where she can go with two children and a nonna. Sometimes Leanne worries that Theresa will have to leave Shelly Bay – it's not the cheapest suburb in the city and without Andrew's income Theresa may have to move further away. Which would make swimming – or walking – difficult, if not impossible, and may also mean she doesn't come back to the hospital, as she plans to eventually.

'But it's possible,' she said that morning as they finished their walk, 'that Nonna is sitting on bags of money. She seems to win a lot at poker. Perhaps I should ask her.' She winked, her voice sounding light, but Leanne doesn't think this phase of her life can be light. She thinks it's probably very hard.

It's selfish of her to wish that Theresa was still at the hospital when there's so much else she needs to do, but Leanne can't help it. Theresa used to wave if they saw each other from afar.

If they passed in the corridor she'd give Leanne a wink and a hello, or she'd make a remark about that morning's swim.

'Like a millpond, wasn't it!' she'd say if the sea was calm.

'That was better than a ride at Luna Park!' she'd reserve for days when the waves were bigger than usual.

The phrases weren't necessary, nor were they always original. But they were thoughtful. They let Leanne know that Theresa *saw* her. Acknowledged her. In return, Leanne is trying to learn how to do that for others.

Leanne is good with the children; she always makes sure they know they're important. Some, like Imogen, turn out to be more important than others. They're the ones she misses when they go home. Or never go home. If they die she tries not to think about them too often; she wouldn't be able to function if she did. It was one of the great reliefs of her life that Imogen actually did go home. She will be in and out of hospitals for years, and Leanne may never see her again, but she can allow herself to think of her, knowing that the thought causes no pain.

The adults she has to deal with, on the other hand, have for so long been – not a cause of pain, really, but a source of vexation. They want to talk to her, and ask questions about her life, which, as far as she's concerned, is none of their business. Children can be nosy but they also respect 'no'. Adults, in her experience, do not. What she didn't allow for, though, is that she's likely been seeing only what she wants to see. She hasn't given many adults a chance to be kind to her – men, for her own very good reasons, but also women.

Yet three women in particular have been very kind to her, each in their own way. Leanne doesn't know what she has done to deserve it, because she's hardly been as kind to them. She saw a chance, though, when Theresa needed help, and has been taking Oliver and Sasha to the park each Saturday morning so Theresa can have some time to herself. It's something practical she can do, to show Theresa that she cares.

Leanne's not good at words – she can't say 'I care about you'. She's confident she will never be able to say 'I love you' to anyone. That's not her. But she can show someone she cares, so that's what she's doing. Theresa understands, Leanne is sure. She doesn't make a fuss about the fact that Leanne has offered to help; she just accepts it and says thank you.

In the past Leanne thought she couldn't accept help from people because there would be a price: she'd have to offer something in return. Watching Theresa, though, and observing her own behaviour has been instructive, if not enlightening, because it occurs to her that people usually only offer to help if they want to – as she has offered help to Theresa – and there is no price other than saying 'thank you'. Not that Leanne wants to rush off and get help from people, but she could be a little less staunch in her independence. Even at work – if she's struggling to carry something, for example, and someone offers to help her carry it, she doesn't have to say no.

When Leanne leaves the hospital today, it's not quite as dark as it was yesterday. They're turning towards summer and she can't wait to get back into the water. She makes an effort to say goodbye to people, where before she would scurry off. Her colleagues showed surprise the first few times she did it, but now everyone's used to it. As is she.

Not that she's confessing details about her life to anyone yet – and she hasn't mentioned that she has a boyfriend. It's hard to say the word even to herself; it was Matt who said it first.

'So . . . we've seen each other a lot,' he said the other night as he was dropping her home.

At first she felt tense, worried he was going to try to rush her into doing something that she isn't unwilling to do – surprisingly – but that she wants to be prepared for. She's attracted to him: her whole body tells her that each time she sees him. He's made it clear he thinks she's 'gorgeous', although she's sure that's an exaggeration. She's never been gorgeous. But she appreciates that he says it without seeming to expect anything in return for saying it. She has come to trust him, not because of what he says but how he acts: respectfully, slowly. It's enabled her to start thinking about what it would be like to take things further. To kiss him somewhere other than in the front seat of his car. But when he made his statement she was still at the stage of thinking about it, not taking steps to make it happen.

'We have,' she said.

He smiled and took her hand. 'Does that mean . . .' He raised an eyebrow and she still felt tense. 'That I can call myself your boyfriend?'

Her mouth gaped and she felt the tension release. 'Oh,' was all she could manage at first. 'Yes.'

'You sure?' He looked worried.

'Yes. Yes!' She smiled reassuringly.

'I know you, um . . . haven't had a boyfriend before.' He squeezed her hand. 'So I didn't want to rush into saying it.'

No, she hasn't had a boyfriend before and she knew what he'd interpret that to mean – that she hasn't *been* with a boy before. That's one of the things she has to work out how to negotiate once they move beyond the front seat of his car.

'It's fine,' she said, squeezing him back.

He kissed her, or she kissed him. These days there is no routine to it. At the start he would always kiss her first because she was still clinging to the ideas of what a 'nice girl' should be – then she remembered that being a nice girl hadn't kept her out of harm's way, so she should do what she feels. And what she feels, often, is that she wants to kiss him first.

Remembering last night's kiss, she smiles to herself as she walks out the hospital's main entrance and starts around the semicircular driveway that allows for patient drop-offs and pick-ups. If she follows the road to the left it'll take her to Casualty; instead she leaves the path and starts to walk through the car park.

'Leanne?'

Her head cracks to the right at the sound. The ancient sound of her name spoken in her mother's voice.

Leanne's heard of people saying 'I just froze' when they're in a bank robbery or something like that, and always thought it a strange reaction. But she's doing it right now, as she sees her mother standing a few metres away, an imploring look on her face.

Her mother has barely changed in eight years, which would seem impossible were it not for something Leanne remembers her saying once: that her own mother always looked the same until she reached sixty, and then looked immediately eighty. 'Her mother too,' she'd said with a knowing nod. Leanne hadn't believed it, but now she thinks she should have.

'Leanne?' her mother says again, taking a tentative step closer. She's clutching a boxy handbag that Leanne remembers.

'M-Mum,' she says, still frozen. 'How did you find me?'

She's never had her number listed in the phone book; she's never been in the newspaper. A clean break is what she wanted and she had it.

'My friend.' Her mother gestures towards the building. 'She works with you.'

'Which friend?' Leanne mentally scans the staff for anyone who might be a candidate. But she knows so little about them – on purpose, of course. She doesn't know where any of them live. For all she knows, one of them is her parents' neighbour.

'Your matron,' her mother says, nodding once, decisively, as if she expects Leanne to argue.

'Matron?' Leanne calculates quickly. Matron is younger than her mother, she's sure of it; not that that rules her out, as Leanne knows: Elaine, Theresa and Marie are older than her.

'She's married to a friend of your father's. She said she has a lovely young nurse here – Leanne. She said Leanne looks like me.'

Her mother seems scared now, as if Leanne is about to get angry at her. She doesn't feel angry. She feels surprised. Startled. Perhaps slightly scared herself, given what happened the last time they saw each other.

They're standing, looking at each other, when a car horn toots and Leanne realises she's in the way. She moves quickly out of its path and towards her mother.

'Leanne,' her mother says again, pleadingly. 'Where have you been?'

Her mother's face crumples, and Leanne feels a pain she hasn't felt in years. The pain of disappointing the person she loves the most. No, not just disappointing her – causing her extreme distress, even as Leanne was in distress herself.

What happened to her, how it happened, the result of what happened – it was all of a piece. A horrible ball of mess from which there could be no good outcome. Leanne chose to do what she thought would reduce the pain the most: she would remove herself and take care of the pregnancy. But the shame never left her. It just trickled into her marrow, where it will stay forever.

'I've been here,' she says, almost choking on the words.

Her mother is right in front of her now, reaching out a hand, taking hers. 'What happened . . . to you?' she says, gasping.

'I gave up the baby, Mum.' Leanne tries to keep her voice steady and fails. She swallows. 'She has her own family now. You don't have to worry about it.'

She knows that's the equivalent of sticking a dagger into her mother's side: implying that the only thing she would be worried about is what became of Leanne and her supposed bad behaviour. So that could be why her mother starts crying. She's holding Leanne with both hands now, shaking her head from side to side, tears dripping off her chin.

Leanne tries not to let her heart break as she sees that, yet again, she is causing her mother distress. She thought she had tied it up neatly back then, made it so her parents could get on with their lives, and she, eventually, would get on with hers. Never did she imagine she'd have to reckon with all that pain again.

'We looked for you,' her mother says, putting a hand to Leanne's cheek. 'We looked and we couldn't find you.'

'You have now,' Leanne says.

Suddenly the noise of the car park fills her ears. They're here in public, making a scene. In front of her workplace. She feels like she's going to be sick.

'I have to go,' she says, breaking free of her mother's grip. She kisses her on the cheek and wipes the tears from her chin. 'I love you, Mum,' she says, then pulls away from her.

'Leanne!'

She hears her mother calling as she runs through the car park and down the long driveway to the street, trying to think of the safest place she can go. It's not something she wants to burden Matt with; Marie is closest and would welcome her but she may not be alone. Theresa's and Elaine's houses seem too far away when what she needs is a shelter, right now.

She runs past the falling-down weatherboard houses; past the sturdier Federation houses; past the frangipanis in front gardens and the dogs yapping at gates and the milk bottles left out for collection. She arrives on the flat ground and smells the salt in the breeze.

The noise of the waves reaches her before she can see them, a ceaseless reassurance that the world keeps turning and this ocean will be here for her for as long as she needs it.

Throwing her bag onto the sand, she rushes to the water's edge, drops to her knees, puts her hands into the white foam, and sobs.

CHAPTER 36

Marie can feel spring in the air as she steps out of the church ahead of the other congregants, but she's glad of her light cardigan as a cool breeze wafts past her neck. They'll be back in the water soon – she announced that to the others this morning. The water is warming, and while it's far from balmy she knows from experience that the temperature will be less of a shock.

She was surprised that Leanne seemed the most enthusiastic about it, considering she's been swimming at the pool over winter. The *heated* pool. Marie isn't sure she approves of that, although Theresa assures her that Leanne is only doing it because her boyfriend works there. Boyfriend! Leanne is certainly a dark horse. Marie had no idea from the very little she says that she has a beau in her life.

Perhaps she is being ungenerous about the swimming, though: Leanne is the one who has been most serious about their endeavours. She would stand on the beach looking as if she was just about to take an exam – a small frown of concentration, a setting of her mouth – before meticulously tucking her hair into her cap. Such lovely, straight, long hair: Marie dreamt about having hair like that most of her life. Instead she has hair that does nothing remarkable.

The breeze finds her again and this time she shivers.

'Are you cold?' Gus says as he touches her elbow, and she feels instantly warm.

She smiles. 'No. Just wishing it was warmer. So how was that?' she asks, standing as close to him as she can without scandalising the church regulars.

They aren't at a stage of being demonstrative in public – although she was never at that stage with Norm, because that's just not what they did – yet she finds that she always wants to be close to him.

'You mean, how does a former altar boy feel about going to mass after decades in the wilderness?' He smiles down at her and she feels his hand lightly touch her back then move away. She marvels that at her age a simple gesture can make her feel so enlivened.

'Something like that.'

Gus is here because, despite his reservations about religion, he said he knows that church is important to her.

'It was all very familiar,' he says, looking over her head to where others are slowly exiting.

Marie moves to a spot where Father Paul will see them. She wants Father Paul to meet Gus. She's mentioned Gus to him in a light, I-have-a-new-friend way, which of course he saw through.

'Do you mean you have a *boyfriend*, Marie?' he said, almost salaciously.

Marie considered being shocked, but reckoned that Father Paul probably knew more gossip than anyone, what with the confessional, so he wouldn't really be that outraged by her news.

Busybody Dulcie looks over and Marie knows she has mere seconds before Gus becomes the subject of an inquisition. Except just as Dulcie steps towards them, Father Paul intervenes and takes her hand. Marie is sure it's to help her – she's never known Father Paul to willingly spend time with Dulcie.

'I like your Father Paul,' Gus says. 'He seems sensible.'

'He is. And he's very kind. He's been . . .'

She stops, not wanting to tell Gus that the Marie he knows now was on dim wattage not that long ago. Their friendship – their relationship – is new enough that she still wants to present the best of herself to him. She's worried that if he knows the sludgier parts of her life he may not like her.

It's not entirely to do with him, either. Marie isn't that honest with Nicole. Although she confessed some of her money worries, she didn't tell her daughter that it took her so long to emerge from Norm's death.

To Nicole, it wouldn't have looked as though her parents had a great romance – and they hadn't, not in an Elizabeth Taylor and Richard Burton way. Tempestuousness isn't Marie's style, and it certainly wasn't Norm's. But in their own way it was a very good marriage: they enjoyed their life together, and she never thought there should be fireworks every day. She loved him for him, and he loved her for her.

When he died, her body and brain seemed to take forever to adjust to her new reality. She was still engaged in the same rituals of life with Norm – she'd start to make him breakfast, for example; and if she heard something interesting on the radio she'd go to tell him. Each of those little slips added up each day and she was exhausted from the adjustments she had to make as she remembered.

And once her brain did catch up to the news, about two years after he died, she felt as though she was unmoored from time and space. Nicole would ask why Marie looked so tired, and she didn't say she was waking up at one o'clock each morning, panicking, unable to go back to sleep. She didn't want Nicole to worry. It hadn't occurred to her that by not being honest with Nicole, she wasn't inviting Nicole to be honest with her. And now that she's feeling more like herself, she realises there may have been unintended consequences of that over the past few years.

'What has he been?' Gus says lightly, and for a second Marie thinks he's talking about Norm. But it's Father Paul he's looking at, and she has to remember, again, that she's in this place now, in this time, with Gus.

She isn't ready yet to tell him the whole truth about the last few years, but she can open the door to it.

'I wasn't doing so well for a while there. It was hard, without Norm.'

'I understand,' Gus says.

'I know you do.' Marie presses his hand quickly. 'Father Paul noticed, although he was subtle about it. I'll always be grateful to him for caring.'

Gus glances over her head once more. 'And he's heading this way.'

The breeze ruffles Father Paul's hair as he approaches.

'Hello, Marie,' he says, taking her hand in both of his. 'It's good to see you, as always.' He turns to Gus. 'I'm Paul,' he says as they shake hands.

'Gus.'

'Marie has told me very little about you,' Father Paul says with mischief in his eyes.

'Maybe because there's not much to say,' Gus replies laconically.

'I can't imagine Marie keeping company with anyone who isn't interesting.' Father Paul tilts his head slightly as he looks at her. 'She's certainly one of the most interesting people I know.'

'That can't be true, Father!' Marie is genuinely surprised. Her quiet suburban seaside life is hardly anyone's definition of interesting.

'Marie, you forget how much I know about you.' Father Paul's eyes twinkle, causing Marie to wonder exactly what Dulcie and some of the other church gossips have been saying. Not that she thinks Father Paul would share anything untoward with Gus.

'Did Marie tell you that she speaks two other languages?' Father Paul went on.

Gus gives her an admiring look. 'No, she didn't.'

'You can't *speak* Latin, Father,' Marie says quickly, not wanting anyone to make a fuss.

'*I* can,' he replies, winking. 'And I wasn't thinking of Latin. Don't you occasionally read novels in French and German for fun?'

'Not for a while,' Marie mutters.

Gus's expression is quizzical. 'You told me those books belonged to Nicole.'

Marie purses her lips. She didn't intend to be the subject of conversation today. This is meant to be the Gus-and-Paul show. Just because she decided to learn some foreign languages while Nicole took them at school, and just because she decided to keep up her studies long after Nicole stopped, doesn't mean everyone needs to know. Men don't like smart women – her mother used to say that.

'Father, I don't think Gus needs to know all of this.'

'I think I do,' Gus says, grinning conspiratorially at the priest.

'There's more to know, Gus,' Father Paul says as he puts a hand on Marie's arm, 'but I think Marie will show you in good time.'

'I look forward to finding out.'

As Gus smiles at her, Marie feels herself relax. She doesn't know why she's so comfortable with him. No, that's not the right word, because he makes her heart beat faster and that's not comfort. Comfort is more anodyne. There is an *ease* between them and the edge of attraction with it. Desire, she would call it if she were allowed, but she's not sure women her age are.

Perhaps the word she is looking for is *trust*. She trusts him – improbably, because they haven't known each other long enough. It's the way he looks at her, though, with such care and regard. She hopes she expresses the same to him, but she can't see her own eyes.

'I should move on,' Father Paul says. 'Marie, I'll see you next Sunday. Gus – until we meet again.'

'Goodbye, Father.' Marie nods once – her own gesture of respect.

Gus offers her the crook of his elbow. 'Shall we stroll? The temperature should be just right by the water.'

'All right, Goldilocks,' she says, taking his arm.

As they walk in the direction of the promenade by the beach, chatting easily, she feels light and carefree, the future full of delicious mystery.

CHAPTER 37

When Marie suggested it was time to return to the water, Elaine was surprised at how excited she was. The temperature will hardly be warm: eighteen degrees, if they're lucky. But she doesn't care. Walking is pleasant, and she's seen more of Shelly Bay than she did during a whole year of living here, but it's plodding and graceless compared with swimming. She's enjoyed keeping fit, and being with the others, but she'll enjoy it more in the water.

She hasn't had a drink for several weeks now and while she resents – at times bitterly – the abstinence, she's sleeping better and feeling far less sad and sorry for herself. It seems that her initial attempts to ameliorate her homesickness by drinking it away had at some point started to exacerbate it. If only she'd been able to identify that point, she wouldn't have ended up having to call herself an alcoholic, which she's been doing with regularity at the meetings.

She once expressed to Derek her dismay that she has to announce this status each time she wants to say something – or, rather, when Gerard expects her to say something. Derek looked at her as if she was growing peonies out of her scalp.

'*Elaine*,' he said, 'do you not *get it* yet?' Then he sighed and shook his head. 'You will be an alcoholic *forever*.'

She opened her mouth to protest – how ridiculous, surely one stops being an alcoholic when one stops drinking all the time – but his facial expression told her not to. Apparently she missed the part where joining AA means the first A appends to you for life.

Afterwards she thought about the fact that she will always have to call herself an alcoholic, and decided she finds it freeing. It means she won't have to make choices: will she drink today or won't she? The answer will always be 'no'; and she can cope with missing the taste of gin, if that's what it takes. What is truly ridiculous is that she once thought she couldn't function without it. The last weeks have clearly proved that she can.

Returning to the water will also help. Each morning in the ocean she can experience the sensation of things being washed off her: the barnacles of bad habit. She might call it a ritual cleansing if that didn't sound so dramatic.

'Hi, Elaine,' says Theresa as she arrives, her smile not as bright as it used to be. She hasn't been herself for a while now.

'Hello!' Elaine feels like wrapping her in a hug to celebrate this auspicious day, but that would be strange: who gives hugs just because they're going for a swim?

'How was your meeting with the lawyer?' she says instead, and Theresa's face gives her the answer.

'Not that good.' She presses her lips together. 'Andrew's saying that he doesn't make an income from the business, and he's living with a friend who's claiming that he doesn't pay rent because he's so broke. So he's not going to pay anything to help me with the children.' She sighs. 'And I haven't worked for years – because he didn't want me to – so it's not as if I can go and get a job.'

'Well, you *do* work,' Elaine says. 'You raise children and run a household. That's work.'

Theresa laughs in a way Elaine has never heard from her: laced with bitterness. 'Except the value of that work is determined by my husband, isn't it? And he's saying that because I volunteer at the hospital and see my friends every morning to exercise, I'm not that committed to my children.'

'Oh, Theresa.'

Elaine decides a hug is now appropriate, and she's glad that Theresa accepts it, her head almost falling onto Elaine's shoulder.

'Do you need some money?' Elaine asks as she draws back. 'Because when I sold the business I just put it all into an account and it's still there – in sterling, which is worth considerably more here!'

She laughs to make light of the fact that she has never faced the financial situation Theresa is now in. She feels slightly guilty about it. Even without her own money, James makes more than enough for both of them.

Theresa looks startled, then her face relaxes. 'That is so lovely, but I couldn't – and it's fine. It's really fine.' She half smiles. 'It turns out Nonna's been stashing her poker winnings under her bed and there are several thousand tax-free dollars there. Don't tell anyone!' Her giggle brings back the old Theresa. 'We can get by. I don't know what will happen with the house but—'

'Good morning, you two,' Marie says.

'Good morning,' says Elaine. 'You look like the cat who ate the cream. What on *earth* is going on?'

Marie's smile becomes bigger. 'Nothing!' she says breezily. 'Or something. Gus and I had a lovely dinner. I'm just in a good mood.'

'He didn't . . . stay *overnight*, did he?' says Theresa, grinning.

'Not in the way you're suggesting, Theresa.' Marie smiles again.

'What!'

'Hi,' Leanne says, walking into the middle of their conversation.

'Hi,' Theresa and Elaine chorus.

'Are you all ready to swim?' Theresa adds. 'Because I am *busting* to get out there. Never thought I'd be so keen on exercise. I guess you're never too old to be surprised.'

Marie snorts. 'As if you're old.'

'As if *you* are!' Theresa says, and laughs, and sighs. 'That feels better. I thought I'd lost my sense of humour when I woke up this morning.'

'I don't blame you,' Elaine murmurs.

'Leanne, you have a face longer than a wet week,' says Marie. 'Whatever is the matter?'

Elaine's eyes widen in alarm. She loves Marie but she can be too direct sometimes, and Leanne has always reminded her of a cat: best not approached directly, allowed to approach on her own terms and in her own time. They've barely coaxed her into drinking milk from the bowl and now Marie's gone and stepped in it.

'Um . . . nothing.' Leanne offers her trademark tight smile and her glance away.

Yes, she's a cat, looking for a ledge to jump onto so she can run away.

'Leanne,' Marie huffs, putting her hands on her hips, 'that worked once upon a time but *not now*.' She wags a finger. 'Thank goodness you don't play poker with Theresa's nonna – you have a lot of tells.'

'Marie!' Theresa says. 'That's not very nice.'

'But it's true. Come on – out with it.'

'Really,' Leanne says, her breathing becoming more rapid, 'I can handle it.'

'So there *is* something,' Marie says more gently, stepping closer. 'Well, you're not taking it into the sea with you. You'll get distracted, you'll swallow water, and the next thing you know I'll be dragging you up the beach so Theresa can give you mouth to mouth.'

'And I'm sure you don't want that!' Theresa says breezily, but she doesn't look as though she's joking.

Leanne bows her head and puts it in her hands. 'I don't know what to do,' she says, her voice muffled.

Elaine is stunned, and she can tell the others are too. Leanne has never expressed a firm opinion, let alone an emotion, and they don't recognise it.

'What's happened?' Theresa asks. 'Is it something to do with Matt?'

Leanne shakes her head, then lifts it. Her face is blank, almost like she's not there any more.

'I'm so sorry I didn't notice you were upset before this,' Theresa says, looking as though she wants to cry. 'I haven't been at the hospital for so long.'

How could she have noticed, Elaine thinks – Leanne keeps everything to herself. For a while she thought it was because Leanne wasn't interested in being friends; she was swimming with them because it was safer than swimming alone. After a while she realised that Leanne is just very self-contained. Elaine's sometimes thought of her as being ascetic, keeping everything minimal, including conversation, so she can serve a higher purpose, such as her work.

'My mother turned up,' Leanne mumbles.

'What?' says Marie, leaning closer.

'My mother,' Leanne says more clearly. 'She turned up at work. A couple of weeks ago. I've been . . .' She stops and blinks slowly. 'It was hard.'

Her head tilts forwards again as Elaine, Theresa and Marie exchange looks of confusion.

'I know . . .' Theresa starts, stops, and bites her lip. 'You don't talk about your family. I didn't realise there was a problem.'

'I haven't seen them for eight years,' Leanne explains, and Elaine thinks this is the most she's ever told them about herself on one day.

'Right,' says Marie calmly. 'Do you want to tell us why?'

Leanne looks at each of them, almost defiantly, as if she's challenging them to accept what she's about to tell them. 'When I was eighteen, I . . . was raped.' She sucks in a breath and doesn't seem to let it out.

Elaine has the strange sensation of her spine going cold and bile rising in her oesophagus. It's shock – it must be – at learning that this tough, quiet girl who has been swimming with them for months has endured something so awful.

'By my brother's friend.' Leanne swallows.

'That's what you were trying to tell me that time,' Theresa says, her voice soft.

Leanne nods. 'I . . .' She gulps air and Theresa puts a hand on her arm.

'You don't have to tell us,' she whispers.

'I want to,' Leanne says quickly, and there's that defiance again.

Elaine admires it. Covets it, almost.

'I got pregnant,' Leanne continues, her eyes blinking rapidly.

Elaine risks a glance at the others and can see them trying to hide their surprise, as is she. Theresa looks as though she wants to ask questions, but they need to let Leanne be in charge here.

'It was too late . . . by the time I found out, it was too late to do anything,' Leanne says quietly, evenly. 'And I wouldn't have known where to go anyway. When I told my parents they said I'd brought shame on them. My father . . .' She closes her eyes. 'He was furious,' she whispers. 'My mother couldn't even look at me. They weren't going to forgive me.'

'But it wasn't your fault!' Theresa interjects.

Leanne smiles sadly. 'It's always our fault, isn't it?'

Elaine feels that shot of cold again as she remembers the two girls at her school who mysteriously vanished and were never seen again. Everyone knew they were pregnant and everyone thought badly of them – including her. Not a single person said anything about the men who made them pregnant. Elaine had judged those girls as much as anyone and she's ashamed of herself. As her cheeks burn she wants to turn her head away, but she knows that will look like she's turning away from Leanne – and she's not going to do that.

'So I left,' Leanne says, and her eyes glint with something that looks like pride. 'Found a job as a cleaner. Saved money. Did what I had to do so I could go to uni. I haven't spoken to them since.'

Simple phrases that describe a journey of pain and strength. Elaine marvels at the achievements of this woman she is only now beginning to know.

'What happened to the baby?' Marie asks.

Such a practical, logical question, and such a heartbreaking one too.

'I gave her up,' Leanne says, and Elaine hears Theresa sniff.

They are all silent for several moments. There's really nothing any of them can say that won't sound ineffectual. And won't be too late.

'I'm fine with it.' Leanne looks at each of them again. 'I couldn't have looked after her. I actually . . .' She grimaces, so briefly it's hard to catch. 'I didn't want to keep her. Because of what happened. Every time I looked at her I'd think about it.' She shakes her head. 'I couldn't.'

She releases a long sigh, then gives them a smile Elaine has never seen before: relaxed, natural.

'So your mother . . .' Marie prompts.

'She wants to see me again,' Leanne says. 'She wants me to see them all. She says they're sorry.'

'Maybe they are?' Elaine says. She doesn't know the details, of course, but if Leanne is distressed enough to tell them the story, her mother must be playing on her mind.

'Maybe.' Leanne's tiny say-nothing smile is back.

Marie pats her shoulder. 'You need to do what's right for you,' she says. 'If you want to see them, see them. If you don't, don't – but don't be hard on yourself if that's your decision.' She glances at Theresa and Elaine. 'You know we'll support you whatever.'

Leanne's eyes widen, then half close. She nods quickly and ducks her head.

'Come here, little one,' Marie says, putting her arms around the smaller, slighter woman and rubbing her back the way Elaine used to rub her sons' backs as they fell asleep. Perhaps all mothers know how to do this; perhaps Leanne's mother used to do it, too, years before her children grew up and there was no chance to do it any more. No way to express her love so simply.

Elaine remembers how painful it was when her sons crossed the threshold into the time when they no longer wanted her to hug them. They were boys becoming men, and her hands felt empty for years when she couldn't use them to convey her love and protection any more. She had to find other ways to do it. Ways to say it. She's not sure she's succeeded and she wishes she could just rub their backs again.

'Can we go swimming now?' says Leanne, muffled against Marie's chest.

'What a good idea,' Marie says, letting her go.

'It's going to be cold.' Theresa makes a face.

'I'm ready,' says Elaine with a smile at Leanne.

'Me too.' Leanne pulls her cap on.

'Last one in's a rotten egg!' cries Theresa as she takes off at a trot, and within a minute they are a mass of arms and legs pushing and kicking and diving, four unlikely mermaids swimming for the distant shore.

CHAPTER 38

Theresa tries to tie her towel like a sarong around her waist after her swim, except it's too thick and now it's falling to her ankles as she arrives home and wrenches open the front door. She really should do something about that handle or she'll end up not being able to get into the house. Andrew kept saying he'd fix it but he never did, and he's not here to fix it any more. Maybe Gus does odd jobs. She'd pay him, of course. Or Nonna would.

They wouldn't be getting by without Nonna's ill-gotten gains, and Theresa tells her that she's grateful every day. Nonna just waves a ciggie in her face and tells her it's better than keeping it under the bed.

Theresa also wouldn't be able to go swimming if Nonna didn't mind watching the children. She suspects Nonna enjoys bossing them around, and if that's the price they're paying for an ordered life, Theresa doesn't mind. It just means her children are growing up the way she did, because Nonna tended to impose discipline where Theresa's mother did not.

Nonna can't fix that door handle, though – or maybe she could, but Theresa isn't going to ask her to. So she tells herself to remember to write it on her to-do list, even if the most likely outcome is that as soon as she steps inside a million other things will happen and she'll forget.

The towel falls off completely as she shuts the door behind her and she almost trips over it just as Oliver runs into the room.

'You're WET!' he says, giggling.

He's always been a happy child, unlike his more solemn sister. No judgements, though – not of her own kids. The happy child isn't worth more than the sad one, even if Sasha gives Theresa more to worry about. Especially lately. Ollie has almost breezed through his father's departure whereas Sasha has been moping. Theresa understands: she wants to mope too some days, for different reasons, but she doesn't have the luxury.

'It's just my hair that's wet, Ollie.' She quite likes the drips on her shoulders – they're reminders that only minutes ago she was in the sea. 'Anyway, you're *nude.*'

He's always loved doing a nude run around the house. Andrew used to think it was naughty, but Theresa doesn't care. In her experience kids like to be nude, and she wouldn't mind walking around the house like that herself sometimes. It must feel like freedom. Except in her case it would also feel slightly uncomfortable because her boobs would be flapping in the breeze. That's what breastfeeding does for you.

Oliver giggles again and runs towards his bedroom, where she knows he'll put on his school uniform. He can be quite conscientious. She supposes eldest children usually are – although Angelo isn't and Theresa's always felt like she's the most responsible child in her family.

'Sasha!' she calls. They should both be dressed for school by now but Sasha is always reluctant.

'Where's Nonna?' she asks Oliver as he comes back into the living room, his school shirt wrongly buttoned.

'She's in the show-ahhhh,' he says.

Theresa peels off her swimming costume. She was hoping to have a shower herself straightaway so she can get the rest of the day going, but she's back a bit later than usual so she's thrown out the timing. If only Andrew had put a shower in the granny flat when Theresa had asked – Nonna is too old to get in and out of her bathtub now.

'Aw, Mum, ew! I don't wanna see you in the nuddy.' Oliver pretends to shield his eyes but she can see him grinning.

She grins back. 'Ollie, you have been seeing me in the nuddy all your life!'

Theresa's always tried to be relaxed about her body around the kids. She doesn't want to hide it from them, especially after they were both breastfed. How confusing would that be? Here, you can see my breasts all the time, put your mouth on them, pat them with your hands, and now I'm going to lock them away like there's something wrong with them.

'Sasha!' she calls again, louder this time. 'Ollie, your shirt isn't done up properly.'

'She's sick,' Oliver says, rebuttoning his shirt.

'What?' Theresa can't have a sick child today. She has so much to do, including taking Nonna to her poker game and to the doctor early in the afternoon. Plus she promised Sarah, another school mum, that she'd take her kids home after school because Sarah's working and her babysitter's away.

'What's that?' Oliver says as Theresa wraps her towel around her torso.

'What?'

He sighs. 'It's gone.'

'Ollie, what are you talking about?'

'That funny thing.' He points to her chest.

'The towel?' She frowns at him, confused.

He points again. 'That thing on your booby.'

'You mean my mole? That's always been there.'

'No!' He shakes his head as if she's the silliest person he's ever met. 'Underneath.'

She doesn't know what he's talking about and has no time to look. Right now she has to check on her daughter, get into the shower and take these kids to school.

'Good morning, *bella*,' Nonna says as she enters the room swaddled in her favourite terry-towelling dressing gown, which bears the strong aroma of the several cigarettes she's already smoked this morning.

'Hi, Nonna, did you have a good sleep?' Theresa tucks the top of her towel in more snugly.

'Why are you naked in front of the boy?' Nonna says crossly.

'I'm not naked! I have a towel on. I'm waiting to have a shower.'

'I've seen Mummy naked heaps, Nonna,' Oliver says seriously.

Nonna's disapproval is evident but Theresa doesn't think she has any right to judge – she's hardly a paragon of virtue. That's one of the reasons Theresa loves her so much.

'I haven't had time to put the coffee on,' she says as she heads towards Sasha's bedroom.

'I'll do it,' Nonna says.

Theresa walks into Sasha's bedroom to find a wan-looking child, her hair still tousled from sleep, bravely trying to pull on her uniform.

'Hi, Mum,' Sasha almost whispers and Theresa's heart contracts. Her baby girl looks like she's trying so hard not to be unwell.

'Hello, darling.' Theresa picks her up and sits on the bed. She kisses the side of Sasha's head and feels the softness of her curls against her face.

Despite that long to-do list she would stay like this all day if she could. She loves being around her children, and always wishes she had more time to simply be with them, without them all flinging themselves around the way life seems to demand they must. School, playing with their friends, ballet lessons for Sasha, tennis lessons for Oliver, reading to them as much as she can, cooking, cleaning, mending clothes, tending to the garden, and maybe, sometimes, getting a few minutes to herself.

She smiles at her daughter and strokes the hair that's sticking up on top of her head. 'You're not well, darling?' she says softly and Sasha shakes her head.

Theresa tries not to sigh. She doesn't want Sasha to see how this complicates her day. Almost everything on her list involves her being elsewhere, rather than home with a sick child. She also can't not turn up to take Sarah's children home from school, never mind Oliver. And Theresa can't put Nonna in a taxi to poker because Nonna thinks all the drivers are stupid, and usually ends up yelling at them.

So Theresa needs to be resourceful today; she needs a solution to look after Sasha and manage all the other things. It won't come from within her own family: Andrew has never been her back-up childcare option, especially now; and it also won't come from his parents, who have a regime of VIEW Club meetings, bridge games and beers at the sailing club to uphold. Her own parents are too far away to get here in time. It's a two-hour drive, and that's on a good day.

She thinks about the school mums, most of whom have their own kids or jobs to worry about. Then she remembers something Marie said to her once, when Theresa was moaning about all the things she had to juggle that day.

'If you ever need a hand with the kids, let me know. I'm not far away.' She had a funny expression on her face, almost like she was hopeful that Theresa would take her up on the offer.

Theresa had thanked Marie but never thought she'd actually ask her to help, not because she wouldn't trust her with the kids – Marie is definitely the responsible type – but because she doesn't want to take advantage of her.

She doesn't have another option, though. Not today.

'It's okay, darling,' she says, kissing Sasha again. 'I just have to make a phone call.'

'Of course I can be there,' Marie says, and Theresa feels herself relax.

'Thank you. What would I do without you?'

'And what would I do without *you*?'

Theresa can hear the smile in Marie's voice and hopes Marie can't hear her sniffling. Some days are hard, and some aren't, but because she sees Marie and the others every day they always start with laughter.

'What time do you need me?' Marie asks.

'I'll run Ollie to school and come back. So . . . nine-thirty?'

'Works for me.'

'Thanks again.' Arrangements made, Theresa heads for the shower. 'Nonna, can you get Ollie's breakfast?' she calls.

'*Si, si,*' comes the slightly grumpy reply and Theresa smiles.

As the water hits her she remembers what Ollie said about seeing something on her breast, so she has a bit of a feel. There, on the bottom side of her right breast, there's a funny little thing. A shape. That's how she thinks of it. Not a lump.

She knows what breast lumps look like because her Aunt Gloria was always keen to show hers, to make sure the rest of the family knew what she was going through. Those lumps were so far gone by the time Gloria did anything about them that she was dead within a few months. This one is little. But visible to her son, so Theresa can't believe she didn't notice it before.

Not that she has time to think about groping her boobs looking for lumps, and it's not as if anyone else has been groping her either. Even before he left it had been a long time since Andrew went anywhere near her 'fun bags', as he used to call them. After she breastfed two babies he started saying that her boobs didn't belong to him any more. She could never tell if he was sad or angry about that.

It's not as if they belonged to *her*, either. It wasn't until breastfeeding that she really understood that her breasts had a purpose other than keeping Andrew happy and sometimes being the cause of remarks as she passed strange men on the street. She thinks they're still remark-worthy. Remarkable, even. Two kids later they haven't lost their shape completely, even if they do hang a bit lower than before.

The knock on the bathroom door startles her.

'Mu-um! I need to do a wee!'

'Okay, Ollie. Come in.'

By the time her son has finished his wee, Theresa has almost pushed the lump to the back of her mind. She'll write it on her to-do list, along with everything else. That's the only way she'll remember to talk to someone about it.

CHAPTER 39

The house is as Leanne remembers it, and not. It looks more aged, and it looks the same. Her memories are a veil over the reality in front of her, telling her that this is her childhood home and also the place she vowed never to see again. If it's possible to feel like you are in two places at once – to be two people at once – then she is.

'You're really, really sure about this?' Elaine says, taking her hands from the steering wheel and swivelling towards her.

'No.' Leanne gives her a weak smile. 'I'm not sure of anything.'

After she told the others her story, after she knew that they wouldn't question her decisions, she felt free. A bad thing had happened to her; she'd accepted the consequences. She'd taken charge of things as much as she could.

There have been days, though, when she wished she could take it all back: she would still have her parents and her siblings; she might even have that baby. It had seemed logical at the time: to divest herself of shame by staying away from its witnesses and removing its cause. After her mother appeared at the hospital that day, though, Leanne hasn't been sure she made the right decision. Except she's created a whole life around that decision, and she doesn't know who she would be otherwise.

'Do you not want to talk to your mother at all?' Marie had asked the other morning after their swim.

'I . . . don't know.'

Leanne had looked out to sea. Her life was so simple when she was out there. Arms and legs moving. Opening her mouth, breathing. The sun starting to rise. The occasional seagull hovering. Her only preoccupations to get to Little Beach and back, and keep track of the others. Not because she's competitive with them but because she likes knowing they're around. Her little tribe.

Tears had come to her eyes unbidden. She never meant to involve other people in her mess. In any part of her life. Yet now she has three friends, and a boyfriend, and while that makes her existence more complicated than it was before, it's also richer. Fuller than she can believe. Which is why she accepted Elaine's offer to accompany her today; she has come to realise that she's allowed to have help. It's too hard, and too exhausting, to do everything on her own.

'I'll sit in the car,' Elaine said when she suggested it. 'I'll be waiting when you're ready to leave.'

Something else Leanne told the others that morning was how she'd regretted running away from her mother at the hospital. She wasn't ready to talk then, but she is now, if her mother is.

'She'll be ready,' Marie said firmly. 'If she's found you after all these years, I'd say talking to you is what she wants most and she's not going to be so easily put off.'

Leanne felt her doubt muddled up with her guilt. 'It wasn't the right thing to do,' she said.

'It was the right thing for you to do at the time.' Marie could be so practical and blunt, and that day Leanne was glad of it.

Now, with the house in front of her, she feels more doubt: what if this still isn't the right thing for her?

'I can come in with you,' Elaine says. 'I don't mind.'

Leanne presses her lips together to stop her chin trembling. 'No,' she says in a half whisper. 'I need to do it. But I really appreciate you being here.'

Elaine smiles kindly.

'I'll go now.' Leanne pulls the handle on the car door without waiting for Elaine to respond.

She closes the door behind her, and takes swift steps towards the gate, up the path, to the familiar wooden door with a new-looking brass knocker on it.

Three firm knocks, and she hears noise behind the door.

It opens, and her mother is there, looking tinier than she did at the hospital.

'Leanne?' she whispers, as if she can't believe what she's seeing.

'Hi, Mum,' Leanne says, trying to smile but her chin wobbles again.

Her mother nods at her and steps closer. 'You came.'

'I shouldn't have left you the other day. I'm sorry.'

Her mother puts her hand on Leanne's hair and strokes it once. 'It's okay,' she says. 'You got a shock.'

Leanne feels something thick, like packed sand and salt water, in her throat. She pushes it down. She's not here to get upset. She's here to make amends. Not to ask for forgiveness or even for them to understand her. They may never understand each other. That's what happens in families, and sometimes amongst friends. You love each other anyway. She hadn't known that when she was eighteen. All she could think about was her own pain.

That's what she kept going over in the car while Elaine drove her here, leaving her alone with her thoughts, not trying even once to intrude. It's what they're used to, after all: being alone together in the water, each woman inside her own head. The comfort of wordless company that understands you implicitly. *We're all here, engaged in the same activity, and you don't have to explain a thing to me.* 'Sisters in swimming', one of them called it once. Probably Theresa. Leanne can't imagine that phrase coming from anyone else, and it's certainly not the sort of sentimental thing she'd come up with herself.

'I missed you,' Leanne says raggedly, although she's never admitted this to herself before, let alone said it out loud.

She couldn't allow herself to miss them. That would lead to regrets and she's been determined to not have those. A whole life can be wasted wishing you'd never done something, but the past can't be changed. The only thing that changes is how you deal with what's happened.

'We've been so sad, Leanne.' Her mother closes her eyes. 'We didn't know what to do. Your brothers. Your sister . . .' She sighs. 'They haven't been the same.'

I haven't been the same, Leanne wants to say, but it seems too obvious.

'I'm sorry, Mum.'

'You're here now.'

Her mother smiles that hopeful, childlike smile Leanne always loved. When she was young it made her think her mother was a co-conspirator: that she saw whimsy in the world the way Leanne did. Once she was a teenager she wished her mother would grow up too. Now she knows that smile is not a relic of her mother's youth but a declaration of optimism: her mother sees every day as an opportunity to start anew. Right now, Leanne sees in it her own fresh start.

'I am.' She reaches for her mother's hand. 'Will you show me the garden?'

Her mother's eyes widen. 'Do you want to see your cumquat trees?'

Leanne smiles. She planted those trees when she was eight or ten or some age like that. They bore fruit that the neighbours made into jam. After a while Leanne ignored them and they flourished in spite of that.

'Yes, please.'

'Your father has been looking after them,' her mother says, opening the sliding door. She stops and turns. 'He misses you too.'

The garden looks as neat as it always has, but the cumquats are definitely taller. At the base of the largest tree Leanne sees a small shrine with stones and trinkets and incense. And a photo of her, covered in plastic. She remembers other shrines her mother made, for relatives in a distant land. They were always in her mother's thoughts and in her murmured pleas for their health and safety.

'I've been praying for you to come home,' her mother says.

Leanne closes her eyes against the memories of the last time she was in this house. The stories she has told herself about what needed to happen. She may not have regrets, but if she could change one thing it would be that she believed her parents' love for her was greater than their shame and their anger. And greater than hers. All this time, there has been love here. All these years, she has denied herself that.

No more. The heart she closed eight years ago is cracking open to let in those who come to her with their own hearts ready to give to her, and to receive. She is loved. She loves. For all the shadows of the past she has kept at bay there is now light. Just like the light of day she sees each morning as salt water washes her clean. Each day new.

'Let's burn some incense, Mum,' she says, kneeling down.

They sit together and light a flame, and Leanne quietly says prayers of thanks that she has found her way home.

SUMMER 1983-1984

CHAPTER 40

Marie isn't given to having butterflies, but she has them right now as she speeds around her kitchen, peeling potatoes for Nicole's favourite potato salad, checking on the turkey, thinking about when to make the gravy. She's been in a frenzy since she woke up but it only seems to make her slower.

'You're working too hard,' Gus says as he walks in carrying the plum pudding she's had hanging in the shed for weeks.

'Not hard enough,' Marie mutters. 'I'm not getting anything done.'

She feels his hand on her arm. 'Stop for a second, love.'

The butterflies' wings beat harder now that he's touching her.

Marie's never been interested in romantic stories, unless they're movies starring Katharine Hepburn or Grace Kelly, so she's been surprised at how swept up in her own romance she's become. She thought she was too mature to think about things being romantic, but that's not the truth, because Gus has reintroduced romance to her life, and her to his. It's not in big gestures like bunches of flowers and elaborate dinners, but in small gestures and close attention. It's listening carefully to each other and remembering what you hear. It's thinking of him first thing each day and last thing at night, especially when he's not there. It's allowing him to suffuse her world, and embracing the fact that she does his.

For all her love for Norm, Marie never felt swept away like this – not because they didn't love each other, but because she felt so responsible, so caught up with concerns. She had a household to run and a daughter to raise. She was always conscious of doing the right thing, her mother's admonishments in her head: *You shouldn't let Nicole do that, she'll develop bad habits. Aren't you going to iron those sheets?* They were lines that her mother would have heard from her own mother, and so on back to who knows which generation started thinking their worth to society, and their self-worth, was tied up with ironed sheets. That's what you get for living in the same house as your parents when you're a parent yourself. Now Marie's in the house alone she can't believe they all lived here without killing each other.

At this stage of her life, she has a lot of care – for Nicole, Pete and the children, for Charlie Brown, for Theresa and Elaine and Leanne, for Gwen, for Father Paul – but very little responsibility. Not that long ago she thought her life was becoming tighter, narrower. Now it feels more open than ever and she wants to explore it. She feels curious about what's to be seen and done in this world – and that's something else that's been dormant for a long time. Strange, how you can start to disappear a little and not realise. Now she feels like a flower unfurling in the sunshine: one petal at a time but gloriously colourful.

Gus has shown her how to be free, and given her a reason to embrace the fullness of each day. Before this she was good at appreciating parts of it, such as her morning swim, but she wasn't alive to the possibility of each moment. He is, and she has learnt from him. Her only sadness about it is that Norm never lived long enough to be this free.

She knows it's weird to be thinking about her dead husband when she's with her new . . . friend? What is she meant to call him? 'Boyfriend' sounds absurd for someone her age. 'Lover' sounds slightly tawdry and not for use in front of children. Besides, they're taking that part slowly. So, yes, she probably shouldn't be thinking about Norm now she has Gus, but she can't exactly make herself stop. How can you prevent a memory or a thought popping into your mind? However long she lives, it's unlikely Gus will be in her life for longer than Norm was. Norm's part of the fabric of her, and he's Nicole's father.

And that's another reason why she's nervous about today.

She starts peeling again.

'Marie – *stop*,' Gus orders. 'It's Christmas lunch, not manoeuvres on the Western Front.'

'I just want it to be *right*,' she says, annoyed at this nasty little streak of perfectionism that she's only recently developed. As in, only over the past few days since she started planning and preparing for Christmas lunch.

'Have you ever worried about it this much?' Gus asks.

She thinks for a second. 'No.'

'So what's the problem today?'

He looks amused, and she wants to say that it's all very well for him but it's not his cooking that will be judged.

'Ahh . . .' She looks around the kitchen as if there's an answer hidden in the fruit bowl or the cutlery drawer. Then she looks into his eyes. 'You,' she says.

'Me?'

'Yes. You're the problem.'

His facial expression suggests that he doesn't know whether to laugh or be upset.

'May I ask why?' he says cautiously.

Marie takes a breath to think about how to phrase it. It's something she's been wanting to say for a while, and she knows she doesn't lack for courage. Or perhaps someone who wilfully ignores the existence of sharks on a daily basis is merely foolhardy.

She starts with the simplest truth. 'Because this is a big day.'

He nods but says nothing.

'Christmas is a time for family. And you're . . .'

'Not?' He frowns.

'No, that's not it.' She swallows, feeling those butterflies again. 'I love you, Gus.'

Now she's said it and she can't take it back. She can only hope that the surprise she can see in his eyes also means he's pleased.

'I wouldn't have asked you to be here if I didn't,' she continues. 'It's a big day because I want it to be right. I want you and Nicole and Pete and the children to all like each other and get along. Nicole and Pete will be fine. You know Pete, of course. You've spoken to Nicole. But Toby remembers Norm a little. Jessie doesn't at all and she's never seen me with anyone. And today's a big day.' She swallows again. 'Maybe I shouldn't have done it. It's too much pressure.'

'Why?' Gus says with a quizzical expression. 'It's just Christmas.'

Marie sighs heavily. 'But . . .' Her heart starts to hammer even though she knows she is the one who has raised the stakes of today because she's told him that she loves him. 'I hope it's not the only Christmas lunch we have together.'

Gus is gazing down at her and she sees the corners of his eyes crinkle. He takes her hands and lifts them to his lips, and for a second she worries it's the prelude to him bidding her adieu.

'I love you too,' he says. 'Which is why *you're* having Christmas dinner with *my* children.' He pinches her cheek lightly. 'I think I forgot to explain that to you, though. In my head, you've always known that I love you. I just wasn't sure how you felt about me.'

Marie's laugh is short and incredulous. 'You love me?'

'Of course.' His smile is confident and wide. 'You're very lovable, you know.'

'Sometimes I wonder,' she mutters, but he stops her saying anything more by kissing her. That kiss is familiar to her now but that doesn't make it any less thrilling.

As he breaks the kiss he hugs her to his side and kisses the top of her head. 'I'll finish here. You have a break.'

'I need to get changed.' She unties her apron and hands it to him. 'Thank you.'

In her bedroom she fluffs around with dresses, pulling them on and off in succession, going back to an earlier choice, deciding against it, choosing another. The whole process manages to muss up her hair so she has to start again with that too, carefully brushing it into its usual unfussy shape. She takes a good, hard look at herself in the mirror and decides that she needs lipstick, she really does, if only she could remember where she put the one lipstick she owns. That Revlon one she bought at the chemist the Christmas before last . . .

In the middle of looking for it she hears the knock at the front door and almost jumps out of her skin. She'll just have to go bare-lipped, as usual.

When the door opens there's her daughter's lovely face and big smile.

Nicole glances curiously at Gus as he walks up behind Marie. 'Hi Mum – Merry Christmas.' She kisses Marie on the cheek then hesitates.

'Darling, I'd like you to meet Gus – at last.' Marie looks from one to the other. 'Although you've spoken on the phone enough that you're almost old friends.'

'Yes, he always seems to be answering the phone. Makes me think he never leaves the place.' Nicole gives Gus a wink while Marie has a moment of startled realisation that the relationship she thought was developing slowly has, to her daughter, seemed like something altogether more permanent.

'Merry Christmas, Nicole,' Gus says heartily before pecking her cheek and stepping back so she can walk past.

'Hello, Pete,' Marie says as her grandchildren mob her legs, hugging tightly and stopping her walking anywhere.

Weeks may elapse between seeing them but Marie knows they'll always be this excited about her – it is one of the unexpected blessings of her life, to have the chance to be joyful with her grandchildren the way she couldn't be with Nicole. When you're directly responsible for a child's wellbeing, education, shelter and care, there are endless opportunities for concern and precious few moments for joy.

'Marie.' Pete kisses her on the cheek and extends his hand to Gus, nodding once as they shake hands.

Her son-in-law is a man of few words but he's also one of magnanimous gestures and kind-heartedness, and Marie is fond of him, even if it's harder to get to know someone when they don't say much.

'Who are you?' says Jessie, looking up at Gus as she lets go of Marie's legs. While Toby, already starting to explore his independence, stands to the side and regards Gus with frank curiosity.

Marie starts to answer Jessie but stops. Gus can handle himself around a six-year-old, she's sure of it.

'I'm Gus.'

He crouches so he's more at Jessie's height, and Marie marvels at his flexibility, as she does whenever he's working in the garden. She may be fit, but everything seems to get stiffer with age. She wonders what he'll be like when he catches up to her and knows, with a certainty in her heart, that she will see that. They will still know each other then. She's completely sure of it, and that makes her calm.

'I'm a friend of your grandmother's,' Gus says, holding out his hand for Jessie to shake it, 'and I love her very much, just as I'm sure you do.'

Marie's breath catches at his admission, and as she looks at Nicole she could swear hers does too. Then Nicole smiles at her – in fact, she beams – and Marie feels any last skerrick of concern evaporate.

'I do,' Jessie says matter-of-factly, then holds out her other hand to Gus. 'Can you take me to the garden so I can visit my fairies?'

Gus glances up at Marie and she feels their exquisite complicity in this moment, in this life and in her family. Her heart felt like bursting once before, when she gave birth to Nicole; and it felt like it would shatter when she lost her son. So she knows the extremes of love; she knows the risks and the rewards and the difficulties and the triumphs of it. And as Gus takes Jessie's hand and straightens up, she feels her heart fit to burst once more.

'Charlie Brown!' Toby cries as the dog trots into view, his tail wagging furiously, and in a flash boy and dog are heading out the back.

'The garden's looking wonderful,' Nicole says as they wander down the hallway, through the living room and out through the kitchen to the back verandah. 'Thank you for taking care of it.'

'I should be thanking you,' Gus says over his shoulder. 'You're the reason I met your mother. Thank you for engaging me to work on the garden.'

Nicole looks pleased with herself. 'You're welcome.'

As Gus and Jessie walk into the garden, a lopsided pair, Nicole puts her arm around Marie.

'I like him,' she says.

After that, Marie knows, everything will be perfect.

CHAPTER 41

'**M**ummy?' Marcus says.

'Darling!' There's silence for a few seconds as Elaine's reply is carried across the world.

'How are you?' he says.

Hearing her son's voice makes Elaine immediately, painfully homesick, but she's not going to dwell on it. Instead she pictures her handsome son with his thick brown hair and nuggetty physique. It feels like an age since she's seen him, because it is, but in her mind's eye and her heart he is right there with her, always.

'It's so lovely to hear you,' she says.

'And you. Are you well?'

Elaine thinks of her day thus far: the morning swim, and some teasing of Marie about her relationship with Gus – Theresa called them 'lovey-dovey' and Marie blushed. Blushed! Elaine didn't think Marie knew how. She had lunch with Leanne at the hospital – they've become closer since she drove her to see her parents. Leanne is still reserved but she laughs more now. She just won't tell Elaine much about Matt. Then she went to an AA meeting, came home and cleaned and made plans for dinner, and read a novel in between gazing at her garden and wondering how she could improve it. Improving things used to be how she made money: doing up houses and making people happy. She misses it. Now she's waiting for James to arrive home. In fact, he's late. He said he'd be home at seven and it's seven-thirty.

'Yes, darling, I am well,' she says truthfully. 'And you?'

'Very.'

There's a pause and Elaine isn't sure whether or not she's meant to speak again. These long-distance phone calls can be confusing.

'I have news, Mummy.'

'Oh?' Her heart seems to pause as her immediate reaction is to think it's bad news. Her eternal worry as a mother is that there will be bad news.

'I've asked Caroline to marry me and she's said yes.' He sounds so pleased, and proud.

Elaine quickly calculates how long he's known Caroline – they hadn't started seeing each other when James and Elaine moved to Australia, although they'd known each other for a while, as friends. Elaine has never seen them together; she has no idea what they're like as a couple. Her son is so grown-up now that he's to be a husband and, probably soon, a father. He'll have his own family. His life is separate to hers and they will never intersect the way they used to. If she felt far away from her children before this, now she feels as though she's on Jupiter while they're happily ensconced on Earth. She doesn't think she has ever felt this lonely before in all her life – yet she can't show it. Mustn't show it. This is happy news.

'Darling, that is wonderful – absolutely wonderful,' she says, her voice as joyous as she can make it. 'You must be thrilled. *She* must be thrilled. Lucky girl.'

'Is Papa there? I'd love to speak to him.'

'Not yet,' she says. 'He's late. Shall I ask him to call you?'

More seconds of silence.

'It's fine,' Marcus says, although she can hear that he's disappointed. She can recognise every variant of every emotion in her sons' voices. 'Would you tell him for me?'

'Of course, and I know he'll be delighted. Have you set a date? We'll come home for the wedding. That's if you want us there,' she adds uncertainly.

'Oh, Mummy! We wouldn't let you *not* come!'

'Lovely.' She smiles, putting on a brave face even if he can't see it. 'I'm so happy for you.'

He chortles. 'I'm pretty happy for myself, I must say. Look, I'd best go. I have to get to work.'

'Love you, darling. I'll give Papa your good news.'

'Love you, Mummy. Bye.'

Then he's gone, and she puts down the receiver and her house has never seemed so empty, her life never so pointless. Her son is engaged – he is making a whole new life without her or James – and she's not there. What is she doing? Why are they *here*? They should be there, with Marcus, with Henry. She doesn't want to be the mother who turns up just for the wedding. She wants to be there for the weeks beforehand. The months afterwards.

She wishes she didn't love her husband; she would never have followed him here. This country is absurd – in a different hemisphere, thousands of miles from another continent, with ridiculous weather and strange animals. The people couldn't round a vowel if their lives depended on it, and they think it's funny to have a prime minister who holds the world record for drinking beer quickly. Yes, she's made friends. Lovely people. And she enjoys the swimming. But is that it? Is that all Australia can offer her?

She has to go home. She doesn't care if she has to leave James to do it. They can love each other and live apart. It might even be romantic. She can't stay here.

But she has to stay here.

What would she be going back to?

She sold her business, so she won't have an income. Henry is at university, and Marcus has his work and soon will have his wife. Her sons' lives have moved on. And the worst part is that they seem completely content. They don't appear to miss her at all. Now she thinks of it, when she and James announced they were moving to Australia the boys seemed to be *happy* for them.

If she returns, all she'll be doing is meddling in their lives. She'll be a pathetic, grasping mother who can't leave her grown-up children alone because she doesn't have enough interests of her own.

Elaine is not that person. But she doesn't want to be the person who is stuck in Australia, either, far from the people she loves.

This is a conundrum. And she knows what she needs to help her with a conundrum: she needs to not think about it. To not think at all.

There's only one way to do that.

Flinging open the French doors, she rushes into the garden. At the time she started going to AA meetings she hid a bottle of gin under the camellia. She liked the idea of testing herself, and she knew that if she disturbed the earth there was a chance James would notice. So she'll just have to be careful, won't she?

She uses her hands to dig into the soil, not caring that there will be dirt under her fingernails. She can wash her hands. Nor does she care about the dirt on the knees of her pale pink trousers. She can wash those too. They don't matter. There's only one thing that matters.

Yanking the bottle out of its grave, she twists the lid and pours it straight into her mouth. She doesn't have any tonic – another part of the test. She believed that if she didn't have tonic she wouldn't drink gin. Ha!

She screws up her face as she tastes juniper, then lets the liquid slide down the back of her throat. It's been months since she had a drink so she really shouldn't have much. Just enough to stop her brain from thinking. Then she'll put the bottle back.

Another slug. Another swallow.

She waits to see if it's taken effect. Not yet.

The bottle is to her lips again when she hears a noise at the doors.

'Elaine!'

The bottle is still at her mouth as she turns. She wants to see James looking disgusted. Disappointed. She's broken her promise to herself, to him, that she won't drink any more. Instead he looks upset.

So now they're both upset, because she's still not drunk and her brain is still working so she's having thoughts about how lovely it is that Marcus is engaged and how awful it is that she can't be with him, and what about when something significant happens to Henry and she's not there for that either? What about her parents? They're old. They could die and she won't be there.

This is all a mistake. She's a mistake. Her life is a mistake. The gin is a mistake.

That's what she's thinking as James pulls the bottle out of her hand and flings it into a garden bed, as he holds her tightly and puts his nose against her neck, as she starts to sob about how she misses her babies, until she lets him carry her inside and lay her on the lounge.

'I'm sorry,' she whispers hoarsely and he strokes her forehead.

'You have nothing to be sorry for.'

'I do.' She gazes out to the garden.

'You'll have to start it all again,' he says softly.

'I know.'

And she does know. Because her life has to be here now. She told James she'd come with him and she won't leave him. That would make her sad too. So she's stuck, torn between her loves, between her loyalty to her husband and the care she owes her children. And while the solution to it all would be to love less, she's not prepared to do that.

'I'll get you some water,' he murmurs.

'Thank you,' she whispers, and while she hears the tap running she closes her eyes and thinks of where she was last happiest: this morning, in the water, with the sand below her and the sky above, and all the time in the world.

That is where she needs to start over again.

CHAPTER 42

Kicking helps. Kicking hard. Kicking as if she's kicking Andrew. That's what Theresa's thinking as she heads for Little Beach. But she's so tired. Tired from staying up late worrying about the future, and the present: the fact that her husband isn't overly interested in seeing his children; the bills she needs to pay that she has to ask Nonna to help with; the question of where they're going to live if she has to sell the house.

Still, she keeps kicking, and moving her arms. Stroke, stroke, kick kick kick, breathe. Repeat. Keeping herself going is the only thing keeping her going.

As she nears Little Beach she almost swims straight into Marie, who is standing in the shallows.

'Sorry!' Theresa says as she pulls up just short.

'Right,' Marie says, and she has her hands on her hips the way she does when she wants to make a point. '*What* is going *on?*'

'Hm?' Theresa gets to her feet.

Elaine is sitting in the shallows with her goggles pushed up onto her head. Leanne is only a few metres offshore now. Nearby there's a man walking his black Labrador, and a couple of joggers are drinking from the bubbler. Theresa likes it over here: it's quiet at this time of day, and she can pretend it's an island, separate from the rest of Shelly Bay and an oasis away from care. Unless Marie is asking her probing questions.

'I've never seen you kick like that – you looked like a deranged whisk.' Marie raises her eyebrows.

'I did not! That was me sprinting!' Theresa looks at Elaine for back-up, but she just shakes her head a little and starts to laugh.

'Don't try it again,' Marie says. 'You're not made to be a sprinter. You're a long-distance swimmer.'

Although Theresa knows she should feel mildly insulted by part of what Marie said, she's quite pleased about the last bit. She smiles. 'Am I?'

'You're getting there.'

Leanne walks towards them. 'Why are we stopped?' she asks.

'Theresa was doing something funny,' says Marie.

'I was not!'

Marie looks at her askance. 'There's something going on. Better you tell us what it is. You know we give good advice.'

Theresa purses her lips. 'I don't know if advice can help me.'

The other three look at her expectantly.

'It's just . . . stuff.' She flaps her hands but doesn't really want to wave this off. Trying to manage it all herself – to work things out, even if there are no solutions – is exhausting.

'Tell us,' Elaine says. 'Please.'

Theresa nods slowly and pulls off her goggles. 'Andrew's still saying he has no money, plus he hardly sees the kids. He keeps saying he's busy, and the kids were fine with not seeing him at first but now they miss him. I don't have an income and I can't keep asking Nonna to help pay for the bills and the mortgage. My parents are pressuring me to move in with them and sell the house, because I'll have to when we divorce anyway. And . . .' She sighs. 'I saw Andrew and his girlfriend going into the pub the other day.'

'How do you know it was his girlfriend?' asks Marie.

'Because he had his hand on her bum,' Theresa says, sighing again.

'Are you sure you're going to divorce?' Elaine asks.

Theresa can't help laughing. 'Um – yes. I am. He has a girlfriend.'

She glances at Marie, who smiles sympathetically.

'Don't rush anything,' says Elaine. 'Marriages have survived worse. This may be a phase.'

'I don't want him back! He'd have to spend a week sitting in a vat of Domestos before I'd touch him again and that's not going to happen!' Theresa blinks. She didn't actually know she felt that strongly until now.

'I'd say you're a woman who knows what she wants, then,' says Marie. 'And we can work with that. We'd better get back, though, because we all have places to be.'

'Oh,' says Theresa. She hadn't been sure what would result from her spilling her guts but didn't think they'd all just listen and keep swimming.

'Don't fret, pet,' says Marie, patting her shoulder. 'I've got my thinking cap on.' She taps the side of her head. 'Working on some ideas.'

Theresa has no idea what they could be, but she allows herself to be led into the water. This time she can't kick hard even if she wants to: it's as if confessing to her friends has made her floppy, because she's practically dragging herself through the water. Leanne passes her, and Marie and Elaine are already ahead.

The swell has changed since they set out and the water gets choppy as she nears Main Beach. She gets tangled up in a wave and a pain in her side causes her to gasp. It's not a stitch – she's had those before – but it feels like her ribs are protesting. She doesn't want the others to know, though, because she's already imposed on them enough, so she rearranges her face as she gets out of the water and tries to keep her breathing slow and even.

'Guess I'm lucky last!' she says as she approaches the others but can't help wincing.

'It became a bit messy out there,' Elaine says.

Theresa smiles at her. 'I think you're just trying to make me feel better.'

'No way,' says Marie. 'It was so rough on the way back I swallowed half the Tasman Sea. Was starting to think I'd need a snorkel.'

Theresa wraps a towel around her shoulders and huddles into herself. 'I just need to get a bit fitter.' She smiles. 'And here I was thinking I was already doing that.'

'Don't be too hard on yourself.' Marie steps towards Theresa and gives her a peck on the cheek. 'Anyway, I have to run.'

'I'll walk with you,' Leanne says, and she smiles briefly at Theresa and Elaine.

'*Ciao*,' Theresa replies. She rubs her back before dropping the towel on the sand. Her next sigh is heavier, longer. 'I must be getting old. That stint on the way over wore me out.'

'You're not old,' Elaine says. 'But you are wincing. Is something hurting?'

Now Theresa's ribcage feels like it's spasming. 'I'm just . . . worn out. And . . .' She blinks rapidly and sniffs, wiping her nose with the back of her hand.

Elaine steps closer and puts a hand on her arm. 'Whatever it is, you can tell me.'

Her face is open and Theresa can tell she's being sincere. She's come to know that Elaine is always sincere, even if her accent and her manner can sometimes make her seem like a snob. She's not, really. She's a friend. A mate. And Theresa didn't tell the others everything she's worried about – but she wants someone to know. She wants to share the burden of it so she can stop carrying the worry on her own.

'There's something . . .' She takes a breath. 'On my breast. I – I found it the other day, then I forgot about it, then I remembered.'

She laughs, then stops herself. Why is she trying to make light of this? Is she trying to tell Elaine that it isn't serious? Or tell herself?

They all do that, don't they? All the time. Try to make the world happier, brighter, less troublesome. It's what good girls do. Theresa should know, because she was raised to be one. To be upset but not show anyone; be worried but don't tell anyone. Everything's fine, it's fine, I'm fine.

'Theresa, you don't have to pretend to be okay.'

Theresa nods quickly.

'You need to see a doctor,' Elaine says.

'Do I?'

'You know you do.'

Yes, she does. She's known it ever since she found that lump, but there just hasn't been time. How is she meant to fit in going to a GP, who's invariably running late, when it means she might not be there to pick up the kids from school or take Nonna to poker, or do the shopping or the washing?

'Let me help you,' Elaine says in a softer tone. 'I'll call and make the appointment.'

'You don't have to do that,' Theresa says, glancing away.

'I know I don't,' Elaine says firmly. 'I want to.'

Theresa feels her breath catching. Her worry is shared, but now it's also more real.

'You're not alone,' Elaine says quietly.

'My aunt died of breast cancer,' Theresa chokes out, and Elaine pulls her into a hug.

'This may not be breast cancer. Try not to worry until you've seen the doctor.'

Theresa wipes her eyes with a finger. 'Can I drive you home?'

'Yes, please,' says Elaine, slinging her towel around her neck.

As they walk their feet sink into the soft sand, and Theresa wonders what it would be like to keep sinking down, down, down into the centre of the earth. Her problems could be left on the surface – along with all the people she loves.

No, she would hate that. She doesn't want to be alone, and Elaine is right: she isn't alone. So Theresa will let her help, and she will try to take things one day at a time and not worry too much. She can't know what the doctor will say, and it's a fool's errand to try to predict the future.

CHAPTER 43

Daylight saving will be over soon and they won't have this light in the early evening – the gentle fading of the day that is a hallmark of summer. Leanne will miss it; although once they turn the clocks back she'll be happy to have more light at the start of the day for a while. They've almost been swimming in the dark, trying to fit it in at a reasonable hour, which means not necessarily waiting for the sun to be over the horizon before they start. That pre-dawn light is pretty, but the water is almost grey, and certainly more mysterious, if not a little intimidating.

It's the light she's looking at when she realises Matt is saying something to her.

'Queen to king's knight five,' he says with raised eyebrows and a tone that suggests he's repeating it.

'Sorry,' she says. 'I'm away with the pixies.'

Matt gives her a funny look and laughs. 'I've never heard you use that phrase before.'

'Theresa says it.' She glances down at the chessboard and can tell that after his last move she's not in a winning position. 'I don't know what to do here.'

'Take your time. You should always take your time. And while you do, I'll go to the bar. Would you like something?'

She shakes her head and he picks up his empty glass.

Leanne looks out the window again. The pub is across the road from the beach, and she can see the spot where she and the other women congregate each morning. Loud laughter brings her attention back to the pub and she sees a woman with her hand on Matt's arm, and the two of them laughing. They look like they know each other, their body language suggesting ease.

Her chest and head feel tight, and nausea starts to swirl in her gut. It comes on so suddenly that her first thought is that there was something wrong with the chicken she ate for dinner. She hadn't wanted to eat at the pub but Matt thought it would be nice to stay in one spot: have dinner then play chess.

No, it's not food poisoning. The edges of the sensations aren't sharp enough for that. This is ... an ache. And with each laugh from Matt it pulses.

Her father used to say, 'Jealousy tells you what you want' – and she thinks that's what this is. She didn't recognise it straightaway because she's never felt it before.

So, she wants Matt. That's what her body is telling her and it's a revelation.

Intellectually, she's interested in him. They've spent considerable amounts of time together over the past few months and he has many qualities she likes. Despite the fact she enjoys kissing him, however, there just hasn't been the pull she was expecting – to the point where she's been wondering if she's attracted to men at all. She hasn't met any women she's attracted to, either, so hasn't had proof one way or the other. But now here it is: a physical manifestation of ... what? Desire? Yes.

She shouldn't be surprised, she supposes: over the past few months she has reconnected with her body after years of separation. It used to be easier to think of it as a necessary companion rather than as part of her. That way she could believe that everything that had happened to it hadn't really happened to *her*. Except it did, and she's accepted that – with help. Help from Elaine, Theresa and Marie. Help from Matt. He was the first person to tell her that her body could achieve things: she could swim. He's been encouraging her ever since, often asking about her times to Little Beach and back, encouraging her to try harder, change her breathing. She's had a built-in coach.

More laughter, and now Matt glances over at her. There must be something written on her face because his own drops and he nods to the woman and returns to their table with his empty glass still in hand.

'That was an old school friend,' he says, looking nervous. 'Haven't seen her in years.'

'Oh,' is Leanne's only response, because she's still not reassured.

'She's here with her husband,' he says.

'Oh.' Now she gives him a quick smile.

Matt puts the glass on the table and tilts his head to the side. 'Are you jealous?'

Leanne stares at him. 'No,' she says. It's her first instinct, because she's sure Matt doesn't want a jealous girlfriend. She doesn't want to be a jealous girlfriend either.

'You are,' he says, a grin starting to form.

'I'm not,' she says, but doesn't sound as convincing this time.

He bends down, putting one hand on the table, his lips not far from hers. 'You don't have to admit it,' he says quietly, 'but I know it's true.'

They stare into each other's eyes and she can see him clearly. He has never tried to lie to her. If he thinks something, he tells her. If he wants to say something, he says it. The Matt he presents to the world is the Matt he is. If not, he's a terrific actor – but she's seen him fail to sugarcoat things too often to believe that. If one of his students isn't doing something right, he tells them. If a kid wants to win a blue ribbon at the school carnival but they're too slow to even come in third, he'll tell them.

She is the one not telling him the truth. But, then, she's had practice. For most of her adult life she's successfully concealed herself from everyone. Literally everyone. It took the ocean and three women who offered her unquestioning friendship for her to stop hiding. They've all embraced her.

'Yes, it is true,' she says after the staring has gone on for long enough.

'Ha!' he says, looking incredibly pleased. 'Well.' He puts his hands on his hips. 'And I was starting to think you were going off me.'

'Why?' She quickly searches her memory for an instance of this.

He frowns briefly. 'You, uh . . . you never let me get further than your front door, for one thing.' He holds up his hands. 'I have no interest in pressuring you for anything. But I would like to see where you live. You don't give me many clues, you know – about who you are.'

Leanne can see a bit of skin peeling off his nose where he's been burnt again. Always forgetting to wear his hat. She knows things about him like that. She knows he likes chocolate and golden Labradors but thinks the black ones are insane, and is no fan of small dogs of any variety. He loves his parents and doesn't see them enough, by his own reckoning. His grandma taught him to knit, and while he doesn't usually wear socks in winter he has knitted himself some to wear around the house to keep warm. He tried out for the national swimming team once but wasn't good enough, and seems cheerful about it. He likes to read the *Daily Mirror*. He listens to FM radio.

He doesn't know equivalent details about her, because revealing the small details might lead to revealing the big story, and she's been wanting to keep that from him. In case *he* goes off *her*. Wouldn't it be better, though, to find that out sooner rather than later?

'Do you really want to know who I am?' she says nervously, scared of the answer.

'Of course,' he says, sitting down.

'There's a reason why . . .' She inhales and closes her eyes for a second. 'Why you haven't been past my door. It's not because I'm messy.'

She's trying for levity, but knows she can't pull it off. She's not a light person.

He reaches across and takes her hands; she feels calmer.

'I didn't think that was the reason,' he says. 'Leanne, I – I kind of guessed there's something. You're . . . guarded. With men.'

She is surprised he's noticed that. 'I'm guarded with most adults,' she says, then smiles shyly. 'Somehow you slipped through.'

'It's because I'm charming,' he says, not smiling but squeezing her hands.

'You are,' she says, 'in your own way.'

His smile is small and kind. She breathes in and out. In and out.

'I've only had one experience with a – a man.'

As she holds his gaze she's proud of herself for pressing on. Of course, she's been practising: pressing on to Little Beach, not giving up on the others. On herself. She's trained for this moment.

'It went further than I wanted. Much, much further.'

She hopes she is conveying the truth to him with her eyes, because she doesn't want to say it all. She doesn't want to give it life by describing it exactly.

'I understand,' he says, his voice deeper. His hands still hold hers, and she's glad of that.

'There's more.' She sniffs and notices his irises growing slightly larger, then contracting. 'I got pregnant.'

Matt's mouth opens slightly and she knows she has to continue quickly, otherwise he's likely to think she has a child stashed away somewhere.

'I went through with it. I gave her up for adoption.'

He closes his mouth and bows his head, then lifts it. His thumbs are pressing into her as he leans across the table – knocking the chess pieces over – and kisses her on the lips.

'I knew you were brave,' he says when he sits back. 'I could tell that by the way you went about your swimming.' He nods slowly. 'Now I think you're the bravest person I know. To give me a chance.' He tilts his head again. 'Thank you.'

Leanne feels something that she'd call light-headedness if she didn't also feel anchored in the room, by his hands. It could be that she wants to laugh from relief. Or float away with happiness that Matt hasn't reacted in any number of other ways he could react. She's not sure what the feeling is, but hopes it lasts.

Releasing her left hand so he can restore the chess pieces, he winks and says, 'Now – queen to king's knight five. What are you going to do about it?'

She grins. 'I'm going to take you on,' she says, and giggles as he leans over for another kiss.

CHAPTER 44

'Thanks so much for looking after them,' Theresa says after Oliver and Sasha have disappeared into the back garden.

Elaine is sitting on the couch, perched forwards, waiting for news. Theresa knows this because she's the keeper of the news, but she's in no hurry to share it.

'And for organising the appointment,' she goes on. 'I don't know how you managed to find someone who does house calls on a Saturday.'

'James knew someone,' Elaine says lightly, as if it was the easiest thing in the world to organise and she didn't have to invite the doctor and his wife and children over for lunch. James hadn't extracted the price – she'd offered it. It seemed the polite thing to do. And, in the wash-up, not onerous. She would have done much more to ensure that Theresa saw a doctor.

'I really do appreciate you taking the kids. I couldn't ask Nonna to watch them while the doctor was here. It was her daughter who . . .' Theresa falters. 'Who, um . . . who died of breast cancer. Gloria. Besides, Nonna went to visit a friend. Who knew she has friends? I thought everyone hated her because she keeps winning their money.'

She can hear herself babbling, delaying the inevitable. As Elaine has probably guessed.

'You don't have to explain,' Elaine says. 'I was happy to have them. They're delightful.'

Theresa looks sceptical. 'That may be going too far.'

'Not at all. Is your grandmother back now?'

Theresa thinks of the moment when Nonna walked in the back door and could see that she'd been crying half the afternoon.

'Theresa,' she said as she waddled into the kitchen, her eyes narrowing, 'what is going on, hmm? You crying.'

Theresa shook her head quickly. 'It's nothing.'

'It's *something*.'

'It's not.'

'It *is*.'

She'd turned away, wishing her face wasn't the open book her mother always said it was.

Count to three, she told herself, *count to three or you'll start crying again.*

It was too late, though, because Nonna's hands were on her shoulders and Theresa's head was resting against her neck, and even though she's taller than Nonna now she felt like the little girl she used to be, crying because some kid at school had called her stupid or smelly or whatever the insult had been.

'*Bella mia*,' Nonna would croon, 'they just don't know you like I do.'

It always made her feel better. Safe.

But Nonna couldn't fix what was happening to her now, so Theresa stiffened her back.

'Theresa, do not hide from me,' Nonna said, her voice low.

'I'm not,' Theresa said softly, except of course she was hiding.

'Okay.' The expression on Nonna's face left no doubt that she didn't believe Theresa for one second. 'You come see me when you ready.'

After that Theresa had calmed down. And she's still feeling calm – relatively speaking.

'Yes, she's home.' Her smile is tight. 'Can't you smell the smoke?'

'Ah.' Elaine nods. 'I can.'

At that moment Oliver runs in, squirting a water pistol. Sasha follows him, squealing.

'*Ollie!*' Theresa cries, getting to her feet.

He stops and gives Theresa that 'who – me?' face all kids perfect at an early age.

'Who said you could use the water pistol in the house?'

She's mortified that her children have chosen *right now* to show how undisciplined they can be – and even more mortified to think they might have been like this with Elaine today. Elaine's children are probably perfectly behaved English gentlemen.

'Nonna asked me to use it to put out her cigarette,' Oliver says innocently, and Theresa can almost hear her grandmother cackling from the back garden.

'Is her cigarette in here?' she says, putting her hands on her hips.

He pouts. 'No.'

'Then I suggest you take the water pistol, and your sister, outside.'

'Mu-um, it's not faaa-irrr!'

Theresa gives him a stern look. 'Life isn't fair, and the sooner you get used to it, the better.' It's exactly what her mother used to say to her in the same kind of situation.

She nods in the direction of the garden, and is only slightly mollified when he takes his sister's hand to lead her out of the room.

'Sorry about that,' she says as she sits down on the couch near Elaine.

'No need to apologise. And there was nothing like that while we were at the zoo.' Elaine winks. 'Just to reassure you.'

'Thanks.' Theresa smooths her dress.

'So?' Elaine says, and she makes it last. *Soooooo?*

'So!' Theresa replies, as if they're playing a game. It's no game, though. No game and no fun.

'Theresa.' Elaine frowns.

Theresa takes a moment to admire her lovely English skin that is completely unmarked because she didn't grow up in the sun.

'*Theresa.*'

'Oh.' She knows she's stalling. She just doesn't want to say a particular thing out loud. 'Yeah, I, um, have to go to a specialist.'

Elaine nods. 'Yes, that's to be expected.'

Theresa makes a face. 'The GP was a bit noncommittal about what it could be but, um . . . he doesn't think it's good. The lump's quite big.' She forces a smile. 'I don't think it's a pimple.'

Elaine doesn't look worried, which makes Theresa relax a little. 'All right, so when's your specialist appointment?' she asks.

'Next week. The doctor made a call and got me in. Said it's his friend from uni or something.'

Theresa remembers how pleased the doctor seemed that he could organise this for her. Like he was doing her a favour. She supposes he was, but she still feels like it's a sentence.

'Great,' Elaine says brightly. 'That's great. I'll take the kids again if you like.'

The fear that's been sitting in Theresa's belly releases a little. If Elaine is being this chirpy, maybe she has nothing to worry about.

'Are you going to tell Marie and Leanne?' Elaine asks.

'Um . . . not yet. No. Nothing to tell, is there?'

Elaine gives her a look. A somewhat scolding look. '*Theresa.*'

'What?'

'Wouldn't you want to know if it were them?'

Theresa's sigh is intentionally one of exasperation. 'I suppose.'

'I know they'll want to know,' Elaine says quietly.

The sound of more shrieking floats in from outside.

'*OLIVER!*' Theresa yells.

The shrieking stops.

'He's not a bad kid,' she says to Elaine. 'He's just . . .' She shrugs. 'Spirited.'

'He's a boy,' Elaine says, smiling wistfully. 'I remember when mine were young – they spent so much time running around that I thought there was something wrong with them. I told my mother. She said, "Little girls sit in the corner and scheme. Little boys let it all out physically. Which would you prefer?"' She arches an eyebrow. 'I won't tell you what I said.'

'Sasha doesn't scheme,' Theresa says with her own wistful smile. Her daughter may still be moping a little but has never been troublesome – not unless she's indulging her brother in one of his activities. Theresa should be grateful they're both healthy. The thought makes her inhale sharply.

'What about Andrew?' Elaine says, breaking into her thoughts.

'Hm?'

'Andrew.' Now both of Elaine's eyebrows are up. 'Are you going to tell him?'

Theresa shakes her head, but not too hard. She wants Elaine to think she's considered it, because that would be the reasonable thing to do: she should tell the man who's still her husband that she has a potentially serious health problem. Except he wouldn't be interested.

'I don't think he's ever once asked me how I am. So I don't think he'll care.'

'I'm sure he would,' Elaine says in a vaguely chastising tone.

Theresa laughs in that harsh way she knows she's developed over the past few months. 'Then you don't know my husband. And before you suggest I tell my parents: no. Mum will just say we're cursed, because of Aunt Gloria. She thinks she has a bad back because the family's cursed – Nonna's brother had a back injury once and Mum keeps saying she's inherited it. An injury!'

She throws up her hands, but it's to hide the fact that she would dearly love to tell her mother. After the GP left today Theresa wanted nothing more than to have her mother hold her and tell her that everything will be all right. Except her mother can't know that, and neither can she.

'Well, I'm not going to push,' Elaine says. 'And I think you probably want to get on with your evening.' She stands, and Theresa joins her.

'I'm sorry,' Theresa says. She tucks her hair behind one ear; it's what she used to do when her parents were cross with her.

'What for?'

'For being difficult.'

'Oh, silly.' Elaine hugs her. 'You are the least difficult person imaginable. I just want to help. And I'm not sure how to go about it, so that's my solution.'

'You *are* helping,' Theresa says. 'Thank you. So much.'

'Mu-um, we're hungry,' Oliver singsongs as he skips into the room.

'That's my cue,' says Elaine. She puts her mouth near Theresa's ear. 'And let me know when that specialist appointment is – I can take the children again if you need.'

Theresa nods quickly and mouths her thanks, then Elaine hops into her Renault and drives home, leaving Theresa to wrangle two children now covered in dirt and grass into a bath, through dinner and bedtime. She is glad of the activity, to have her mind filled with the minutiae of running a household and caring for others, instead of the yawning uncertainty that will take her over as soon as the house is quiet.

CHAPTER 45

Marie would recognise Theresa's figure anywhere: she has seen it so many times now, in dim light, walking towards her across the sand. But soon she'll have to make adjustments to the familiar image that's stored in her memory, because as Theresa said when she called the other day to tell her about the surgery: 'I'm going to be lopsided!' She was so chirpy, as if she was talking about a pair of socks that aren't both the same length. Not the kind of lopsided where they take off a breast.

Theresa tried to make light of it. 'It's not that big a lump – well, it's not a golf ball or anything. Still, big or small, they take off the boob. That's what the doctor said. They take it off then find out what the problem is.' She made a sound too much like a laugh to be appropriate. 'Which seems like a lot of fuss, really, but he's not giving me a choice. Guess it's just as well I've finished breastfeeding.'

Despite the forced jollity, Marie felt numb. Her Theresa – *their* Theresa – with cancer? Not confirmed yet, of course – they won't know until they do the pathology – but that's what it seems like. Theresa said her aunt had it. Died of it.

Marie's family was big on arthritis and bad hearts, which is part of her reason for keeping up the swimming; cancer has never darkened her door. Not up close. Not like this.

As Theresa draws nearer, Marie puts on her biggest smile then realises that Theresa will recognise it's fake. She doesn't need fake now. She needs friends.

'My last swim and the sky can't even be bothered smiling,' Theresa says, gesturing at the low cloud. 'How dare it!'

Now Marie's smile is real. 'How are you, love?' she says, throwing one arm around her and planting a kiss on her cheek.

'That's new,' says Theresa. 'You've never greeted me with a kiss for a swim. You must think I'm not coming back.'

'Don't be ridiculous,' Marie says, although she had the fleeting thought earlier today. And banished it, in case it was bad luck. She's not superstitious, but she said a quick prayer to ask forgiveness for her thoughts.

Theresa exhales loudly. 'I haven't told Leanne yet.'

'Oh.'

'I haven't had the chance. I haven't been at the hospital in ages, and I didn't want to tell her before a swim. And when I've called her place she hasn't been home.' Theresa makes the face of a child who hopes she's not in trouble. 'But I'm going to have to tell her today.'

'Yes, you are. Morning, Elaine.'

'Hello.' Elaine kisses Theresa too, and now Theresa looks upset.

'You *both* think I'm not coming back!' she says.

'Not true!' Elaine says with assurance. 'I'd kiss you every morning if I thought I could get away with it, but that would make Trevor far too happy.'

Marie glances towards the clubhouse, where Trev is animatedly discussing something with a younger man. He's been keeping his distance lately – ever since Leanne beat him one morning after he decided he'd race her to the point. She didn't know she was racing him but was faster regardless.

'Here's Leanne now,' Marie says under her breath.

'Have you told her yet?' asks Elaine, a little more loudly. 'Oh,' she adds, as Theresa looks at her with alarm.

'Good morning,' Leanne says happily.

She's now in the habit of smiling each morning and Marie barely recognises the girl who didn't say boo a few months ago. She's crediting the boyfriend for the change, although Leanne doesn't say much about him.

They busy themselves folding towels and clothing, picking up goggles and caps.

'So this is my last swim for a while,' Theresa says as she pulls her cap over her head.

Leanne stares at her. 'What are you talking about?'

'Sorry, Leanne,' Theresa says. 'I tried calling you but you haven't been home.'

'I've been at Matt's,' Leanne says quickly. 'What do you mean – your last swim?' She looks at Marie then Elaine.

Marie tries to keep her face in neutral because this is Theresa's story to tell, but what she really wants to do is say that she's worried for her friend, that she wishes Theresa didn't have to go through something this brutal, and that she would take it all away from her if she could.

'I'm having a bit of surgery at the hospital in a couple of days.' Theresa takes a breath. 'I need to have a mastectomy.'

'What?' Leanne says. '*What?*'

Theresa shrugs casually, like she's just said she's going to trade in her car. Marie doesn't know if she's playing it down as a way of managing her own worries, and can't begrudge her that if she is.

'I have this lump,' Theresa is saying. 'I . . . let it go too long.'

'When did you find out?' Leanne says sharply.

'I've had the lump for a while,' Theresa explains. 'I just didn't do anything about it. The specialist told me a couple of days ago about the surgery. I'm lucky he can fit me in so soon.'

Leanne stares at Theresa.

'I'm still me,' Theresa says, her mouth puckering and a vertical crease appearing on her forehead. 'I'm not different. I'm not going to be different. Leanne?'

Leanne lets out her breath in a rush. 'Yes,' she says. 'Sorry.'

'Are you all right?' Elaine asks, putting a hand on Leanne's shoulder, startling her.

'Yes!' Leanne says shrilly.

'It's okay, Lee,' Marie says, squeezing her other shoulder. 'She's not dying.'

'Not yet!' Theresa says, too brightly.

Marie can see it now: Theresa's bravado is indeed covering her fear. It's there in the slight twitch of her eye and the way she's twisting her mouth. She never used to do that.

'I'm sorry,' Leanne says, dabbing at her eyes with her towel.

'Don't be,' says Theresa and smiles awkwardly. Then she looks down at the sand and wipes her eyes. 'I'm flattered I can get that kind of reaction out of you! You're usually as cool as a cucumber.' She tries to laugh but tears now spill onto her cheeks. 'Christ, this is inconvenient,' she mutters, putting her hands on her hips and turning towards the ocean. 'Sorry, Marie.'

'That's quite all right. I'm sure He'd understand.'

Theresa sniffs. 'I always saw myself going into old age with two boobs, you know?'

'You can get a falsie,' says Marie. 'No one'll know the difference.'

'They bloody well will!' Theresa isn't looking at them now. Marie can see her shoulders shaking. 'Anyway, *I'll* know,' she says, so softly they almost can't hear it.

Marie steps in front of Theresa and takes hold of both her shoulders. 'You'll always be the complete package to me. I don't care if you have one breast, three or none. You're our girl.'

Theresa starts hiccup-crying.

Elaine turns half away, one hand against the side of her head to hide her tears.

'Come on, you lot,' says Marie. 'We need to wash off this salt water with some salt water.'

'I'm certainly ready for a swim,' Leanne says loudly, surprising Marie. 'Theresa, how about you?'

Theresa turns towards her. 'Yes,' she replies. 'I'm ready.'

'Let's go,' Leanne says. 'Elaine, I'll race you.'

'Race me?' Elaine pulls off her T-shirt and shorts and throws them to the sand. 'You'll need a head start if you have any chance of winning.'

Elaine scoops up her cap and goggles and is halfway to the water's edge before Marie even thinks to get ready.

'You go,' she calls to Theresa, who is looking at her enquiringly.

Theresa shakes her head. 'I'll wait. I'm in no hurry.'

Within seconds Marie is by her side and they walk together into the water, the foam hitting their shins at the same time. Pulling their goggles over their heads, they dive under a wave and strike out in the same direction as Leanne and Elaine, keeping pace on their way to Little Beach. Marie lets the others go ahead of her, watching three forms that are now so familiar, and which will not be in this formation again for quite some time. But she will not let herself become maudlin. This is not an ending, just a change. She has become used to change, and she'll become used to this one – but she will look forward to the day when the four of them will swim to Little Beach once more.

AUTUMN 1984

AUTUMN 1984

CHAPTER 46

Theresa remembers counting backwards from ten and making it as far as eight. Right before that, she heard the surgeon say hello to her. A little while before that, she had an injection to relax her before the anaesthetic. The anaesthetist had gentle hands and hard eyes. Theresa didn't know if that was the right combination, but obviously he knew what he was doing because here she is, waking up.

'Theresa,' a woman's voice is saying. She doesn't recognise it. Should she? Where is she?

'Theresa, you're in Recovery. The operation is over. Mr Phillips said it went well.'

Mr Phillips – that's her surgeon. She was calling him Dr Phillips until one of the nurses corrected her and said that surgeons are called 'Mr'. Although she never found out why.

'How are you feeling?' The nurse is bending over her now, not smiling, but not looking worried. That must be a good thing.

'A bit . . . um, woozy.' Theresa tries to swallow and it feels like her mouth is sticking together. 'Am I going to be sick?'

'Not likely.' The nurse pats her hand. 'Although it can feel like that. You'll be here for a little while, then we'll move you to the ward.'

And after that? What am I meant to do with one boob?

That's the question she really wants to ask but she doesn't think anyone has an answer.

Her bravado in front of Marie and Elaine and Leanne – talking about how she's going to use a falsie and it will all be fine – never took root in her. She can be a good actress when she needs to be and she thinks she had them all believing she's okay with all of this. Except she's not.

She swallows again as her head seems to swirl, and wishes her mother were here. In the end she decided to tell her parents and grandmother that she was having 'a procedure', because the stress of keeping it secret was worse than any reaction they could come up with. They don't know everything, though – she didn't give details, just said she would be in hospital for a couple of days or so.

Although now she's wondering why she insisted this surgery would be 'nothing, Mum, just a little op'. It was to spare her parents the worry, except she's set herself up to feel like the loneliest person in the world right now, with no one to sit by her bed and hold her hand and tell her everything's going to be all right, the way her mum used to do when she was a child and sick in bed, with lemonade and a straw, and a cool hand on her forehead and a lullaby to help her go to sleep.

It's horrible, this business of being alone after they've cut off a part of you. Nurses bustle around to other patients who all seem to be more important, although everyone probably gets the same amount of attention. Everyone's coming around from being out of it. There's probably someone worse off than her. Maybe they had a leg off. Now *that* would be bad. You can get by with one boob, but one leg would be a lot harder. She's lucky, and she needs to remember that when they come back and tell her it's cancer. Because she knows it will be, just like Aunt Gloria.

Then what? That's the bit she doesn't want to think about.

Aunt Gloria withered away and died within a few months. Her kids were grown-up though. Oliver and Sasha are only in primary school.

Theresa has no interest in dying just yet. She feels pretty good too – well, not right now, because of the anaesthetic, but with the swimming she's been feeling fit. It's bloody inconvenient, this lump business, and not least because she'll have to miss swimming for who knows how long.

That's all ahead of her. Right now she needs to get through the aftermath of this surgery, get back to the kids and keep going with the business of being a single mum. She's been putting that off, given this other pressing matter, but she can't do it forever.

'We're ready to take you up now, Theresa.'

It's the same nurse. Theresa must have been daydreaming for longer than she realised if it's time to go to the ward.

She closes her eyes as they wheel her into a lift and up to another floor. She doesn't want to see the rest of the hospital because she's going to try to focus just on herself and her recovery. That's what Elaine suggested she do.

'Here we are,' says a different nurse – she must have appeared while Theresa was in transit. 'Let's get you settled. How's your pain?'

'Fine. I mean – I don't have any.'

Which strikes Theresa as strange: she's had a breast removed and she feels . . . nothing. Except misshapen, sure, because she has dressings and whatnot over her chest, but there's no pain. There should be. She should have the sensation of having lost something she was quite fond of, really, if she thinks about it. Her boobs have seen better days, but they fed her babies and looked all right in a tight dress, with the right bra. Thankfully tight dresses have been in her past for a while, because she's not likely to wear anything form-fitting for the rest of her life. No matter how good the falsie is, it's hardly going to match her remaining boob.

'Now, you have a visitor,' says the nurse, smiling brightly.

'Do I?'

Maybe Elaine is here – although she said she wouldn't visit today because no patient wants anyone to see them straight out of surgery. 'Not even the people who love you the most,' she'd said, 'because you feel horrendous and it's just too much work to be polite.' So it's probably not Elaine.

'Your husband's here,' the nurse says, and before Theresa can protest she's out the door and returning with Andrew.

'I'll leave you to it!'

The nurse is gone but Theresa wishes she wasn't, because Andrew is glaring at her and if she thought she didn't have the energy to deal with people who care about her, she really doesn't have anything in the tank to deal with him.

'When were you going to tell me, hey?'

Andrew's arms are crossed and his feet are planted wide apart. She's seen him use that stance when he's arguing with someone who thinks they're being charged too much for a new muffler.

'Andrew, I'm not feeling great,' she says, leaning back against the pillow. 'I've just had surgery.'

And I haven't seen you in weeks, so why would I tell you? That's what she really wants to say, but she certainly doesn't want to have an argument right now.

'Which you *didn't tell me about.*'

'I *did* tell you,' she says, trying not to waste any energy getting upset.

'You just said surgery. You didn't say what for.'

'And you didn't ask!' Her voice is shrill and she clenches and unclenches her hands, telling herself to stay calm.

She hadn't wanted to give him the details of the operation because she was sure he'd use it as an excuse to say she isn't looking after 'his house' properly. That's what he's been calling it since he moved out. His house. Not their home.

'I shouldn't have to!'

He steps closer and she flinches. Which makes him stop and drop his arms. And a look crosses his face – Theresa could swear it was concern, if she didn't know better.

'Theresa, look,' he says, his voice calmer, 'I just wanted to see how you are.'

'How did you find out?'

'One of the nurses here is married to one of my boys. She told him you were admitted this morning. He asked me how I felt about you having a breast off.' He's glaring again. 'I had to pretend I knew.'

Theresa feels the white heat of shame that her private business is known by Andrew's employees. 'Nurses aren't meant to talk about patients like that.'

He keeps glaring.

'Why is he asking you about it anyway? Don't they know you're not at home any more?' she says, not able to resist making that point. Why should she cop his frustration because she didn't tell him something that, as far as she's concerned, he no longer has a right to know?

He looks down and shakes his head slowly. 'Nuh. I told Chook to keep it quiet.'

Because, of course, Chook's sister knows exactly why Andrew isn't at home. But it's not the time to say that. It's never going to be the time. She's not going to focus on the past when she has to concentrate on getting out of here and back home to the people who really love her.

'Well, sorry if I made things difficult for you,' she says. Appeasing him is the fastest way to ensure he leaves. 'I didn't want to bother you.'

'Where are the kids?'

'With Marie.'

'Who's Marie?'

'I swim with her. I've told you about her.' She winces as she shifts so she can sit up straighter. She may not be in pain but she is restricted by whatever it is the doctor has done to sew her back together.

'You let someone else take our kids so you could come in here and have your boob cut off?'

'You've been a bit *busy*,' Theresa snaps.

She can see he's surprised, because she's not given to losing her temper, but all she can perceive is a man who is thinking only of himself and not caring one iota about her. It's the story of their marriage, and of the end of their marriage, and now he's even making the removal of her breast about him and what she hasn't told him. If she wasn't already starting to feel relieved that Susie's taken him off her hands, she would be now.

'So?' he says. 'You still could have told me.'

'So you could do *what*, *exactly*, Andrew? You wouldn't have given up work to look after the kids. I would still have had to make arrangements. And you have *not once* asked me how I am.'

'Is everything all right in here?' It's the nurse, poking her head into the room.

Theresa wants to tell her that it's not all right, but you're not meant to air your dirty laundry, are you? Even if it's managed to drag itself into your hospital room.

She stares at the nurse, then at Andrew. Then says, 'I'm feeling tired. I wasn't expecting to see anyone so soon after surgery.'

The nurse steps all the way into the room. 'Best leave her to rest now,' she tells Andrew. 'You can come back later.'

'Or tomorrow,' Theresa says.

Andrew glances from the nurse to Theresa. 'Fine,' he says, before shoving his hands in the pockets of his work shorts and stalking from the room.

'Or come back never,' Theresa mutters.

'Get some rest,' the nurse says pointedly, drawing the curtains around Theresa's bed.

For the first time Theresa is alone with her solitary breast, and her wound and her dressings and the drip that is attached to her arm. She's alone with thoughts of her children and how much she wants to see them. Alone with her fears of what comes next, of the unknown.

But she knows one thing for sure: she doesn't want to be married to Andrew any more, and as soon as she can she's going to get that divorce, even if it means she no longer has the house.

As hard as it is to get comfortable so she can sleep, Theresa closes her eyes and thinks of her last swim with the others. She goes over each stroke, each kick, each wave – and each laugh, each smile, each kind word. The memories comfort her until she drifts off.

CHAPTER 47

'Look at you, all gussied up in bandages,' Marie says at Theresa's bedside.

On her walk up the hill to the hospital she decided she'd be cheerful, and now she's seen how forlorn Theresa is looking she's glad she did.

'I'd rather be gussied up in a nice dress and going out for cocktails,' Theresa says. She lifts her arm. 'Of course, my friend the intravenous drip would have to come too.'

'We all need a dance partner, love.' Marie bends down and kisses Theresa's cheek. 'We missed you this morning.'

'You went swimming without me?' Theresa's mouth drops open. 'How dare you!'

'We dared. It wasn't the same, of course.'

'You have to say that.'

'I think you know me well enough to know that just because I have to do something, it doesn't mean I will.' Marie puts two books on the bedside table. 'Here you go – some Barbara Cartlands. Quick, easy, and you can leave them behind.'

Theresa makes a face. 'Maybe I'll get some tips about how to pick a better husband next time.' Her expression softens. 'Thank you, that's very thoughtful.'

'The kids are with Gus,' Marie says, gesturing to the sole chair. Theresa nods and she sits down. 'In case you're wondering. And he was with them this morning while we were swimming. He took them for a run along the sand.'

'They were up that early?' Theresa looks sceptical.

'We didn't give them a choice. Besides, he promised them an ice cream.' Marie winks. 'We figure a few days of bribery won't hurt, then you can have them back.'

'Gee, thanks.' Theresa's smile is tight. 'Are they okay?'

Marie waves a hand. 'They're fine. They're tormenting Charlie Brown and helping me make cakes. They've barely noticed you're not around.'

It was mostly true. Last night both children insisted that they had to see their mother before going to sleep and Marie ended up singing lullabies and rubbing their backs until they calmed down. Sasha is too young to think of what specifically is happening to her mother but Marie is sure that Oliver has worked out something is wrong – he may be rambunctious but he's sharp, and she saw the worried look on his face when he asked about Theresa.

Theresa shifts position and looks uncomfortable doing it. 'They've always wanted a dog.'

'Well, they have one now,' Marie says brightly. 'For a few days.'

She sits back and looks at Theresa, who looks at her. A thousand small emotions flit across her friend's face.

'There aren't many things as difficult as this,' Marie says after a time. 'You're being very calm about it, but I know it's hard to cope with.'

'I don't feel calm,' Theresa says, strangling the last word. 'I feel like I don't know what I'm going to do next and how I'm going to manage.'

Marie wants to be reassuring but she also doesn't want to lie. 'That's because you *can't* know what you're going to do next. You just have to get through this day. And the next. Then the next. There's no other option.'

She looks away from Theresa. When she looks back, she can tell she is being scrutinised.

'Norm's death must have been hard,' Theresa says quietly. 'It was.'

The look they exchange is frank: one wounded bird to another, both of them flapping their remaining wing and hoping they can still fly away.

The patient in the next bed is listening to the radio. Marie didn't realise this is a shared ward, although the curtain drawn around the next bed should have tipped her off. She looks towards the window, which gives her a glimpse of harbour but no encouragement. Despite her deepening friendship with Theresa, she hasn't revealed that much of herself yet, and they don't have the shorthand that Marie has with Gwen.

'Mainly because it made me remember a lot of things I'd forgotten,' she says. 'Or tried to forget. When I lost my boy.'

Marie immediately thinks it's selfish to say this to Theresa now. Then she thinks it's a distraction, so may be a good thing. When she sees Theresa crying, she knows it's neither.

'Oh, Marie,' Theresa says, her chin puckering and her forehead collapsing. 'I forgot.'

'Don't you cry, or I will,' Marie says. She tries to blink back her own tears, because she's been brave about this for a long time, so she should keep it going now.

'We haven't spoken about it really, have we?' Theresa sighs heavily. 'I didn't want to pry at the time. And then there was no other time, was there? It's so sad, Marie. That you lost him.'

Marie nods. 'It is. But my life is how it's been. You know what I mean? There is no other life in which he lives.'

Theresa looks down and pulls at the sheet that covers her abdomen. 'I'm wondering . . .' she starts, then lifts her eyes to meet Marie's, and there is anguish in them. 'I'm wondering if there's another life in which I live.'

Although Marie saw Theresa's fear before this operation, it still strikes her as discordant: Theresa, who attacks waves and open water with laughter and brio, hasn't seemed like a candidate for fear. But of course she's afraid. Of course a woman who's had a breast cut off is worried about what it means. If Marie had thought for half a second about her friend and not about herself, she'd have realised that.

'Don't be ridiculous, my girl,' she says with as much authority as she can muster. If Theresa is scared, Marie needs to be the bossy boots who makes her feel as though there's nothing to be worried about. 'We'll get you sorted. You're going to be out of here in no time, and then we'll tackle the next steps. You're not alone in this. I won't allow it.'

'But my aunt died of breast cancer,' Theresa says softly.

'You don't even know if it's cancer yet!' Marie says.

Theresa stares at her. '*Marie.*'

'All right.' Marie sighs. 'It probably is. But you're not your aunt. You're my friend and we're getting you through this. And by "we" I mean Elaine and Leanne too. If we can see each other half naked every morning, we can certainly help you with one breast missing.'

Theresa looks surprised, then she starts to laugh. 'How did this happen?' she says.

'What? The breast cancer?'

'No!' She keeps laughing. 'How did we get here – you and me? Elaine and Leanne? I didn't even know you two years ago.'

Marie looks at this woman she has come to hold so dear and it feels like she's known her for aeons. Perhaps she has, and it has just taken them until now to recognise it.

'Bluebottles have a way of bonding people,' is what she offers instead.

'Nasty buggers,' Theresa says knowingly.

'Just like your husband, right?' Marie says.

She is rewarded with Theresa's shrieking laugh, and the nurse checking in to see if everything is fine.

Then the lunch trolley arrives and Marie makes a retort about the parlous state of the jelly on the tray, before she is told that visiting hours are over. She leaves Theresa trying to negotiate a chicken sandwich she doesn't want to eat.

She's about to walk out of the hospital and home when she decides to make a detour.

The hospital's chapel is non-denominational and Marie believes – hopes – the Lord will forgive her for that, and also for the fact that she's been so happy lately she hasn't felt as though she's needed Him as much. She's been feeling some guilt about that happiness while Theresa has her travails, yet knows Theresa would be the first to tell her not to do that.

Still, there it is, and here she is, crossing herself and kneeling in a pew.

Her prayer is the same one she's been making every day since Theresa told her about the surgery. Usually she says it to herself while she swims, but today she feels the need for rein-forcements. In this quiet space she can be more direct. More demanding, maybe. Because she wants her God to pull Theresa through this victoriously.

After she's made her request, Marie leaves the hospital and walks down the hill. The day is cool, verging on cold. Autumn is becoming entrenched and soon they may take up walking again. Or maybe not. Elaine and Leanne are veterans now. Like her, they may find it harder to give up the winter sea than to embrace it.

Before long she sees Gus at the side gate, holding Oliver's and Sasha's hands, and she gives thanks for the bounty that is in her life even as she continues to pray to God to take care of Theresa, one of the greatest bounties of all. Because Marie is firmly of the belief that everything that has come into her life over the past year – almost two years – is because of that woman. Theresa, her big heart, and a stretch of water that has drawn in companions Marie never dared to dream she would find; companions who've opened her heart to a possibility she never thought existed: a new love, with all its strangeness and familiarity.

'Hello, darling,' Gus says, kissing her on the lips as she reaches them. 'We've missed you.'

'And I've missed you,' she says, as the children rush to tell her about their day, and Charlie Brown sits by the door, waiting for her, and the smell of whatever Gus is making for dinner wafts down the hall.

CHAPTER 48

Leanne dips a toe in the water then steps back. It seems to be colder than yesterday. However, she won't be deterred. She's already decided to keep going as long as she can stand it, and perhaps beyond, because as nice as walking is, it's just not the same. There's no sense of achievement at the end of a walk the way there is each day she swims. Even though they're still swimming the same distance, she can experiment with going faster and changing strokes. Matt has been encouraging her to try backstroke. She feels like she's going to drown half the time but she's improving. She may even practise this morning and surprise him when he's back.

For the Easter long weekend he's gone to his family's beach house a couple of hours away. He called her yesterday to say his brother had turned up unexpectedly and he didn't know if he wanted to stay.

'I'm not sure if I can give you advice about that,' Leanne said. 'I'm not the best at family relationships.'

'But you're talking to them,' Matt said, and she could almost see the look of pride on his face. He'd told her he was proud of her for staying in contact with her mother and, slowly, her father. Her father's is the anger she's found the hardest to forget.

She puts her whole foot in the water and smiles as she thinks of Matt's warm hand taking hers as they walked back to her place after dinner on Thursday night. He felt strong, and safe. Each time she sees him she feels less on guard. Hardly at all now.

'Good morning, Lee,' says Marie. She puts a hand on Leanne's back and kisses her on the cheek.

They're all kissing each other hello now. It's not a sporting group any more; it's a meeting of friends.

'Hello, ladies,' Elaine says as she strides over the last of the soft sand and meets them on the hard. 'How was your Good Friday lunch, Marie?'

'Wonderful. We went for a barbecue in that park on the headland. Gus did the cooking.' She smiles.

'Fish, I presume?' Elaine says, taking off her long-sleeved top.

'Of course. Morning mass, fish for lunch – I like the rituals.' She winks. 'What about you, Lee? A bit of time to yourself with Matt gone?'

Leanne nods. 'And I'm working today. I thought I'd take the long weekend so some of the others could go away.' She shrugs. 'I don't mind it over Easter. It's quiet. Like Christmas.'

They stand there looking at each other.

'It's funny,' says Marie. 'I still keep waiting for Theresa to arrive.'

Elaine laughs with relief. 'Me too. I spoke to her last night and she said she wished she could join us.'

'I called her in the afternoon,' says Leanne.

'So did I,' says Marie. 'She probably felt bombarded.'

They all know, though, that it's better to bombard her than not. They all call every day, and visit when they can. No one wants to overload her with visits, because even though she says she enjoys them she's still recovering, and simply being with the children takes energy, let alone having conversations. Besides, Theresa's nonna has turned into a bodyguard and none of them thinks she'll let them in if they turn up more regularly.

'How are you going, Lee?' Marie says. 'You keep so quiet I forget to ask sometimes.'

'You don't have to ask,' Leanne says, because she's content to not be the focus of enquiry.

'I wouldn't find out otherwise, would I?' Marie says drily. 'You are what is known in the business as a closed shop. Which I understand,' she adds quickly. 'But that doesn't mean I'm not going to ask questions.'

Leanne accepts her fate. 'I'm well,' she says as a seagull hops by. Then she notices something different. 'Is that . . . a pelican?' she says, gasping.

'Sure is,' says Marie. 'I haven't seen those here for years.' She looks around. 'There have to be others. They're rarely alone.' Her head swivels to the left. 'There – two more.'

Elaine looks delighted as she takes a step closer to the water.

'I loved *Storm Boy* when I was little,' Leanne says dreamily.

'Nicole loved it too.' Marie's eyes follow the majestic birds. 'I preferred *Sun on the Stubble* when I was reading to her. It's a riot.'

'I've never seen a pelican before,' Elaine says, watching as one of them takes flight. 'They're magnificent.'

'The other two will go now – watch,' Marie says, and within seconds they do.

'Maybe they're parents following their young.' Elaine's neck is craned to watch them as they fly towards Little Beach.

'Speaking of which . . .' Leanne can feel Marie staring at her. 'It's been a while since we've had an update, Lee.'

That's true. Theresa's medical condition has engrossed them all; and Leanne's also been talking to Matt about her family, so she hasn't felt the need to talk to Marie and Elaine. But that doesn't mean she shouldn't. It occurs to her that they might be interested in her life without expecting her to need them for anything.

'Mum wants us all to have lunch together at home,' she starts. 'But I'm not sure. There are . . .' She considers how to phrase it. 'There are some things that are hard to forget.'

She closes her eyes and sees her father's furious face, hears the things he said to her, feels the sensation of him slapping her. Being there with him, with them all, would seem too much like a re-enactment of the last time they were all there.

Matt has suggested she invite them to Shelly Bay and she's thinking about it. 'I could be there,' he'd said, looking hopeful. 'For back-up.'

'Has your mother said if your father is sorry for what happened?' Elaine prods gently.

'Yes. But maybe she's just saying that because she wants it all to stay in the past.'

Leanne isn't sure whether she believes that or just wants to, because it's easier to not reconcile with them all. There's work ahead if she walks down that path, just when her life feels carefree for the first time.

'I guess you won't know unless you talk to him,' Marie says. 'You'll hear it in his voice. Were you close before?'

Leanne thinks of the man who built her a cubby house – just for her, so she had a space away from her brothers, even though they'd always try to get into it. She thinks of him patiently drawing illustrations for her school projects because she was hopeless at drawing.

'Yes,' she says.

'Then that's not gone, love,' Marie says. 'Now, let's get in the water. It's colder out here than it will be in there.'

They've been talking so long the sun is further above the horizon than usual and its light turns the bay into a pool of gold. Near them the first surfer of the day is paddling out.

They quickly discard their clothes and wade in. After a few seconds underwater, the cold disappears and the water becomes the balm it always is.

CHAPTER 49

Elaine parks her old Renault in front of Marie's charming home. She's noticed this house before on her many long walks around Shelly Bay and wondered at its age. Sometimes even wished she were living there.

As she gets out of the car she glances across the street to a building that has the name *Therese* over its doorway and smiles at the coincidence. Not exactly the same, but close enough.

Theresa is the reason Elaine's here today: to help Marie with Oliver and Sasha. Gus is working and when Marie mentioned this morning, after the swim, that she'd be alone with the children after she picks them up from school, Elaine asked if she could join her. She has grown fond of Theresa's pigeon pair.

Theresa has been insisting that she's 'all right, really' and doesn't need any more help, but Marie's been insisting that she rests as much as she can. If she takes the children for a few hours, Theresa can sleep or read or watch television – whatever she likes.

'*Bonjour*,' Marie says as she opens the door and kisses Elaine on the cheek.

'You speak French?'

Marie colours. 'A little.'

'*On peut parler en français si tu veux,*' Elaine offers, although her French skills have grown rusty since she left the northern hemisphere.

'Maybe. One day. I'm, uh . . . not that fluent.'

Elaine gets the message and steps inside. As they walk down the hall she hears the sound of chattering children.

'How are they?' she asks.

'They're kids,' Marie says, smiling. 'They're focused on what's going on right now. Which happens to be making mud pies.'

She leads the way out the back, to where Sasha and Oliver are sitting in a garden bed, dirt on their faces and hands and feet, talking about who has the bigger clump of dirt and what they're going to do with it.

'I told them I'd hose them off at the end,' Marie says, folding her arms and looking down at the children with something resembling pride. 'I think they like the idea of that more than anything, so they're getting as dirty as possible.'

Elaine smiles to see the children unworried about their mother, or anything other than what they're doing right now. She wishes she could be like that, but she left it behind as soon as adolescence arrived.

'Hello, Ollie, hi, Sasha,' she calls.

'Hi, Lainey!' Sasha waves.

Oliver looks up and gives a nonchalant little-boy nod.

'That's new,' Elaine says. 'He used to be very happy to see me.'

'He's too cool sometimes, that kid,' Marie says, laughing. 'Come on, let's get a cuppa. We'll hear if they get into strife.'

The children burble away to each other as Elaine follows Marie into the house, noticing the shift from the warmth of the garden to the cool interior. Autumn is vacillating between cool and heat, throwing up the occasional day that recalls summer not long past. Elaine's own house doesn't give the same relief from this city's high temperatures, although she has started to adjust to the climate. She doesn't find herself resenting it any more; she doesn't grumble to herself about how lovely and mild English summers are. It would be ungrateful to do so when she has an ocean at the bottom of the hill and can stay in it all day if she wishes.

'So how are things?' Marie says as she turns on the kettle. 'I see you every day but we don't really chat much, do we?'

It's true: they don't. Elaine has found that the language created by swimming together – the way she has come to recognise the other women's facial expressions and signs of fatigue or joy or fear sometimes – obviates the need for much discussion. On many subjects, at least.

'Things are . . .' she starts, before realising that she doesn't have a neat answer. And Marie has enough to think about at the moment – she doesn't need Elaine whingeing about her transgressions. 'Fine,' she says with a tight-lipped smile.

'Love, I didn't come down in the last shower. I know you far too well to believe that little performance.' Marie cocks her head as if she's issuing a challenge.

Elaine inhales sharply through her nostrils. 'Yes. Perhaps you do.' Another tight smile.

'So?'

Elaine folds her arms. 'It's been easier to not say anything. Easier to hide.'

Marie's expression softens. 'You don't have to say, love. I didn't think it was anything serious.'

'Oh, it's not,' Elaine says breezily. 'Not really, in the scheme of things. I'm just a failure, that's all.'

'AA,' Marie states.

'Still going,' Elaine says, her chin lifting slightly, 'but I had to start again.'

Marie looks relieved. 'So you had a slip?'

'Yes.'

'That's all?'

Elaine frowns. 'Yes.'

'Well . . .' Marie starts laughing. 'If you thought it was going to stick the first time . . .'

'Shouldn't it?'

'No!' Marie chuckles. 'I'm sure you think that just because you're disciplined enough to turn up for a swim every morning, you should be able to stay off the grog. So now you're wondering what on earth happened, because you had a drink, and clearly if you'd just applied yourself the way you do to swimming, you'd be fine.'

'Yes,' Elaine mumbles.

'Elaine, my dear, that is not how it works.' Marie sighs. 'I wish it were. Alcohol is not sea water. Drinking is not good for you.'

'But giving it up is! Like swimming is good for me.' Elaine can hear that she sounds like she wants a gold star.

'True. But it's not the same thing. Slipping up just means you're human.' She gives Elaine a piercing look. 'Or maybe that's the part you don't like.'

Elaine stares at her, because she knows there's truth in that. She would like to think herself preternaturally able to cope, to rise above life's challenges. To glide, dare she say it, like a swan over troubles. Her behaviour over the past few months has been more like that of a fish caught in a net, flapping away, futilely searching for escape. She's been kidding herself about who she really is and Marie has seen right through it.

'You may be right,' she murmurs.

'I usually am.' Marie smiles and lifts the tea tray. 'Shall we sit on the verandah?'

'Sure.'

'And why don't you tell me more about your sons,' she adds, 'because we don't talk about them on the beach.' As she smiles, her eyes almost disappear inside her crow's feet.

'Only if you tell me about Gus,' Elaine says. 'I have a feeling Theresa knows more than I do.'

Marie shrugs. 'Maybe.' She winks and gestures to a chair that overlooks the garden where Sasha and Oliver are still busy getting themselves dirty.

'Is Theresa going to be all right?' Elaine asks as she sits.

'That's only for God to know,' Marie responds, pouring the tea for them both.

'So you believe in God?' Elaine asks, genuinely interested.

Her religious upbringing was unobservant Anglican and she can hardly say she has a spiritual life. And religion hasn't been a subject during their swims. Elaine was brought up to never discuss religion or politics and she's found Australians in concordance on the first point, but not the second. They're all very keen to discuss politics and politicians and why they think they're a 'pack of mongrels', as Derek said once.

'Of course,' Marie replies. 'Do you?'

'I don't know.'

'Hm.' Marie smiles mysteriously as she sips her tea. 'Don't they make you submit to a higher power in AA?'

God has never been a consideration for Elaine. The world has always turned, the grass has grown and the sun has shone. After she left childhood, her curiosity about it all faded. But she looks at the children squealing with laughter as they play, at Charlie Brown as he decides where he's going to sit, at the flowers in the garden and the flower pattern on her china teacup. She is aware of Marie sitting next to her and how two years ago they didn't know each other. She thinks of the mornings spent in each other's company and the friendship each of the women has given her. If it's not God doing all of this, then who? What? How is it possible that two years ago she was miserable and friendless, and then the kindness of Theresa and Marie and even Leanne, in her quiet way, changed that for her? She was heading for a serious drinking problem, then she was offered support without judgement. All that came from the ether, not from her. Someone – something – has given her these riches.

'Yes, they do,' she says at last. 'So I'm thinking about it.'

Marie nods approvingly, then they sit and sip their tea – Elaine wincing because it's stewed just a little too long for her taste – and talk of men and marriages, of bad decisions and recovering from them, as the breeze comes up, chasing the heat away, and the late afternoon brings the children to the verandah. Marie washes off the evidence of the garden on their skin, before Elaine drives them home to their mother.

CHAPTER 50

It's taken Theresa several pep talks to herself and from Marie to get to the beach this morning. Not because she doesn't want to be here – she's missed her morning outings – but because she knows it won't be the same. While the others swim, she will have to stay on the beach. Her surgical wound – the thing that's holding her together to cover the place where her breast used to be – is still healing; and even if it wasn't she doesn't know how she'd go about presenting herself in a swimming costume. The falsie might be fine for lying around on the sand, but what is she meant to do if she wants to swim like she used to? That's been one of the pep talks: how to get back into swimming with a false breast.

The house is silent as she prepares to leave. Marie suggested that Ollie and Sasha stay with her last night so Gus could watch them this morning, because Nonna's been doing more than her fair share of childminding. Theresa forgets that Nonna is in her eighties, and sometimes a woman that age doesn't want to be bothered with children, even if she's been preserved in nicotine and chianti.

It was so kind of Marie and Gus to offer to have them – although it did make Theresa wonder how often Gus stays the night at Marie's place. That's as far as she lets her imagination wander, though, because while she's curious she really doesn't want to think about Marie having a more active love life than she has. Theresa can only hope that if she makes it to Marie's age she'll find herself a nice bloke who's handy around the house and doesn't mind looking after other people's children. He's a bit dishy, too, Gus is. Not that Theresa's ever been interested in older men, but she certainly understands what Marie sees in him.

She's not allowed to drive yet so she's going to walk down to the beach and Elaine will drive her home. It's a decent walk but she has time: she'll arrive after they've all started swimming and wait for them to get out of the water. No sense sitting there while they do the full swim. She might get upset at what she's missing out on. There's been a bit of that going on lately.

The light is dim as she walks down the road to meet the beach. At this end there are surfers already in the water and not many waves to keep them busy. But she knows that likely doesn't bother them: surfers seem to enjoy the peaceful times sitting out there on the board. Theresa never really understood it until she spent more time in the water – until she got deeper, that is.

Her childhood weekends were spent playing in the shallows, then venturing out further as she grew older, but never too far. Even when she was in Nippers she was reluctant to go too far out. Her mother wasn't a keen swimmer – although she loved living by the beach – and thought that dangers lurked beyond the waves. Perhaps they did. Theresa never found out, because she obeyed her mother and kept within a few metres of the shore.

Swimming to Little Beach, however, has given her a different understanding of the water. The world of that swim is so different to the one she knew growing up. While she was scared the first few times, once she realised she was going to be fine she opened her eyes and saw what was there. Not just fish – although there are some of those – but a place that's strange yet so much like home. She was free there. She was graceful. She was able. Sometimes she even felt fierce.

She was never a fan of mermaid stories when she was younger, but once she started ocean swimming she wanted nothing more than to grow gills and a tail and be able to stay underwater for hours. Out there, in the open water, she wasn't Theresa, she wasn't Mum, she wasn't anyone's wife or daughter or friend. She was part of something huge. Part of the planet. The rhythms of the water felt like they belonged to her and she belonged to them. The swell felt like the undulations of her own blood. It was bliss, being there. Then she'd have to leave and go home.

She once told Marie about what she felt; she figured that if anyone was going to understand it would be the person who's been swimming every day for decades.

Marie had nodded, a serious look on her face. 'That's it, yes. We're part of something much bigger than ourselves. I find it a relief.' Her face had clouded briefly. 'A salvation, sometimes. We're nothing in the ocean, and we're everything. Every drop of water is us. Every grain of sand.' She turned to Theresa. 'Which means we're not so different, you and me. So don't go thinking I won't understand things that are going on in your life, and I won't think that about you in respect of my life either.'

It took Theresa a while to appreciate what Marie was offering her right then, but she did eventually. Which is how she's found herself accepting help from the three women while she recovers. She honestly doesn't know how she would have managed the children and the cooking and cleaning and washing if she hadn't had them. It was hard enough managing before.

As she continues walking she sees fewer surfers in the middle stretch of the beach. She looks ahead to the southern end: somewhere up there Marie, Elaine and Leanne are already in the water. Her longing to join them is physical, and closely followed by a pain in her chest where her breast used to be.

'Yeah, yeah, I hear you,' she mutters, glad that the only other people around are jogging too fast to notice what she says.

Maybe she's overdoing it, walking this far, but she can't stay on the couch forever. Before the surgery she was fitter than she'd been in years, and she doesn't want to lose more of that than she needs to. She also needed to get out of the house – it's been quiet without the kids there. Without Andrew around.

Theresa's had plenty of time to think about their marriage, especially during the night when she can't fall asleep, or when she wakes in the wee hours and can't get back to sleep. Perhaps she should have been a different wife. A better wife. She could have been a little less loud and a little more subservient. Andrew would have liked that. Every man she knows would like that. She just doesn't know a lot of women who like doing that.

That's the conundrum, isn't it: the way men want the world to run isn't the way that women want it to run, but men are bigger and stronger so women do what men want. For all time, that's how it's gone.

Thank god for friends or you'd go spare.

She can see them now: Elaine in the lead as they leave the water, then Marie. Leanne is . . . Theresa can see her, trying to catch a wave. That's an achievement in itself, because Leanne has never been keen on body surfing.

They look fine without her. They look like a group of friends having a laugh. Enjoying their swimming. Maybe they don't need her after all.

'Theresa!'

Elaine is waving so vigorously Theresa thinks her arm may fall out of its socket.

And that's all it takes for her insecurity to be gone: a wave, a call, a big smile, and Marie and Leanne and Elaine walking towards her as she descends the stairs to the sand.

'Let me give you a hug,' says Marie, 'even though I'm all wet.'

'Hi,' says Leanne, and Theresa could swear she sees a smile.

'Hello, hello.' Elaine kisses her on both cheeks and leaves sea water behind.

'Did you have a good swim?' Theresa asks.

'We did,' Marie says slowly. 'But it was definitely not as much fun without you. It hasn't been as much fun any day.'

'Oh, sure,' says Theresa, although she's quietly thrilled.

'It's true,' says Elaine with a kind smile. 'Without you I'm far less entertained than I was.'

'I'm still really slow,' says Leanne, pulling a face. 'So you're definitely going to swim faster than me. When you're back.'

'Yes . . . when I'm back.'

Theresa feels her breath catch in her chest. She didn't think she'd feel sad coming here – she thought she'd be happy to see them, and invigorated at the idea of getting into the ocean again. Instead, she feels like she's lost something before it had time to really start. Although that's a ridiculous idea, and she's being overly dramatic. Her mother always called her 'my little Sarah Bernhardt'.

'It'll take a while, love,' Marie says. 'It's cold now, so you may want to wait until winter's over.'

'Really?' says Elaine with a mischievous look on her face. 'Does that mean we get to take a break?'

'No such luck,' says Marie. 'I'm used to having you around. So you'll just have to buy a wetsuit or something.'

Theresa smiles, although she doesn't like the idea of waiting until after winter to swim again. She'll have to ask the doctor about it when she goes for her appointment tomorrow. That's when they're going to talk about what happens next. She hasn't let herself worry about it because she can't control the outcome. Very mature of herself, she thinks.

'How about you all come back to my place for a while?' says Marie. 'The children will be up.'

'That sounds lovely,' says Theresa. 'Thank you.'

'All right, well, let's get dry and get our clothes on, then off we go.'

Theresa relaxes as Marie takes charge and lets herself be led first to Elaine's car, then into Marie's house, where even Leanne participates in the conversation. She feels warm and loved, and for a little while her mind is quiet and focused.

She tries to make the feeling last as long as she can, knowing that tonight she'll be lying awake again, her thoughts racing, trying not to worry about her present and her future.

WINTER 1984

CHAPTER 51

The days are so short now that on an afternoon walk there is barely time to enjoy the last light of the day from the headland looking west, with the Tasman Sea behind them and the city in front of them. The city Marie barely visits, despite her fears that her world is too small, because she's been content to stay close to Shelly Bay. She's also found that keeping herself confined physically has not stopped her world breaking its bounds in other ways.

Meeting Gus, falling in love with him, has made her grow. If her heart has expanded to accommodate Elaine, Leanne and Theresa, it has ballooned to take in this wondrous man who goes for walks with her and calls her just to say hello. The man who is sitting here with her now as they hold hands, share kisses and dream of a future together.

'Theresa's been in the wars, hasn't she?' Gus says, rubbing the back of Marie's neck with one hand while he leans on his other.

'She has,' Marie mumbles, 'but if you keep doing that I'm not going to know what you're talking about.'

'Enjoying it, are you?'

'Mm-hm.'

'I'm glad.'

She feels his lips on her cheek and smiles, then the smile vanishes. 'I think she's worrying a lot but she's not telling us, so it's hard to know how to help. She doesn't want us to go round there to do the housework any more, but I don't think her grandmother can do as much as she says she can.'

'How do you know?'

Marie feels guilty and it probably shows on her face. 'Because the kids told me.'

'Marie!' Gus laughs. 'You weren't extracting information from minors?'

'Maybe.'

'I'm outraged.' He starts rubbing her neck again. 'But it's a good tactic. I doubt Theresa would tell you herself.'

'I wish she would, because the three of us would be in there like a shot. We had a roster going. We can start it up again.' She sighs. 'I don't think it's that she's too proud. I think she just doesn't want us to know what it's really like. As if she's failed or something.'

Gus stops again and moves so she can see him better. Marie aches for the feeling of his hand on her skin.

'Tell me,' he says, 'after Norm died did you let anyone help you?'

'I didn't have a choice. Gwen kept barging in with casseroles and baked goods.'

Marie remembers a fridge overflowing with Gwen's generosity, and not a moment to herself to think for quite a while. At the time she'd found herself getting irritated, holding back from being short with Gwen. It wasn't until the activity had stopped that she appreciated it.

She remembers another time, too, many decades before, when Gwen didn't bring food but her presence, sitting with Marie while she wept for the child who didn't come home from hospital. Did she thank Gwen on either occasion? She thinks not, and Gwen wouldn't have expected it. Tomorrow Marie's going to visit her old friend and put that right.

'But Gwen was trying to help me through grief,' she says. 'With Theresa—'

She stops because she sees it now: Theresa, too, is grieving. Perhaps for the loss of her breast, but more likely for the end of the life she once knew. Her marriage is over and although she expresses no regrets, it's still a fundamental change. Combined with the illness, she'll never be the same person again. She may not even realise it yet but that won't stop her feeling a sorrow she can't name.

'I think you need to go back there,' Gus says gently. 'Don't take no for an answer, just help her.'

'I can't barge in! She has her grandmother there.'

'She *needs* a friend.' He rubs her back. 'And you're a good friend.'

There's a deepening orange in the western sky. Soon it will be night and they'll have trouble seeing their way down the path.

'Am I?' Marie says quietly.

'You're a good friend to me.' Gus kisses her temple. 'The best.'

She leans into his chest. 'And you are to me.'

They sit in silence that is broken only by the calls of birds flying home for the night. Kookaburras busy themselves in nearby trees, chattering about who knows what. A magpie calls as it flies overhead.

'It's busy up there,' Gus says.

'It is. We should think about getting home to the nest too.'

'Another minute or so, eh?'

He squeezes her shoulder and she's glad of the warmth of him as a guard against the cooling of the evening. And for other reasons: it's a reminder that he's real and he's here; that he's properly in her life no matter how unlikely and unexpected that is.

'You make me very happy, Marie Kathleen Veronica,' he murmurs, and she smiles. He recently discovered her confirmation name when he read it in her Bible and he's been using it liberally ever since.

'You make me very happy too, Angus George.'

'I know we haven't been acquainted very long,' he says, 'but I hope you don't mind me asking if you've ever considered getting married again? Not that I'm proposing. Yet. Don't want to scare you off.'

At that moment Marie feels the purest sensation of joy she's had in ages. Uncensored and unbridled. She is a long way from being scared.

Then she pulls away from him because she wants to see his face, to work out if he's joking. He's not the kind to joke about something like this, but she has to check. It's too dark to see him properly, though, so she'll have to ask instead.

'Are you being serious?' she says.

'Of course I àm. So what's your answer?'

She takes a breath. 'I would consider it,' she says. 'And aren't you full of surprises?'

'A lifetime's worth,' he says, and she can hear the smile in his voice. His hand finds hers in the gloom. 'Come on. Time to get back and start dinner.'

'That's it?' She gets to her feet as he does. 'You're not going to say anything else?'

'That was a reccy,' he says. This time when he kisses her it's on the lips.

He produces a torch from inside his windcheater and switches it on so they can see the footpath.

'I didn't know you brought that,' she says.

'As I said, a lifetime of surprises.'

He shines the light ahead, and beyond it she can see the lights of the first line of houses starting to be switched on.

His hand is strong on hers as they walk and she likes to imagine hers is strong in his. But she's prepared to let him take the lead and help her get home. Tonight, and every night.

CHAPTER 52

'So tell me again,' James says as he leans against the kitchen table, his eyes dancing.

'Why?' Elaine says, although she's giddy enough to do it.

'Because I want to see how happy you look when you say it.' He gives her that smile she still falls for, over and over.

'Henry's coming to visit!' she declares, laughing. 'Before Marcus's wedding!'

'And?'

'And I've booked our flights so we can go back together for the wedding!'

Now James is laughing. 'Come here,' he says, opening his arms and closing them around her as she giggles into his neck.

'You know something?' he says into her hair.

'What?'

'That's the first time you've said "go back" instead of "go home".'

She's so surprised she loosens her grip on him a little. 'I think you're right. Although it sounds as if you've been keeping track.'

He shakes his head. 'Not at all. I've only noticed because you used to wince a little each time you said it.'

No doubt he's right, although she's never been conscious of doing that. Taking his hands, she kisses him gently. 'I'm sorry.'

He stares into her eyes. 'For what?'

'That was hurtful of me, to do that.' She kisses him again. 'My home is with you.'

'Darling, I understand. I've always understood.' His smile has a tinge of sadness to it. 'Even if sometimes you've seemed very far away.'

She nods. 'I have been. But I'm here now.'

The kitchen clock chimes seven.

'We have to leave!' she says. 'We need to be at your friends' place at half past.'

'I would hope they're your friends too,' he says, starting to undo his tie so he can change his shirt for the one she's put out on the bed.

'That's a lovely hope, darling, but I have my friends.' She winks, such an uncharacteristic action for her that James looks taken aback.

'Don't you think I should meet these mysterious swimmers?' he says as he walks down the hall towards their bedroom and she follows.

She's been dressed for an hour but that doesn't mean she won't want to watch him undress and dress again. It's one of her favourite pastimes.

'Honestly, it is *so* hard to corral them at night. Leanne has a boyfriend. Marie has a . . . a Gus. Theresa has the children.' She has a thought. 'Perhaps we could all go there for dinner. That would save her needing to make arrangements. In a little while, I mean. When she's up to it.'

'I really would like to meet them,' he says as he pulls his shirt over his head and drops it on the floor. She frowns. 'Oh, right – washing basket,' he says, grinning, and picks it up.

In the few seconds it takes him to walk to the basket in the corner by the door, Elaine lets her mind flit to the other news of her day. Although not news, really, so much as a thought, or a thought process.

'What are you worrying about?' James says as he puts on the clean shirt and starts to button.

'Nothing!' she says brightly. 'I'm not worrying. Just pondering.'

'About . . . ?'

She gazes at him and considers how much to say. It's a new plan and it may come to nothing. Or something. When she first started considering it she panicked. In England she had friends who supported her business initially, and she was forever grateful for that. She didn't have any such contacts here. She would hardly ask James to see if any of the other doctors' wives want their homes decorated. She didn't even know if Australians liked decorating their homes. From what she was able to tell, they spend most of their time outside. Perhaps she should become a horticulturist instead, then she could decorate gardens. And without any clue of how to find clients, there seemed little point going to the trouble of sourcing suppliers and finding a shopfront or other space. Their house was charming but not big enough for what she needed.

All that talking herself out of the job made her loathe herself, briefly. She was being lazy. Or scared. She spent a few days wearing herself out with ruminations, then decided to look at what was really bothering her.

Her hesitations mainly stemmed from the fact that, despite her robust friendships with the ladies in her swimming circle, she is, truly, shy. It was masked when she was in her home environment and her friends were women she'd known since school. It didn't manifest in her business either because she was playing a role. It took a move to the other side of the world for that veneer to fall away and leave her exposed as someone who doesn't make friends as easily as she thought. Her boat had never been rocked until it came ashore here in Shelly Bay, and for quite a while she didn't have the resources to handle it.

She had to be brave, in the end. Brave enough to believe that Marie, Theresa and Leanne would like her. Brave enough to believe that she'd like them. That was the realisation that spurred her on: if she can swim to Little Beach and back every day with three people who were strangers when she arrived here, she can certainly create a business in a place where she has to make new connections.

It would be good not to have to rely on James financially any more too. She still hasn't grown used to that – for years she had her own income and loved not being dependent on anyone. James doesn't seem to mind; indeed, he appears to relish the fact that she needs him. Which is a pity, as he'll have to give that up.

'I'm going to start a new business,' she says. 'Much like the old one. I've been doing some research about what's needed.'

James's face lights up. 'That is *sensational*!' he says, and she almost believes he's going to do a jig on the spot. 'Interior decorating?' he prompts.

'Yes. Or . . . perhaps a shop.' She smiles mysteriously. 'I might have looked at a couple of properties for rent.'

The idea of the shop came to her when she conceded she wouldn't have the appropriate space at home. She could run the design business from a shop, and that would give her room for storage and display and a space separate from home all at once.

James loops his tie around his neck. 'Can we drive past them on the way?'

'It's dark! You won't be able to see anything,' she says, although she can't help smiling at his enthusiasm.

'I don't care. Show me.'

'Oh, all right.'

She picks up her evening bag and lets him take her by the hand as he almost trots down the hall, collecting his keys and jacket from the chair by the front door, then out into the street.

As he closes the passenger door and jogs around to the driver's side, she laughs at his boyishness, and marvels that she can be married to someone who cares about her so much. Theresa has a husband who seemed to have only disdain for her. For some reason Elaine has ended up with a man who has nothing but regard for her.

There is so much luck in this world, she thinks, and very little design. Although she is closer to believing in that higher power – whatever it is – that Marie asked her about. For now, though, she will be grateful for her luck.

It's taken her a long time to realise that moving to Australia was luck, not tragedy, but now she is going to grab that luck with both hands and see where it takes her.

CHAPTER 53

If Matt squeezes her hand any more tightly Leanne is sure her circulation will never be restored. He is probably thinking the same thing, because she is squeezing him back. The plan – to meet her parents next to the beach, so they could take a walk in full public view, thereby reducing the chances of her father becoming angry with her – seemed sound, until now. Standing here, surrounded by tourists and seagulls stealing their hot chips, she thinks that all she's done is create an audience for what may turn out to be a failed meeting.

Her mother reassured her that it would all go well. She and Leanne's father are so happy she wants to see them, she said. Of course they will come to Shelly Bay, even if they've never been before. In Shelly Bay Leanne knew she'd feel most at ease, if not safe.

Matt is the other piece of the insurance plan. He appeared genuinely pleased to be asked.

'Are you sure?' he said. 'It's a big deal.'

Which she knows, of course. Such a big deal that she's felt queasy about it for weeks.

'It would be a bigger deal without you there,' she told him, because it's true, then realised it sounded strange. 'I mean, it would be harder. To deal with.'

'Lee,' he kissed her forehead, 'I know it's scary but they really do want to see you. You just need to create some new memories with them. That last memory is the main one you have so it feels like it's the only one. It's kind of . . .' He paused and his eyes flickered away. 'When I was a kid, I got dumped by a wave. Full washing machine. Thought I was going to drown. Worst experience of my *life*. And it was a wave my dad told me to catch. He was gutted, obviously, but I blamed him – and I *never* wanted to catch another wave. But Dad told me I had to. Right away, that day. He said I needed to catch a better wave so I didn't think that being dumped was all there was.' He grinned. 'So I did. And I went on to be a bloody good swimmer, as you know.'

She understood the analogy but wanted to tell him that in her memory her family aren't so much washing machine as terrifying carnival ride. That wouldn't have been kind, though – he was trying to be understanding. And he was. He is. Which is why he's here now.

'There they are,' she whispers urgently, seeing a man who is smaller and more bent over than she remembers, with her mother holding his arm tightly.

'Leanne,' her mother's mellifluous voice calls. 'Leanne!'

She's waving, so Leanne waves back. As they approach she lets go of Matt's hand.

'Mum,' she says, kissing her hello. 'Dad.'

His eyes are still blue, although their colour has faded. He looks like a little old man instead of the fit, tough father of her youth.

'Leanne,' he rasps, holding out his hand to clasp hers.

'Mum, Dad, I'd like you to meet Matt, my boyfriend.' She feels Matt's hand squeeze her shoulder. 'Matt, I'd like you to meet my mother, Ji-woo, and my father, Pádraic.'

'Good to meet you both.' Matt extends his hand to each of them. 'Pádraic – are you Irish?' he asks as the handshake ends.

'My mother was. It's a family name,' her father says, his eyes coming to rest on Leanne.

'Shall we walk for a while?' she says, smiling as hard as she can, feeling the forced nature of it.

'Leanne.' Her father puts a hand on her arm. 'Please. It's been so long.'

She stiffens and draws in a breath. Is he going to cause a scene? She really doesn't want a scene.

'New wave,' Matt whispers in her ear and she relaxes.

As she turns towards her father she sees pain in his eyes, and in her mother's. The difference between who she is now, though, and who she was then is that this time she doesn't blame herself for it.

Her father takes one of her hands in both of his. 'Can you forgive me?'

Leanne looks from him to her mother and back again. Perhaps forgiveness is what they came for. It's not something she has ever thought to ask of them. She has asked it of herself, and given it. Withholding it from them would be cruel, and she may be many things but she is not that.

What is that saying? To err is human; to forgive, divine. She doesn't need to be divine to grant them something that is so intrinsically a part of being human.

'Leanne!' calls a familiar voice, and her father's face falls.

Turning towards the sound, Leanne sees Marie walking in their direction from the Little Beach end of the promenade.

'Lee!' she calls again, and Leanne waves. If she thought she needed a benediction to grant forgiveness to her parents, she could not have asked for a better person to appear. If Elaine and Theresa also turned up she wouldn't be surprised.

'Hello, love,' Marie says, kissing Leanne's cheek. 'Can you believe we see each other down here every morning and we've never bumped into each other at any other time of day?' She laughs, then registers the presence of three other people. 'Oops,' she says. 'Sorry – I'm interrupting.'

Leanne hesitates over who to introduce first, and decides to go with the order in which Marie knew of their existence.

'Marie, this is Matt,' she says, beaming for a second because she's conscious that at this point in her life Marie knows her better than her parents do, and knows more about Matt than they do too.

'The famous Matt,' Marie says, shaking his hand vigorously. 'You're right, Lee – he *is* ugly.'

Matt's momentary surprise is replaced by a good-natured shake of the head. 'Don't worry, I've heard things about you too,' he says as Leanne's eyes flicker sideways to watch her parents' reactions.

She has told her mother about her morning swims, and mentioned the women's names, but she's never said enough for her mother to know how close she has become to them.

'And these are . . .' Leanne takes a breath. 'My parents.'

Marie stops and stares at her, then gives her a tiny nod and a wink.

'Hello, Mrs Leanne and Mr Leanne.' She smiles, and adds, 'I think I'd best keep walking. Gus is waiting for me somewhere. Oh, there he is.' She raises an arm and waves. 'We're heading off to visit his sister. It's a day for meeting the family.' A reassuring smile for Leanne as she starts to move away. 'Lovely to meet you all. See you tomorrow, Lee.'

Leanne watches her go. Although she doesn't believe in angels or kismet or anything mystical, she is tempted to believe that Marie was sent to her at just that moment, by something or someone, to remind her of how far she's come. Her lonely life – the one she chose, after she felt she didn't have a choice – is no more. It's time to catch that new wave.

'Yes, Dad,' she says, turning back to face her father, 'I forgive you.'

His eyes tremble and he bows his head.

Leanne steps beside him and offers her his arm, while Matt takes her other hand. Four astride, they stroll along the promenade, taking their time.

SPRING 1984

CHAPTER 54

The cancer wasn't content with taking Theresa's breast – it came for her lymph nodes too. The doctor said taking them out was a 'precautionary measure'. She wanted to ask him what he thought he was precautioning against, but she's not a doctor – not an expert in anything – so she has to trust him.

'We need to go back in,' was the way he phrased it.

Back in where? That was the first thing that came into her mind. She didn't want to sound stupid, though, so she played along. 'Oh, yes. Right,' she said, nodding, as if that was a helpful thing to do.

'We took a sample of one of your lymph nodes and the pathology suggests the cancer might have spread. So we'd like to take them all out.'

He had this flat tone of voice, like he was discussing whether a lamb roast should be in the oven at two hundred degrees or one eighty. To him she probably was just a piece of meat, so that explained it. Just one of his patients. After she left he'd probably talk to some other poor woman about her lymph nodes. Or worse.

That's what Theresa has to keep reminding herself: it could be worse. She could be living in a place without a doctor or a hospital. She could be in a country town and have to leave her children behind to come to the city for treatment.

She met someone like that when she was still volunteering in the hospital: a young woman who needed an operation on something she wasn't prepared to discuss. Theresa learnt that she had three kids who had to go back to the far west of the state – several hundred kilometres away – with their dad while she stayed. They were on holiday in Shelly Bay when whatever the problem was came up. That was tough, Theresa thought – to be so far from home when something so serious was happening. She had her friends to help her, and Ollie and Sasha and Nonna to make her smile, and that poor woman had no one. So it could be worse. For sure.

But it could also be better, and this time she took Marie's advice and told her parents the full story and asked them if they could come and help. Theresa doesn't want to burden Marie, Leanne and Elaine with helping out with the kids and the house because it just isn't fair.

'It has nothing to do with fair!' Marie protested, but Theresa doesn't agree. How can she ever even up this ledger?

Marie also asked – as she did the last time – if Theresa was going to tell Andrew about the second round of surgery.

'No way,' was her response.

'Theresa, this is more serious now,' Marie said.

'And so am I. If I tell him he might try to take the kids away.'

'Love, he hardly sees them – wasn't the last visit a fortnight ago and all he did was take them to McDonald's? Don't you think it's unlikely he'll want them all the time?'

'He'd make his parents look after them,' she said, starting to panic as she imagined a scenario where her in-laws left Ollie and Sasha behind at the sailing club after they had too much to drink one day and the children weren't found until morning.

'Theresa, whatever you're thinking, stop it,' Marie said. 'You look like you're going to explode.'

'I'll tell him I'm having more surgery but I'm not going to tell him why,' she said defiantly.

That was when Marie pointed out that in that case there was only one solution, and it was to ask Theresa's parents to move in for a while.

Her parents fairly flew down from the Central Coast and arrived on the doorstep only a few hours after Theresa called them.

'You should have told me sooner!' her mother admonished the minute she was in the door.

Theresa wanted to point out that this really wasn't the time for her mum to be telling her off, except she guessed some things would never change and it didn't matter if you had cancer. She'd like to think she wouldn't say that to Sasha in the same circumstances.

She hates the idea that this could happen to Sasha. She hates the idea of anything bad happening to her children. So she'll give her mum the benefit of the doubt and presume that she's covering her fear by switching into strict-parent mode. Or a different sort of strict-parent mode.

Theresa's always felt that her mother has been tough on her, and for no reason other than that she seems to think daughters are to be treated differently to sons. Theresa's brothers never had to apologise for wrongdoings as kids; never had to explain where they were or why they wanted to do something.

Her mother once hinted that Nonna had been tough on her, too, but Theresa has no proof of that. All she knows is that Nonna was never harder on her granddaughter than on her grandsons. If anything, she treated Theresa like a friend and her brothers like irritants. 'Silly little boys,' she would say, shaking her head each time Theresa's mother indulged them.

Once her mother knew that Theresa was having this surgery, though, something seemed to shift. 'You need us,' she said, and in that simple statement was a clue Theresa had waited a lifetime to find: perhaps her mother had simply wanted her daughter to need her. Or perhaps she'd been waiting for an excuse to show her daughter that she cares.

Before recent events, Theresa had pretty much mimicked her mother's life. When she gave birth, that was no different to anything her mother had done. But now their paths have diverged. And there her mother was, wishing Theresa had told her sooner.

'I didn't want to worry you,' was Theresa's excuse, and her mum looked at her the way she used to when Theresa was little and tried to 'help' make cakes by throwing flour all around the kitchen.

Now her parents are set up in the spare room and saying nothing about Andrew not being in the house. They've been invaluable, giving Theresa time to be convalescent; but at the same time she hasn't been left alone long enough to dwell on things. Marie and the others were so helpful last time, but what they couldn't do was be there every minute, filling up her time so she didn't sit around worrying.

The kids have had enough red frogs 'as a treat' to keep them bouncing off the walls until Christmas. And Theresa has time to see 'her ladies', as her mother once referred to them. Her swimming circle.

Elaine had called them that once, in her posh accent: 'the Shelly Bay ladies swimming circle'. Theresa thought that meant they may need to learn synchronised swimming, because otherwise where was the circle going to come from? She said as much and Elaine laughed.

'It's just a turn of phrase,' she said, 'and perhaps not a good one.'

But afterwards Theresa thought it sounded right. They feel like a circle – not a square, not a rectangle, not a straight line. They are a group. They are a collective hug, and what could that be but a circle?

She may not have been swimming with them for months now, and she isn't always there to meet them at the end of a swim, but they call, they visit, they chat to her parents so she can have time to herself. They have helped her cope.

She said that to Marie once, and was surprised to see Marie get teary.

'Don't you know,' she said, 'what *you* have done for *us*?'

No, Theresa doesn't know. She's just herself, muddling through each day and trying to make it the best it can be. Life is hard enough without everyone being grumpy. If she can bring a smile to someone's face, that's a good day's work. If she still went to church, she might think what she does is religiously motivated: she's doing the work of the Lord. Instead she likes to think she's doing the work of being human. What's that phrase she heard the other day? Good karma. She's spreading good karma. Or something.

Besides, she has to be an example to her children. If Ollie and Sasha see her smiling each day, if they remember their mum being happy even when she's really not, that has to be a good thing.

Theresa's started to think like that since the news about the lymph nodes: thinking about the kids remembering her. It's so bloody morbid, she knows that, but she has to be practical too. What if this gets worse? What if they keep chopping bits off her until there's nothing left? She has to prepare the kids.

It's probably bad to think like this. She needs to *be positive*. That's what Elaine said.

Theresa said it sounded like AA was having an effect. The Elaine she first met would never have popped out with a phrase like that.

'I agree,' Elaine said, looking surprised. 'I'm still not sure I said it.'

'You did,' Theresa said. 'But I can pretend I never heard it if you like.'

Elaine snorted. 'No, it's fine. It's a good thing. I'm *changing*. And didn't I need to?'

Theresa isn't sure she did. She likes Elaine just as she is.

Last night Theresa's mum came in and sat on her bed, taking her hand. 'How's my girl?' she said, in a tone Theresa had never heard her use.

'I'm . . .' Theresa tried to be brave but it didn't work. Besides, her mum can read her like a book. 'I'm afraid,' she said and her mum nodded.

'Of course you are. I would be too. But they're on top of things – your doctors. It must be so hard to go through all this, but it's good they acted quickly.'

Theresa nodded. 'I know. I just wish they could tell me what happens next.'

Her mother had smiled that smile mothers give when they want to be reassuring.

'We'd all like to know that,' she said. 'Or maybe we wouldn't. Sometimes it's better to think that nothing is decided. It's too much worry otherwise.'

That had worked – as her mother probably knew it would – and Theresa slept for more hours than usual.

Today she's moved to a chair in the garden, and is watching the kids running through the hose their grandfather is holding for them, even though they've been wet for so long they're turning blue.

Theresa remembers him doing it for her too. He was hard on her a lot of the time, but not always.

Simple pleasures – she's never lost sight of them. Swimming is that for her now. Was that. She feels that longing in her bones again, growing more intense with each day she can't be in the water. As her body becomes more of a battleground she wishes more fervently that the water could take her away from it.

'Here you go,' her mum says, handing her a lemonade.

'Thanks, Mum.'

Theresa tries to get comfortable in the flimsy outdoor chair she's had for years, and watches her mother attempt to do the same in the folding chair she brought with her from home. They're like two little old ladies sitting in the garden, except even Mum isn't particularly old.

'How's your pain?' she asks in a light tone.

'It's fine,' Theresa replies, trying to match it. 'The pain-killers are pretty good. Even if I need to take a nap every now and again.'

Her mother nods.

'Does Andrew know about all of this?' she says, in that same tone. Like it's a bog-standard question.

Mind you, Theresa should have expected it. They could hardly not talk about Andrew all this time.

'No.' She takes a sip of lemonade.

'Don't you think he should?' Her mother is watching the kids but Theresa hears the scold meant for her.

'No.'

'Theresa.' Her mother looks at her, but Theresa can't see her eyes behind the cat's-eye sunglasses she always wears. 'That's not reasonable.'

'*He's* not reasonable!' She wants to storm off but she can't move quickly enough.

'Theresa.' Now her mother has that you're-not-in-trouble-but-you-might-be-soon tone of voice that she's never quite lost even though Theresa has been an adult for, oh, twenty-odd years.

'What?' She attempts to huff, but it makes her stitches pull and she ends up saying 'ow' instead.

'He's Oliver and Sasha's father, and their mother is sick. And not able to look after them all the time. He needs to do his share.'

'He wouldn't know what his share is.'

'Then it's time he learnt. He has an easy life, swanning around Shelly Bay like it's his personal kingdom. His job's here, his house is here. He probably has palpitations each time he has to go further than City Road.'

Theresa can't hide her surprise.

'Well,' her mother says primly, 'I've never been a fan.'

Theresa giggles. 'Really?'

'He was never good enough for you. But it was your choice.' Her mother holds up a hand. 'Not my place to interfere. And he's given me two beautiful grandchildren, so I have to tolerate him. He has time, though, that's my point. Time to help you with the kids.'

'I don't want him to know,' Theresa says firmly.

'You don't want *him* to know,' her mother's head swivels towards her again, 'or you don't want the *girlfriend* to know?'

'What's the difference?' Now she *really* wants to huff but she accepts her limitations.

Her mother keeps watching her and Theresa wishes she could see her eyes, to know what she's thinking. She's always been hard to read, whereas Theresa couldn't hide an emotion if her life depended on it.

'Your dad and I won't be staying forever,' her mother says. 'We'll drive you mad if we do. And I know you have friends, but it's not fair to them either. Andrew has to pull his weight. He won't do everything the way you would do it – you're just going to have to let that go.'

Theresa knows her mother is right. The children will likely say something to him anyway, and he might try to use her secrecy against her. Not that she thinks he'll want to have the kids full time – that would cramp his style, and his lifestyle. He might do it to be mean, though, because all bets are off when your marriage breaks down and you're the guilty party. You'll do what you can to save face.

'I don't want to talk to him,' Theresa mumbles.

'You don't have to,' her mother says, so cheerily that Theresa knows she expected her to fold. 'I'll do it.'

'Ollie, doooon't!' Sasha wails, and Theresa looks up in time to see Oliver turning the hose directly on his sister.

'Oliver, put that down,' she says with as much force as she can muster.

'Wouldn't it be good,' her mother says, 'if you didn't have to do this all the time?'

Theresa nods resignedly.

'Close your eyes, love,' her mother instructs, as Sasha's cries turn to laughter once more. 'Have a snooze. I'll go and make the call.'

CHAPTER 55

Elaine pulls into Theresa's driveway and turns off the engine. The street runs along the ridge between Main Beach and Sunrise Beach, so there are ocean views wherever you look. Theresa told her that she and Andrew have lived here, on Royalist Road, since they married. Andrew's childhood home is one street away and he didn't want to move far, although his parents were already on their way to a new place half an hour's drive away by then.

'Early retirement,' Theresa had said, 'which means they're usually too busy to look after the kids.' She sighed. 'So my parents are on the coast and his parents are on acreage, and they all love their grandchildren but don't want to see them very often. Did your parents help you out?'

'They did,' Elaine said, feeling slightly guilty. 'I was very lucky. They lived close by and they were happy to help. It meant I could run my business.'

Whenever Theresa asks questions about the business – as she does from time to time – she makes Elaine feel as if running a business while having children is a superhuman achievement. Perhaps it is. At the time it was simply her life and she didn't think it extraordinary. Now she wonders if she should have given herself more credit.

Since that conversation Elaine's been determined to do for Theresa what her parents did for her – especially as Andrew's involvement with the children seems to be short on the responsible side and long on the side that's all about fun. The meagre times he spends with them he takes them to the mall for donuts or to the beach for fish and chips, and they're only gone an hour at best.

It's made Elaine cast James differently. She never thought him a bad father, although his work always kept him away from the children each weeknight and sometimes on weekends. But she never fussed about it, because she hadn't minded, which meant the children didn't mind either. What she hadn't appreciated was that during the times James was with the boys he didn't try to make up for those absences by being 'fun dad'. When he was there, family life carried on as normal. He always praised Elaine in front of the boys, and told them how lucky they were to have such a wonderful mother – to which they'd either groan or not respond at all – and told her that he was lucky to have such a wonderful wife. In other words: he didn't use fatherhood to boost his ego.

As she approaches Theresa's front door, Elaine can hear Oliver and Sasha playing in the back garden so she knows that Theresa is home. Theresa's parents have gone to Canberra to stay with one of her brothers for a couple of days – 'to give me a break from always getting in trouble', as Theresa explained it.

'Mum keeps saying I need to do this and I need to do that,' she said when Elaine called a couple of days ago. 'She even rang Andrew to tell him that he should be looking after the kids a bit. I didn't hear the call, but she told me she said he's the laziest father she's ever met and if he doesn't get his act together she and my father are going to give me money to sue for full custody. It didn't work. He says he's too busy,' Theresa went on.

Elaine could hear the false levity in her voice, the sign that she was making an effort to not be disappointed. But she must be – Elaine would be. Anyone would be upset that their children's father can't be bothered to fulfil basic parenting duties.

'I'm not too busy,' Elaine had said, knowing it would be no hardship for her to continue to assist Theresa, nor to take the children to school.

'Theresa?' she calls through the screen door into the living room beyond. Seconds pass and all she can hear is the children.

'Theresa?' She calls a little more loudly now.

'It's open,' a faint voice responds.

As Elaine opens the screen door and steps inside she can barely see Theresa on the couch because the blinds are closed. She's never seen the blinds closed – Theresa is a fan of letting in the light, even if it means her neighbours from across the street can look into her sitting room.

'Theresa?' she says, almost whispering, because the darkness suggests it.

'Yes. Hi.' The shape on the couch shifts. 'Elaine.' Theresa's voice sounds off – weak and thin.

'Can I turn on the light?' Elaine says.

'Um . . . okay.'

Theresa moves slowly to sit upright. With the light on Elaine can see that she's not a good colour – in fact, she looks almost yellow.

Elaine last saw her four days ago when she popped over briefly; they've been talking on the phone since and Theresa hasn't mentioned feeling unwell. Marie and Leanne haven't seen her for a few days either. They've all been calling, though – they talk about it each morning before the swim.

'Theresa, what's wrong?' Elaine says, moving quickly to sit next to her.

'Oh, I'm . . .' Theresa trails off and looks towards the window. 'Why are the blinds down?'

'I don't know.' Elaine puts a hand to Theresa's forehead – years of raising children have made this action an instinct. If her children looked the wrong colour, it was the first thing she'd do. 'You're hot,' she says. 'How long have you been feeling unwell?'

Theresa looks confused. 'A couple of days.' She frowns. 'Where are the children?'

'In the back garden.'

Elaine tries to stay calm but she can't help feeling a flicker of panic. Theresa isn't careless with her children, even if she's appeared carefree. She always knows where they are.

'Oh.' Theresa licks her lips.

'Do you need some water?'

Elaine goes to the kitchen without waiting for a response. She fills a glass and brings it to Theresa, who sips a little and puts it down.

'I feel a bit sick,' she says.

'I'd say you *are* a bit sick.' Elaine keeps her voice as light as possible. 'Where's your nonna?'

Theresa frowns. 'I think she's here,' she says slowly.

'I'll check,' Elaine says with false brightness.

She doesn't want to believe that the other adult in the house hasn't noticed that Theresa is clearly unwell, so there must be something wrong with Nonna too. Through the screen door of the granny flat Elaine can hear a radio and smell cigarette smoke.

'Nonna?' she calls.

'Who is it?'

'It's Elaine, Theresa's friend. We've met before.'

'Lainey!' Oliver cries as he rushes up to her. 'What are you doing here?'

'I've come to see your mum,' she says.

The screen door opens and Nonna stands there, looking a little more wizened than the last time Elaine saw her.

'Yes?' she draws out.

'Oliver, how about you and Sasha put all that dirt you've dug up back into the garden?' Elaine says, patting his shoulder.

'Okay.' He grins before racing off. 'Saaa-shhhha, Lainey says we need to put it all baack!'

Elaine turns to Nonna and folds her arms, wanting to contain her rising tide of worry. 'Theresa's not well,' she says.

Nonna stares at her and Elaine sees a glimpse of the tyrannical poker player Theresa has described. 'I know. She has the cancer.'

'No, I mean she's not well *today*. She's listless, she has a temperature – she's not herself.'

'What is *listless*?' Nonna sniffs.

'She's . . . she's . . .' Elaine didn't reckon on being a dictionary. 'She's not focusing, she can't remember where the children are – where you are.'

'I thought she just tired. She don't make breakfast so I make it.' Nonna shrugged. 'I don't mind.'

'She didn't get like this quickly,' Elaine says. 'How long has she been so unlike herself?'

It's the best indication Elaine can think of that something is profoundly wrong. She's seen infections develop before – and she suspects that's what this is. She saw it in Henry, when he had an ear infection that raged too far and ended with him in hospital. While an infection can escalate at speed, the infected person usually shows some symptoms before that point. Elaine has still never forgiven herself for missing the signs in Henry so she knows she should be more gentle with Nonna, except she doesn't feel gentle.

'Maybe one day. Maybe two.' Nonna's eyebrow twitches. 'I noticed. I did not want to . . . what is it? Make a big fuss.'

Elaine wants to laugh from dismay, because she understands too well: it's the story of her life, to not make a big fuss. She is sure Theresa doesn't make big fusses either, nor Marie or Leanne. They're all so well trained. They're women. Nothing that happens to them is a big fuss, the subtext being that they're not important enough to have big fusses. They exist to take care of other people's big fusses. And what's most mortifying is that this lifetime of what amounts to submission to others' needs before their own has, Elaine is sure, led to Theresa being in this situation today. Theresa has likely been feeling ghastly for a while, but when it began she would have told herself she couldn't make a fuss about it – not even to her or Marie or Leanne. Now Theresa is past the point of worrying about that, but if she'd only said something sooner she wouldn't be so sick.

At what point, Elaine thinks, does the relentless rampage of an illness become so great that you're prepared to overthrow years of believing you're not important enough to worry about your health? It was the same story with the lump: Theresa noticed it weeks before she told Elaine, but was too busy looking after the children and everyone else to make herself a priority.

Today, however, Elaine is going to make her the priority.

'I think she needs to see a doctor,' she says to Nonna. 'Can you please watch the children?'

'As long as they are not naughty.' Nonna glares in their direction.

'I'm afraid you'll have to regardless of how naughty they are.' Elaine smiles as politely as she can but she has no time for nonsense.

Nonna's glare falters. 'Is she really sick?'

This time Elaine tries a reassuring smile instead. No sense causing unproductive amounts of worry. 'I think she's sick enough to see a doctor.'

She isn't going to say that the first doctor she plans to consult is James, but that's only because the main person she doesn't want to worry is Theresa. No sense packing her off to the hospital without checking first.

Elaine walks back into the sitting room and dials the number for James's rooms while Theresa lies unmoving on the couch.

'Mr Schaeffer's office,' says a voice Elaine knows well.

'Hello, Barbara, it's Elaine.'

'Elaine, hello.'

'Is he in?'

'He's with a patient,' Barbara says, as Elaine expected.

'I really need to speak with him. It's fairly urgent.'

As that's not a word Elaine is prone to using, she hopes it has the intended effect.

'Putting you through,' Barbara says, then there are seconds of silence in which Elaine glances over to see that Theresa still has her eyes closed.

'Darling,' James says and Elaine feels the relief of knowing someone else is going to help her make decisions.

'Hello. I'm sorry to bother you but I'm at my friend Theresa's house.' She takes a quick breath, aware that she's starting to panic and trying not to. 'She's not a good colour. Remember I told you she had surgery recently – a mastectomy? Then some lymph nodes removed a week or so ago. She's been fine – getting back to normal, I thought. I saw her four days ago. Spoke to her two days ago. Now she's hot to the touch and seems to just want to sleep.'

There is silence for a few seconds and Elaine knows James

will be formulating the right answer. He is careful, bordering on cautious, when it comes to giving advice.

'Have you checked the wound site?' he says.

'No. Shall I?'

'Actually, don't. Just take her to Casualty, right away.'

He sounds calm and she wishes she could match it, but that's not the instruction she was expecting.

'What do you think it is?' she says.

'I'd rather not say. Can you get her to the hospital?'

'Yes. We'll go now.'

'Call me when you get there. I'll come and meet you if I can.'

'All right. Thank you.'

The line goes dead and Elaine knows that James will be back with his patient. Which isn't to say he doesn't care, but she's the one here, in this moment, with a responsibility to her friend.

Her next call is to Marie, who says she will meet Elaine at the house and help her put Theresa into the car.

Then Elaine sits by Theresa, taking her hot hand and stroking it. 'Theresa?' she says softly.

'Mm.' Theresa moves her mouth as if she's trying to swallow.

'We need to go to the hospital.'

Elaine feels the sting of new tears as she watches the lack of reaction from Theresa. How sick she must be – how far from herself – to not even register what Elaine has said. But Elaine's tears are useless; she has to take charge, and be competent, and steadfast. All the things she once believed herself to be. All the things she can be.

She can hear the children in the back garden while she waits for Marie to arrive. It's only then that she wonders if she should try to find Andrew. As little regard as Elaine has for him, Theresa is going to be in hospital for a while and he should know.

But Elaine doesn't have time for him now, just as he hasn't had time for his wife and children. If only he'd been paying attention – if only they all had – Theresa wouldn't be in this situation.

CHAPTER 56

When Leanne pokes her head into Theresa's hospital room she expects to see her friend sitting up, bright-eyed, the way she always looks. Instead she finds her lying down with an IV in each arm, her skin a strange greyish-white colour and her hair matted. Theresa's eyes are closed and for that Leanne is grateful, because it gives her time to rearrange her face so she doesn't look so shocked.

Leanne feels guilty for not knowing her friend was in trouble. They all rely on Theresa to jolly them along, and when she couldn't they didn't stop to wonder why. *She* didn't wonder why. She hasn't been to visit Theresa since before her last operation because Theresa's parents were staying with her and Leanne didn't want to intrude. That's the excuse she's been giving herself, but the truth is that she didn't want to have to make small talk with strangers. She let her own neuroses prevent her from checking on her friend and for that she can't quite forgive herself.

Elaine told her it was bad. She missed yesterday's swim and turned up this morning, explaining that she's helping Nonna look after Oliver and Sasha so that's why she missed the day before. Explaining that Theresa is very sick and in hospital again.

'She's septic,' Elaine said simply, and Leanne knew what that meant.

Leanne caught the expression on Marie's face as she looked back at Elaine: fear.

'How did she get it?' Leanne asked.

Anything can happen with wounds, she knows, but Theresa hasn't seemed more unwell than she should have been after the surgery.

'Her surgical wound became infected and she mustn't have noticed that it was spreading,' Elaine explained. 'She's been on painkillers. They might have masked the symptoms. That's what James . . .' Elaine stopped and glanced away, looking stricken.

'I should have checked on her earlier,' Marie said.

'We've all been talking to her,' Elaine said. 'She didn't say anything. She didn't sound any different – I mean, she hasn't been sounding like herself anyway.'

'What happens now?' Leanne said.

'Ideally they cut out the infected flesh, but because it's so close to her mastectomy site they're . . .' Elaine's exhalation was ragged. 'They're not doing it. Yet. They have her on antibiotics.'

'Is she improving?' Marie asked.

'I don't know. I've been focused on the children.'

'Isn't – isn't Andrew taking care of them?' Leanne said, feeling like it was the least contribution she could make to this conversation. She knew why Elaine and Marie didn't tell her yesterday: she was at work, unable to help them with anything. For the first time, she resented her job.

Marie turned towards her with an expression of slight amusement. 'Well, he might if he seemed to think it was important. But either he doesn't want to believe Theresa is that sick or he doesn't think he can take the time off, because he seems to think her grandmother can do it all.'

'I think Theresa's parents will take over, though,' Elaine continued. 'I spoke to her mother last night and they're coming back today.'

After they swam – slower than usual, and slower to leave the beach too – Leanne decided she'd visit Theresa after work. At lunchtime she took a jar to the beach and scooped up some sea water. It was the only thing she could think of to give Theresa that might mean something more than flowers would.

If it's guilt that brought Leanne here, it's concern that takes her to Theresa's bedside, holding the jar of water with both hands as if it's the most precious thing she owns.

Theresa's eyelids flutter open.

'Hi,' Leanne says softly.

Theresa half smiles. 'Leanne,' she says croakily.

'Hi,' Leanne repeats, finding it hard to think of the right words.

There is an intimacy in visiting someone in hospital – implicit in the visit is the acknowledgement that the person is weak and vulnerable. There is no pretending that everything is fine. Trite phrases, expressions that are familiar yet mean nothing, are emptier than usual. 'How are you?' has no purpose here. For Leanne, who has taken refuge behind social niceties, who has ducked and weaved out of intimacy's way for most of her adult life by replying 'Very well, thank you' each time she is asked how she is, who uses 'please' and 'thank you' like protection spells so that no one looks any closer, being here with Theresa is a test – and one she has no right to be worried about. She's here because Theresa created their friendship by inviting Leanne to come closer. Theresa wasn't afraid of knowing her better; she has never minded if someone's answer is not 'Very well, thank you'. So Leanne cannot mind now.

'I brought you some water,' she says, putting the jar on the bedside table, 'from our end of the beach. I thought . . .' She looks at the jar and feels slightly foolish for imagining this could be any kind of gift. But it's here now and she needs to explain it. 'I thought if you can't get to the beach, I could bring it to you.' She shrugs casually. 'It's a bit silly,' she says, feeling silly herself.

'No,' Theresa says, pushing herself up a little. 'It's lovely.' Her words are slow, deliberate. 'So thoughtful.'

They sit looking at each other, and Leanne searches for the light that is usually in Theresa's eyes. She can't find it.

'How long do you have to be here?' she asks.

Theresa smiles, and it looks like it takes an effort. 'As long as they decide it's necessary.'

'Are you in pain?'

'No. I'm just . . . whacked.' Theresa's eyelids half close. 'I never knew I could feel this tired.'

'I won't stay long,' Leanne says. She should have considered that Theresa might not want visitors.

Theresa shakes her head. 'No, you're fine. It's really nice for me to have a visitor. I'm so bored of my own company.' She closes her eyes again for a few seconds, then half opens them. 'Marie told me . . .' She licks her lips. 'That she saw you. With your parents.' A smile appears and disappears. 'And Matt.'

'She did, but we don't need to talk about that. You have other things to think about.'

'What if I want to talk about it?' The smile stays this time. 'I'm missing out on the gossip.'

Leanne nods. 'Not so much gossip, really.'

'So . . .' Theresa swallows slowly. 'How was it?'

'It was strange, but good. Comforting, in a way.'

Theresa looks at her encouragingly.

'We talked about the hospital,' Leanne goes on. 'My parents asked lots of questions. That was the strange bit. They don't know . . .' She stops, trying to recall all the details of that day, wanting to tell Theresa a good story. 'There's a lot they didn't know because we haven't seen each other. They asked Matt a lot of questions too.'

'And what happens next?' Theresa prompts.

There's a noise at the door and they both look towards it.

'Sorry, I'm, um, I'm interrupting.'

It's a man Leanne has never seen before. He's tall and slightly overweight. His hair is shaggy, his skin is half sunburnt and his eyes are bloodshot.

Leanne turns to Theresa for guidance and sees her tense.

'Andrew,' Theresa says flatly. She catches Leanne's eye but it's impossible to tell if she wants her husband there or not.

'I should go,' Leanne says, because she can see Andrew is irritated by her presence.

'No, you shouldn't,' Theresa says with more force than Leanne has heard from her so far. Her face is hard now; Leanne has never seen it like this.

'The, uh, the kids want to see you,' Andrew says.

Theresa looks furious. 'Why are they with you?'

'Your mum told me . . .' He scratches behind his ear. 'She said I couldn't leave them with Nonna or your friends.'

A flash of something resembling anger comes Leanne's way.

Theresa's eyelids flutter closed for a few seconds. 'They do need their father. Despite what you think.'

Leanne wishes there was another exit to the room, because she thinks if Theresa was in her right mind she wouldn't want anyone to witness this.

'Look, do ya want to see them or not?' Andrew says.

'You didn't bring them here?' Theresa says, glowering.

'They're in the car.'

'Jesus, Andrew.' Theresa slumps back against the pillows.

'I'll go to them,' Leanne says. She turns to Andrew, who is frowning at her. 'I'm Leanne. I swim with Theresa. Sasha and Oliver know me.'

'Right,' he says, still frowning.

'What does the car look like?'

'It's a Falcon. Station wagon. Red.' His face relaxes.

Leanne turns back to Theresa. 'I'll take them for a walk while you two talk.'

It sounds like a directive, and she means it to. She's not going to bring them to Theresa's bed, because no children should see their mother with drips in her arms. They wouldn't understand it and the scene would, no doubt, upset them. She will do the only thing that makes sense and keep them away.

'You've got twenty minutes,' she says to Andrew before giving Theresa a quick kiss on the cheek. She's never kissed her before so it's no wonder Theresa looks surprised.

'I'll be back,' Leanne says, and almost runs from the room, leaving the complication of Theresa's marriage behind, heading for the much more straightforward business of looking after her children.

CHAPTER 57

'So you're managing to stay off the booze?' Marie asks as Elaine puts on her indicator. Left up this street, then right, right again and they'll be at Theresa's house.

'Mm,' Elaine says, not really wanting to have the conversation but appreciative that Marie is prepared to talk about the subject. Not everyone wants to address the hard things.

'That doesn't sound confident.'

'I haven't had a drink since that relapse I told you about.'

'But . . . you've been thinking about it.'

'Yes. I have,' Elaine says grimly. 'I know I shouldn't.'

'Of course you should,' Marie says. 'That's why it's so hard giving it up – as previously discussed. I'm not an alcoholic, but my understanding is that you're going to be thinking about it for a long time. Maybe for the rest of your life.'

'That can't be true!' Elaine says, aghast even though she knows it is.

She doesn't want to have these thoughts forever. She needs to free her mind to contemplate other things. Better things. Which is proving impossible with Theresa so sick, and it's occurred to her more than once that thinking about gin is a reflexive distraction, the way actually drinking it used to be. So maybe the thoughts are useful: she doesn't need to drink because simply thinking about it is having a similar effect. Or maybe that, too, is a self-deception and she's stuck in a pattern that will, as Marie suggests, go on for the rest of her life.

'Well, you'll find out,' Marie says, not unkindly.

There's silence as Elaine makes the last turn.

'How about Leanne?' Marie adds. 'They say still waters run deep – she's the living example.'

'Yes,' Elaine says. 'It's wonderful that her life is coming together. At last. She's had a difficult time.'

She turns the engine off and looks to the house.

'Yes, she has,' Marie murmurs. 'She's been brave, our little Leanne. She has more courage than I do.'

'I don't believe that,' Elaine says as she opens the screen door.

Three sharp raps of the knocker bring a man to the front door. Andrew, they presume, because it was Andrew who answered the phone when Elaine rang to see if Nonna needed anything. He said he'd moved back in. For now.

'Oh,' Elaine had said. 'May I ask why?'

'Mum told me I had to. She said Nonna's too old to look after the kids.'

Elaine couldn't help feeling irritated that it took his mother's admonishment to get him to do anything. But she kept it to herself. It's good for the children to have their father around. No matter how indifferent he might be to them – or seem to be – he's their only other parent.

'G'day,' Andrew says now, holding the door open to let them in. 'Thanks for comin'.'

His eyes are bleary – whether from lack of sleep or over-consumption of beer, Elaine doesn't know.

'Where are the children?' asks Marie.

Andrew scratches his head. 'Nonna's taken them to the park.'

'Is she up to that?' Elaine has never seen Nonna walk a longer distance than the path from her granny flat to the kitchen.

He shrugs. 'She suggested it. Can I get you anything?'

'No, thank you,' says Marie. 'We're just here to see how you are.'

'Shithouse,' he says. 'How do ya reckon?'

Elaine flinches. She's not used to men swearing in front of her; it's another characteristic of this country she has to learn to accommodate.

'Have you been to the hospital today?' Marie asks him.

'Nuh.' He folds his arms across his chest. 'The kids want to come with me and Theresa doesn't want to see them.'

'That can't be true,' Elaine says, then realises it sounds as if she doubts him, and that's not what she came here to express.

Andrew looks momentarily upset. 'She, uh . . . she doesn't want *them* to see her. Yeah. That's what I meant. With all the tubes and everythin'.'

Elaine thinks of the way Theresa looked yesterday: like she was fading to the point of disappearing into the white hospital sheets. The light that has always been so bright in her seems to have dimmed to the point of being extinguished, and Elaine didn't mind admitting to Marie that she's scared of what that means.

James has spoken of how the difference between someone living and dying can so often be an element that doctors can't see or describe. 'It's the will to live,' he said. 'You can have two patients with the same life-threatening problem and all the factors that you think will influence the outcome – weight, age, general health, whether or not they smoke – don't have as much of an impact as the will to live.'

When Elaine met Theresa she thought she had the biggest life force of anyone; now she wonders if there has been a cost. If being so bright and capacious for everyone else has diminished

Theresa so greatly that she doesn't have the reserves to draw on to come back from a shock to the system like this. Or that she may not want to. Theresa adores her children, she loves her parents and her grandmother. But all that love goes out, and Elaine isn't sure it comes back in sufficient quantities to make up for the deficit.

It's the first time she's thought that being a little reserved, the way she is, the way Leanne is – even the way Marie can be – might have benefits she hadn't reckoned on. She worries that if the mastectomy didn't get it all, if Theresa still has cancer and all that follows that diagnosis, she may not have the strength to make it through if she doesn't learn to pull back from being herself.

There is pure selfishness in this concern, because Elaine loves Theresa as she is. She wants her to always be the same, just as she wants Marie and Leanne to be – and she knows that, in return, they feel that way about her. To be accepted like this, to know that there are three other people who have arrived at the same place, who have decided to be her friend just as she has decided to be theirs, has been perhaps the greatest act of grace in her life. So unexpected, so beautiful, and so rare.

'Andrew, what have you told the children?' Marie says with a softness to her voice that Elaine hasn't heard before.

His forehead wrinkles. 'Not much. Just that their mum's sick but she'll get better again.'

As Marie glances her way, Elaine can see the same fear she has, and she feels as if her guts are turning themselves inside out. If Marie, who has seen more of life than she has, is worried about Theresa, that means they can't tell themselves lies about what happens next, and they can't encourage Andrew to stay in the dark either.

'You know,' Marie starts, 'that this infection has weakened her. A lot.'

Andrew looks as if he has no idea what she's saying. 'So?' he replies, almost resentfully. 'She'll be all right.'

'They haven't said what's in her lymph nodes yet, have they?' Elaine asks.

He shakes his head slowly. 'They want to wait until she's better. To talk about treatment.'

Another glance from Marie, and Elaine knows she understands what that means: there is something sinister inside their friend, and a long road ahead. And because Andrew is still her husband, he is her next of kin and will be in the position to make decisions about it if she can't.

'Andrew, everything has to change,' Marie says evenly. 'Your business, the way this household runs ... it can't go on the way it was. Not for the foreseeable future. Theresa is going to need care.'

'Someone has to pay the mortgage!' he says with an edge, but it's weak. 'It's still my house too.'

'We understand that. But someone also has to get these children to school and wash their clothes and make their dinner. Theresa is not going to be capable for a long time. Nonna can't do it.'

'So what are you saying? That I give up the garage and go on the dole just so I can pick the kids up from school? I'm not gonna do that.' His eyes flash.

'No, Andrew,' Elaine says as calmly as she can. She and Marie are there to help but they can't if he keeps fighting them. 'Marie and I are prepared to do a lot of that work for you. Leanne wants to but she has a full-time job.' She looks at Marie, who nods encouragingly. 'We have the time and we want to do it. What we don't want to do is force ourselves on you. But we don't think you can manage on your own.'

He juts out his chin then looks at his feet. 'I'm not a charity case,' he mutters.

'For goodness' sake, stop being so pig-headed,' Marie remonstrates. 'Your wife's in trouble. No one's offering *charity*, Andrew, we're offering *housework*. There's a difference.'

Elaine wants to smile, because she quite likes seeing Marie riled up.

Andrew sniffs a couple of times then shoves his hands in his pockets as he looks up. Elaine sees the outline of the face he used to have and understands how he might have appealed to Theresa. He was good-looking once; perhaps he was good too. She'll never know.

'What does she tell you about me?' he says, still defiant.

'Not much,' says Marie. 'Because from what I understand you're not here very often, so there's not much to tell.'

'That's because she doesn't want me here,' he says. 'Does she tell you that too?'

Marie sighs and Elaine knows why: neither of them wants to get involved in Theresa's marriage more than they need to. However, they have to defend their friend.

'That's not true, Andrew,' Elaine says. 'But we're not going into it now.'

'None of this had to happen if she just loved me like she used to,' he says, quick as a flash and hard.

Marie raises her eyebrows. 'I didn't love my husband the way I used to, either, after we had our daughter and all the other concerns that come with being a family. That's how marriage works.'

'Yeah, well, I still love her the way I used to,' he says, so softly it's almost inaudible.

They stand in silence, and Elaine feels the impossibility of responding to what he's said. He still loves his wife but he chooses to protest the way their lives have changed by not being around her, which leads her to think he doesn't love her, and she responds accordingly.

It is a miracle, Elaine thinks – a large one, not a small, domestic one – that she and James have never arrived at this point. Perhaps there's nothing either of them has done to achieve it, or deserve it.

'Will you let us help you, Andrew?' Marie says after a time. 'We want to.'

He sniffs again and pushes his hands deeper into his jeans pockets. 'Yeah, okay.'

Elaine wishes she could feel more relieved, but the reason they're here isn't one they ever wanted. They'll make the best of it, though. She and Marie will work out their days between them and ensure the children are looked after. And when Theresa comes home they'll figure that out too.

'Thank you,' Marie says. 'We'll be in touch.'

As they leave she gives Andrew a quick kiss on the cheek, so Elaine does the same. He looks surprised, but says nothing as they go.

CHAPTER 58

It took Theresa a while to ask to be moved to the bed nearest the window. She wanted to see trees and sky and a glimpse of the harbour. It's not the ocean side of Shelly Bay, where she swam all those mornings; where she found so much happiness, even if it only lasted while she was in the water. Happiness, and tired muscles. That was the story of her swimming.

She still has these drips attached to her, but from the little she can hear of the nurses' conversations, what's in the drips isn't helping her as much as it should. Not that they will tell her that. Apparently the deal with medical treatment is that the patient is kept in the dark up to, during and after procedures. She's been jabbed at by random people taking blood samples; other people have stuck warfarin needles in her abdomen so she doesn't develop blood clots, leaving a colourful bruise display; nurses check the chart at the end of her bed and disinterestedly measure her blood pressure. Not a single one of these strangers asks her how she is. If they did, she'd tell them she's bewildered, and overwhelmed, and scared. She feels like her insides have melted, her wound is still throbbing, and they haven't told her if they're going to take her back into surgery to fix it.

Leanne came to visit last night. That was a bright spot. And Marie and Elaine have called. She hasn't seen Andrew for a while.

She hasn't seen the children in days. It was her decision, because she doesn't want to scare them, but she regrets it now. She misses them. She misses Sasha's fluffy hair and Oliver's eyes full of sparkle. Sometimes she closes her eyes so she can daydream about them. Her precious babies.

She tries to take a breath. Breathing has been getting harder, but she can't seem to convince the nurses of that. They tell her that she's tired. And that's true, she is. Although tiredness is too meagre a description for what feels like nothing she has ever known. She carried two humans inside her and that didn't feel as alien as what is happening to her now.

None of the nurses has mentioned something that's been bothering her for a day or so: she feels like she's swelling. Her skin is tight. If she pushes a finger into her forearm – which takes some effort, but she does it – the dent stays for a while. That's not normal. But she has a lot of time to think, and worry. Maybe she's making this worse than it is. All of these signs could be normal for what she has.

It feels hard though. To stay alive. She's been here for days now – she's lost track of how many. Visitors come and go, but she already sees how they leave her and slip back into their lives. She's a blip; an errand to run.

It's not that she doesn't think she's loved – she knows she is. She can see it in the eyes of her parents, of her friends.

There is something else she knows, though: they would be all right without her. Even Sasha and Oliver would be all right. She is more important to them than to anyone else, but they would continue to grow and learn. They would be loved too.

So she's been thinking it may not be so bad. In fact, it may be easier. If she were to simply step off this planet and go into the universe, that would be the easiest thing of all. For all that time she spent in church as a child, she doesn't believe it's God waiting for her. But she's pretty sure this big, beautiful universe with all its stars and planets and moons and rocks is going to look after her. Sometimes she feels its pull. Like now, when it's so hard to take a breath.

Her next breath might be the hardest. She just doesn't know.

'Theresa?'

There's a feeling on her shoulder ... someone's hand, perhaps. Whoever it is, they're pushing her. But she can't see because the light outside the window is bright and she's closed her eyes against it.

'Theresa? Theresa, it's Leanne.'

She thinks of that first day she met Marie. From that point on, swimming didn't seem like a chore, something she was suffering through in order to get in shape. It became the highlight of each day.

She smiles to herself, even though it hurts. Everything hurts her now.

Better to think of more pleasant times. If she concentrates she can conjure the feeling of the foam against her legs. That first shock of cold, because the ocean in Shelly Bay is never as warm as you want it to be. She's dreamt of going to Queensland for a holiday because the water is warmer there. To the tropics, where it's like a bath. Or so she's heard.

Now there's a hand on her wrist. It feels cool. Or maybe she's warm. The nurses were talking about her temperature this morning. She didn't catch whether it was good or bad.

'Theresa, can you open your eyes?'

When she waded in at Main Beach she would make it quick. Some people like a slow adjustment to the temperature but that was never her style. Rip off that band-aid, she liked to say. Head under, full immersion, and gasp if you have to. It never took long to adjust. Especially once she started moving.

She tries to remember the fish she would see swimming off Little Beach. What colour were they?

'I need some help in here! Sister! *Sister! Now!*'

There's Marie, ahead of her. Always ahead of her. So fit and fast.

Elaine's passing her. She really does like Elaine. It took a while to get to know her but it was worth it.

And Leanne, close behind. She's worked so hard to keep up with them. To achieve something. It's admirable.

They're all women she loves, and she knows they love her in return. It's been enough to get her through some days, and she knows what Marie would say: it never ends. Love is eternal, just like the good book says.

Theresa believes it.

CHAPTER 59

'Oliver, take your sister's hand, please.' Marie watches as Oliver and Sasha walk slowly down the steps onto the sand, Sasha a step behind her impatient brother. 'Stop there, please, while we wait for the others.'

She turns around to see Elaine and Leanne carrying towels and bottles of soft drink: Leanne with her efficient walk and precise steps, and Elaine with her more loping stride. They are talking to each other but they're still too far away for her to hear what they're discussing.

Gus will walk down the hill from Marie's home in a little while. 'Let them have some time with the three of you first,' he said.

The sun is behind them in the western sky, still an hour or so from setting. Marie loves the waning light. These last few evenings she's been making a point of watching it. Delaying the time when she goes inside and sits with her thoughts. Then goes to bed with those same thoughts and barely sleeps. The last few nights she's had an hour, maybe, or two.

Gus has been staying with her and she's envied his heavy slumber. He's been caring of her in the mornings, bringing her breakfast in bed. She doesn't know if Elaine and Leanne have anyone doing that for them, but she knows they, too, are having sleepless nights. She can see it on their faces each morning. Leanne, especially, looks haunted.

It was such a scare for Leanne when she found Theresa like that. She's tried to tell them what she felt – they've encouraged her to – but she loses her words each time. She gets as far as, 'I just went down to see her on my lunch break.' Then the story skips to where Theresa is in intensive care.

For a few days they didn't know if they'd get to keep her. If they could hold her here on earth and never let her go. They weren't able to see her. One visitor at a time, they were told, and her parents had priority. So they called to check. And Leanne used her connections to find out what she could.

It was only two days ago that they allowed Theresa back on the ward. It's been many more days than that since her children have seen her. Marie doesn't mind, not for a second, taking care of them as often as she can.

She and Elaine and Leanne are still swimming; of course they are. They're all awake in the early hours anyway. And swimming gives them purpose now in a way it never has before. In the past it was for fitness, and the fun of seeing each other. Now it's a chance to be together and understand each other so well that they don't have to speak, while knowing that if they do speak they're safe among friends. True friends. Because they're still shocked. On some level they may always be. Their friend, their beloved friend, almost slipped away from them while they were watching. Nothing feels safe now. Everything is unstable. Yet never has it all been so sure. Nothing matters, and everything does. In almost losing their friend they have all found their purpose, and it is to let love guide them. To say 'I love you' to those they love; to receive it joyfully. If they thought Theresa was a gift before, they are convinced of it now. If only they could tell her in person.

In good time.

Meanwhile, they are focusing on her children. Initially Andrew resisted but a few days ago he was more agreeable.

'I'm not trying to be their grandmother,' Marie said when he consented to her taking them that day. 'I know they have two of those. But I've spent a bit of time with them and I miss them.'

'Right. Okay,' he said.

'I'll pick them up at nine,' she said, before he could change his mind. 'I presume you're in the house?'

'Yeah.'

'You're welcome to come too, Andrew. You and Nonna.'

'Nah, it's all right,' he said. There was silence for a few moments. 'Reckon I should have some time alone with Nonna. She's a bit cut up about the whole thing.'

We all are, Marie wanted to say. Instead she told him that was a good idea.

This afternoon when she picked up the children, with Elaine driving, she promised Andrew she'd give them dinner and have them home by seven. He nodded, then kissed each child goodbye on the top of their heads. Marie was pleased to see the children didn't seem too different to their normal selves as they fought over who got to sit on which side of the car.

As Elaine and Leanne reach her, Marie takes a towel and a bottle of drink from them.

'Shall we set up over there?' She nods towards the boat ramp next to the surf club. 'Or more out here in the middle?'

'I like the middle,' Leanne says. 'We get a better view of the ocean.'

They find a spot amongst the people still soaking up the last hours of Sunday. No matter the season, there are always people on this beach.

'Kids, over here,' Elaine calls as Sasha and Oliver reach the water's edge.

They run squealing as a wave comes in and froths around their ankles.

'They're going to get wet,' Marie says, smiling.

'They should,' says Elaine. 'They're kids.'

'Your mum does that sometimes,' Marie tells Oliver and Sasha as they approach. 'If the water's cold, she'll make a face and laugh.'

Oliver squints into the setting sun as he turns to her. 'But she likes swimming?' he asks.

'She does.' Marie pats a spot next to her on the towel. 'Come and sit here and I'll tell you all about it. Sasha, you take my other side.'

'I'll go and get the fish and chips,' Leanne offers.

'I'll come with you.' Elaine smiles but Marie can see the strain in it. She's seen that strain in her own mirror.

'Ollie likes lots of salt on his chips, don't you?' Marie says. 'Lots and lots.'

Oliver looks aghast. 'No, I don't!'

'Oh, it must be Sasha who likes it.'

'Noooo!' Sasha shakes her head so hard her hair flies around.

'Guess it's no one then.' Marie shrugs. 'Just normal chips for us.'

Leanne and Elaine walk slowly in the direction of the shops, their heads turned to look at the water. They probably don't even realise they're doing it, Marie thinks. It happens, though, after you've been swimming for a while – you unconsciously check the waves and see how big they are, how constant. You start to chart your path out the back. Theresa once told her that she wishes she had gills, and Marie understands completely. She has the same desire herself. To be able to swim indefinitely, to see more of the world underwater – that would be worth more than riches.

'Did you know that your mum's got caught in dumpers a few times?' she says to the children.

'What are dumpers?' Oliver asks.

'They're waves that pick you up and toss you all around. Not like normal waves that you can bodysurf on. See, like that man is doing.'

They watch as the man's head bobs out of the white wash, then he gets to his feet in the shallows.

'How do you know which one is a dumper?' Oliver looks serious.

'They curl over at the top. So if you're looking at a wave as it's coming towards you, watch the top and see what it does.'

'Huh?' He frowns.

'How about I show you one day?' Marie says. 'We'll have a bodysurfing lesson.'

'Okay,' he says in the way children do: agreeing without really understanding what they're agreeing to.

'Now, why don't you tell me about school,' she says to Sasha. 'Is your teacher being nice?'

Marie listens as the children fill her in about their teachers, about the new boy in third class who is taller than all the other boys and meaner too. About the books they were allowed to take home from the library, and how Dad forgot to dress them in their sports uniform on Wednesday.

Leanne and Elaine come walking across the sand, each carrying fish and chips in one hand and their shoes in the other. Marie checks her watch: Gus should be here soon.

The light is softening further and the seagulls are getting louder, competing for the last scraps of the day. On the other side of Shelly Bay the tourists will be boarding the ferry that will take them back to the city. Patrons will be sipping beer in the pub as the shops nearby start to close for the day. Everything is the same as it ever was, Marie thinks, even when it's not.

Another wave rolls in. And another. As they always will, for eternity. No two the same. Her whole life, she has seen God's design in the waves, and the sky, and the earth. Through her greatest sadnesses, she has always trusted in God's will.

She's been tested these last few days, though, and has been mad at herself. She should hold her friend closer. She should tell her that she is loved more than she knows. Gestures are all well and good, but there is no substitute for saying the words that every single human being longs to hear: *You are loved, Theresa. I love you. Elaine loves you. Leanne loves you.*

She will say it soon, though; as soon as she can, as soon as Theresa is allowed visitors. For now, though, she will offer it to the water and let it roll back in with each wave, over and over, here on the beach that has come to mean so much to them all.

'Whoa! Look at that wave, Marie!' Oliver says as a dumper crashes to the shore.

'That was a big one,' she says.

As the children continue to chatter away she puts her hands on their shoulders and looks out to sea. To the place she loves, where she'll be tomorrow morning, with her friends. They will swim to Little Beach and back, and they'll do it every day. She doesn't know how long this time will last. She doesn't know what her life holds. It is profoundly clear now that none of them can rely on anything. She is, however, sure about this: once summer arrives, Theresa will be strong again. Marie will make her be.

The four of them will get in the water, even if all Theresa can do is float on her back. Marie will float with her. So will Elaine. So will Leanne. Then the next day they'll get her to float a bit further. The day after, maybe dog paddle. Bit by bit. That's how she'll get better. That's how they all will.

SUMMER 1984

CHAPTER 60

'You ready?' Marie holds out her hand.

'Can you tell?' Theresa says, looking down at her chest as she takes Marie's hand. 'That it's fake?'

Leanne and Elaine watch with amusement. Leanne is tempted to rub her eyes to check that it really is Theresa standing there in a swimming costume, whole if not entirely hearty.

Marie rolls her eyes. 'Only if I'm really staring at your chest. And you're an attractive woman, Theresa, but I have no interest in looking at your breasts.'

Theresa grimaces. 'I don't feel too attractive. I look like a stringy hag. But I guess Andrew got what he wanted.'

'How do you mean?' Marie frowns.

'He said I was fat. Needed to lose some weight. Ta-da!' She giggles.

Theresa lost a lot of weight during those nightmare days in hospital and hasn't put it back on. So she doesn't look like herself, especially as she also lost some of her hair because of the trauma. Those bouncy brown locks will come back, though; Leanne has seen it before.

'He's left, by the way,' Theresa says, and Leanne can see how hard she's gripping Marie's hand.

'What?' says Elaine. 'After everything?'

'All that "everything" is why I'm happy he's gone,' Theresa says, taking a step into the water. 'Nonna was annoyed all the time and he was shirty with her. Whenever Mum and Dad stayed they got on each other's nerves. It was making the kids upset.'

'I'm sorry that happened,' Elaine says with an expression of regret.

Theresa throws up her free hand. 'It was never going to be a fairytale ending. Seeing me sick wasn't going to make him behave better. He saw me cut in half to get Sasha out and it barely bothered him.' Her face clouds. 'I should have left then.'

'So he's . . . ?' Elaine prompts.

'Back with his parents. Or with his girlfriend.'

'Don't tell me she's still around!' Marie cries.

'I honestly don't know and I don't care.' Theresa takes another tentative step. 'I have other things to care about.'

She doesn't look at any of them and they know why: she's out of the woods, but not the forest. There was no cancer in the other lymph nodes that were taken months ago, but her doctors gave her no assurances that there wouldn't be at some stage. She needs to be vigilant.

They will be vigilant with her, Leanne thinks, even if they drive her mad.

'Elaine, could you take her other hand?' Marie asks.

'Sure.' Elaine reaches out.

'Lee, why don't you take Elaine's hand. Safety in numbers.'

Leanne complies, although she knows it's nothing to do with numbers. Marie just doesn't want her to feel left out.

'Right, ladies, heads up. Take a good look at that amazing sunrise.' Marie gestures with her chin.

Theresa sighs contentedly. 'I can't believe I'm back here.'

'We can,' says Elaine. 'We weren't giving up on you.'

For a second Theresa looks as though she's going to falter. 'No, you didn't give up on me,' she says. 'I'll never forget it.'

'As I've said before, it was a team effort,' Elaine says briskly. 'I just happened to be there at a critical point.' She pauses. 'No pun intended.'

Theresa smiles.

'Besides, I was just the start of the chain.' Elaine nods towards Leanne. 'This one was the end. The lucky end.'

That moment – that luck – visits Leanne at odd times of the day. She sees Theresa lying in the bed. She feels time slowing down. She remembers telling herself to not panic. To think of Theresa as a patient, not as her friend. To make decisions as she would for a patient.

'Why were you even there?' Theresa asked her the first time they were able to speak alone, once she was past the worst. 'You'd just visited me the night before.'

Leanne didn't have a good answer. The truth is, she had a feeling. A hunch. An intuition. She was on her way to the canteen for lunch when something made her deviate towards Theresa's room. The thought popped into her head, that she had to go to Theresa immediately, and she obeyed it. She hasn't always obeyed those sorts of thoughts, and has always regretted it when she hasn't. That day, she wasn't going to take the risk.

She hasn't told Theresa that, though, because she's superstitious about it. If Leanne says what really happened it might all unravel. There's no proof that it won't, only her sense that everything is too fragile to be taken for granted. So the answer she gave Theresa was an element of the truth, if not the whole: 'I wanted to see you,' she said.

Now she is able to see Theresa again every morning, because while Theresa isn't ready to swim yet, she's pledged to be there at the beach every day.

'Do you want to go all the way in?' Marie asks. 'Or are you worried the falsie will escape?'

Theresa blows air out of her mouth. 'Only one way to find out!'

They hold steady as they walk in, all keeping an eye on the waves that are strong, if small, and breaking close to shore.

'Let's go a bit further,' Theresa instructs, and soon they're up to their waists, then chests, then they let go of each other's hands and push off the bottom so their legs rise into a float.

'Ah, this is the life,' Theresa says.

'Sure is,' Marie responds.

Leanne giggles as Elaine bumps into her.

'Sorry!' says Elaine as she rights herself. 'It's hard to float when there's a swell.'

Leanne, too, stops floating, and she and Elaine watch as a wave breaks on top of Theresa, who shrieks and disappears.

She emerges with her hair plastered across her face, laughing.

'All right, sunshine, that's enough for you for today,' Marie says.

Still laughing, Theresa nods her agreement. 'Okay. But it was fun.'

As they walk back towards the sand, Theresa stops. 'Wait a second! We can't go!'

'Why not?' says Elaine.

'I've lost my falsie!'

Marie's incredulous expression says it all. 'On your *first swim*?'

'Quick!' Theresa says, looking around her, patting the water. 'We have to find it before it floats away!'

The women turn in circles but there's too much movement in the water to see anything.

'Oh, love,' says Marie. 'I think it's gone.'

Theresa grins and pulls out something from the side of her costume. 'Got you!' she says, brandishing the falsie aloft before sticking it back into place.

Marie and Elaine roll their eyes.

'Good Lord,' says Elaine. 'Please do *not* try that again.'

'How did you manage that?' Leanne asks.

'I took my chance under that wave.' Theresa sashays through the shallows and swings her arms from side to side. 'Ladies,' she says, turning around to face them, 'it is bloody amazing to be alive.' Her face lights up. 'And I like it even better with you three along for the ride.'

'So do we, love,' says Marie, taking the hand Theresa offers as they climb up the steep portion of the hard sand.

They are slow to reach for their towels as they watch the day break over the surf.

Marie's head jerks in the direction of the surf club. 'Oh no – Trev incoming.'

'Shall we adjourn to the promenade?' says Elaine.

'Even better – to my place,' says Marie. 'Gus made some Anzac biscuits. He's taken over my recipe.'

'Sounds good,' says Theresa, and the friends hustle their way towards the steps and onto the footpath, chattering away.

At the top of the steps Leanne turns to look back at the beach. She sees Trev gazing after them longingly, and a jogger going past him on the sand, and a father and son heading for the water hand in hand. She knows she'll be back tomorrow, but she wants to take it all in today.

Today is all she has; and tomorrow will be another today, as will the day after, and she will cherish them all.

ACKNOWLEDGEMENTS

Thank you to Rebecca Saunders and Fiona Hazard, the publishers of this book, for taking such good care of it. Thank you to my literary agent, Melanie Ostell, for being a kind listener and a great reader.

Thank you to Sarah Brooks for carrying the ladies of Shelly Bay beyond Australian waters; to Abby Parsons and Cath Burke at Sphere, and to Andy Hine and the Little, Brown UK rights team.

At Hachette Australia, thanks to Vanessa Radnidge, Louise Sherwin-Stark, Justin Ractliffe, Daniel Pilkington, Anna Egelstaff, Ella Chapman and, actually, everyone else!

I have been so fortunate to work with Karen Ward as the editor of this book and of *Fairvale*. Oceans of gratitude to Celine Kelly for her editorial eye, and to Nicola O'Shea and to Fiona Daniels for theirs.

Books have been a central part of my life because my parents, Robbie and David, ensured they would be. Eternal love and gratitude to them and to my brother, Nicholas.

Love and thanks to Jen Bradley, Isabelle Benton, Chris Kunz, Ashleigh Barton, Amelia Rowe, Neralyn and Col Porter, Richard and Robbie Hille, Kate Farquharson, Katie and Brian Sampson, Jill Wunderlich and Marg Cruikshank for their interest and support.

The inspiration and teaching provided by Shiva Rea keep my creative fire alight.

This book has a long lineage that includes *Home and Away* and *All Saints* – two masterclasses in Australian storytelling. It also includes Australian country music artists such as Fanny Lumsden, Harmony James, Brad Butcher, Beccy Cole, The McClymonts, Lachlan Bryan, Lyn Bowtell, Felicity Urquhart and Kasey Chambers, who open their hearts and shape their songs to bring joy and meaning to their audiences.

And to all the readers, including readers of *Fairvale* who sent me tweets and messages, or who spoke to me at events – thank you so much for spending time with my stories.

Loved spending time with the ladies of Shelly Bay?

Read on for an extract from Sophie Green's
bestselling debut novel

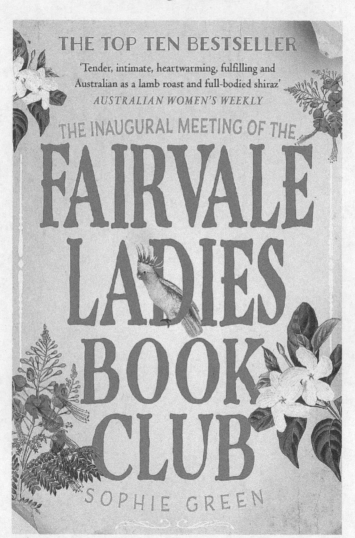

THE INAUGURAL MEETING OF THE

FAIRVALE LADIES BOOK CLUB

SOPHIE GREEN

CHAPTER ONE

The morning sky was its usual muted dry-season blue as Sybil paused to gaze out of the kitchen window. Before she'd moved to the Northern Territory she'd thought it would be a land of perpetual brilliance: blood-red dirt, sapphire skies and emerald trees, and a luminous, pendulous sun reigning over the land. All of that was true – just not at the same time.

The palette of the place changed with the seasons. The light of the dry season was pallid at dawn and dusk, and during the wet the sky was often so heavy with cloud that it was hard to say what sort of blue it was. When it rained – and rained and rained – the trees turned so bright and the earth, even the rocks, became so alive with new growth that it was like living in a greenhouse; but during the dry season the colours of the trees seemed subdued, almost as if the persistent foliage felt like it didn't have permission to be any more vibrant. The wet season was the star up here: it had the power to turn the Katherine River into a swollen force, waterfalls cascading down the sides of the gorges; it made the air leaden with moisture and turned people into molasses. And it could kill.

Everyone knew of someone who had died trying to cross a river during a wet, or a child who had wandered off to a water-hole or creek they thought they knew well, only to discover that the usual friendly trickle was now a roiling torrent in which lurked traps for small feet: tangled branches, rotting animal carcasses, strong currents. It was too easy for the wet to claim an unwary child – or adult. That's what had shocked Sybil the most when she'd arrived here. She'd grown up in Sydney, with all its traffic and bustle and urgency, but she'd never known anyone to die because of the weather. Yet in her first year here on Fairvale Station, she knew two. It had been an unwelcome lesson: the Territory would always be the boss. Humans could try to bend the land and the seasons to their will, but they would fail. They would fail forever. All they could do was surrender completely and make the best of what was there. And the best was plentiful.

It was impossible not to fall in love with the place. So many colours and contradictions; so many secrets and surprises. She had been here for twenty-six years, since she was twenty-five, and she knew enough to realise that she would never know the Territory completely, even though it felt like the Territory knew her. It knew her weaknesses, that was for sure; it also brought out her strengths. Of all the relationships in her life, this was the one that seemed to contain the most challenges and rewards. Not that she'd tell her husband that.

As if on cue, Joe walked into her field of vision. She smiled as she saw him lift his battered Akubra and scratch his head. He did that a lot, usually when he was trying to work out how to say something stern to a worker without actually sounding stern. He was a gentle man, in so many ways. She was lucky to be married to him; lucky that he had taken her away from a life that was pressing in on her. She hadn't loved him then but she loved him now. And it was time to call him in to breakfast.

She waved vigorously through the window, hoping to catch his eye; his lifted finger was the sign that she had. She saw him turn towards the cattle yards and cup his hands to his mouth, no doubt calling to their son Ben, who had also started the day early. Everyone on Fairvale was up with the sun, if not before, and they worked long after the moon rose. Sometimes Sybil wondered whether she'd have chosen this life if she'd known that it was relentless: seven days a week, so many hours a day. There seemed to be very little time even to read a book, because they were all so tired they'd fall into bed at night. Except they did end up making time for the things that mattered, and if Sybil thought she was missing out on being a lady of leisure she was also aware that life wasn't made for sitting around and doing nothing. Human bodies were built to work, and the hard, long toil of each day made the snatched hours of relaxation all the more precious.

Sybil watched as her husband and son pushed open the gate to enter the garden. Despite the fact that they lived in the middle of hundreds of thousands of hectares with apparently no need for fences, where the land threw up its own natural barriers, the gate kept out the working dogs and any stray cattle that might trample through the green-lawned garden that Sybil had defied nature and good sense to create. That garden still carried the signs of the lush growth of the wet season just past. Before too long, though, the dry would start to bite and she'd need to draw on the bore water to keep the garden at its best.

She'd fashioned it – perhaps ridiculously – as if it was a garden belonging to a quaint English cottage instead of a large, squat outback home. Fairvale's big house had a generous verandah that wrapped around three of its sides, but it was no more genteel than that. The garden was Sybil's attempt at bringing something refined into her immediate world. She had fashioned long garden beds to border the lawn. A bird bath sat in the middle of the grass; instead of swallows dipping their beaks into it, however, the local cockatoos used it as a swimming pool, raucously announcing their activities every time. It often sounded like they were laughing at her – laughing at her delusions of order and grace – and they probably were. She'd started this garden as a bride, trying to bring something of her old, organised life into her new. If she'd waited five years, it wouldn't have mattered so much. By that point in her marriage she had realised that she would never be able to control anything much around here, apart from herself.

After the beds had been dug she had, at great expense, ordered poinciana saplings and a jacaranda tree from a supplier in Darwin. African trees, she'd thought, might have a chance of surviving here. She had installed some camellias, hoping they would reach a fair height even if this wasn't their natural habitat. They had survived, although they weren't always happy about it.

Maidenhair ferns hugged the ground; she'd planted them hoping they would keep the beds together, and moist, to encourage the other plants to grow. The ferns loved the wet season and hated the dry; some years Sybil thought she'd lose them all, yet they'd endured. She supposed that plants that had been growing on earth for millions of years could outlast the tough seasons.

The lawn had been the hardest part. It was a risk, when the wet season was likely to turn it into mush, but Joe had gone to Darwin one day and returned with enough lawn to cover the patch of dirt that was left after the beds had been planted. Sometimes he'd laugh at her, slowly shaking his head, as he watched her curse the weather and offer up the occasional prayer that her lawn would be saved.

'Why are you laughing?' she'd said once, irritated that he could be so amused while she was so annoyed.

'Because that lawn is the only thing that can make you believe in God.' He'd laughed more heartily then and she'd wanted to stomp away from him – because he was right. Instead she'd pressed her lips together, turned away and started pruning a camellia.

The garden had been many things to Sybil over the years: a source of pride and frustration; a refuge when she needed a few minutes to herself; a place for her children to learn to take care of nature; and a spot where she and Joe could sometimes sit quietly as the sun set on a dry-season day, listening to those cockatoos, still laughing at her.

Mainly, though, the garden was her work of art – the only one she had. Out here on Fairvale, two hours from the nearest town and a long way from the culture and sophistication of her childhood, Sybil needed something to gaze upon. Something that wasn't stampeding cattle and mangy dogs, coals in a fire or a creek bed full of animal skeletons.

As the two men approached the flyscreen door, she could hear them talking about one of the workers. It was as she'd suspected: Joe needed to pull the man back into line and he didn't have the heart to do it.

'If you don't, I will,' she could hear Ben saying. 'And I won't be half as nice as you.'

'Now, now,' came Joe's deep, measured tones; he sounded just as he had when Ben had misbehaved as a boy and Joe had tried to discipline him. *Now, now, Ben*, he'd say. *You don't really want to do that, do you?* Amazingly, this tactic had often been effective. As it no doubt would be with the worker.

'Hello, love,' Joe said as he opened the door, removing his hat and hanging it on the hook by the door. Sybil liked the way he always greeted her as if he hadn't seen her just half an hour ago, wrapped in her towel as she exited the shower, her hair wet, her face unadorned. He always made it sound as though seeing her was an occasion.

'Smells good, Mum,' Ben said as he pulled out a chair and sat.

'There's nothing cooking yet, Ben,' she said.

'I know.' He winked. 'Get a wriggle on.'

'You can go and eat with the others in the dining room if you don't like it,' Sybil said. The residents of Fairvale – the community of stockmen, workers, and their wives and children if they had them – usually ate together, with all the food cooked by Ruby, who had been with them for years. Sybil always liked to make breakfast for her family in their home, however. The days could become so frenetic for Joe – so many people wanting to talk to him, to ask him things, to have him do things for them – that providing him with a quiet start, with a meal where he could eat in peace, was, she felt, important.

Joe tapped his son on the shoulder. 'Be kind to your mother,' he said. 'We're lucky to have our breakfast made for us.'

'Yeah, yeah.' Ben grinned at his mother, taking off his own dusty Akubra and putting it on the table. Sybil knew that grin: it was Ben's good-luck charm, his means of getting out of trouble. He'd been using it on her since before he could talk and she always fell for it, even though she tried not to let him see that.

'Do you reckon the rain's finished?' Sybil said, turning her head briefly towards the kitchen window.

'Could be a bit more.' Joe squinted at the sky. 'Sometimes we get fooled. It's been a good wet, though, so we shouldn't be greedy. The bores are full. We'll last through the dry.'

'Where's Katie?' Ben said to his mother.

'She's your wife, Ben,' Sybil replied. 'How should I know?' Her son was twenty-three years of age – old enough not to be lazy. Although she had a motherly impulse to want to take care of everything, he was a grown-up.

'Because you've been in the house together.' He tried his grin again.

'And I've been in here,' Sybil said.

'All right,' Ben said, sounding weary and getting to his feet. 'I'll get her.'

'Thank you,' Sybil said, turning to a loaf of bread next to the stove, picking up the knife so she could start to hack out the many slices she'd need just for this one meal.

'Ka-aaate!' Ben called as he walked through to the rest of the house, and Sybil turned to Joe and raised an eyebrow. Only he could understand the paradox of loving Ben and being exasperated by him at the same time.

Joe smiled. 'Cup of tea, love?' he said and Sybil nodded.

'Thank you,' she said as she started to slice.

Another day on Fairvale was beginning.

CHAPTER TWO

Sallyanne sat in the car with the ignition off, turning her wedding ring round and round on her finger, feeling the sun already burning through the side window. It wasn't even ten o'clock.

The car was almost new, although that didn't make her love it any more. It had been her husband's choice, but Mick rarely drove it; he had a ute for work and he'd drive that on weekends too. Sallyanne would rather have had one of those little Japanese numbers instead of a burnt-orange 1976 Kingswood station wagon that felt as wieldy as a truck and was as hot as an oven inside.

She sighed and kept turning her ring. She didn't know why she did that when she was nervous; it wasn't as if the ring looked any different whichever way she moved it.

The ring was a plain platinum band. Platinum, her mother had once told her, was more valuable than gold. That had been years ago, of course – her mother had been dead for half of Sallyanne's life. She never forgot anything her mother told her, though. Or anything her mother did.

Sallyanne remembered arriving home from school and finding her mother cackling – yes, actually cackling, almost bent over with laughter – in the presence of other women who crowded their small sitting room. There were cups of tea in her mother's best china and half-full plates of Arnott's biscuits. Lemon Crisps, Scotch Fingers and Venetians. Her mother had barely noticed her only daughter arriving, apart from saying, 'Hello, darling, it's just the CWA,' before she continued laughing.

There had never been another meeting at their house but her mother had remained a member of the Country Women's Association until she died. Sallyanne had always thought it was an organisation for women far older than her who wanted to talk about their grandchildren, but her mother hadn't been that old. Not that much older than Sallyanne was now.

The blast of a horn made her jump and she looked up to see a woman waving at a car in the street. It was the same wave her daughter, Gretel, had given her as she'd left this morning, her fingers waggling as she'd chewed on some of her hair, a new habit that Sallyanne would have to stop.

She'd left Gretel with Mick's mother, who was a reliable babysitter, if a somewhat unenthusiastic one. Colleen had never been keen on watching Gretel's brothers, Tim and Billy, declaring boys to be 'nothing but trouble – and *exhausting*, Sally, they're *exhausting*', although she'd softened once Gretel had arrived. However, Sallyanne reflected with another twist of the ring, the woman had never learnt to call her daughter-in-law by her proper name.

The boys were at school now. Probably looking forward to recess. And here was their mother, acting like it was her own first day of school.

Sallyanne had thought about doing something with her days ever since Billy had started kindergarten. With only Gretel at home, she'd really had no excuse not to try to make better use of her time. So when she'd seen the little advertisement in the local paper, announcing the next CWA meeting and welcoming new members, she had called the number in the ad and stammered out her question about whether she could attend. Of course she could, a kindly lady had told her.

'And you sound young, dear,' the lady had gone on to say. 'We need some young ones.'

Sallyanne was glad she sounded young because she had been feeling so old lately. Her body was worn out from carrying and feeding three babies, from running a household of five people. This morning had been like all the others: she was up early to make Mick his tea and toast, never receiving any words of thanks, just the glowering that now seemed to be a fixture. He was drinking more and smiling less, and she didn't know why – she knew only that he'd decided it was her fault that he needed six beers in quick succession at night, which was probably why he was morose in the mornings. That was her fault, too, apparently. He'd always had a temper, arriving quickly and violently and gone in the same way, but this latest turn in his personality was settling into his foundations and she didn't like it. Didn't like the way he looked at her, as if she was provocation and prey. Didn't like the way he snapped at the kids, when their only offence was to be young.

So she made the best of it: she would be chirpy with the children as they woke and tumbled into the kitchen for their breakfast and Mick grunted his goodbyes. She would bustle around, packing the boys' lunches, making sure their shoes were polished, answering Gretel's constant questions about why puppies barked and trees were green. It was exhausting and she always felt there was nothing left over for her. No time, no energy, no motivation.

Still, she had to make an effort. Thirty-four years of age was too young not to try. Not to live.

She'd decided to drive past the front entrance of the building on the main street. She could have parked out the front. Instead, her throat feeling like someone's hand was on it, she'd turned left at the corner and gone around the block to First Street, thinking she'd park out the back. She wouldn't feel so exposed if she was waiting there.

Yet she could see there was a rear entrance to the building, and now two women walked past her car, laughing, as they headed for it. They had the short haircuts that were so practical in this hot place and the short-sleeved cotton dresses that were also advisable, but she was sure they were wearing stockings. Sallyanne looked down at her own cotton dress and her bare legs. Was she meant to have worn stockings? Was that what proper CWA ladies did? Even in a place where the air was so stifling that people sat in the hot springs – a pool of water that was thirty-eight degrees Celsius – in preference to being on dry land?

It was too late now for stockings so she'd just have to hope no one would notice. Maybe this particular cotton dress hadn't been such a good idea, though: her belly, so slack after three babies had grown in it, was pushing out prominently with nothing to hold it in. If she'd worn a different, more structured dress – if she wasn't so fond of biscuits and cakes – she wouldn't look so plump. Those other women didn't look plump. They looked like they'd been working out in the sun every day of their lives: sturdy and strong and hearty. She'd never been hearty.

Feeling sick with uncertainty about what would happen once she stepped inside the building, Sallyanne pushed open the creaky car door and put one tentative foot onto the road. She tucked her wispy blonde hair behind her ears, licked her lips, and then sent a silent plea to her mum to give her strength as she emerged fully from the car and slammed the door shut – it was the only way to get it to stick. Trying to remember to keep her shoulders back, she walked across the sparse lawn at the back of the building, then, falteringly, opened the screen door that took her into a room that was smaller than she had imagined.

Sallyanne guessed that there were about twenty women standing around – she'd never been good at estimating the size of a crowd, though. They were all older than her, although some not by much. There was an array of dresses in various unremarkable patterns, and sturdy handbags placed on or next to the large table that dominated the space.

Almost to a woman they had short or shoulder-length hair, which made Sallyanne conscious of her own long locks, which she had wanted to cut for years except Mick kept telling her not to. She looked like Rapunzel, he'd say; certainly there were days when Sallyanne felt like her, too.

Sallyanne realised that a moderately tall, middle-aged woman was looking at her curiously. She was sure she'd never seen the woman before – she'd have remembered such a striking face. The woman looked like Ava Gardner before Frank Sinatra got to her. She had short grey hair cut close to her head and she was wearing something no one else in the room was: boots, and a Western shirt tucked into her slim waist above a pair of sensible-looking pants with a flare at the hem. Sallyanne had seen those shirts in cowboy movies, always worn by men. A large silver buckle adorned the woman's belt. She looked like she was about to go to work on a property, which meant she probably wasn't from town. Sallyanne was sure she'd have noticed her if she was – she knew pretty much everyone by sight. That's what happened when you'd lived your whole life in one place.

'You're Sallyanne Morris, aren't you?' the woman said.

'Yes,' Sallyanne replied cautiously. 'How did you know?'

The woman smiled enigmatically. 'I'm Sybil Baxter. From Fairvale.'

Sallyanne knew about Fairvale. Everyone in the area did. The Baxter family had lived on Fairvale for so long that no one in town could remember them not being there. Well, no one except the local Aboriginal tribe, but people didn't really talk about that.

'And you're joining us?' Sybil's smile was more generous now.

Sallyanne nodded and let out the breath she didn't know she'd been holding onto.

'It's my first meeting,' she said, sure she was spluttering.

Sybil nodded towards the women gathering around a table laden with cups, saucers and scones. 'Shall we?'

Sallyanne felt herself relaxing, just a little.

'What made you want to join us?' Sybil said, walking slowly.

Because I need some new friends, Sallyanne almost said but realised how that would sound. 'I heard that you talk about books sometimes,' she said instead, and was rewarded with a look of delight on Sybil's face.

'You like to read?' Sybil said, stopping before they reached the table.

Sallyanne nodded vigorously. 'I love it,' she said. 'It's my escape. It gives me—'

She bit her lip. She would sound loony if she told this woman that she loved books because they let her exist in different worlds, far from the dusty, hot town in which she'd grown up. In books she could live in London and Crete and New York City; she could inhabit the eighteenth century or

New Kingdom Egypt. In books she could find tips on how to be a proper lady, what it felt like to have a grand romance, how to say 'fiddle-dee-dee' when you really wanted to tell someone to *get lost*. Not that Sallyanne said 'fiddle-dee-dee' to anyone. She'd tried it when she was a teenager, convinced that Scarlett O'Hara was her role model, and her friends had teased her for a week.

The quizzical look Sybil was giving her told Sallyanne that she'd let her mind wander again, in full view of another human being. Her mother always used to say she was 'off with the fairies', which she'd never quite understood – fairies didn't interest her so much as pharaohs.

'Sorry,' Sallyanne said quietly.

'For what?' Sybil now looked amused.

'I lost my train of thought.'

'That doesn't need an apology.' Sybil smiled sympathetically and Sallyanne felt a pang of something she recognised from her earliest school days: the desire for a friendship.

'So you've grown up in Katherine?' Sybil said, although her intonation suggested she knew the answer.

'Yes. Born here. Raised here.' Sallyanne grimaced. 'It sounds boring when I say it like that.'

'Not at all,' Sybil said. 'It's a fine town. I wish I could spend more time here.'

'And you're from . . . ?' Sallyanne guessed it was somewhere far away. Sybil held herself as if she knew her place in the world and was comfortable with it. It wasn't the sort of confidence that came from growing up in a country town – one glance around the room at the slightly rounded shoulders and the universally deferential postures, even on the most robust-looking women, could tell anyone that. All these women, with lives and families they'd made their own, holding themselves as if they had something to apologise for.

'Sydney,' Sybil said.

'I've always wanted to go there,' Sallyanne said. 'Some of my favourite books are set there.'

'Oh? Which ones?'

'*Harp in the South* is the main one. I—'

'Sybil!'

A short, wide woman with a rigidly set perm was waving at them, and Sallyanne felt immediately disappointed that her conversation with Sybil Baxter was clearly about to end.

Sybil gave her an apologetic look and touched her arm lightly.

'Come and I'll introduce you to Peg,' she said, waving briefly at the other woman. 'And . . . I may have an idea.'

Sallyanne frowned.

'A book-related idea,' Sybil said. 'I'll ring you, if that's all right?'

'Shall I give you my number?' Sallyanne said, not daring to hope that it was this easy to make a friend.

'I don't need it. I'll just ask the operator to connect me.' Sybil squeezed her arm. 'Come on. Peg's a hoot.'

Perhaps it *was* that easy. Or perhaps Sybil felt sorry for her. Whatever the truth, Sallyanne allowed Sybil to lead her into the CWA fray.

Sophie Green is an author and publisher who lives in Sydney. She has written several fiction and non-fiction books, some under other names. In her spare time she writes about country music on her blog, Jolene. She grew up by the water in Sydney and will holiday by the ocean in preference to anywhere else. Sophie's debut novel, *The Inaugural Meeting of the Fairvale Ladies Book Club*, a Top 10 bestseller, was shortlisted for the Australian Book Industry Awards for General Fiction Book of the Year 2018, longlisted for the Matt Richell Award for New Writer of the Year 2018 and longlisted for the Indie Book Award for Debut Fiction 2018.

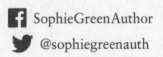

SophieGreenAuthor
@sophiegreenauth